THE
BRIDGE

BILL
KONIGSBERG

SCHOLASTIC PRESS
NEW YORK

ISBN 978-1-338-32503-4

1 2020

Printed in the U.S.A.   23

First edition, September 2020

Book design by Baily Crawford

For Ned and Amy

and

*For every human being who has ever felt
the world would be better off without them*

Can't I have this one moment to myself, please?

This thought sears in Aaron Boroff's mind as the sobbing girl passes behind him. She's interrupted his solitude as he stares down at the undulating Hudson River from the south side of the George Washington Bridge.

He senses her presence as strongly as he feels the concrete walkway shaking frantically below him. He glances right and watches her walk toward New Jersey, head down. Then she stops maybe a hundred feet from him, approaches the ledge, and stands there, looking down at the empty space below her, just as he'd been doing.

He turns and glares at her. It's hard to see details from this distance. She's short, with long jet-black hair. Devastated, definitely. Same reason for being here? Probably.

He wonders: *Which one of us is worse off?* His gut twists. *Her, of course. I'm such a fucking coward to even be thinking of ending my life. People will forget about me because thinking about me is too embarrassing. I'm a failure in every way and I probably won't even manage to kill myself right.*

At the same time, he can't imagine withstanding this hole in his chest even a moment longer. Too, too much. It's like when he was eight and he wanted his mommy—only to remember she wasn't living with them anymore. Thinking this makes him sob audibly, and even though the vehicles and the wind and the buckling bridge are louder and more chaotic than anything he's ever blared on his headphones, the girl turns her head toward the sound, toward Aaron.

It is too far for eye contact, really. What they share is the basic idea of eye contact. And Aaron feels it for both of them. Awkwardness.

Why couldn't she have walked just a little farther?

×

This is Tillie Stanley's time, and here is this interruption, this lost waif of a boy, his hair blowing in the hectic, wild wind. Tall, narrow, leaning in on himself like a branch about to snap. And she thinks, *Does this boy have to be here?* And then she thinks, *You know what? Fuck him. I am so tired of letting other people dictate my life.*

She looks away and grasps the nearly petrified metal railing with her hand and lifts her leg onto the other side so that she's straddling it. If he even tries to walk in her direction, she'll let go and end it. That's how serious she is. Her throat bone-dry. Her chest empty. Her head spinning wild.

Then the boy straddles the railing, too, and Tillie is like, *Oh, come on.* Suddenly they're facing each other like they're playing a deadly game of dare.

×

Aaron wants to scream at her—*Leave me alone! This moment is mine. This is all I have left.*

×

Tillie's brain is mottled with warring thoughts she can't quite decipher—she only knows they're getting in her way. *Be a big girl,* she berates herself. *Pick up your damn thick leg and walk far enough away that he can't see you anymore.* But she's stuck there. She is too far gone, much too far gone to imagine suffering even one more minute of this life. No. Oblivion is the only answer. Whatever comes after—nothing or a lot of something unknown—cannot be worse than this. It's time to stop. To end.

×

They remain that way for a few seconds. Then a few seconds more. Eye contact without being able to see each other's eyes.

And then, at 3:57—

Aaron watches as the nameless girl throws her other leg over the railing and pushes off. Before his eyes, she is diving, dropping. Sideways, upside down. Falling.

It does not look like Aaron expects it to look. It's not beautiful or noble or anything that makes sense. It's a bungee jump without a cord, then a smack into the waves, a hole in the water, and she's consumed.

No sound comes from his mouth. He cannot breathe. The girl was there. And now she's not.

He cannot even consider doing what she just did.

Panicked, he pulls his leg back to the safe side of the barrier, his entire body jittering. The whir of cars blitzes his reality and steals his ability to process. This is outside his realm of understanding. He was supposed to die but he didn't, and a stranger did.

Should I call 911? And say what? How will that help her?

But her family! They'll never know if I don't—

Holy shit. Holy shit holy shit holy shit.

He takes his phone out of his pocket and dials.

"Nine-one-one. What's your emergency?"

He has to scream to be heard and his throat is too dry, too hoarse. "I just—a girl. Jumped."

"What's your location, sir?"

He shouts it like it's a question. "George Washington Bridge?"

"Stay right there. What level? South side or north side?"

He wonders if this happens all the time. It must.

"Upper level—"

"I can't hear you. You have to speak up."

He screams it. "Upper level! Um. South side. I—"

"Are you a danger to yourself?" the woman asks, and he thinks, *Good question.*

He yells, "I don't know! Maybe?"

"Stay right there. I'll stay on the line with you. Stay. Right. There. You hear me?"

Nothing freaks him out more than hearing her say these words in this tone. Like he's in danger.

Oh my God. Oh my God oh my God oh my God.

It's hitting him:

He almost jumped to his death.

So close.

He came so close.

And she came closer.

He starts crying. "Okay," he chokes out, closing his eyes and feeling the wind chill the tears dripping down his cheeks. He wants hot chocolate. Hot chocolate and a blanket and his dad playing old records. And a window. A window safely separating him from all this.

He stays on the line with her, and she keeps him talking, asking him questions. He gets that she's only doing it because it's her job, but it's nice just the same, and she doesn't seem to mind his short answers, and soon he kind of likes hearing her breathing and snapping her gum—orange flavored, he imagines. He thinks about asking her what her name is. What if he spoke to her boss and got her a commendation or something? He hears sirens blaring in the distance and thinks about his father being notified. How it would break him. No.

"Shit."

"What, hon?"

"I can't . . . I'm okay. I just. The ambulance. That's not for me, is it?"

"Just stay on the line with me," she says, her voice remaining calm.

He hangs up and runs. Back to Manhattan, down the winding, rotting metal staircase. He runs because if he's not there, then none of this ever happened. He can try to be normal, and make this a normal Wednesday.

He sees her falling. He can't stop seeing her fall. He can't stop her from falling. He wants to stop it. He wants it to stop. He wants to stop everything—except, apparently, his life.

When he gets to the park on 178th, he numbly walks east, toward the subway. He replays the back of her sad head as she walked over to the spot. Her sobs. Her eyes that he couldn't see clearly then—he sees them clearly now.

He starts to ask himself:

What kind of person jumps—

Then he thinks:

Oh. Right.

He puts his earphones back in, taking the time to graze his ear with his finger. It feels spiritual, almost. This skin, these organs. Alive, unalive. The fine edge between the two. It could have happened so easily. He knows it. If she hadn't shown up and taken his place, this living ear is never again touched by human fingers. It never again hears music, never again hears—anything.

He felt it, the momentum that would have ended with a splash and oblivion.

He shouldn't be here anymore.

He captures every detail of this scene, savors every single

thing that he can still sense as an alive person. It all feels so tentative, this edge between living and dying, and he tunes in to the way the breeze, gentler down here off the bridge, brushes through his hair.

He begins to laughsobhyperventilate. He bends at the waist and tries to expel the crazy pent-up energy from everywhere it's been hiding in his body.

Behind his eyes.

His toenails.

Every inch of his skin.

X

On the other side of Manhattan, the Upper East Side, Britt is practicing her routine to Cardi B's "I Like It" in the living room. She's wondering when Tillie will be home. She cannot wait to show her older sister her new moves. She has this thing where she turns her body away like she's shy, and then she jumps to face forward and does this shimmy thing. Tillie is totally going to love it! When Tillie watches her create her dance moves, she always pretends like she's a talent scout trying to decide if Britt makes the cut. It's fun. And Britt has this new joke she heard in her fifth-grade art class that will make Tillie laugh, and making Tillie laugh is the best because when Tillie's dimples come out, Britt can't help but be happy, too. Her sister is the only one who can make her feel that way, and she tries really hard to make Tillie feel it back.

Okay, Britt thinks. *Back to practice.*

She wants it to be perfect for when Tillie comes home.

X

Across town, Molly Tobin languishes in her comfortable bed, in her comfortable home, feeling bored and pissed. She's been stuck inside basically all day, which is what happens when you get suspended.

Spence has a zero-tolerance policy for bullying. But what Molly did? It wasn't *meant* to be bullying. If she was laughing in the video, it was in a *this is so wrong* way, not a *make this girl's life a living hell* way.

She was just trying to . . . whatever. She was there, Gretchen and Isabella were there, and the group mentality kicked in. This is how the Nazis happened, she realizes, and she hates that she's so easily swayed, but more than that she can't get over the injustice. Gretchen's sex kitten video never got leaked, and it was way over the line. Way worse than what Molly did minutes later.

God. It was just too easy. What girl who has even a slight weight issue, let alone an obvious one, does a spoken word poem in which she likens herself to a cow? And now Molly's suspended, and she can forget Brown, forget Michigan (probably).

If she had to do it all over again, obviously she wouldn't.

But it's not like anyone's offering her a do-over.

×

In his bedroom on the Upper East Side, Amir Rahimi stares at a spot on the wall.

Tomorrow, he'll do it. Not *it* it. He can never do *that*. It would kill his mom. But what he can do is text Tillie. She deserves that, at least, and maybe it will help him feel less ashamed, because the feeling is too much.

He can trust her with the truth, can't he?

She's a very cool girl, after all. The coolest he's ever met.

×

"How was your day?" Aaron's father asks when he gets home from work at 8:45.

"Good," Aaron says. He is eating a bowl of Froot Loops.

"Did you eat?"

Aaron points down at his bowl, and his dad rolls his eyes.

"Did you eat anything with nutrition?"

Aaron shakes his head.

"Was I wrong to let Magda go?"

Magda was the latest in a conga line of Columbia University graduate students Aaron's father had given free room and board in exchange for adult supervision for Aaron. Magda was from Israel, smelled like sweet melon, and had once interrupted Aaron's homework to say, "I'm going out with my sweater. See you in a few hours." Now, sometimes when Aaron and his dad go out, they text each other, *I'm going out with my sweater.*

"Nah," Aaron says, focused on the one surviving Froot Loop, attempting to rescue it from the milk. He shivers, thinking of the nameless girl somewhere in the Hudson. Did she sink to the bottom? Did they get her body out? Could she possibly still be alive? Could he have possibly saved her life with that call?

Don't be stupid, he berates himself. *She's dead. You're not. You failed her. Jury's out on whether you failed yourself.*

He picks up his phone and retypes the words into the search engine: *girl rescued Hudson George Washington Bridge jump.* Still nothing from today. Maybe not every attempted suicide is covered? Maybe there are too many? And what does that tell you about the shittiness of this particular world?

His dad sighs, puts his briefcase down on the kitchen table, and says, "Check in?"

Aaron nods. His father has been insisting on check-ins ever since he went to that Warrior Weekend thing a couple years back. He came back filled with passion for life and regret for the times he had put work before fatherhood. He'd promptly quit his job at the bank and went back to school to become a social worker. Now Aaron and his dad are cash poor, apartment rich, and they *check in* every night.

Of course, Aaron doesn't tell him anything. Or at least not the kind of things that lead to a bridge.

"You first?" Dad asks.

Aaron shakes his head, and his dad relents and goes first.

"Physically: bone-tired. Who knew that a freakin' practicum would be more taxing than investment banking? I tell you what: I can't wait until I have my own practice and I don't have to do the endless rotation at Montefiore. Emotionally: joyful and angry. Mostly joyful, but this prick in a BMW ran a red light even though there were about a hundred of us waiting in the crosswalk, just about to cross, and you know that stupid, selfish drivers make me homicidal. Spiritually: somewhat connected. I meditated on my second break, but that doesn't always last through a spate of bulimic teens. Mentally: pretty sharp for nearly nine o'clock, I must say. How about you, bud?"

Aaron puts down his spoon and stares at his father's forehead. That's as close as he can comfortably get to his eyes, but he makes sure to make intermittent contact because if he doesn't, Dad will ask questions. Aaron cannot answer questions today.

"Physically: okay. My legs itch. Probably the grass allergy because I went to Riverside Park after school. Just to hang and do some writing."

His dad smiles that inimitable smile he has, the one where his right dimple rises perhaps two millimeters higher than his left yet his right eye stays still—a leftover from the Bell's palsy he had in his twenties.

"Emotionally: fine. Good. Joyful and a little sad, I guess."

"A little?" his dad asks.

"Okay, sad," Aaron says, rolling his eyes.

His tone is playful. It is complete bullshit and it makes him sick of himself.

Sad?

Sad is hearing about a jumper on the news.

Sad is not seeing it right next to you.

Sad is not knowing it should have been you.

"Go on," Dad answers with an impish grin.

"Spiritually: the same as yesterday. Not sure what to believe. Mentally: sharp as a tack. Done. Fini."

The *fini* gets stuck in his dry throat. It comes with a series of images of the falling girl and the gentle smack when she hit the water, a smack that was in reality anything but gentle. His dad is looking directly at him. Aaron averts his eyes.

Dad goes over and kisses him on top of the head. "My dad radar is going off and I don't know why. Am I projecting? You sure you're fine?"

Aaron shrugs. "I didn't find out about *Avenue Q* yet. Thought today was the day but apparently not. And anyway, I'm not sure . . ."

Dad looks at him, waiting for him to finish. Aaron won't. He can't. It's too close to the truth. The stupid reason he wound up on the bridge.

It wasn't one thing, of course. And thank God for that, since killing yourself because someone didn't like you in a play is too self-absorbed, even for him. But that was basically the last straw. On the subway home from school, when Sarah Palmer mentioned she'd seen their school production of *Rent*, stupidly—he was so painfully stupid—he asked how she'd liked it.

"It was . . . okay," she said. The train was heading into Manhattan, over the Bronx River.

"Is that all?" he asked.

She ran her fingers through her long brown hair. "I thought Kelly Jameson was really good."

Kelly Jameson had been Mimi to his Roger. Kelly was on the fast track to AMDA—the American Musical and Dramatic Academy—and everyone knew she was awesome. Sarah's elusive statement ought to have been enough to get a normal kid to stop digging. But Aaron wasn't normal and he sucked with social cues, and mostly he didn't want to walk around miserable all night if she was simply forgetting to compliment him. They were pretty good friends, after all. And everyone had said he'd been a really good Roger. Marissa Jones had said his and Kelly's duet of "Without You" was almost better than the Broadway cast album version. So he followed up.

"What about me?"

Sarah pursed her lips.

That ought to have been enough, but it wasn't. Nothing was ever enough for him, and he hated himself for it.

"What? Did I, like, suck?" he persisted. "I don't care. You can tell me."

Sarah took a deep breath and tapped her fingers against the window.

"I thought you were not great," she said. "Your voice is just okay. I thought you kind of knew that. Sorry. I'm just being honest."

He laughed. He always laughed when his feelings were hurt. Also because it was a pile-on, and maybe she didn't know it, but it was, and he was thinking, *Great. Awesome. Thank you, Sarah. I cannot take a single thing more. Thanks a lot.*

But instead he said, "Yeah. I know. I kinda sucked."

Sarah looked relieved. "For what it's worth, I thought almost everyone was really bad."

It wasn't worth much, and when he stood to get off at the George Washington Bridge stop, he expected someone would ask why he was getting off there when he lived a hundred blocks south, but no one did. As he climbed the steps to the street, he thought: *No one can ever know that this was the last straw. That I killed myself because Sarah Palmer didn't like me in* Rent. *That's too pathetic, even for me.*

It wasn't just that, though. It was a lot of stuff.

It was that he was tired of being so deeply sick of himself and his stupid brain.

It was that he was tired of always fucking up.

It was that he couldn't see this ever changing.

It was that the world ignored him so much that he figured it wouldn't make a difference if one day he didn't show up to life.

It was that he even sucked at the things he thought he was good at.

Witness the severely underwhelming performance of the video he'd posted last night on YouTube. Insignificant, but symbolic in its insignificance. "Walking Alone" was the track, and while he'd recorded it, he'd had a sense that this was the one where it all came together. The lyrics were real and he felt them deep inside. Maybe it was a little retro . . . but people liked retro, right? It was going to be his breakthrough on Spotify, make the Viral 50. He felt it in his bones.

He'd come up with the lyrics in a fit of inspiration.

Spending time on my own
Right now it's all I can do
Taking walks all alone
Because I can't be with y

There were times when his lyrics stabbed him in the gut. He'd come to know that feeling, when he wrote something that begged to be heard by others. He'd come to understand that those moments were real, and that's why out of his maybe two hundred songs, he'd written music for only twelve.

This was one of those.

He opened GarageBand and in about an hour he came up with the music. He banged out a slow, somber dirge of a melody on the electric piano, and then he slowed down a retro beat from 120 bpm to 75, and the resulting sound was—haunting. He added a bass track that looped, and then his vocals. His singing, people said, was like Bob Dylan's. (He knew this meant it wasn't naturally pretty, but gritty was good to a lot of people, so it was good enough for him.) There was a yearning in the vocals that made his stomach buzz because people would hear it, and they'd just get it. They'd get *him*. They'd admire *him*.

It was one of Dad's late nights at Montefiore, so a long chat in his bedroom and a sharing of the new music wasn't in the cards, and this one needed to be heard immediately. So he got on his YouTube channel and played it, and then came up with the genius idea to record a harmony and sing the vocals live. That's the one he published, and then he sent out an email to every single person he knew, telling them he had recorded his best song ever.

This was how it worked. This was how you went Viral 50. You made a good song, you got people talking about it on YouTube, you paid to send it off to Spotify, you caught the attention of an influential playlist maker, and bam! You're Ed Sheeran.

Then he waited. Hours. Seventy-four people on his email list. The number of plays? Six. Four or five of them were his, he was pretty sure.

Out of seventy-four people, maybe one or two people had clicked play. And not a single comment or like.

Was he that bad? What did everyone else know about him that he didn't know? No comments or likes cut him from the inside, pierced his organs and hollowed him out until he was utterly cored.

He remembers how he lay there last night, and he found a spot on his bedroom wall and he stared at it, the beige wall, so plain, so I-need-something-to-change-but-nothing-ever-does. He stared and he stared, thinking, *This isn't normal.* Because he hadn't ever stared at a spot before for hours, and if he could have moved, he would have gone online and searched *staring at a spot on the wall for hours*, but he couldn't actually move. When his father came home and stopped by his open doorway, Aaron closed his eyes and pretended to be asleep with the lights on, and then, when Dad turned the lights out, he opened his eyes again, staring back at that same spot he could no longer see, and he wondered whether anyone would miss him if he just disappeared from the world.

"Aar—?" his dad says now.

"Wha— Yeah."

"Where are you, Aaron Boroff?"

He pastes a smile on his face. One that even he'd believe. He's that good an actor.

"Bermuda," he says. "Sorry, thinking of something funny."

Dad smiles. "Okay. You're sure you're all right?"

Aaron cocks his head and looks at his dad out of the side of his eye. Dad laughs. "Okay. Just checking. Sleep tight?"

"Bedbugs, you'd better not bite or there will be hell to pay," Aaron says.

Dad laughs again, hugs him, kisses him on the top of the head, and goes to his bedroom.

Aaron is left alone, wondering how on earth his father would have reacted had Aaron been the one to jump.

The news finally comes through overnight. When Aaron checks his phone after he wakes up, there it is on the *Daily News* website.

Private School Girl Jumps from Bridge

An Upper East Side private school girl was pronounced dead after she apparently jumped from the George Washington Bridge on Wednesday afternoon.

The body of the 17-year-old girl was found on Wednesday evening in the Hudson River close to the bridge, authorities said. The injuries were consistent with someone who had jumped from a high distance.

Port Authority police are notifying the family. The teenager's name has not been disclosed.

In the first four months of this year, there have been eleven suicides at the bridge. Seven of those have been teenagers.

Simultaneously numb and peeved by the lack of information, Aaron tries Heavy.com, because they tend to sometimes go further than the traditional news sites in terms of publishing information, and he needs her name. There's been nothing in the last twenty-four hours about a jumper. He tries Twitter, typing in the names of various private schools and the word *suicide*. Once he types *Spence*, a post comes up from fifteen minutes earlier.

LYT @lyt_tenor
It was a Spence girl who committed suicide. omg I didn't know her! Tillie something?

And then a response:

MoseDuBose @mosedubose
@lyt_tenor That's seriously fukked up. Don't know her

Aaron types in *Tillie Spence suicide*, and a bunch of tweets come up.

SammiLovesLemons @SammiQ10028
Omg Spence people. Tillie Stanley suicide. Poor Molly 😞
This is gonna kill her I can't even

And then there's this response:

Natasha Out! @mikedropnatNYC
@SammiQ10028 did you really just gloss over the fact that Tillie is dead and worry about fucking Molly Tobin, aka the reason why? You are literally the worst person.

Followed by this:

SammiLovesLemons @SammiQ10028
@mikedropnatNYC First off RIP Tillie Stanley. Second no one is talking to you. Ever. Remember that.

Followed by this:

Natasha Out! @mikedropnatNYC
@SammiQ10028 This. This is a lovely example of just the kind of online bullying that killed Tillie, so . . . congratulations on that. #worldsworstperson

SammiLovesLemons @SammiQ10028
@mikedropnatNYC so you calling me the world's worst person isn't online bullying but what I said is? Because I have friends and you don't? #wrongpersonjumped

Aaron closes his eyes. Tillie Stanley. He didn't see her up close, but she didn't look like a Tillie Stanley. Could it have been another jumper? He types Tillie's full name into Google Images and one of the photos that comes up is of three teenage girls at a formal dance or a gala of some sort. One is Black and has a large smile. Another is white, short, and skinny with pale blond hair. The third is Asian, short and wide, and she looks like she's been caught mid-sentence, because her mouth is half-open. Aaron's heart crashes into his stomach as he realizes it's the third girl. He stares into her eyes and mouths, *Sorry, Tillie Stanley, rest in peace.* Why why why didn't he just—say something? Go over to her? Stop being so damn selfish all the time. He's so selfish, so useless.

His father knocks on the door with his usual knock-pause-knock-knock-pause-knock-knock-knock rhythm.

"How's Aaron?"

Aaron groans. It's like he's on autopilot. This is the role he plays. Tired, lazy teenager. But his heart isn't in it today.

"You almost ready for school?"

"Yes," Aaron says, remembering he did zero homework yesterday, because, well. "Coming."

It's silent on the other side of the door, and he doesn't hear footsteps walking away.

Aaron gets up, lunges into his open closet, and puts on a tattered gray robe he sometimes wears. He opens the door.

"Morning, Father dearest," he says.

His dad wrinkles his nose and lunges his face forward to sniff. "Aaron. You gotta wash that. Immediately. Or burn it. I think I need to get another Magda, don't I?"

"I can do laundry, Dad."

"You can, yes. But you don't. And I'm sorry. Not the way to greet a day. I apologize. Good morning, dearest son."

Aaron bows respectfully. Inside his rib cage is the remnant of what he just read, but he pushes it down, caches it in his gut, along with all the other stuff from yesterday.

His dad is regarding him with much the same expression he had last night. "I swear that something's not right. Are you depressed, bud? You know you can tell me, right? That I would do anything, anytime, anyhow, to help you? That I'd stop the world for you?"

"Yeah," Aaron says. "You'd stop the world. I know."

It's the word. *Depression*. He gets it, that less than twenty-four hours ago he nearly died. But the word doesn't feel . . . apt. Insofar as depression means sad, it's kind of like, yeah. He has sadness. But also he has happiness, at random moments, and silliness, most of the time, and weirdness, just about always. His feelings are his. They don't fit in a box and have a tidy label. A lot of things could happen and he'd feel better. Like if people commented on his songs, or laughed when he said things. He's experienced it. One laugh, and then the rib crush? It's like it never existed. That's not *depressed*; that's

Aaron-esque, he guesses. Anyway, depression is interior. He knows that from his dad. This thing is just—his life is broken. Not his brain.

His dad is studying him like he's a science project, perhaps something he's grown in a petri dish.

"I got my eye on you, mister," he says.

Aaron closes his left eye and squints his right. "And I got my eye on you, madame."

His dad smirks and rolls his eyes. "Breakfast?"

"Cinnamon toast up. Orange juice, two small ice cubes. The round kind."

His dad bows, which Aaron knows is a tribute to one of Aaron's signature moves. "Showerup. And burn that robe, okay? I love you?"

Aaron laughs. If there's one thing in the world that's not in question, it's his dad's love.

"And you I love?" he says back, à la Yoda, and his dad smirks again and leaves him alone with his thoughts and his odiferous robe.

In the shower his brain does its Aaron thing, skipping from one random thought to another, which is why he'll never be a scientist or a doctor or a lawyer or anyone who needs to have cogent, normal, focused thoughts. He thinks about Tillie Stanley, and a shiver runs through him despite the piping hot water running down his back, so his brain switches over to Mr. O'Mahoney from middle school, who still is and will always be his go-to, and his butt in gray coach's shorts, and *Avenue Q*, and today is a new day, and he's gonna push all the awful down, and no one will ever, ever know about yesterday, and thank god he didn't succeed, and simultaneously he wishes he did, because he didn't do his creative writing assignment and Ms. Hooper will give disappointed face, which is his least favorite Hooper expression, and Mr. O'Mahoney, bending down to pick up a soccer ball, and good god, man, they should sculpt that thing out of marble and make a monument, and is he ever going to have actual sex, and soap! He's standing there, wet-but-soapless. How is it he sometimes forgets the soap, that might be a slight issue if he ever does want to have actual sex, and is it possible that Evan Hanson is gay? Not Evan Hansen from the show. Real Evan Hanson from school. Can you imagine having a name and then suddenly your name is a show and the rest of your life, every time you meet someone, it's like, *Are you Evan Hansen from the show?* He would change it. He would totally, totally change it, and but so anyhow Evan Hanson, senior, sometimes theater-doer, and that taxi ride to the west side from Cecil's party together and it was so awkward and so delicious and maybe touched by a little sexual tension? Hard to know, hard to know. But Tillie, Tillie Stanley falling, what's next, what happens after? His mother—what would she have thought if he had—would she have thought it was her fault? His dad definitely should know it wasn't—

There's a knock on the bathroom door, and he comes to, realizing he has no idea how long he's been standing there getting pelted by water.

"You okay in there?"

"Uh, yeah. Peachy!"

"There's cinnamon toast up, getting soggy."

"Okay!"

Aaron finishes up. He tries to focus. But every time he does, he returns to the photo of Tillie, playing in his mind.

So he unfocuses again.

X

Across town, Winnie and Frank Stanley sit on a couch in their living room, motionless.

Winnie feels like the police cut her midsection open and pulled out her organs one at a time with their news, saving her heart for last. She isn't sure a time will come when she'll be able to get up from this couch. She may live here now.

Frank is silent. No surprise there.

For his part, Frank holds his breath. He ignores the devastation lodged in his torso, the wreckage that is his throat and neck, and he refuses to breathe. He has to get out of here. As soon as he can.

Britt is in her room, staring at her phone, which isn't on. Maybe if she keeps staring, the world will rewind to before the police came. Before this thing. Which doesn't make sense. She wants her dad to come in and tell her it isn't true. It's just a bad joke. A prank. She wants her mom to make it go away.

Nobody comes by. She keeps staring at the blank screen.

✕

On the subway, Aaron sits next to Topher Flaherty, who goes on and on about Nimbus and Rage, the Flower, and some rave he went to that interests Aaron not in the least. Sarah gets on at Eighty-Sixth and sits on the other side of him.

"Hey, did you do Spanish?" she asks.

Aaron shakes his head, forcing his brain to forget what she said yesterday about him in *Rent*.

"Shit," she says. "What, were you, like, gaming all night?"

He scratches his nose. "Something like that."

"Maybe Ms. Higuera won't check today."

"I hope she wears something floral, is all I know."

Sarah laughs. "I think there's a decent chance of that."

"Maybe it's the trend in old people? To have big orange and pink lilies instead of breasts?"

Sarah laughs again. "Probably."

"I'm considering a line of clothing for boys, pants where the crotch is a huge tulip."

"Put your tulips on my crotch," Topher says, and Sarah and Aaron stare at him like, *Did you just say that?*

As they get closer to 242nd, the row across from Aaron fills up with Fieldstonians, kids he likes. Vonte Mendoza. Emily Claiborne. Jebeze. And he smiles, feeling a little at home for the moment, and utterly free of the hollowness in his gut. When it's gone, it's kind of hard to imagine it was ever there in the first place.

Getting off the subway and waiting for the shuttle bus to school is always kind of sobering, because almost all the other students take a private bus from Manhattan. His dad can't swing it financially. The kids are too nice to openly look down on a scholarship kid, but he feels the separation nonetheless. He's a subway kid.

The streets of the Van Cortlandt Park area and its elevated subway tracks covered in graffiti and its pizzerias and smoke shops quickly morph into the quiet, tree-lined suburban streets of River-dale, and then here he is: another day at one of the most expensive private schools in the country.

One time over the summer after ninth grade, when he was out at his mom's place on Cape Cod—Sandwich, not a Hyannis mansion or anything like that—she paged through his yearbook and shook her head.

"All the kids look like models. How do you even cope?"

"Um," Aaron said, screwing up his face.

"Oh, honey," his mom replied. "You're nice-looking, too. I just mean. These kids are all so gorgeous!"

"I know you think you just made it better, but you kind of didn't," he said, and she dismissed him with a wave of her hand.

As he walks the quad toward the main building, this disparity morphs and multiplies in the fun-house mirror of his brain. The only reason they live in a nice apartment on Seventy-Eighth and Riverside overlooking the Hudson River is that his grandmother willed it to his dad when she died, back when Aaron was ten. The only reason he's at the most expensive private school in the country is that his dad pulled strings and got him a nearly full scholarship. He's not fabulous, he doesn't really belong there, and he's not good enough, and he's an idiot dork moron geek loser sad clown bad bad bad.

Walking to homeroom, he passes the *Avenue Q* sign and sees no cast list, still, which sucks. Then he spies a sign-up sheet for the talent show two weeks from Saturday. He stops and stares at it. He cracks up and rolls his eyes. *Right. You people can't even be bothered to listen to one song when I send it to you. I'm not wasting my—*

A second thought trips over the first. *But they didn't even hear it.* There were so few clicks, so it's not like people rejected it. They just didn't listen.

And then, as he stands there, staring at the Sharpie hanging from a string attached to the bottom of the sign-up sheet with a blue thumbtack, he has a fantasy. He's onstage, performing "Walking Alone." The rapt attention as he gets to the chorus: *Taking walks all alone, because I can't be with you . . .* and his eyes meet Evan Hanson's, and they have a moment, a thing where the curtain rises between two people and there's that heart shimmy that happens when someone sees him, really sees him, and he hears Evan's voice: *You, Aaron Boroff. You have layers. You're so much more than they know. Is the* you *in the song . . . me? Could it be, please?* And

Aaron smiles dopily, because he knows it's just a fantasy but it's a scrumptious fantasy nonetheless, and that's enough to make him add his name to the list.

×

Molly Tobin's mom cancels her Pilates class to hang with her.

"You okay, darling?" her mom asks, sitting at Molly's bedside.

Molly stares at her with red-rimmed eyes. There's oblivious and then there's *oblivious*.

The girl she got suspended for making fun of, her old best friend from sixth grade, just jumped off a bridge. Committed suicide. She's dead.

Safe to say Molly is not exactly okay.

×

A few blocks north, at Browning School, a boy sits on the stage in the theater, in the dark, stunned. He was going to text her. Today. Why oh why did he have to wait? Why?

When his buddy Mike sent the link—*Is this her???*—Amir Rahimi was in English class.

Mike had been there when Amir met Tillie. All Mike knows is the few details Amir shared: that she fell for Amir and then he jetted.

Amir's story is more than that. Way more.

And yes, it was her. He clicked on the link and promptly ran out of class. He made it to within five feet of the bathroom before spewing vomit all over the floor. Then he looked both ways, saw he was alone in the hallway, and ran off to the theater, where he could be alone with his overwhelming shock and shame.

He had been intending to make things right. He had just been waiting for the right time. For the jitteriness to subside. So he could be real with her. Why couldn't she have given him one more day?

Sometimes ghosting isn't ghosting, he thinks, sitting there, his forehead resting in his palms. Sometimes what seems like an aggressive move to get rid of someone, actively ignore them, is something else entirely.

But the other person. They don't know that.

And that's the shittiest part of it all.

✕

As soon as he gets to the hospital for his rotation, an unsettled feeling creeps into Michael Boroff's gut.

"Are you feeling sad?" he asked his son, knowing the answer already. Aaron thought he was a better actor than he really was.

Michael calls his warrior brother Morris.

"You have a few minutes?" he asks, ducking into a supply closet. "Need to check in on something."

"Just doing my morning sudoku," Morris says. "What's up?"

"I can't get Aaron to talk. I can't get him to say anything. He's freezing me out."

"I hear that," Morris says. "What's the feeling?"

As much as the warrior speak helped him, sometimes it makes him a little homicidal.

"It feels fucking shitty!" he answers testily.

"Good awareness." Morris remains calm. "Say more about that."

And Michael allows himself to yell it out. "I have no control! It feels like I'm driving blind and I fucking hate it!"

The two men breathe together for a bit. And soon Michael feels better. Not good, but better. He laughs. Morris laughs, too.

"Yeah," Morris says. "Thank you. I believe that."

A calmness overcomes Michael. His heart is open. Thank God for that. For years, the world of finance had closed it. Not feeling things almost killed him. He hadn't even known. And now. Not easy. Not easy almost ever. But so much better. So much more real.

"Thank you," Michael says. "And thank you for not giving me advice. Because if you had given me advice, I would have hunted you down and killed you."

Morris laughs. "Wow. Aggressive."

The men both laugh.

"Thanks," Michael says again, his voice much softer now. "Thanks for holding space."

"No problem, brother."

X

In creative writing class, it's Aaron's day to be critiqued. On the positive side, that means he didn't neglect to read someone else's story last night. On the negative, he hasn't written anything new. Luckily, he has something ready to go because he's Aaron and of course he does, so he emails it around so they can follow along and he starts to get that jittery feeling in his throat that comes when he's about to be the center of attention, because he loves loves loves that and he'll never ever ever tell a soul just how much he loves it.

While everyone is opening the file, Ms. Hooper smiles at him and strolls over to his front-row desk. She points at him with a wiggle of her finger.

"I really loved that song," she says. "Wow."

Aaron feels his face heat up. Mystery solved on one of the two other listeners. "Um, thanks. I know it's kind of bad."

"Not at all. It's the opposite. I love how you emote in your songs. It's such a good outlet for you."

Aaron swallows. He knows this isn't what gets said to future music legends, necessarily, but he's too tired to focus there, so he smiles again and focuses on the *wow*.

"Thanks."

He reads his piece, which is a change-of-pace story for him. Pretty much everything he writes is from his life, thinly veiled versions of things that had happened to him or were on his mind. Like when he wrote about a kid who was scared to come out. It said what he couldn't, and everybody was really supportive and three girls came up after and gave him a hug and said he should sit with them at lunch. The lunchtime arrangement lasted only a couple days, but he was always grateful for how the kids in the class had rallied by his side. And he came out shortly after, so that was good.

Today's piece, though, is more funny. He does dialogue straight from his weirdo social-worker-in-training, men's-group-going dad, and then he gives a pretty random but amusing inner monologue from the subway. A friend makes an offhanded joke that Aaron considers really weird, and he thinks, in response, *What are you, autistic?*

When the story is done and the critique starts, Staci Raimey raises her hand.

"I just think it's interesting that Aaron asks for total support and acceptance of his gayness," she says, twirling her frizzy brown hair around her finger, "but, like, autism is funny to him."

He isn't supposed to speak during the workshop, but this catches him off guard.

"What?" he asks. It was a throwaway line. He didn't mean anything by it. "I—"

Ms. Hooper shushes him. "No talking when it's your story being critiqued."

"That was super offensive," Staci says. "Using *autistic* like it's something bad."

Aaron knows he made a dumb mistake. He'd written it without thinking, and when Kwan talks about how mean people are to his brother, who has Asperger's, and how words really can hurt people, and that Aaron should know that, a little bit of him dies inside.

He walks to Spanish feeling like the worst person in the world. Which he is. Because he's been mean, and him being mean indicates that he must have abandoned himself, lost himself somewhere, because nothing about Aaron has ever really been mean, and it isn't acceptable to him to think of himself as a hurter rather than a hurtee, as someone who lets a girl jump off a bridge instead of someone who jumps himself. Ms. Higuera asks him *cómo está*, and Aaron says *bien*, but he's anything but *bien*, and he hears almost nothing the rest of class.

He sits alone at lunch, a dark fog settling over him, thoughts reaching low into an abyss that reminds him of the bridge yesterday. How can feelings actually hurt his body? But they do. They push out against his rib cage like an expanding devil bubble, and he finds it's hard to breathe.

Kwan puts his tray down and says, "Can I sit here?"

Aaron nods and says "sure" softly. It's all the voice he has at the moment.

Kwan waves, and suddenly Ratiya Song and Ebony McClendon and Josh Porter join them, and dread seeps into Aaron's chest. He's not gonna be able to handle whatever's coming. Not by a long shot.

"So in diversity club," Ratiya says, "we have this ouch/oops policy."

"Yeah," says Ebony. "When you microaggress, a person interrupts and says, 'Ouch.' And then they explain why they said it, and then the microaggressor has a chance to say, 'Oops,' and make things right."

"Oops," Aaron says to the table in front of him, avoiding everyone's eyes because he's afraid if he looks at them they'll see that he's just about through. With life. With everything. Everything feels tight. They don't know, and it's not something you can tell people. That they should be kind to a microaggressor because he almost jumped off a bridge the day before and is feeling kinda jumpy again. It's not a thing you say, and he doesn't deserve it anyway.

As his classmates talk him through it, Aaron nods and nods and nods and says sorry, sorry, sorry until they finally go away, which is about a minute after he feels his system failing, like a computer spinning, spinning until you have to just shut it down, and his head is buzzing and things feel out of perspective, like the walls in the hall tilt slightly to the left and his feet feel like they might stumble on the uneven floor beneath him.

He finds himself avoiding the eyes of everyone in the dizzy-making, skewed hallway, sure word has gotten out that he wrote something hurtful and that everyone is talking about it. If he'd jumped yesterday, people would be saying nice things about him, but instead he's still alive and everyone hates hates hates him and what in the world are they saying in the hallways at Spence about Tillie, and it's probably mostly nice, and could he get that without the dying part, could he just get everyone to be nice even when he's bad, even when he's wrong.

Tillie, is it better where you are? Are you finally at peace? Was it worth it? Did it work?

In physics class, he struggles to pay attention, and the difference between centripetal and centrifugal goes right through him and he feels it not landing, and he realizes he doesn't actually care anymore. It just goes through him. And when the bell rings, the funniest thing ever happens.

He doesn't move.

Aaron is staring at the whiteboard. A crack in the upper-left quadrant that is almost a diagonal line, almost leading toward the top-left corner, but not quite. It's imperfect and random.

"Aaron?" Dr. Sengupta says from the front of the classroom. It may be empty, it may be emptying. Aaron doesn't know. He cannot move his head.

Hmm, he thinks. *This is new. This is interesting.* Aaron likes new and interesting, but not this new and interesting in particular. It's petrifying because he literally cannot move and if he had feelings left he would feel deeply scared. But feelings are gone.

"Aaron?" Dr. Sengupta repeats, and it's as if Aaron is watching a movie but not seeing it. He knows there's a classroom, and he's in it, but he can't quite see the scene, and his mind tells him, *It might be good for you to stand now and walk out of the classroom, because there will be repercussions*—but that's not a choice he has. He can't. Move.

The next fifteen minutes are notable in that he is aware that a class is not starting, despite the bell. Something, someone, must be keeping the kids out of the classroom. Sengupta and the Nameless They were talking to him and then not talking to him, trying to roust him and then accepting the unmovable object that is Aaron Boroff, who is so, so weird, and this will not help his reputation but also, again, he doesn't care anymore. He can't.

The stretcher feels new. A new form of transport from the physics room. And as he's carried out as a sort of problematic Egyptian king, the thought he has is that he'd better not come to right now, because probably nothing would be more alarming to him than what is happening right at the moment, except it's not quite happening to him, is it? It's the idea of an event, happening to someone else. His brain is cushioned by white cloud. His eyes are very much open but unseeing. His ears are swathed with a puff of toilet tissue from the inside, clogging up the canal.

The ambulance is.

The hospital hallway, too. Is.

Is. Is. Is. Time undulates, goes copper. Then silver-white.

The questions the doctor asks are not for him and it seems from the tone of what he can hear that this is understood, much like an agreement in math, when it's understood that X is a positive integer, perhaps. Solve for Y. He is Y. Someone is there with him, and the presence of this person is a color, off blue, like a grayish version that dulls at the corners and will never take anyone to prom. No one likes this blue or invites it to hang out in front of the Museum of Natural History on Friday nights.

Is Topher? Is Sengupta? Is the assistant principal? Who has a name, too? They?

Dad?

"So I heard you had quite a day yesterday," Dr. Laudner says.

Aaron nods, but he's elsewhere. Not elsewhere like yesterday, when he really wasn't present. More like contemplative, tired. He's sitting in a small, faded, gray-walled office that is packed with ferns, as if this dude should have gone into horticulture and started a greenhouse rather than becoming a shrink. The doctor, a tall, lanky middle-aged guy with a well-trimmed blond beard, sits across the room in a high-backed beige leather chair, taking Aaron in with a look that is not unkind.

For Aaron, it feels like he's taken a vacation from his life. Like by not going to school on a Friday, and having his dad take the day off, too, it's as if it's summer break without the heat. He's stepped outside the bounds of what is usual and it feels a bit like the end of the world. And he's not sure it will ever feel any better, ever again.

"Aaron?" Dr. Laudner says.

"Sorry."

"So the last couple days. Tell me about them."

Aaron goes through the experience as best he can, and it's all so exhausting to relive. He leaves out the part about Tillie; that's not something he's up for sharing. He finds that when he gets to the part where he's carried out of the classroom on a stretcher, he has to pause. Not because he's going to cry; he's far too numb for that. It's more that he's so, so tired. Of talking. Of everything.

Thankfully, Dr. Laudner doesn't push. They just sit there in silence for a bit, and then the doctor grabs a clipboard from his desk and hands it to Aaron.

"How about if we just have you fill this out," he says, and at that moment Aaron decides he likes Dr. Laudner.

The doctor hands him a questionnaire. There are eighteen questions, and each has six multiple choice responses: *Not at All, Just a Little, Somewhat, Moderately, Quite a Lot,* or *Very Much.* If he weren't nearly comatose, he knows he'd probably find the British-sounding responses charming. Instead, he just stares for a bit and then gets to work.

It's not hard to answer the first. He realizes he's been staring at the statement *I do things slowly* for a long time, so that one gets an easy *Very Much.*

Does his future seem hopeless? What future? Check. *Very Much.*

Has the pleasure and joy gone out of his life? Check. If there ever was any, it's now totally gone. *Very Much.*

He stares at the column of *Very Much,* and suddenly the word *Much* looks like it's misspelled, or not a word, or it's lost its meaning.

The eighth question is the first one that doesn't get a *Very Much. I am agitated and keep moving around.* Um, no. *Not at All.*

But the rest are all *Very Much,* and when he gets to fifteen, which asks if he spends a lot of time thinking about how he might kill himself, his hand starts shaking and he overfills the circle. *Very Much.*

In the end, he has fifteen *Very Much,* one *Quite a Lot,* one *Moderately,* and one *Not at All.* He motions the clipboard at Dr. Laudner, who jumps up and collects it. He then sits down and scores it with a blue pen.

When he's done, he looks up at Aaron. "So you scored an eighty-two," he says.

Aaron asks, "Is that good?"

"Zero to nine is not depressed. Anything over fifty-four is severely depressed."

"Just like me to pick the worst time to get a B-minus."

This makes Dr. Laudner laugh, Quite a Lot, and Aaron, despite himself, perks up Just a Little.

"So let's talk," the doctor says, and Aaron tells a little bit. How he felt going up to the bridge and deciding not to jump. And about his dad sobbing in the hospital, when he heard, and how that made Aaron feel like the worst person in the world. Super Guilty. And all the background of his life. Just the facts, ma'am. His dad and his mom. The divorce when he was eight, which multiplied his holiday presents by two, basically. Living with Dad ten months a year, visits to Mom during the summer and over Christmas, which makes sense since she's Christian and Dad is Jewish. The doctor nods at all the right places, and Aaron finds that he's pretty comfortable, actually. For a guy who went, like, full-on catatonic a day earlier, for a guy who just aced the severely depressed test, just talking feels okay, like a warm sweater and a log on the fireplace at his mom's place in Sandwich, writing a song or maybe a funny short story. *Hygge*. Which is a word his dad taught him.

"So tell me about your mom," the doctor says, crossing his legs.

Aaron presses his tongue against the top of his mouth like he's trying to stop brain freeze. He bites his lip.

"She's a person," he says.

"Well, that's encouraging."

Aaron cracks a mild smile. "It *is* encouraging."

"Tell me about her."

"Not much to tell," Aaron says, and for some reason he thinks about the beach thing.

He's eight years old. It's a bright, sunny summer day and Dad is still working in a bank. It's just before the split, before his dad's Big Change, and Mom is home, one of those meandering days in Forest Hills, with Mom at the helm, once in a while going to auditions but mostly just hanging. They've settled into a routine. Cocoa Puffs and Pillsbury croissants rising in the oven, watching cartoon DVDs—*Ren & Stimpy*, his mom's favorite—on the family room couch. Then it's across the street to the park, where he joins the other kids running in circles through the sprinkler while his mom sits alone, away from the other moms who congregate by the same row of benches every day. Aaron's mom is not a *plays well with other moms* sort of person. Aaron loves these days. The predictability of the endless hours with nothing that they need to do.

But on this day, they don't have their usual breakfast. Mom wakes him early. Her eyes are puffy and pink.

"C'mon," she says. "We're going for a train ride."

Aaron lights up. He loves his mom, and he adores a good adventure.

The train leaves from Penn Station. His mom says they're going to Jones Beach. Aaron cheers, wondering: *Where's our stuff?* His mom isn't carrying any bags, and for the beach, you usually want a blanket, bathing suits, towels, maybe a pail and shovel to play with, that gooey sunblock in the orange squeeze bottle.

"Don't we need things?" he asks.

"It's an adventure," she says. "Stop worrying."

On the train, Mom starts saying things she's never said before.

She puts her hand on his knee. "I'm so completely bored, Aaron. Do you know what that's like?"

"No."

"I hope you never know. It's torture."

They take a train and then a jam-packed bus, and once they reach the beach, they walk onto the sand and keep walking, aimlessly. Aaron keeps spotting places that would be good for building a sandcastle but they don't stop anywhere, and he keeps stealing glances at his mom, who just looks blank—tired, maybe. Finally, without warning, she plops down in the sand like an unstrung marionette. Aaron looks around, wondering if someone will bring them a blanket or towels.

"What should we do? We can go in the water or we can build a sandcastle," he offers. "We can draw pictures in the sand."

She nods, doesn't answer, looking off at the horizon, sitting on her hands on the warm, slightly wet sand. She smokes a cigarette, which he's never seen her do before. He sits next to her and breathes in the chalky fumes, and he starts to dig a little, and he finds himself getting thirsty and his head is on fire from the sun but it's fun to just dig, dig, so he does and then he starts to feel the heat in his cheeks and he remembers the time he got a burn when he was five in Cape May, and they had to put lotion on him and his skin peeled for a week.

After about an hour and a half, his mother stands and wipes sand off her knees and hands.

"This is stupid," she says. "Mom screwed up."

They walk back toward the bus, away from the water they never got to play in.

"Sometimes you try new things," she says as they walk. "Occasionally they work."

Aaron remembers so clearly staring down at the sand as they walked, trying to step entirely in big people's footsteps. *You have to make your own fun* was the thought he had. Which turns out to be true, Aaron realizes, and he smiles, and he crosses his arms over his chest.

"What are you thinking about?" the doctor asks.

"Nothing," he says, remembering that moments ago he was noticing it was hygge in here, and he wants his hygge back. He offers a tight-lipped smile. "A good memory."

×

Aaron's father is seated in the waiting area when Aaron comes out with a prescription and a bunch of business cards, which is weird, like the doctor wants Aaron to hand them out on a street corner or something. He hands them to his dad.

"He wants me here every day this coming week. I told him I didn't know if I could because—"

"You can," his father says. "Of course. This is the only thing right now. Nothing else matters but getting you better."

"Also I guess I'm going to be on medicine because there was this depression-ometer in there and I broke it. We owe him money because he has a 'you break it, you buy it' policy."

His dad hugs him tight and buries his chin into the back of Aaron's neck. "I am so sorry. I feel like I let you down. How could you go up there—how did I miss this?"

Aaron doesn't answer. He doesn't know what to say. He's thinking about Tillie. If his score was eighty-two, what was hers?

×

Even though the body is barely recognizable, barely what it was, they still need to pick out clothes for the funeral.

Winnie asks Frank to do it. Frank says yes and then he gets a business call, and he has to take it, and he's so sorry, but would she mind, and Winnie says of course, she'll do it, of course, and she walks into the room and it steals her breath. She has to steady herself against the doorframe. It's like she's walked into an actual physical barrier and it slammed her in the stomach.

How does anyone do this? How can a parent be asked to—

And suddenly Britt is there, standing next to her mom, and it happens with no words. Britt goes in, and maybe she heard them talking about picking out clothes? She goes in and steps into the closet and looks around. Even at this moment when she has never understood Tillie less, she tries to figure out what she would want to be buried in.

Something black, it seems to Britt, makes sense. Tillie liked black. And pink. White is for weddings. But it doesn't matter what she wears, also, because it's not really her. She's in a box but she isn't. She'll be wearing clothes but she's dead.

None of it makes any sense.

✕

The text comes from a number Molly's never seen before.

> Are you happy now? You know you killed Tillie, right?

The breath gets caught in Molly's throat, and the weird thing that happens next is that she pictures her old friend from sixth grade, Tillie with pigtails and pink scrunchies, and then she pictures *that* girl, not the weird one who'd changed so much, jumping off the bridge. And her eyes well up.

She doesn't answer the text. What is there to say? The texter is right, but that's not, like, something you agree with on the record. Could she go to jail?

A second text comes in from the same number.

You need to die for what you did.

Molly turns off her phone. As if whatever that was—a threat?—will cease to exist if she powers down.

"Are you up for a trip to Sephora?" her mom asks through the door.

Fury catches in her throat. How is it possible that her mother is thinking about makeup right now?

"No thanks," Molly says, as neutral as possible, hoping her mother will just go away.

And when her mom goes, Molly decides it's time for a new look.

Her beautiful blond hair. It's always been her calling card. It's natural, and it's gorgeous, and she doesn't deserve to have it anymore.

She goes into her mom's bathroom and rifles through the drawers until she finds the electric clippers, and she removes the guard. She wants blade on scalp for sure.

Her first stroke is right down the middle, and she watches the hair disappear like she's watching the guy mow the lawn out in East Hampton. And as she does more strokes, and as the massive pile of blond accumulates at her feet, she thinks, *Me. My fault. I did this to Tillie.*

X

Amir has never had detention before. But he'd do it again in a second.

Of course he punched Jason Mathes in the face. Who wouldn't have punched him and broken his nose?

"You fucked that girl to death, dude."

Who thinks to say such a thing?

Of course he punched him. How could he not?

Thank God the other kids who witnessed this had more sense and talked Jason and his dad out of pressing charges.

So Amir sits there in Mr. Boswell's classroom, alone except for Mr. Boswell. He cannot focus on homework. He's tried to, but every time he pulls out his calc book, the words swim across the page like uninterested fish in an aquarium.

He pulls out a piece of paper and tries to write something. Anything to approximate the guilt he feels.

A girl is dead.

A girl I liked is dead.

Because I was a coward.

He reads it and he crumples it up into a ball. Garbage. Words can never come close to expressing anything he's feeling. And anyway, he can never say it now. He's caused enough trouble.

If he comes out now, he's the boy who killed a girl because he was too chickenshit to be who he was.

X

Aaron and his dad go to Barney Greengrass at Eighty-Sixth and Amsterdam for lunch. A treat, his father says. Since he left the bank and went into social work, they eat out almost never. As they open the door, Aaron is assaulted by the intermingling smells of pastrami, garlic, and cabbage, and the shouting of patrons trying to be heard at the insanely busy deli counter. He follows his dad to the hostess station at the entranceway to the dining area, his senses reeling from the smells and noise and the old Jewish people noshing on bagels and lox and it's a lot, a lot.

The old guy with the gray-white beard and crusty voice tells them five minutes and they stand there, cocooned between the noisy deli and the busy dining area, and Aaron feels trapped and like he can't breathe and he tries to go somewhere else, anywhere else.

"My dad used to take me here," his dad says. "It's a hoot."

Aaron nods and smiles as much as he can but the walls are closing in on him and he closes his eyes.

"Did he hate you?" Aaron asks.

His dad gives him a look. "Is this too much? Am I an idiot? I really just thought—"

"It's fine," Aaron says. "It's a lot but it's fine."

His father looks pained and glances at the door, but just at that moment, the bearded host calls their name.

"Is this what you want?" his dad asks.

Aaron shrugs. "Let's make some Jewish delicatessen memories."

They follow the host through the dining area, tables stuffed together like it's a clown car and they're all a bunch of clowns. The host takes them to the far diagonal corner, and they come to a standstill at a table of miraculously old people who block their way. The old guy sitting across from his wife looks up and laughs.

"I guess I'm the gatekeeper," he says, slowly standing, and Aaron's stomach twists. As he follows his dad and the host around the old man, all Aaron can feel is his own pulsing heartbeat, which is so strange to him because, yes, depressed, but he's been in crowds before. He doesn't have an issue with crowds. He made his dad go with him to Columbus Avenue to watch the balloons get blown up the night before Thanksgiving every year until last because there was something nice about the smell of chestnuts and hot chocolate, and the swarm of people made him feel alive. But suddenly it's the opposite and he's broken and he wonders what his claustrophobia score would be now: one sixty-six? Forty-nine? The scales are undefined and everything's unfixably wrong.

He sits against the wall, looking out on the messy mass of diners, and he stares at his menu, hoping to quiet his pulsing chest.

A Dr. Brown's cherry soda helps some, as do pickles, as Aaron sits there and tries to make sure his newfound claustrophobia doesn't show up.

"I would never eat the latkes," Dad says.

"No?"

"Definite no. 'Pancakes are not potatoes,' I used to explain. Your grandmother thought I was nuts. She basically foisted them upon me. For years, I could not eat at a table where someone else was eating any latke-like substance."

Aaron laughs, but he's checked out.

"Where is Aaron?"

Aaron looks around dramatically, but it's not really computing, the Aaron-Dad banter thing. He's just. Not. There. But he does it anyway because it's what they do.

"He's in one of the circles of hell, where they seat you in the back at a table where every time the waiter wants to get to you, a man who can barely stand is made to stand, and at some point he and his father die of hunger."

His dad screws up his face at him. "That's dark."

"Dark times are these," Aaron intones, channeling Yoda.

His father bends his head down and shakes it, which is not the reaction Aaron is expecting. He crosses his arms over his chest.

"I just . . ." Dad says.

"You just?"

"I just can't understand. Why you didn't tell me. I asked you. Like right after you went to the bridge. Like just yesterday morning. I asked you a thousand times. Why wouldn't you tell me? Did you think you couldn't tell me? I just. Help me understand, Aaron. Help me."

Aaron feels the jitters in his throat and his instinct is to yell but it wouldn't be words, it would be more like a roar of exasperation because it's too much, much too much. Here in this fetid pastrami palace, this cacophonous cabbage chaos. He's a fuckup. He gets it. Everything he does is wrong. He really, really gets it.

"What's going on? Aaron. You okay? Do we need to get you out of here?"

His dad is looking at him funny, looming over him, and it reminds Aaron of this Natasha balloon that one time on Thanksgiving was being blown up and it seemed to be staring down at him like . . . *Hello? Hello?* It was hard to explain but it cracked him up, and suddenly his dad is Natasha, and Aaron's laughing, and the laughter is guttural, or lower, it's a full-body laugh, and he convulses with it and his dad keeps looking at him, super concerned, and that's even more funny and he slides to the floor like this is the funniest thing that's ever happened and his body shakes and oh my God! Two out of two! Two days in a row, crazy body things! What's happening to him, to his body, these days, and this would be such a funny thing to tell Sarah on the bus and she'd laugh but no, no, no. It's actually not that funny and he's crying on the sticky, mustard-stained floor of a restaurant, hugging the wooden table leg, and he wants to disappear from the world. Forever.

His dad comes and tries to sit next to him but more like leans against the octogenarian woman's chair, and he kneels and cradles Aaron's head in his chest and Aaron slowly relaxes into his father's care, all the while breathing, slow, slow, as his dad offers the saddest, kindest litany he's ever heard.

"I'm sorry. I'm sorry. I'm sorry."

X

After the funeral, Britt hides in her room, playing Candy Crush.

She thinks, *Tillie didn't even say goodbye,* and she slashes a row of grape candy, and she imagines it's Tillie's face.

It's stupid when people don't say goodbye. And if Tillie was sad, she should have said so. Britt could have made her feel better. With a hug.

Explode three rows of lemon drops. Make them go bye. She won't cry. Not like Mom.

Dad didn't cry like a baby at the funeral, and she won't, either. Dad just stood there, and then after that he packed up and went on his business trip. Kissed Britt on the top of the head and went off with his suitcase because that's his job as a dad. Which is normal. Act normal, like Dad. Don't get all sad like Mom.

She smiles. That's her job. So while she crushes the stupid candy, she pastes a smile on her face.

X

Aaron lies in bed, alone, staring at the ceiling, on his first post-medicine Friday night. He feels like he has entered a club of one: the End of the World Club.

He thinks about the girl who would have understood, could

have joined him in the club. Tillie Stanley. He's curious about her in a way, but also he's afraid of knowing more. Of finding out that she was an amazing, shiny person, so much more necessary to the world than he is. That he should have died and she should have lived. He'll never unsee that moment, and the less he knows about her awesomeness, in some ways, the better.

He's always wanted things to be different but this isn't the way he was hoping. Suddenly he has a medication making its way slowly, painfully slowly, into his bloodstream, and who knows what it will do to him, or if he'll even recognize himself in a few days, or a week, or up to three weeks, as Dr. Laudner said.

What kind of masochist creates a medication to help people who are in emotional crises, and makes it so that it's only effective after three weeks? Is this a normal phase others have gone through? Just waiting around, hoping to wake up and not want to die?

He picks up his phone. Lots of text messages. From Sarah. From Marissa Jones. One from Ebony.

> Hey Aaron. I feel so bad. I didn't know what was up. Get well soon and we'll hang out.

Aaron types:

> thx and you didn't do anything wrong I did

There's no response right away, so Aaron puts the phone down and then picks it up again to turn it off.

"How you doing?" His dad sticks his head into the room. He's been coming and going with some regularity, bringing cups of tea and chicken soup as if Aaron has the flu and not a broken brain.

Aaron doesn't sit up. "I just won the Critics' Choice Award for Greatest Person."

His dad kisses the top of his head and scruffs his hair. After his dad leaves, Aaron sighs and reaches for the notebook his dad gave him after they got back from therapy and the restaurant meltdown.

"It may be good for you to just write," his dad said. "This time, when you're going through so much, it might be nice to have a place to put thoughts and ideas."

He nodded, but really he thought, *My time to write is over. No one cares.*

But now he stares at the space for a title, and an idea comes to him: *Aaron Boroff: Songs from Up Top, Never to Fall.*

He rereads it and laughs. It reminds him of when his dad says, "Fake it till you make it." Usually in regard to feeling awkward as fuck socially before going to some party. It's decent advice that sometimes goes terribly wrong, like at Chloe Vick's '70s party, where he thought it would be hilarious to show up as a septuagenarian rather than a person *of* the 1970s, and his dad talked him into just owning it, going in confident. It did not go well. There's nothing worse than going to a party in old people's clothes, walking up to someone like Kiersten Haas, all smiles and fake confidence, and have them look at your outfit and go, "Okay . . ." and then walk away. It had been somehow worse than had he just been real and stood there in his ridiculous outfit alone by the bathroom door feeling authentically awkward.

He opens to the first blank page and decides to write a song.

Lying in bed
Junk in my head

He rolls his eyes. Not exactly the stuff of Spotify viral charts.

He could be the next Ed Sheeran if he could just write the right song. It's so frustrating. And worse, it's so alone.

He tries again.

I sit alone
in my corner
I sit alone
in my corner
I sit alone
depression goes down to the bone
won't call nobody on the phone
I oughta by myself a home
So I can sit alone
in my corner

He looks at what he's written and thinks: *Yeah. Not my best. Not exactly what everyone wants to hear. I could call the album* Kill Me, Please. It's like his brain is jelly and thoughts are not connecting and not in a *boy, what an amazing tortured artist* sort of way. More like a Debbie Downer sort of way. Nothing grabs him.

It's the first night of his post-medication life. He now has one Petralor pill in him. Petralor. It sounds like the name of a heroine in a postapocalyptic novel, some girl whose family has died, who has to forage through this city for dead vermin to eat.

A lot of his life is lived in his head, he realizes, which makes it all the more ironic that he is, as of today, diseased in the head.

Jesus. If he can't trust his brain, what can he trust?

On Sunday morning, Aaron's dad bursts into Aaron's room without knocking.

"Are you ready?" he asks.

Aaron has been in bed for the better part of thirty-six hours, and when he sits up, his head spins.

"Ready for what, exactly?"

His arms and legs feel super restless, like he wants to do something—anything—that would get him out of his head. The other parts of him, though, are pretty okay with continuing to avoid the real world indefinitely. Yesterday, Aaron told his dad he was ready to venture out and they made a plan to see a movie, but in the shower the negative thoughts attacked, and he started thinking about his music career in the past tense, and realized that probably everyone was humoring him, and they all knew he was terrible, and the joke was totally on him, and by the time he got out of the shower, it was all he could do to get back into bed. His dad, it seemed, wasn't particularly surprised when he came in all dressed for a movie. He simply sat on the bed and silently rubbed Aaron's temples until Aaron fell asleep again.

But today, apparently, is a new day.

"Time to reprise Aaron Day," his dad says, and Aaron rolls his eyes. Aaron Day was something he and his dad did right after his mom left. Aaron got to choose what they did, and his dad had no veto power. Aaron knew this was one of those things parents do to make up for divorcing, but he loved it nonetheless and still has memories of the candy binge they did, hitting eight different candy stores and loading up on all Aaron's favorites. But now he's seventeen and depressed, and he's not sure he has it in him to make one choice, let alone six, or ten.

"Is it, though?"

His dad does that thing he does when he's trying to be Cool Dad. It's a bit like pantomiming, and Aaron has no idea why his dad thinks this is a good look. He pretends to grab for a gun holstered to his left side, and then does the same on the right side, and he pretends to shoot in Aaron's direction as if life were a Western movie. "C'mon, partner. Think of all the fun we can have with you at the helm. We can drive to Pennsylvania and find a shooting range. We can . . . do a pottery class. A foreign film binge at Lincoln Center."

Aaron cracks up. "It's like you know all my favorite things."

This makes his dad smile. "C'mon. Jump in the shower. This time we're gonna make it, okay?"

Aaron slowly stands. The blood rushes from his head again and he feels momentarily dizzy. "Deal," he says.

And this time, unlike yesterday, they do make it out the door.

X

At the Time Warner Center, Aaron gets two Thomas Keller Oreos, which are as big as his hand and filled with white chocolate ganache instead of whatever they usually put in Oreos. When he's scarfed those down, because it's his day and it seems like he's supposed to do unusual stuff, he makes his dad stop at a vendor for two dirty-water hot dogs, extra sauerkraut. They messily devour them on the way to the Bethesda Terrace in Central Park.

"Does Mom know?" Aaron asks as they stroll.

"I put in a few calls Friday and yesterday but haven't heard back," his dad says, dodging a young woman who walks like she's in a speed-walking race despite wearing headphones and texting.

"Beautiful," Aaron says.

"You know she never listens to messages."

Aaron almost says, *You know what might get her attention? Telling her that she almost lost her son to the Hudson River.* But he doesn't say it. The sun is out, he's finally outside, and he doesn't have the energy to fight.

Nice that your parents have that option, Tillie says in his head. *Mine didn't have a choice about whether or not they'd be told.*

Aaron shudders. His dad doesn't notice.

When they arrive at the Bethesda Fountain, with its gallant angel overlooking all the activity, there's an impromptu concert going on. A busker stands in the center of a tan circle between the terrace and fountain, and he's surrounded by a swarm of New Yorkers. He has a guitar, a harp, a couple wind instruments, and a drumbeat emanating from a keyboard.

They stop and listen. The guy records loops of each instrument, one at a time, so that the drumbeat is suddenly joined by a flute, and then the guitar broadens the sound, and a harp punctuates with a harmony, and finally his voice, like the voice of that Bethesda angel behind him—fluttering, diving down, lifting up. Aaron's bathed in sound that shivers the peach fuzz hairs on his arms.

He looks at his dad, who is swaying to the music, as if in a trance, and Aaron is filled with palpable love and something that feels like grace, like for a second he sees his dad and he's so damn happy he didn't die four days ago, so damn relieved, and he wants to memorize his dad's profile, that slight curve down in his nose, because it all seems so fleeting right now, so random, how another choice could have so altered this moment and every moment forever after. He could so easily not *be* right now. And what would that experience be like, to terminate being? Can you cease to exist and still know?

In a moment that overtakes him, he grasps his father from the side and hugs him, and his dad, as if he knows, as if he understands exactly why this music has led to this embrace, turns and suddenly there, on the Bethesda Terrace, a father and son hold on to each other for dear, precious life.

And all is good in the world.

Then, out of the corner of his eye, Aaron sees a guy maybe a year or two older than him glancing their way and whispering to his friend, who wears a Yankee hat, who laughs at whatever his friend whispers.

Aaron's heart drops.

He doesn't want it to. He needs it not to, but it's as if he's allowed himself to be seen, and now he's been judged, as if this awful kid sees the terrible truth about Aaron and his dad that he can't possibly know because he is Aaron, and his stomach falls into his groin and he lets go of his dad and looks away and all that beauty of that moment, gone, judged as stupid, corny, weak.

Averting his body from his dad, Aaron can feel the eyes of his father on him, and he wants to pull away. He wants to walk away. The world is so terrible and something so pure has been tarnished and he wants to cry out but can you even just imagine what the kid would say about that?

"Let's just go," Aaron says.

His dad, incredulous, says, "What? What happened?"

And Aaron won't tell, ever. It's all too embarrassing, being Aaron. So he just says, "I need to go. Now."

On the walk home, Aaron's mood drops to that all-too-familiar place where he feels no one can touch him, he is untouchable, unreachable, in an impenetrable vacuum.

His dad speaks softly to him. "I dealt with some depression when I was your age. A little older. Came home from college late freshman year and Nan took care of me for a while."

Aaron doesn't look at his dad. "I didn't know that," he says.

"I never told you. Didn't want to burden you but, yeah."

"Did you—"

Aaron can feel his dad shake his head without looking at him. "I sure thought about it, though. It felt like I'd been sad my whole life and it was never going to get any better. Depression does that. It changes your brain and makes you think things that aren't true."

Aaron thinks, *What things? Maybe the stuff about my music? Like, that I suck?*

"I've been worried forever that you'd have to go through it, too," his dad says.

"Well," Aaron says, monotone, "here we are."

×

In the evening, back home and safely in bed, Aaron notices a pattern. Days start better, end worse.

His heart is hurting again and he's not really sure why, or what constitutes a broken heart, because he hasn't had his heart broken. He's never been in love, or at least not with anyone who loved him back or knew that Aaron loved them.

None of this makes sense, he thinks as he lies in bed, staring at the ceiling. His dad is hanging out with him, sitting in the blue rocking chair across the room, reading a book of essays. *This thing? It's a sham*, Aaron thinks. Dr. Laudner made him take a test and diagnosed him based on it. He could absolutely, one hundred percent have answered the questions differently, and then the diagnosis would have been different.

"Do you think maybe I'm faking?" Aaron says.

His dad looks up. His reading glasses make him look like an owl, a bit. "What?"

"Maybe I'm faking. Like maybe I just need to try harder to be normal, and I have these, like, dramatic tendencies, and I'm making the problem bigger than it is."

His father puts his book down and takes off his glasses. "What are you talking about? You're depressed, Aaron. You've been depressed for a while. Even you aren't that good an actor. Why do you think you're being dramatic?"

"I don't know. I just. I don't believe in this, maybe."

"You don't believe in how you're feeling?"

"Well, what kind of god would allow a person to have a brain that undermines them, or even kills them? That doesn't make sense."

His dad leans forward. "I hear that. What's the emotion? What are you feeling, Aaron?"

Aaron resists groaning. Sometimes his dad can't help but bring his work home with him. "I don't know. Sad. I mean, who wants to live in a world with a god that's so mean? It's so . . . disappointing."

"Disappointing?"

Aaron's eyes tear up. "I don't want to be here. In that kind of world. It's all so bleak."

The rocking chair squeaks as his dad drags it toward Aaron a couple inches.

"That's depression, Aaron. What you just said. That's your brain on depression. I know. I've been there, kiddo. It sucks."

Aaron just stares at the blue paisley sheets below him. "It really does."

His dad tilts his head and gives him that super-supportive smile that he should really patent.

Aaron smiles back and he knows, without seeing it, that it must look like a sad smile. And suddenly all the unsaid stuff feels like it's tickling his uvula.

"I'm sorry," he says when he can't keep quiet any longer.

"Whatever for?"

"You shouldn't have to have a son who has a broken brain. You didn't sign up for this."

His dad kisses him on the top of the head and grasps his hands.

"I most definitely did sign up for this," he says.

Aaron knows it's the truth.

The hand squeeze tells him it's true. But he can just barely feel the truth of it.

At therapy on Monday, Aaron learns that Dr. Laudner celebrates weird things.

The doctor gives him the same test he took on Friday. Aaron tries to answer the questions as accurately as possible, because he wants—needs—to believe the diagnosis. He's still not convinced this is real.

He hands the test over and watches the bearded doctor as he scores the test this time, the way he mouths words while he reads. Then Laudner looks up, smiling, and hands him the test back. On top is the score: thirty-seven.

"Moderate depression," the doctor says, a big smile on his face. "That's a huge difference in three days. Massive, actually. The meds often take weeks to work. Congratulations!"

Aaron imagines a surprise party, a banner reading *Congratulations! You're moderately depressed!* hanging in the doorway.

"Yay," Aaron says, deadpan. Dr. Laudner smirks. He'd be a decent audience if Aaron were to be a comedian.

"So how are we feeling today?" the doctor asks as he waters the fern that sits directly to his right. He did this same thing Friday. Aaron imagines it as a nervous tic his doc has, that he does it at the start of every appointment. He imagines a waterlogged fern being taken out of the doctor's office on a gurney.

"My emoji would be, like, not a sad face. I mean. I'm still kinda sad, but. Maybe more of a constipated face."

This makes the doctor laugh. "Is that becoming something of a problem?"

Aaron nods dramatically.

"Petralor can do that. I can give you something," the doctor says, and Aaron puts his two hands together and bows in his direction.

Dr. Laudner says, "So let's talk about school. Let's talk about a plan. Had you asked me on Friday, I would have said you were going to be out awhile. Now I have to say I'm simply not sure. Do you think you'd want to go back this week if you keep feeling better?"

"Yeah. I dunno. Maybe?"

"That about covers all the options," Dr. Laudner says.

"I like to make sure I leave no qualifier unturned."

"You're a smart kid, aren't you?"

"Guilty, I guess. I don't get the grades of a smart kid, but that's probably on account of my not enjoying the whole homework thing."

"Ah. What do you enjoy instead?"

"Not. Not doing homework."

"Ah. And do you sit in silent prayer when you are not doing this homework?"

"Sometimes I write songs."

"Oh. Okay. That's great."

"Well, depends who you ask, I guess."

"Say more about that."

Aaron crosses his arms over his chest. "Well. My dad likes my songs. When he listens to them, anyway. And that's not fair, 'cause he does listen to them, he just didn't that one night, the night before the . . . you know. I sent out a YouTube clip of a new song to a bunch of people, like seventy. I got two hits."

"Ouch."

The doctor saying this has a funny effect on Aaron. It's like he expected the doctor to make excuses for other people—they're busy, or whatever—and when he doesn't, it makes Aaron's jaw feel tight.

"Well, usually I get more. I mean, I'm not a total loser. I'm not . . ."

"Say more about that. Do you think I think you're a loser? Because I don't."

Aaron throws his head back in frustration. "Never mind, okay?"

"Okay. But I'd like to come back to that sometime, okay?"

"Oh, good," Aaron says, and the doctor grins again, which makes Aaron feel a little bit more understood, at least.

"So . . . going back to school. What feelings come up around that?"

Aaron shrugs. "Scared, I guess."

"So let's see how you feel tomorrow and make a decision then. Sometimes normalizing life is the way to go. Sooner rather than later. Let's talk about the fear, though. What's the fear for you? That it will happen again, what happened?"

Aaron rubs his forehead. "More like dealing with people about it. Everyone's going to know I'm crazy."

"You're not crazy. You suffer from depression, like many, many other people. You had a frightening episode where you nearly attempted suicide. What's actually going to happen, if you're at all like my other private school patients, is that all day long people are going to treat you like their own private confessional or therapist."

"Oh, good," Aaron says. "That sounds fun."

Dr. Laudner takes a sip of his coffee and crosses one leg over the other in a way that makes Aaron wonder if he's gay. Aaron thinks about the fact that the doctor has a penis in his pants and a butt around the other side and how weird it is that every man he passes on the street has both, and how do men even deal with everything, and what even is sex? And how is it that people don't just combust from strangeness, from this odd desire, and his dad must, too, ew, ew, ew, and god would it be so, so good to finally get to—and how normal the perverted, and how perverted the normal, and it's all just about enough to make you go insane.

"So what's on that interesting mind of yours?" the doctor asks.

Aaron shrugs again.

"I'm thinking it's time to push you a bit. We've stayed pretty general to this point, but I want to get a little deeper now. Medicine is just one of the tools we use here. The pills are there to help you with the chemicals in your brain. We also do talk therapy. And so far, you've been a little—uninterested in that part. Why, do you think?"

Aaron glances around the office. He has so many books on his bookshelf. The one he always sees is called *The Road Less Traveled*, and because he's Aaron and there's no cure, he keeps reading it as *The Roadless Traveler*, imagining it's a story about a traveler who refuses to take roads. And then he thinks about highways, and different states, and whether sex feels different depending on what state you're in. Then he looks up, realizes he's being stared at by a doctor, and scratches his left temple.

"Well, it doesn't make sense, for one thing," he says.

"What doesn't?"

"Talk therapy. You told me it's an illness. Would you give a cancer patient medicine and then ask them to tell you about their mother?"

Laudner laughs. "Perhaps I would. Is it strange for a doctor to ask a patient personal questions?"

"It's a little strange. I mean, how is talking about what's happening between a cancer patient and his absent mom going to help him get better?"

This makes Laudner sit up taller and stare at Aaron, as if waiting for more. No. *No more*, Aaron thinks. *This is exhausting and too much.* He imagines the faces Laudner must make when he has sex with his husband/wife/partner/self. This gives Aaron a boner.

When Aaron doesn't say anything, Laudner says, "Well, I don't know. It's not a terrible question. How do you think it might help?

And can you see any differences between cancer and depression? What differences might exist there?"

Aaron scratches his knee through his jeans and yawns. Too many questions. It's beginning to feel like Aaron's the kid in that old karate movie, Laudner is his wise sensei, and Aaron has to answer endless riddles.

It's exhausting.

✕

At Marie France's suggestion, Winnie brings Britt to their appointment. Britt sits on the floor, legs splayed like an M.

"So, Britt. I've heard so much about you," Marie France says, her voice warm and honeyed.

Britt stares at her. For Winnie, the difference in Britt is beyond stark. Two weeks ago, Marie France would have gotten a hug.

"I hear you like to dance?"

A shrug.

Marie France crosses and uncrosses her legs. "I understand that your family has had some really bad news."

Britt picks at the hardwood floor with a fingernail.

"Do you want to talk about that?"

Not even a shrug this time. Winnie looks to Marie France, whose return look says, *I got this. It's okay.*

"Britt, do you like to draw?"

A nod without looking up.

"Would you like to draw?"

A half shrug, half nod.

Marie France grabs a sketch pad and some magic markers out of her drawer. She places them on the floor in front of Britt.

"Do you want to go to the table or stay there?"

"Here is okay."

Marie France goes back to her desk, and the two adults watch Britt sit there with a red marker in her hand, staring at a piece of blank paper.

×

Tillie went away, Britt thinks. *She didn't leave me a note saying goodbye, or anything.*

That means she didn't love me.

Why do people say they love you if they don't? Why do people go away without saying goodbye?

The lady with the nice black skirt wants me to draw. I don't want to but I will, anyway.

I draw a house. It's square and red. I scribble in the paint. I put clouds above it in gray, and some green grass below.

"What do you have there?" the lady asks.

"A house."

"And who lives in that house?"

It's just a drawing, Britt wants to tell her. *No one lives there. I just want to take a nap.*

"Me and my dad," Britt answers. She thinks of her daddy, who is on a business trip. He was away last night and probably will be again tonight.

She looks up and the lady and her mom are looking at each other. Mom is wiping her eyes. Again.

"Mom, also," Britt says, hoping she'll stop crying. She hates when her mom cries. She cried when she told Britt what Tillie did and Britt didn't like it at all. Her dad didn't cry and that was good.

Britt just wanted to play pretend. Like pretend it was before Tillie did suicide, and when her mom wasn't so sad all the time.

Her mom doesn't stop crying, though. Britt is sorry about her drawing. She thought it was too small for three people. She didn't know the rules.

×

Amir's mother is horrified that her son's been suspended. Utterly horrified to the point that she barely spoke to him all weekend.

The one thing she did say: "How could you put everything in jeopardy?"

He tried to explain but nope. She wasn't having it.

He spent most of the weekend in his bedroom, lying in bed, because his mom took away his phone, his laptop, everything. No TV privileges.

"I want you to really think about whether this is the kind of man you want to be," she said on Monday morning, before going off to show an apartment on East End Avenue.

Now he sits in the living room, in the dark, knowing that the TV is off-limits, and the funny thing is, he's glad she's taken things away.

She should take away more.

×

Molly braves turning on her phone for the first time in three days, and it's worse than she expected.

Forty-three messages. Forty-one of them death threats or in that general arena. Two of them from Gretchen.

What's up, ho? reads one.

The other: Fine, be that way. Everybody here hates you by the way

Somehow, this hurts even more than the threats, which she mostly doesn't read. Well, she reads some of them. Glances over to see if any names come up. Only one. Sammi Petrowski, who is an Emma, which is what Gretchen, Isabella, and she always have called the B girls who would run each other over to be A, because they're all named Emma. Sammi has always been sort of a shark, on the perimeter of their posse, circling around, waiting for blood.

Sammi's text reads, well this is awkward . . . what do you say to a murderer? Sorry not sorry

Molly feels a squeezing on her heart, like the air is being taken from her chest. Her head feels dizzy. Dizzy and cold, because now it's bald.

She texts Gretchen.

> Hey. Not ignoring you. Didn't see the texts bc
> I'm getting death threats. Nice right?

She waits. For the bubbles to form so she'll know a response is coming. No bubbles.

Then some. Her heart lurches.

Then they disappear, and Molly stares and stares, waiting for them to come back. Because they need to. Because without Gretchen she has no one left.

X

In the afternoon, Aaron sits in his room with his computer open to GarageBand. He's riffing on the synth, thinking about how groups like Vicetone aren't shiny, in the same way he isn't shiny. They just make great beats.

He could be like that, maybe?

He tries an '80s synth beat and speeds up the RPM until it sounds almost hypnotically fast, and an idea comes to him. With "Walking Alone," he went slow to match the lyrics. What about a somber high-energy song? He'd started that "In My Corner" thing. Maybe it needs to be fully written and made into a celebration?

He smiles. Yes. This is the kind of über-random, crazy idea that makes people famous.

He grabs his notebook, keeping the sped-up beat on to inspire him. His pen stays motionless on the paper for quite some time, and he laughs. Yeah, not so easy to write a dance dirge.

sit alone,
my corner
sit alone
epression goes down to the bone
don't call nobody on the phone
oughta buy myself a throne
I can sit alone
my corner

He rereads it, and unlike the other day, when he thought it sucked, this time it lights him up a bit and he feels a warmth pass through his chest and perk up his shoulders. That's the chorus, he realizes. He needs a verse. A couple verses. And maybe a bridge.

A shiver passes through his rib cage. He finds the melody so easily he has to wonder if it's something someone else came up with, but he can't think of what it is. It's just . . . not half bad.

Maybe his dream isn't over after all? Maybe the Viral 50 is within his reach? He lies down in his bed and goes into a happy trance, listening to the loop of the frantic beat, singing the lyrics over and over in his head and imagining the synth and how it will sound with that melody. Then he's thinking about his Grammy acceptance speech for "In My Corner," and Sarah's expression when it hits 41 on the Viral 50, and the cool kids like Chloe at his lunch table, watching his video on his phone over his shoulder, and Evan Hanson saying, *Hey, can I talk to you about something?* And making out with Evan in a broom closet in the main building's entrance hallway . . .

The lyrics just come to him like sometimes they do. How does that happen? Why is it that other times he can't write a single word, but times like this, fully formed verses come to him and they're great? This one's just two lines, with a repetition for the end of the first verse, and it just . . . works.

He sets up to record it, realizing his depression is lifting because for the first time in a few days—weeks, really—he is really imagining a future again, and it's not entirely un-bright, and he knows he's special and there's something about his life that is different and maybe it's not fully shiny but it's there.

He finds the melody, and sped up it sounds trippy and happy and it makes him laugh as he bangs it out and lays it down, and then a super-subversive bass line in bass guitar, and he imagines telling the story of how he came up with that incredible bass line. *Oh, I was severely depressed. It was days after I almost committed suicide. Now that, that was a story.*

His dad knocks on the door.

"You have a phone call."

Aaron's heart jumps. He somehow knows. He slowly stands, takes the phone from his dad, and sits in the rocking chair.

"Hello?"

"Aaron!"

His mother's voice cracks and he can tell from the plaintive way she says his name that she's crying. He closes his eyes and feels like a piece of dirt.

"Hi, Mom."

"Why would you—you don't do that, okay? You don't jump off a bridge. You have your dad. You have me. You can call me anytime, right? You get that, right?"

"Yep," he says, thinking, *That happened five days ago and you're just calling back now, so.*

"Do I need to come down there?"

His heart pulses in a way that he knows is instinctual, biological. Mother bear and cub. The promise of proximity. Needed like oxygen.

"I guess. If you want," he says.

She pauses. "Well, do you need me? I mean, if you need me . . . I'll have to cancel, um. Well, it's only just started rehearsal and it's not exactly a major part. It's a supporting, but forty-three lines so major supporting. But yeah, of course. Sure. I'll quit. It's not a big deal. Or if it is a big deal, I'll deal with it. I'll deal. Yes. It's basically fine. Nothing is such a calamity if you think about it. Even if I were to get blacklisted in the Boston theater community—"

"It's okay."

"Are you sure?"

"I'm sure."

"Well, listen. You have so much to live for. Your music! Right? You love your music."

His esophagus tightens and a heavy blanket envelops his shoulders and pushes down. It's the *you.* She makes it sound singular, which it is. You, and only you.

"You're just a good person, Aaron. You are. I'm so very pleased with how you've turned out. If I could have chosen a child to be mine, it would have been you. Well, without the depression. I would not choose that, of course."

"Thanks."

"Just . . . you'll be here in a few months and I promise. I absolutely promise. No big productions. I'll hold off until the fall. I mean. That's not such a huge problem that I can't—for you, anything."

"Thanks, Mom."

"Oh, shit. I'm late. I love you so very much. You're perfect just the way you are. Okay?"

"Okay."

He gets off the phone and climbs into bed, under the blue paisley comforter, turning to face the wall. He feels the mattress shift as his dad sits down. He's ready for the talk. Expectations. Limitations. Narcissism. Not personal. He has it memorized.

But he doesn't get it, or any words. He just gets a sturdy hand on his midsection. What would be called obliques if he wasn't so lazy and he worked out, like, ever.

That hand is better than any words could be, so he closes his eyes and allows himself to disappear into sleep.

X

Amir is waiting at the kitchen table when his mother comes home from work. It's time. To tell her. Even if it means she kicks him out. Maybe he wants her to. He deserves to be punished.

She bursts in and puts her keys and the mail on the kitchen table, sorts through it, pours herself a glass of water. All without saying anything to Amir.

"Mom. I need to talk to you. About something."

She stops and looks at him. "Unless it's to apologize, there isn't anything to talk about."

He rubs his head. "Mom. Stop. There's something I need to—"

She takes a sip of water and doesn't look at him. "That suspension is on your record. What if Georgetown rescinds your admission? How could you do something like this?"

"Do you know what that guy said to me?"

"I really don't care, Amir. Nothing is worth this. Nothing."

Amir says, "A girl is dead, Mom."

She puts a piece of mail down. Suddenly he has her attention. "What?"

"A girl. Is dead. The girl I was dating. Tillie. She killed herself."

His mother's mouth gapes open.

"You see, she killed herself, probably because I broke up with her. Well, worse. I didn't break up with her. I was too much of a coward to do that."

Amir's tears come now.

"She killed herself because I was such a coward and I didn't even text her to break it off. And then, at school, Jason Mathes comes up to me, like, the next day, and he says, 'You bleeped that girl to death.' So yeah. I punched him. I couldn't help it. And now my life is ruined, not because of what could happen to Georgetown, but because I killed a girl with my secret—"

His mother comes to him. She hugs him. She's not a hugger, and it feels weird to Amir, but also nice. Necessary. She doesn't seem to hear the thing he says about a secret.

It's now or never, he realizes. He needs to keep going. Rip the Band-Aid off quick. Tell her why. Why he ghosted her.

She says, "Oh, Amir. Dear god. That's a lot, Amir."

The words approximate kindness to him. He holds on for dear life to the moment, swallowing down the thing he absolutely needs to tell her, knowing that it might take this moment away, and he cannot possibly deal with losing it right now.

Aaron's first day back at school is Weird with a capital *W*.

"My best friend from summer camp, Paige Johansen, is on anti-depressants," Sarah says to him as the subway arrives at the 110th Street stop.

"Ah," Aaron says, thinking that Paige Johansen may not be a big fan of a friend sharing her personal business, and that soon enough Paige Johansen will surely know that Aaron Boroff takes antidepressants, too. Stop the presses.

"Yeah, and they totally help her, and we all know in the bunk and we're super down with supporting her."

"Cool." Aaron nods, thinking that this is vaguely reminiscent of the *I have gay friends* period that followed his coming out last year.

The conversation is sporadic, as Aaron's attention is split. The idea of walking back through the front doors of the main building at Fieldston has him feeling jittery all over. Clearly everyone knows about the physics event. Shit like that gets passed around like prescription pills at a party.

"Well, look at the bright side," Sarah says as they coast into 168th. "You get a three-day week. I'd die for one of those."

"Absolutely. Bright side attained," Aaron says, wishing the word *die* didn't hit him right in the solar plexus, didn't make him think of the photos he saw of Tillie Stanley online.

"I didn't mean—"

He smiles. "It's fine, Sarah. I'm fucking with you. I'm actually fine. Nervous, but fine."

She puts her head on his shoulder, which is oddly intimate for their friendship level, and Aaron realizes this is somehow related to his depression and he's not sure how. "I'm just glad you're okay."

"Thanks."

"And by the way. That thing I said? About *Rent*? That wasn't—"

He laughs. "Yeah, I really had a mental breakdown because you told me I'm a bad singer."

"You're not that bad a singer," she says. "You just—"

"Sarah. Dude," says Topher. Aaron hadn't noticed he was sitting on his other side. Or if he had noticed, he'd forgotten.

"It's fine," Aaron says, and he stares at the ads for a storage company above the seats across from him and thinks about how nice it would be to grow up and have space for all his stuff.

X

On his way to homeroom, Aaron's intercepted by Dr. Flores, whose ultra-white teeth glimmer too loudly when he smiles. He shakes Aaron's hand like he's the next contestant on *The Price Is Right*, or they've just done a real estate transaction and Aaron is now the owner of a charming one-bedroom in Tribeca. Then he beckons Aaron into his office.

The walls are brown, slightly darker than the well-filled bookshelves, about the same as the leather chair behind the mahogany desk, about the same as the wooden chair into which Aaron slides. Flores definitely has a brown fetish.

"I just wanted to touch base with you," Dr. Flores says, sitting down across from Aaron. On his desk is a picture of him in front of the Eiffel Tower with a blond woman whose teeth are also a little too white.

Aaron stifles his desire to say, "Base touched." He looks around and wonders if vice principals at private schools are rich. He's never been in the vice principal's office before. It's weird. He looks around at the various posters about reading and safe zones and wonders whether vice principaling would be a good fallback for viral music sensation.

"I'm okay," he says.

Dr. Flores takes a sip of brown coffee from his brown mug and smiles all white.

"You have support here. If you need anything, come to me. Come to Ms. Marshall. She's aware of the situation. We're both allies, okay? We know how hard it is to come out, how challenging it is to be different."

Aaron freezes. *Wait, what?* But he nods, because, yeah, he's seen *Love, Simon*. He knows it's hard to be gay. Just not so much at Fieldston to this point, for him. He's told people in hopes that some other gay kid will want to date him, but so far his gayness is entirely theoretical and no one seems to really give a shit about who, theoretically, he might sleep with.

Dr. Flores seems to be waiting for him to say something, so he says, "Um, thanks. That's cool. Thanks."

"Do we need to have an assembly?"

Aaron freezes. An assembly? On him? Being depressed? What? Why?

"Um, I'm okay, thanks."

Dr. Flores frowns. "You can tell me. If there's problematic behavior in terms of LGBTQIA+ issues and we need to do something on sensitivity, on being an ally, we'll do it. We'll preempt tomorrow's assembly."

"Um. I don't know?" Aaron says, because he really doesn't. "Probably not?"

"I actually already have a speaker, so. I think maybe we should. Surely there's something problematic going on, and you know we have a zero-tolerance policy for harassing LGBTQIA+ people here. You know that, right?"

This is the most I've been harassed about my sexuality ever, Aaron thinks, but he swallows down a smile and tries to match Dr. Flores's serious expression.

"Honestly? I think this is like garden-variety sadness or whatever. Depression. I mean, I think this school is great vis-à-vis my gayness. Really, truly. No problem. No assembly required."

Dr. Flores nods, and his eyes go distant and his ultra-white smile dims somewhat, and Aaron thinks, *Outstanding. I have disappointed someone because I haven't been bullied for being gay.*

✕

Winnie's makeup isn't quite right. She put it on during what felt like an out-of-body experience. She's out of bed because of Britt, and because normalcy is everything right now for her daughter. But the biggest part of her is still in bed, and will be in bed, for a long time. Forever, maybe.

Forever in bed sounds about right at this point.

"Yogurt or an egg?" she asks Britt, who is Candy Crushing while sitting at the breakfast nook.

Britt says, "Okay."

The part of Winnie that isn't a zombie wants to take the phone from Britt, pull it out of her hands, and yell, "It's okay to have feelings! It's okay to let them out!"

The part of Winnie that is a zombie takes *okay* to mean yogurt, because yogurt is easier. She scoops out a dollop of yogurt. She brings the bowl over to the table and Britt ignores it, continuing to play her game.

"Do you have any questions, Britt?"

Britt doesn't respond.

So Winnie keeps Britt silent company until it's time for Britt to go downstairs for the bus, and she gives her daughter a tight hug, which Britt doesn't return, and then Winnie trudges to her bedroom, disrobing as she walks, and she gets in bed, and she sets an alarm for thirty minutes before Britt will be back from school.

So she can pick up her clothes from the hallway, and reapply her makeup, and throw out the yogurt, and make everything look okay again.

And before she goes to bed, she uses every last bit of her remaining juice to text her husband.

She can't help but think about how much she'd rather be texting Tillie instead.

✕

Aaron gets looks in the hallway. Lots of looks. They vary, from the super sympathetic to the borderline pathetic. Dr. Sengupta pulls him out of the classroom right before physics to ask him if he thinks he'll be okay this time.

No. I'm back in school because I find catatonia in the physics classroom refreshingly droll. I hope to do it again very soon.

"I promise," he says, and Sengupta gives him that look that says, *I'd like to believe you, but I really don't.* It is unpleasant.

At lunch he sits with Wylie Jones and Marissa Jones, no relation—hopefully. They are band geeks in love, and he wonders what happens if two allegedly unrelated people with the same name get married. Do they go Jones-Jones? A single Jones but for the rest of their lives they have to deal with the fact that no one took anyone's name? There has to be some drawback to that situation. He, for instance, would not date another Boroff and potentially become Aaron Boroff-Boroff. Aaron considers Marissa and Wylie the kind of people he'd be friends with if he were to have actual friends.

"How are you?" Marissa asks, becoming the thirty-trillionth person to ask him that same question.

He surprises himself by answering the question honestly. He doesn't know why, exactly. Maybe he's tired of fronting.

"Exhausted," he says.

"Exhausted?" she asks.

"Today is an exercise in humiliation," he says.

Marissa and Wylie share the kind of look that people who have been intimate share with each other. It makes Aaron want to punch them both in the face with something large.

"Humiliation," Marissa echoes. She'd make a terrific background singer if they were to assemble a '60s doo-wop band or something, Aaron thinks.

"Generally, people pay just about no attention to me, and today I'm like a roadside attraction at a suicide fair."

Another look between Marissa and Wylie, and Aaron's chest gets tight. "Sorry," he says. "I'm just. It's really nice that people care but it's all a little overwhelming, I guess."

"I get that," Wylie says, and Marissa, because she'd be a fantastic background vocalist, repeats, "I get that."

"A lot of us were really worried about you," Marissa adds.

Aaron opens his mouth to say something, but there are no words. Until there are. "Um. Really? I didn't really think . . ."

"What?" Marissa asks, and, sweetly, she comes and sits next to him, so close he can smell her perfume. It smells like the beach and money.

"I just don't feel like . . . I have friends, but. Not anyone close."

Wylie and Marissa share another look.

Aaron says, "Permission to speak freely. Seriously. Like, what do people think of me?"

A fourth look. "People like you," Marissa says. "There's no one who doesn't like you. It's just—"

A fifth look. "What?" Aaron asks. "Please. I really am curious."

"You don't really let anyone in. You're a good singer and actor and all that, but it's like no one really knows what makes you tick or anything. Offstage, I mean. You're like Blank Slate Kid. If there's anyone in our grade who is more blank slate than you, I don't know who they are."

"Wow," Aaron says, genuinely pleased to be hearing this information. "Thank you, Marissa. This is actually helpful to hear. I want to be less blank."

"Good!" she says, almost too enthusiastically.

"But, like, my songs suck, right?"

"I love your songs!" Marissa says. "Oh my god! What was that one you did at the talent show before winter break?"

"'For You I Would Lie'?"

"How does that one go?"

Aaron's eyes go up and to the left. It's hard, because it doesn't really have a chorus, that one. "'Your picture is in my mind'? 'Careful not to put it on my wall'?"

There's no recognition, but she keeps staring at him, like she wants him to continue. He blushes a bit, because it's weird to recite your own lyrics to someone in the cafeteria. But he goes on, focusing in on a part that might be more memorable or catchy.

"'Stay in my viewing room, my fantasy. Wanna hear your voice from inside of me'?"

"Maybe . . ." she says skeptically.

"'Even though it sounds very funny, even though you could never care for me, I want you next to me so . . . that I'd kiss you, head to toe'?"

Her eyes light up! "Yes! Oh my god, Aaron." She closes her eyes. "And then it's like, 'I'm lying, but I would lie for you'?"

Now it's Aaron's turn to illuminate. He feels it inside his rib cage, like a warm light, spreading.

"'Okay, that was a lie, but for you I would lie, any day.'"

"Yes! Oh my god. I was totally into that. It's catchy. You're so talented. I like that your voice isn't like a pretty-boy Troye Sivan voice. It's so much more . . . real, gritty. I was talking about that for days after."

"That's true," Wylie says, glancing at her. "She wouldn't shut up about it. I got, like, a smidge jealous."

Aaron holds his breath, hoping that it will allow his face not to go beet red. "Thanks," he says, but really he feels like he could fly out of the cafeteria, like his feet could not touch the ground ever again.

"Who was that about?" she asks, a smirk crossing her face. "I am so all about the m-for-m romance. You can tell me. I mean. Please. Tell me!"

He lowers his chin. "Honestly?"

"Yes!"

"No one."

"What?"

"No one. It's about a fantasy. It's about that feeling of wanting something. Someone, I guess I mean. I wrote it about no one?"

"Wow," she says, and Wylie nods and says, "Cool."

"So there's no one you stan for?"

"Well, Evan Hanson, obviously," he says before he can stop the words from coming out of his mouth. And then the blushing again.

"What? Get out! Evan is really, really, really cute. Is he gay?" She whispers that last part.

"Well, probably not, but. We did have like the best silent cab ride ever. Last fall."

She laughs. "Oh my god, I am loving you and Evan so much. I ship you so hard."

"Me too, clearly," Aaron says.

They decide to have lunch again the next day, and Aaron does almost float out of the lunchroom. It seems so easy. Almost too easy. How did he not know how much a conversation with nice people could mean to him? Or the song. And he realizes: This is the thing. It's happening. It was one thing when his dad liked his music. Another to know that someone was loving his song and he didn't even know it. All this time. He almost died over this. It's like, how could that happen?

And how could Tillie . . . He doesn't know why she did what she did, but he wonders if a simple conversation would have made her feel like life was worth living.

He'll never know, though. Because she died. And there's no coming back from that.

The thought makes Aaron shudder. Hard.

X

Frank's eyes slowly open when he feels the not-so-gentle nudge on his shoulder.

"Mr. Stanley? You seem to have fallen asleep on the floor."

The voice belongs to a woman with a European accent of some sort. He grunts in response.

"Are you certain you would like me to refill the bar? It seems as though you may want to give your body a rest."

Frank looks up at her. He wants someone to take him where he belongs. To make it all go away, be better. To bathe him, clean him up, and fix this thing that's happened. Fix it so he doesn't have to, because it's unfixable.

She lifts him up, and, aware that he's utterly disgusting—unshowered, soaked in a week's worth of booze—he averts his eyes.

"Will you take me to the shower?" he asks.

It turns out she will not.

✕

The afternoon of Amir's third and final day of suspension, he and his mother go to Central Park and race model sailboats.

It's so far from something they've ever done, but then again, so is his mom playing hooky. So is her being fun. His mom has always been a great provider and a whiz at keeping Amir on track, but playing? Almost never.

But then again, nothing's been remotely normal since Tillie's suicide. It still hurts, like a blade in the center of his back that keeps twisting. But ever since he told his mom, her love and support have definitely helped ease the horrible ache.

"Mine won't turn," his mother shouts as she jerks the remote control hard to the left, as if moving the entire console will move her boat.

"What do you mean? You're doing circles," he says.

"What? No . . . Oh, shit," she says, laughing. "I thought I was the blue one!"

Amir laughs back and puts his head on her shoulder. "Oh, Mom," he says. "You probably won't ever do this professionally."

She puts her head on top of his, and Amir wants to memorize this feeling. This unconditional love. It's the most ironic thing ever, that him getting suspended from school has brought them closer. In a million years he could not have imagined this.

"Can I be honest with you?" his mom asks. He hears the words vibrate in his head as she says them.

"Sure."

"Truth is, I'm relieved. You're so secretive, and I think I wondered if you were gay. I'm so sorry about your friend, your ex. I really am, Amir. But honestly I'm glad to know you had a girlfriend."

"Oh."

"They say these things run in families, and you know, Aunt Nava. Who is a perfectly fine person, to tell the truth. Just so you don't think I'm a monster. I just think she needs to grow up and stop—anyway. Not important. And anyway, you're not gay, so."

He moves his head in a way that makes her pick her head up so that he can, too. He stares out at the model boats, the placid water. His heart feels heavy, and he knows. He just knows.

As much as this might end this beautiful moment, he can't—not.

And it won't change anything. His mom is a lot of things—driven, typically no-nonsense. But also she's a great mom. He's been being dramatic, and he knows it, and now, out of nowhere, he'll find out what happens next. Because, oh god. It's happening.

"But I am," he says, not turning his face toward hers.

She laughs. "You are what?"

He whispers, "Gay."

The air changes. Like he can feel it. The afternoon, which had stretched out around them like pillows, like softness, hardens. A steep intake of air marks it.

His mother stands. He doesn't look at her. It's like he can't, but he can feel the judgment.

"Oh, for fuck's sake, Amir," she says.

Then she walks off. Actually walks away from him. And Amir sits on the concrete bench with the two remote controls, trying to ignore the little part of himself that feels like it was just assaulted.

×

"So . . . your first day back at school," Dr. Laudner says as Aaron parks himself in his usual cushy chair.

"Yes," Aaron says. "My first day back."

"And the verdict?"

"Total confessional. I feel like I should have brought a rosary or something. And I'm half Jewish, so . . ."

Dr. Laudner laughs. Aaron laughs. He's feeling—it's hard to explain, really. Just a week ago he was lower than low, and one well-placed compliment about his music and he feels like he can't even imagine his life ending, or wanting it to. Is this that Petralor drug? It doesn't feel connected, like he doesn't get how a drug could change him so much, but a compliment? That, either. It's magic, and whatever it is, he should bottle it and sell it. World peace would be attained in like a half a minute, and he'd become a bazillionaire.

"Should we even—yes, we should. Take the test, please. I want to see what you score."

Aaron looks at the form when Dr. Laudner hands it to him and it just looks different to him. Like he can barely remember how it was, just five days ago.

The truth is that he's on this medicine, and the clouds are lifting. And even if he can't feel the connection, it has to be—it's a little uncanny, really. All his life, he's been living under a cloud without knowing it. The thing in his stomach, that thing that was always rolled tight in a horrible ball of pain, isn't normal. Not everyone has that. And it's not like he really thought everyone did; it's more like he never noticed that it existed in the first place. It was just how things were. And all this time, it was a sickness? And yeah, he'd heard his dad talk about depression, plenty. But it always seemed like he was listening to something theoretical, not real, and certainly not inside him.

Now he gets it, and he feels himself about ninety percent out of it, and it's a little goddamn difficult not to cry out of gratitude, because his life! He's going to have a life! And it's not all going to hurt!

Dr. Laudner smiles at him and says, "I see it, you know."

And he doesn't have to ask him what he means. Because he knows. He sees it, too.

He watches the doctor score the test this time, staring into his eyes as he marks away, filled with this tender anticipation in his belly.

The doctor looks up, smiling, and hands him back the test.

On top is the score: nineteen.

"Borderline depression," he says. "That's amazing, Aaron. Utterly amazing. Five days. You're doing great . . . This is a long journey we're on, but I must say . . . we're off and running!"

And yeah, it's hard for him not to feel a little proud about that.

×

Walking down West End Avenue after the appointment, Aaron finds himself enjoying the old-timeyness of the buildings and their awnings. The buildings on West End are like unassuming acquaintances from middle school who don't ask much of you. Internally he salutes each one he passes and he absentmindedly plays the game where he can't step on any lines in the pavement. He finds himself giggling a little. He'd never in a million years have guessed he'd feel good again. And yeah. He feels good! He feels . . . new! He finds himself smiling at passersby and thinking a good thought for each of them. And for the yellow cabs blaring by. And for the guy trying to park his black Tesla in a too-small spot, and for the line of cars behind him, honking incessantly, as if that will make him go faster. The sounds of New York life.

All his life everything's been so hard. And in actuality it's so easy! So much of life is how you approach it, he realizes as he passes Eighty-Third Street, and for so long he's been shackled to these beliefs. That he's lesser. That he's no good. That he's unlovable. And suddenly the veil has been lifted, and he sees behind the curtain, and it's good! He's not lesser! He's totally good! He's absolutely lovable, and some day, the right guy—or who knows, the right girl, maybe, gotta keep the options open—will show up, and he'll be ready, and he'll treat them so well, and they'll love him for exactly who he is. He'll have a Wylie or a Marissa to share looks with. He'll tell them his innermost secrets, and they'll divulge theirs, and the feeling will be so, so good, and oh my God. It's so sunny today! The sun and the glistening of the sidewalks on West End and he actually twirls on the street out of goddamn gratitude for whatever this feeling is. Because he loves loves loves it! So much!

He finds himself singing to himself. One of his songs. Not "In My Corner," because that's too bleak for this gorgeous moment.

> *If we had to be apart*
> *For a very long time*
> *I'd count the days that you were gone*
> *Inside I'd never let you go*

He sings softly at first, but then the feeling builds inside him. It feels like a victory lap, like he's succeeded. Like he has a new lease on life, and the second verse and the chorus come out with a little gusto, like he doesn't care who hears. And he doesn't.

> *Because to me you're the sun*
> *I cannot shine without you*
> *And all of our memories*
> *They're all that I ever do*
>
> *Because I can't forget your smile*
> *You know it's all that I can see*
> *I never will forget your smile*
> *Now you've become a part of me*

And the *be-come* part, from D to G, takes him right to the top of his vocal range, and sometimes his voice cracks when he does it; it's the highest part of the song. But crossing Eighty-Second Street, he nails it, hitting the G right in its center, and feeling it in his core. *Be-COME!*

"Sing!" this guy shouts. He's on the corner of Eighty-Second, waiting for the light to cross to the east side of West End. He's kind of hippie-ish—maybe thirty, maybe less, white, with a bushy ponytail and a bright, blissed-out smile. Old Aaron might have thought he was weird, but new and improved Aaron has such goodwill toward humankind, so he guffaws—actually guffaws—to the guy, who holds up his hand for a high five, which Aaron gives him.

"That sounds awesome. What song is that?" the guy asks.

"I actually wrote it."

"What? Are you serious? That there's a track! Retro. Like singer-songwriter stuff from the eighties or nineties. I miss that shit."

"Naw," Aaron says, but the guy shakes his head like, *C'mon, man, no need for modesty! Own it!* So Aaron adds, "Thanks."

"Singing on the street. Do you know that they say it's impossible to sing and be unhappy at the same time? True fact."

"That makes sense," Aaron says, and the light turns green.

"I admire when a person isn't afraid to show their happiness. That's how things will change," the guy says, and he starts crossing the street while he says it, so Aaron crosses with him.

"Yeah," Aaron says. "I always feel like I can make the world a better place by just being nicer to people. Like on the street." Despite the fact that he's never felt that way before today, nonetheless it feels true to him now.

"Right! And you know what? New Yorkers? We get a bad rap but we're friendly people. You just have to get out the way, but you know. That's just common sense there." The guy laughs, so Aaron laughs, too, and Aaron feels like he knows this guy, like he should know this guy. He can tell he's good. Inside and out. Just good.

"I'm starting something new," Aaron says. "Like trying a new way. I used to be really shy, so today I'm like, no. No more shyness. From now on, I will, you know, sing on the street. And talk to people.

Because how do you get to know someone without talking to them? Taking the chance."

The guy stops walking, turns to Aaron, and upturns the left side of his upper lip into a kind smirk.

"I really like the sound of that, man. Maybe it's time to start a movement. Of people who talk to other people on the streets of Manhattan."

Other people might be walking by. They might be looking at this odd pairing of adult and kid. They might not. For once, Aaron simply does not care.

"Yes. That. We should do that," Aaron just about yells. He feels like he could jump out of his skin, he feels so damn good.

"And that song! I produce. Haven't in a while, but I used to, I mean. What if . . . nah."

"What?" Aaron says.

"What if we get that song going? Work in some percussion, add some guitar. That's the kind of song . . . I'm just saying."

Aaron imagines going up onstage and accepting his American Music Award for "Can't Forget Your Smile." It's too juicy to imagine. He thanks his dad, and his friends, all his great friends, especially Marissa and Wylie, the Jones-Joneses, and then this guy—

But no. "I actually have a better one," Aaron says.

"Really?"

"Yeah. It's called 'In My Corner,' and it's kinda sad, but—okay, I'm gonna let you in on my idea. Can I trust you?"

The guy nods, looking like he's on the edge of his seat.

"Dance dirge," he says.

"What?"

Aaron thinks he may have lost him, so he starts talking really fast.

"Maybe it's stupid, I don't know, it's just like, a new genre, like depressing lyrics but dance beat? I don't know, that's dumb."

The guy laughs. "That's not dumb. I like that, actually. What's the song like?"

Aaron's heart flutters. Someone wants to hear his song. "Really?"

"You were singing a second ago. C'mon. Let me hear it."

They're on Broadway and Eighty-Second, in front of Barnes & Noble, and people are rushing by because it's just about rush hour, and somehow none of it matters. So Aaron takes a deep breath and sings the slow version.

"Holy shit," the guy says when he's done.

Aaron blushes and looks down at the concrete beneath his feet. He kicks at an ancient gum stain. "It's terrible, I know. I'm terrible."

The guy surprises him by touching his arm, and a shiver travels up Aaron's spine.

"It's not even in the same zip code as terrible. I really fucking love it. And with, like, a beat? Like a hundred twenty BPM, like house, maybe? I think you have something amazing there, really. What's your name?"

"Aaron."

"I'm Darrell. I've been kinda looking to get back into the game, and you know what? The best things are by chance. Like this. Know what I mean?"

"Totally," Aaron says. "Like random." And they both laugh.

The guy smiles and puts out his fist for a bump. "So. Are we gonna do this?"

Aaron is knocked out. Utterly. Every dream he's ever had, everything, everything, has led to this moment. And you wouldn't believe it but it's true. It's happening, and he just lets his face go and the widest smile he's ever made feels like a victory, like a moment that's so juicy that it's just. It's wrong enough to be so right. And he's always thought he was the ugliest guy in the world. But he's sure, in this moment, that his smile is expressing his essential inner beauty in a brand-new way.

"We are SO doing this," Aaron says.

On Thursday morning, Aaron wakes up well before usual and jumps right onto his phone.

You up? he texts.

Darrell hits him right back. Yeah, dude. Totally buzzing about everything.

> Me too! Can't wait for tomorrow!

I know! Feel like the sooner we hit this song, the sooner it'll get out into the world and we can get to Stage B.

> Shivers . . .

Lol look out world, Aaron Boroff is coming!

> Why are you so nice to me? I feel like meeting you is this once in a lifetime thing

Dude. Meeting you is that. For me! Get ready because we're gonna change the world!

Aaron lies in bed fantasizing about six things at once. Is Darrell gay? How do I find out? What if he isn't? What if he is? What is his place like? What will everyone at school think when I become famous? Will I still be nice to them or will I be all, *You guys had no time for me before, and suddenly you're like my best friends? I don't think so!* Except Marissa and Wylie, of course. They'll be invited to the American Music Awards for sure. And the winner of the Best New Artist Award is . . . Aaron Boroff!

This thought makes him giggle and writhe in bed. He hasn't taken his Petralor yet, but, Jesus, he wants to, because this is what life should BE like!

×

Lexington Avenue feels particularly cold and lonely on the morning Amir is supposed to head back to school.

He's been chilly for hours now. Ever since he got home and his mother gave him the silent treatment, going so far as to take her dinner into her bedroom and not even leave anything for him. And then, this morning, as they both scurried around—his mom getting ready to show an apartment and Amir preparing for what was certain to be a weird return to school—he might as well have been invisible.

So many times he thought about saying something, making sure his mom was okay. Apologizing, even. Because if he could take it back? If he could take back the momentary insanity that led him to come out to his mom? He would. In a heartbeat.

And then, as he gets on the subway, of course he sees Stu Bees-meyer and his gang, and he braces for the assault of stupidity. After all, it was Stu who saw him at Oath Pizza the day of the fight, before it all went down, who said some stupid shit about halal food and then mistook Pakistan for Iran. Amir braces for whatever idiocy is coming, and then—nothing. They ignore him, don't even notice.

He's not sure why that's worse, or even if it is worse.

All he knows is that when the train gets to the Sixty-Eighth Street stop, he doesn't get off. Instead, he stays on, then transfers to Penn Station. Numbly, knowing what he's doing but also not allowing the seriousness of the moment to fully penetrate his consciousness, he thinks of his aunt Nava, and what she'll say. What he'll say to her. All that stuff. Too much for one brain to really conjure.

"One one-way for Washington, DC," he tells the ticket guy.

✕

At lunch Aaron rushes up to Marissa and Wylie's table, slams down his tray, which holds two slices of pizza with pineapple on them, and gives them an uncharacteristic "Hey!"

"Hey, Aaron," Marissa says, her smile earnest and kind.

"I am SO on a roll," Aaron says. "I crushed my essay on Toni Morrison. I actually understood what Sengupta was saying, which is a HUGE win given my usual level of physics comprehension, and my texting game is at a new level. Do you know I never, ever texted in class before today? And now I'm, like, comprehending shit AND staying in touch with . . . well, someone really cool, actually. I feel like I found the keys to the castle, you know?"

The table is silent for a while. He knows Marissa and Wylie now because of the great talk yesterday, but the others are people he only knows in theory, like Jonas Campbell, who is one of those quiet kids—like him, like he used to be, oh, he could mentor him!—and Dora Sanchez, who he once did a project with in ninth-grade English. They got a C-plus.

"That's . . . awesome, Aaron," Wylie says. "You're like a different person!"

"I know! It feels like all this time I've been holding back on letting people know me, and I don't actually know what I was afraid of. I mean, we're all just people, right? And I think part of life is about saying hello to people on the streets. I mean, can you imagine if we did that? How the world would change? I think we should do that. From now on, that's my plan. No one's a stranger. No one."

"Well, that's . . . good," says, Marissa, but something in the way she says it makes him laugh, more like guffaw, as a thought rushes into his brain.

"Oh my god. People are going to start to realize they liked me better depressed!" he says, and this gets everyone laughing, and that makes him feel better because, yeah, so he's hyped up and it's a lot. Better than jumping off a bridge or being unable to move in his physics classroom, and his new friends know that, and they will be with him now, and he'll never be alone, and that's beautiful.

Aaron laughs more at lunch than he ever has before, and he just about snorts milk out of his nose at a story Wylie tells about him and Marissa getting carded at a club, and it's so, so good to be part of something, and how many times did he sit alone, and oh! He should text Darrell, no. Oh! He should . . . yes!

"So can I show you something? It's a secret, and it's pretty outrageously exciting. It's probably the reason I'm like this right now. And I haven't told anyone!"

Everyone leans in. Aaron has them in the palm of his (beautiful) hand—that's a song he wrote once—and he loves loves loves it.

"What is it?" Wylie says. "Tell us."

"So I met a producer . . ."

"What?" Marissa says, nearly matching Aaron's excitement.

"I know! I was actually, like, singing one of my songs on the street—"

"Like you were busking?" asks Dora.

"No! Ha! No. I was just . . . singing. Because I was so happy."

"Aw," says Marissa.

"So his name is Darrell, and he's a freaking producer! And he heard me singing, and he wants to help me put music to it and record it. He thinks it's, like, singer-songwriter retro nineties or eighties or something. I don't know. So then I sang a different one, the one I'm working on now, which is definitely better, and he got that one, too, plus the idea of dance dirge. So tomorrow, after school. Or, I don't know, during school. We haven't exactly figured out the specifics. I'm going to his studio on Forty-Fourth and Ninth, and we're gonna lay down some tracks."

The table is awash with looks. A little like yesterday with the Jones-Joneses, but Aaron's head is spinning too fast to really read them, or maybe it's that he's more confident today, he's not sure. He just . . . waits.

"What's dance dirge?" Dora asks.

X

The church is freaking freezing when Molly Tobin enters it, and she finds she has to bundle herself in her pink tweed coat.

Some of it is the temperature, sure. But it's also just massive inside, with towering stained-glass windows everywhere she looks, staring down at her. She feels miraculously little there.

Molly is not religious. Her family thinks God is for weak people, and she's basically taken that belief and run with it. But today, right now? She feels like one of those weak people. Particularly weak, and even though she's not Catholic, it feels like confession time.

The confessional is small and red-velvety, and it smells like salty soup. There's a tiny window between her and the priest—she guesses? She's not sure how it all works—and momentarily, when nothing happens, she wonders how this is supposed to work.

"Um," she says.

The window slides open. She exhales.

"Yes?" the voice says. It's old and somewhat impatient.

"I, um."

"Is this your first confession?"

"I'm not, um, Catholic," she says.

"Do you wish to convert?"

"Um? Maybe? I don't know?"

The voice behind the screen exhales dramatically. "So why are you here?"

Molly feels tears in the back of her throat. She sucks them down. "I did something," she says.

"What did you do?" the voice says.

And Molly runs out, slamming the door behind her, sprinting out of the church and not looking back.

X

Winnie arranges for Britt to hang out at her friend Carly's place after school and uses the extra time for an emergency session at Marie France's.

"I just can't be with people right now," Winnie says.

"Why not?"

Winnie throws her hands up in the air. She thinks of Luna, who called to see how she was holding up.

"I'd be happy to make you an appointment with my acupuncturist. When my mother died, I went to her and I swear I felt better so much faster than I would have otherwise," she'd said.

Or Carly's mom, Patti, who had said, "At a time like this, it's important to remember you have a second child. This is a chance to remember what a blessing Britt is. Pour your love into Britt."

Winnie looks at Marie France and says, "Everyone has an answer. I don't want a fucking answer. Everyone wants to make me better. I know they mean well, but in reality, I'd like to mow them down with an SUV."

Marie France nods. "I totally hear that."

"Thank you. That's actually all I need. It feels like everyone is telling me not to feel, or how to fix it. I don't want to fix it. I want to mourn her. Tillie. She was . . . a lot. She was always struggling, but she was . . . she was everything. Everything. How do I go from having everything to nothing and then just have it be okay? Fixed? I can't. I won't."

Marie France smiles in a way that make Winnie feel understood.

"So beyond that, it's over. With Frank. He's just . . . totally checked out. Disappeared, and no, it's not a business trip. I know it isn't. He insists on using credit cards I have access to, so I'm well aware he's at the Trump International."

"This is a pattern?"

"He's done it before, but frankly I don't care if he needs a little staycation once in a while. Who doesn't? But our daughter just died, so. No. Not okay. Not even a little. I love Britt to the moon and back, and in the end, is it really better for her to have him around? I mean, he's not here. Literally."

Marie France nods and nods. "Well. That's big. Are you sure?"

Winnie runs her hands through her hair and bites her lip. "I'm sure."

"Sounds like you know what you need to do," Marie France says.

Winnie laughs. "Well, a week ago I had a daughter—two daughters—and a husband. Now I have . . ." She starts to cry.

Marie France hands her a box of tissues.

×

Aunt Nava's persona makes her more like an older sister than an aunt. So perhaps it's kind of fitting that when Amir arrives, she and her girlfriend, Ciena, are basically in nightshirts, watching Netflix in the middle of the day.

"Of course you can crash here," Nava says, enveloping Amir in a strong hug. "We have a futon."

So Amir gingerly sits next to Nava and Ciena on the couch, and the three of them watch some sort of true crime story thing.

For a long time, Amir doesn't say anything. Until it feels weird. Because, um. He's a teenager and he lives in New York, and here he is, having shown up unannounced at his aunt's house, where he hasn't been since he was seven.

Amir finally says, "She found out I'm gay and she's ignoring me."

Now Nava clicks pause on the show. "Fucking Laleh," she says, shaking her head. "Your mom is the worst. Can I just say that?"

No, Amir thinks. But he doesn't say it.

×

Carly's mom takes Carly and Britt to Dylan's Candy Bar, down the street from Bloomingdale's, as an after-school treat.

"Get whatever you want, okay? Anything, sweetie."

Britt knows this is how adults talk to you after a thing happens, like them being nice to you will make it all better. It doesn't. But, candy. So. She shrugs and pockets the two twenties Carly's mom gives her, and she walks toward the penny candy bins on the first floor. She loads up on sour belts and sour cherries and sour peaches and pink gummy bears. As Carly runs around giving Britt updates on where she's going next—"C'mon! Let's hit the Jelly Bellys! We can get unicorn gummy kabobs!"—Britt silently but intently gets a little bit of everything she loves.

Then she sees the tiny, colorful, tinfoil-wrapped chocolate bottles that look like the bottles Dad has in the big cabinet in the living room. One is gold and reads JIM BEAM. Another is reddish orange and reads COINTREAU.

How funny would it be . . . ? she thinks.

The cashier, though, doesn't find it so funny.

"Yeah, you can't even close to buy these," the girl says. She's a few years older than Tillie was, maybe, before she died. "There's alcohol in there."

"Oh," says Britt, and she pays for the rest.

Then, before she goes to meet Carly and her mom at the front door, she detours back to where the tinfoil bottles were. She takes three Jim Beams and one Cointreau and she stuffs them in her down jacket pocket when no one's looking.

She's pretty surprised when the security lady stops her as she and Carly and her mom get to the door.

"Excuse me, please. Will you empty your jacket pockets, please?"

X

Aaron calls Dr. Laudner's office after school and says he can't make it in. He leaves a message.

Why bother with a doctor? He feels great! Better than great! Pretty sure talk therapy isn't needed anymore, thanks!

Instead, he goes to Riverside Park and he stands on the green benches, facing the field of dust and grass where he used to play tag with his friends back in third grade, and the West Side Highway, and beyond that, the frigid Hudson, where . . . What a difference less than a week makes! He thinks of the falling girl, of Tillie, and then he shakes his head—no. No time for those feelings right now. He throws his jacket down and allows the chilly breeze to raise the light blond hairs that are beginning to appear on his arm. He's got a whisper of approaching manhood there, of the fur he'll have, like his dad. He wishes his dad were here, that he could see him more confident, could see the new, improved, becoming-a-man Aaron, and he stands on the bench and belts "In My Corner" at the top of his lungs, over the highway noise, the barking dogs, the screaming kids in the enclosed playground down about a hundred feet. He half hopes someone will ask him what he's doing so he can say, *I'm practicing. For the studio tomorrow. This is going to be a huge hit. Just you wait. You'll want to remember this moment.* It's okay that no one asks, but he kinds of wishes they would.

Back home, he makes dinner for his dad, which is not something he generally does, but he decides to experiment a little with an amuse-bouche and microwave a couple of French bread pizzas. He gives his dad the one with mushrooms because *ew.*

"So what is all this?" Dad asks when Aaron meets him at the door with a napkin tucked into his shirt. He put it there because it was his best way of approximating a maître d'.

"Bonjour, monsieur!" he says. "Velcome to Chez Boroff!"

His dad laughs and shakes his head. "We gotta lower your dose, dude," he says. "By the way, did you skip your appointment? Got a call from your doctor."

"Had to stay after school," Aaron says, and Michael is about to launch into a whole thing about priorities and how nothing is more important right now than getting better, but then he sees his son and the look in his eye, that expression he gets when he's playing, which he hasn't seen in a while. So he gives Aaron a hug and Aaron resists hugging him so tight that he'd almost lift him, although he wants to, in a way. Instead, he says, "Put down ze briefcase. Ze dinner ees thees way."

"Your accent," his dad says. "It's like being in Paris. Paris, Texas."

"Ah, oui," Aaron says. "J'aime les cowboys."

His dad cackles. "Oh boy," he says, but he follows Aaron to the dinner table.

"For ze first course, ve have what is called, ze French onion zoup."

His dad looks down. In a bowl, Aaron has heated up a half a can of onion soup. On top of it, he's put a slice of American cheese, which is all they had. It floats uncertainly, like a half-melted impostor afraid of being made.

"You are too much," his dad says, and he laughs, and Aaron is glad because, yeah, it's meant as a joke and for a moment there he thought maybe he misfired but now he sees how fucking funny this is. And his dad laughs more and their mirth trips over each other until they both sit and try to eat their not-so-French soups.

"So what, exactly, is going on, kiddo?" his dad says. "You are so extremely different in just about a day or two. Have you talked to Laudner about this shift in your mood? Should I be worried?"

"Worried? About me being happy? Yeah, probably not. I feel great, Dad. I feel like I'm becoming—"

Aaron feels tears behind his eyes and he gulps down some air, trying to steady himself. So many emotions. He loves them and fears them because he can't hardly keep them in.

"What?" his dad asks. "What are you becoming?"

"A man," Aaron says, and his voice squeaks on the word *man*, which makes them both laugh some more, and the conversation just goes like that, and Aaron, who was thinking about telling his dad about Darrell, decides he'll tell him later. After.

It'll be something to celebrate.

✕

Winnie feels utterly beat down and humiliated when Carly's mom delivers Britt.

Patti is nothing but nice. The fucking bitch. Try having a dead daughter and an AWOL husband and now, apparently, a thief. She's doing the best she can, and all she wants to do is wipe that simpering smile off Patti's face.

"It's to be expected," Patti says as Britt hightails it to her room, and Winnie nods and averts her eyes, not because she's going to cry, but because she's going to fucking scream.

"Thanks. She's never—"

"She's acting out," Patti says. "You know what you should do? Have a spa day. Why don't I stay for a bit and the girls can—"

"Please just leave," Winnie says as the first tear falls. Better than the scream it's holding back.

"Of course," Patti says. "Call. Anytime. Really, Winn."

Winnie nods, and when Patti leaves, Winnie counts to twenty and then groans like she's going through childbirth again. She groans and she rests her head against the wall and she thinks maybe Tillie had it right. Because she sure as hell doesn't want to be here right now, either.

She collects herself and knocks on Britt's door and enters before her daughter can answer.

Britt's lying in bed, eating sour belts. She doesn't look up. She doesn't say she's sorry. She just lies there, like nothing's happening.

Winnie sees it again, just more clearly this time. Who Britt is a little bit like. And it scares the fucking shit out of her.

When Aaron wakes up on Friday, he has the beginning of a rap in his head.

I am who I am
And that's important, because
What you think of me
is secondary

He's not a rapper. In fact, when he raps it out loud, it sounds totally wrong. Like a (relatively) privileged white kid co-opting someone else's culture, which is what he is. And it's too bad, because he has a whole story in his mind about being the first gay, white rapper—is that true? He'll have to google it, but he's certainly never heard of one. The first mainstream, famous one, maybe.

So maybe this isn't for him, but more like a featured rap in "Can't Forget Your Smile," like between the chorus and the third verse, or, like, the song doesn't actually have a bridge—some of his do, this one doesn't—so maybe this is the bridge, and he sees it as it would be written on Spotify: Aaron B. Feat. X, where X is the rapper's name, and who from school could he ask? Vonte Mendoza? It would be so cool to be the kind of person who offers fame to someone else; that would be awesome. And no, he's not sure how *I am who I am* relates to "Can't Forget Your Smile," but there has to be an angle; there's always an angle.

There's a knock on the door.

"You up? Getting ready for school?"

"Yes and yes!" yells Aaron.

"Good. I wanna talk to you before you go, okay? Can you come out here? Like now, or in five?"

"In five," Aaron says, and he gets up, looks in the mirror at his body. He's never been to the gym but what he has is thin and tight and maybe he should start working out? He flexes his muscles and nothing jumps out but maybe it does a bit. Just a little gym time and he'd look even better, and Darrell, would Darrell like him more if he—wait. Darrell might like him exactly as he is. He did say hi on the street after all, and he might not even be gay but he might be, and that part of the intrigue just makes today almost unbearably exciting, and he shimmies his hips in the mirror and smiles and tries to imagine an album cover with Aaron Boroff's face on it.

X

Aaron's dad is waiting for him when he pokes his head out the door.

"It's been ten," his dad says.

"Sorry."

"Did you even shower yet?"

"Been busy with other stuff."

"Aaron . . . I was going to say something last night, but you had that whole dinner thing planned. I'm a little concerned about what I see."

"What? Why? I just went from depressed to not in, like, three minutes. You should be thrilled. I'm thrilled, obviously. I feel like I've been reborn into this new person and I have plans for the world, I actually have plans, and you know? I've never had plans before,

I—do you think it's possible that I was meant to be famous? For my music. I mean, would that be okay? I wouldn't change. If I were famous I wouldn't treat you any different, it would not change our thing at all. I'd just be Aaron-but-famous."

"What? What are you—so this is hard for me, but you know I'm always real with you, right?"

Aaron stares. His chest feels tight, and he feels coiled up and ready to attack.

His father goes on. "I'm concerned that you're manic. I see all this energy—and in general, energy is a good thing. But this feels extreme. To me it does. Do you understand what I'm saying to you?"

Aaron looks at his dad like he's never seen him before.

"Are you fucking kidding me?"

"Aaron!"

"Are you *fucking kidding*? I almost jumped off a bridge last week. You should be, like, celebrating. I'm celebrating, Dad. Because I don't feel like jumping off a bridge for once in my goddamn fucking life. There are people—like this one girl I know, she didn't know how to feel like this, so she jumped. I don't want that. So maybe you can stop shitting on my good mood and celebrate with me?"

"Aaron," his dad says.

"I mean. I'm trying new things. Is that a crime? Would you rather me mope around like I was doing for all my life?"

"I—no. I want you to be happy."

"Which I am! You should have seen me at school yesterday. I have friends, Dad! Did you know that? I've never actually had friends, because I'm a fucking drag to be around, let alone be. So now I'm being new. Different."

"I see that, I just—"

"Maybe don't interrupt?" Aaron says it and looks away. He

meant it like don't interrupt my good mood, but it sounds like he's saying his dad interrupted him while he was speaking, which is assholish and not like him. But he's on a roll, and he's not going to stop now.

"Yeah," he adds. "Yeah."

His dad looks punched. Like punched in the chest, maybe. His face would be comical if it weren't his dad, his closest everything. Instead it's just, like, sad. That his dad is caught up in the cross fire of something he couldn't even possibly understand. He doesn't even know about Darrell. The music. He wants to surprise his dad, and he doesn't want him to worry. It just seems smarter that way.

"So. I'm gonna, you know, go off now. To school. And you. Don't worry so much. Maybe it's a boomerang thing. And I know I'm different. But different is good because same was almost terminal. Got it?"

His dad nods, speechless.

✕

As soon as Aaron leaves, his father makes a phone call that has him feeling right on the edge of a cliff.

"He's manic. He's absolutely, definitely manic."

"So what do you want to do?" Morris asks.

"I don't know. This is so much fucking easier when it's someone else's kid."

"Is there any way I can support you?"

"No, I'm good. I just need to get off my ass and call his doctor. He's not right. I know it."

"Make it happen," Morris says.

"I will."

X

As Aaron walks south on Broadway to the subway, passing the outdoor fruit market of the Westside Market with its bright red tomatoes and the orangest of tangelos, passing all the specialty shops with high-end shaving accoutrements and French patisserie and luxury fragrance—imagine a whole store that sells air! Maybe he could become an oxygen mogul?—Aaron feels oddly dirty, unshowered. He feels like he's been awake thirty hours straight and this plaintive voice in his head is screaming for his daddy and his mommy and he pushes it down, away, because no. He's this person now, he doesn't need anything, anyone. He just needs—this. His burgeoning célébrité, his face on billboards, his arrival at school with an entourage, maybe, Evan Hanson fawning over him. He giggles, walking, and covers his mouth with his hands like people are watching. They aren't, but soon they will be.

He takes the subway south instead of north, feeling dangerously free and on the precipice of something—*just you wait, just you wait*—he hears it in Lin-Manuel Miranda's voice, as Hamilton. History has its eyes on him, oh boy, oh boy, and for some reason he thinks of his mother, and that day in Central Park, fifth-grade baseball. He rolls his eyes because—stupid memory.

His dad couldn't make it, and she was going to be there. And there was this moment the night before, when she kissed him good night, that it was like he knew she didn't want to come. That he wasn't worth watching, and he wanted to say to her that it was okay. That she didn't have to, that he knew he was terrible at baseball. But he didn't, and then the next day, he sat on the bench, and he saw Manny Sanchez's mom, and Corey's dad, and Yanni's moms. All of the kids' parents, so far as he could tell. But his mom didn't show, and he totally didn't care. Not even a bit. He didn't feel numb in his chest and he didn't think, *I'm all alone and no one cares*. Because he was a burden and anyway he was just sitting his skinny butt on a frigid metal bench, chattering his twig legs like a loser. In short, he was no one special, and it didn't matter, anyway.

The subway screeches into the Fiftieth Street station, and everyone is New Yorking. The college-aged kid sitting there playing some game on his phone. The Orthodox Jew reading his Hebrew newspaper. The older Black lady twisting worry beads around her fingers while staring into space.

No one sees anything. No one looks. And he's had enough. Enough of that. He sees people. He says hello on the street now. He's worth others looking back at and he cannot wait hardly a second more until the world realizes that it should see Aaron Boroff. That he is worthy of a look.

And then Aaron is standing in front of the building: 430 W. Forty-Fourth Street. It's an orange-brick brownstone next to the Actors Studio. It doesn't look like a recording studio, and momentarily Aaron feels a twinge of something sour waft through his gut. And then he realizes: *Of course. He said it was a home studio.*

He climbs the steps to the entrance and peruses the buzzers. None say *Clancy. Darrell Clancy.* He's thought about that name a lot since two days ago, and he knows it's the right name because of Facebook.

He texts Darrell.

> Hey! I'm here!

He waits for the bubble to appear that shows Darrell is typing.

It does appear, and more bubbles form . . . in Aaron's throat and esophagus.

Then the bubble goes away.

Aaron resists the urge to repeat the text or send question marks. *Patience*, he tells himself.

He tells himself that again after a minute. Again after two. Then four. The sour feeling comes back.

> Hey Darrell! I'm here! Can't wait to do this!

No bubble this time.

Darrell has never not responded before. Not once.

Aaron sits on the steps and stares at his phone. It's 11:36 a.m. on a Friday, he's playing hooky, and he's in front of an address in Hell's Kitchen. Darrell is not responding. How long does he wait? He thinks this and then he laughs because where else does he have to be? He'll wait here forever if he has to.

There's no backup plan. They are recording the song today. It's more than his hopes that are up. His entire everything is hooked into this happening.

It has to.

But 11:36 becomes 12:12. There's no response. He calls the number and it goes straight to voice mail, like the way a call goes to voice mail when someone rejects the call. He goes back to texting.

> Darrell. What's happening. I'm here.
> Just please answer back please

Nothing.

> Did I do something wrong?

> Did you change your mind?

He zips up his down jacket and squeezes his gloved hands into the poofy pockets. He thinks of the day his mom came in and told him.

He was sitting on the floor doing a puzzle. What eight-year-old does puzzles alone on their floor? Ones like Aaron. His mother came in. She was wearing skinny jeans. They were fundamentally not mommyish. He knew that even then. He saw it and it registered but he didn't know why, or how, it mattered. But it did.

She sat down on the floor, also un-mommyish behavior. Her flowing blond hair was so, so pretty. She looked like a movie star, almost.

"So I'm moving to Boston," she said, as if she were saying, *I'm going to the store.*

Aaron nodded. He knew better than to ask why. There were questions you didn't want the answer to. Instead, he just said, "Oh."

"You'll come to visit. Like all the time. Probably in the summer. Maybe half the summer. At least a month, probably. I don't know. We'll see."

"Okay."

"Sometimes you change things up. Something's gotta give. When you're older, you'll understand."

And Aaron nodded and nodded, and she told him he was such a good kid, and he knew that he was. But he wondered: Would he one day understand? Because he fundamentally didn't, but he knew better than to ask.

Nine years later, he doesn't, really. Understand. Or he does, kind of.

There are levels of shininess in the world. There's glitter, like the kind that shocks your eyes when you glance at it and it's like looking into a million pieces of the sun, glimmering. There's the shininess of a chocolate cake in a patisserie window, the chocolate frosting seemingly lacquered on, and you think it's almost too shiny to eat but boy would you like to. There's normal shiny, like people in Central

Park, and depending on the angle of the sun there might be a glint off a forehead or there might not be, there might be shade and shadow showing their fundamental unworthiness. And then there's dull. The things, the people, upon whom the sun never shines. The invisible, really.

His mom loves shiny things. The world does.

He is invisible. He will become shiny if it kills him.

Facing an outcome that's simply not tenable, he tries a different tactic with Darrell.

> You can do anything to me if you just record the song . . . I'm fine with that

A bubble appears again. Aaron's heart lurches. The bubble disappears. His heart drops.

Whatever you want I'll do, he texts.

No bubbles, no nothing.

His dad calls him. It's weird, because his dad doesn't call him during school hours usually. Aaron stares at the phone. Gingerly with his index finger, he declines.

Another call. He closes his eyes and does to the phone what's just been done to him. Declined. His fundamental lack of sheen pulses within him, and he knows it goes unnoticed on the New York street, with all the New Yorkers New Yorking.

A text: Aaron where are you? School says you're not there. I'm worried. Please tell me where you are I'll come get you I won't be angry I promise.

A tear falls from Aaron's left eye. He's on the steps of a brownstone where he shouldn't be, where he wouldn't be if he wasn't so unshiny and hopeless and gullible and . . . every good feeling from the past forty-eight hours seeps out of his bloodstream until he is empty.

And he's lower, even. Lower than before.

He thinks of Tillie and it's like he gets it. Gets how she must have felt when she jumped. How it was just ever so slightly more than he felt at the moment, and now he knows the feeling. He knows.

The empty stomach pain, the one that feels like it could swallow him whole, is back with a vengeance, and this time there's an anchor tied to it, and he cannot move. Like his legs are stuck and why is he so fucked up? And everyone knows at school, and—oh man. He went on and on about how he was about to be a famous singer to those kids yesterday, and hubris, and they know. They know. He was probably opaque in the cafeteria when he couldn't shut up. Unlistenable. Unwatchable, which is worse. And his dad knows exactly who he is, and the words about how great he is, how special? Just a tactic to keep him alive, and it's so embarrassing. To be Aaron Boroff is to be humiliating at a cellular level.

> Please, Aaron. You are the most important thing in my life and I would be devastated if you hurt yourself. I will help you regardless. Just let me

> PLEASE!!!

> PLEASE!!!

But there's no help for him to be had. It's too late. There are no real options. Asking his dad for help is not an option. He doesn't deserve help.

The world deserves to spin on without the atrocity that is Aaron Boroff.

X

Michael finally gets to speak with Aaron's doctor.

"So you're thinking the Petralor kicked him into a hypomanic state?" Dr. Laudner says.

"Manic, hypomanic. I have no idea. I just . . . what I'm seeing is not normal. I'm worried. He skipped school today."

"That's . . . very worrisome. If you had to guess where he was, where would he be?"

Michael cannot answer. He can't say the words.

Oh my god.

The bridge.

✕

Molly stares into the bathroom mirror.

She wants to rip her face off. Or more like, she wants to rip her face back.

Back to before.

Before the stupid video. Before she lost her friends, her standing.

What if she—no. She doesn't want to die, exactly.

What if she could almost die? Like take enough pills to pass out and her mom would find her after Pilates and—

She looks in her own eyes and realizes how messed up that idea is. And how messed up she is. And she wants it to stop. She needs it over.

She grabs her phone.

> Come home, Mom. Please. Not okay.

✕

Aaron stands on the subway, wondering what's next.

After he gets to the bridge. After he jumps, submerges. He shivers. He almost moans out loud, thinking of the moment when he goes from on to off. The moment when the unknown overwhelms his being. What happens? Will Tillie be there, waiting for him?

And what happens to the people around him? His heart hurts, thinking about his dad. It's not his fault that Aaron's matte, that he doesn't deserve to live, that he has no options left. And his dad's gonna feel pain. So much pain.

An old, gray woman gets on the train. Her eyelids droop all the way to her ankles. She looks like Aaron feels. She needs a seat, so obviously. There are young people all around the train. People his age, sitting. Some playing on their phones, some zoned out on headphones. No one looks up to see her, or they do see her and they don't care. They are New Yorking. As you do in New York. The subway car is so far underground that there can be no shine, and this is the endgame of no shine. No one cares.

He wraps his jacket around him for one of the last times ever. The world is a cold place. It's all just so unacceptably mean.

X

Frank returns home for the first time since his daughter's funeral. He swings open the door and doesn't even close it behind him.

"Hello?" he calls out.

Winnie saunters into the living room and walks toward him, calm as can be. She's wearing a cream-colored turtleneck and her best skinny jeans. When he texted he was coming home, she put on eyeliner and blush and lipstick. She calmly showered and made herself pretty. Just for this moment.

"Where's Britt?" he asks, looking behind her.

She pounds her fist down on the top of his head.

He grabs at his head and shrinks away, but she's not letting him get away this time. She grabs him by his filthy shirt and throws him onto the floor behind her, and then she gets on top of him and pummels down, down, with fists, with hands, onto his face, onto his torso, everywhere.

He doesn't fight back. It's like he gets it. He knows that he deserves this, and he's almost grateful for the physical release, because at least it's something.

She hits and hits until she's tired, and then she rolls off him and crawls over to the wall, where she sits.

"It's over," she says. "Everything's over."

✕

Aaron's walk up the stairs to the bridge is almost too easy. It's like he can't believe no one's stopping him, but there's no one there to do so. Every step, every grasp of the dingy fading gray banister is a last. The last time he feels chill through his gloves. The last time he gets a little winded walking up stairs. The last time he pushes off on his toes while ascending to the top step.

In the after, what replaces the feelings of body? The mundane? What if he never feels his lungs take in air again? How is that possible?

And how is it avoidable? *This is me on medicine*, Aaron thinks. *There's no cure.*

He feels Tillie Stanley's presence. Calling for him. Calling for him to join. To come to the land of the unsustainable. Those unshining souls with not enough going to make it, not in this world. Not in the world as it is.

The world in which he'll never be a star, because—didn't he see it? The looks on their faces? Marissa and Wylie and all them? He saw it but he chose not to take it in. Their embarrassment for him.

He'll never be a famous musician because he's not a good musician. And those who become famous for music without being musicians are hot and popular, and he's neither. He's weird and stupid and shameful—and who was the last weird, stupid, shameful superstar? That's not how it works.

He stands at the very same spot where he stood nine days ago, when he was so sad and the girl, Tillie, beat him to the jump. He looks south, all the way down to the new World Trade Center, the one that replaced the one where all those people jumped because it was on fire and about to collapse, back before he was born. He shivers, thinking that they'd be so angry, seeing him voluntarily do what they didn't want to have to do. But they had life force. Something he lacks. He thinks about Wylie and Marissa and all them, and how they'll always wonder. It'll be like, the day before, he was laughing and alive. Then he jumped. What the fuck? How does that—he thinks about his last conversation with his dad, and how his dad was worried for him, and he told him not to—and Aaron thought, yeah. Worry about me being too happy. Worry about—

Jesus.

I'm worried you're manic.

Manic.

He honestly always thought of manic as a joke. It's funny, really, if you think about it. Who gets so happy they jump off a bridge? Aaron, standing there at the ledge, shivers from his toes to the tips of his hair.

He's too tired to deal. Maybe he should just—

But what if—

What if it's just my brain? And what if this is the worst, biggest, awful-est mistake I ever make? And the last?

Shit. And what if I have to live even more of this because of this one thought? And living it is so, so painful?

Exhausted by the combinations and permutations, Aaron reaches into his pocket and fishes out his phone. He does so while looking at the impossibly blue New York sky, and the alley of green-blue below him, the Hudson, teeming with workboats and kayaks and what is that, the Circle Line? People enjoying the world while he stands there, twisted beyond what is humanly possible.

On his phone, there's one last text from his dad:

please?

That's all it says.

It's the lowercased-ness of it that gets Aaron. The meekness.

His hand shakes and he braces the banister in front of him, like he's securing himself so that he doesn't fall, and he leans all the way the other way, so that his phone doesn't drop, either. And with one finger while still grasping his phone like it's his life, he types:

Daddy!

Aaron!

Daddy! I'm sorry!

Where are you???

I'm on the GW bridge

Aaron!

I don't want to die, daddy

Don't! Meet me?

Where??

Just down the stairs, kiddo. I'll be there as soon as I can. I love you, Aaron! So so much!

I love you too

And he walks, slowly but surely, away from the saddest place on earth. The place that was almost his end. To the unknown, which he knows will be all kinds of painful. Because it always is. But what's the alternative?

Quite a Lot and *Very Much*, indeed.

Aaron is tempted to avoid these two responses to the questions on the new test Dr. Laudner gives him, but the part of the directions written **IN BOLD LETTERS** on top of the form makes it impossible.

DURING THE LAST WEEK, it reads.

So the responses to *My mind has never been sharper* and *I talk so fast that people have a hard time keeping up with me* can't be *Not at All*, which is how he feels at this particular moment.

He's certainly not manic right now. That's for damn sure. In fact, he feels worse than before, if that's even possible.

The statement that really gets him, though, is number fifteen: *I have special plans for the world.*

Were the writers of this test actually living in his brain?

He used to have special plans, and now he feels stupid and simple thinking about that. He believed what was up in his brain was special and good, and in fact it was so typical that psychiatrists he's never met know exactly how he felt.

That's like the definition of not special. Of unshiny.

When Dr. Laudner scores the test, Aaron finds out that he wasn't quite as manic by the numbers as he once was depressed; sixty-nine as compared to that first eighty-two. Nevertheless, it's enough to put him in the severely manic range.

"It's fairly uncommon," Dr. Laudner says, his voice a little subdued. He's come into the office on a Saturday because of Aaron's emergency, and it's pretty clear he'd rather be watering his plants, or whatever shrinks do on their time off. "Very rarely patients are kicked into what we call a manic or hypomanic state when they're put on an antidepressant. Especially an SSRI, which Petralor is."

"Aah," says Aaron, thinking: *Maybe that would have been a good thing to tell me so I wouldn't have gone through this not knowing what was up with me.*

As if reading his mind, Dr. Laudner says, "I'm so sorry, Aaron. When you called in yesterday, I called your dad but I should have done more. It's okay if you're angry with me. Are you?"

Aaron shrugs.

"Well, it's okay if you are. And what's most important is you're here, and you're safe now. I'm so glad you texted your father when you did, Aaron. That shows an incredible maturity on your part."

The story is too embarrassing to go into when Dr. Laudner asks him to talk about things, so Aaron skirts around it a little. He goes a little hazy on the reasons he wound up on the bridge, preferring to mention how he was at school and with his dad.

Dr. Laudner seems aware there's something missing.

"You know, what you tell me in here is confidential. I won't tell your dad. Did something happen, Aaron? Something beyond what you've told me?"

Aaron stares at the carpet. "Maybe. I don't want to talk about it."

Dr. Laudner nods. "Maybe over time you'll consider telling me?"

"Maybe. Not today."

"Fair enough. Though I need to ask: Did you put yourself in any trouble legally or health-wise? Anything we need to deal with?"

This snaps Aaron out of his carpet stare. "What? No."

"Well, that can happen. During a manic episode, people do all sorts of things that can jeopardize their lives. Gamble away fortunes, have unprotected sex, make new enemies."

"None of those. I was just stupid. I'm embarrassed, okay?"

"I get that. And, Aaron, there's really nothing that you need to feel embarrassed about. It was your brain chemicals. They acted in a way they normally don't."

"And don't you think that's embarrassing? I'm fucking humiliated. I acted like an asshole at school and at . . . never mind."

"I hear you. What we're going to do today is put you on a different antidepressant. One that works for people who are bipolar."

Bipolar. Aaron has heard this word many times before. Mostly as a punch line, really. Saying someone was bipolar was a way of saying they were a little off, a little out of their minds. Now he knows. Not so much a punch line.

"So this could happen? Like, anytime?"

"Probably not, with proper medication. We'll watch things very carefully, okay? I'm going to give you my cell phone number and ask that if something isn't feeling right, you call me. Anytime, okay? You've been through a lot, Aaron. I don't know what's going to happen, but I can tell you that I care about you. And your father . . . he'd be so very sad if something happened to you. So please. Let's work closely together on this, okay?"

Aaron puts his hand over his face. What he wouldn't give to erase these past forty-eight hours. And he can't, which is the worst thing.

×

Winnie can't bear to imagine what her monthly bill from Marie France will be. Enough to buy a small country, she guesses. And totally, utterly worth it. Where would she be without Marie France? And anyway, Frank can worry about that.

She sits on the couch that's beginning to have a permanent

indentation from her ass, and she fills Marie France in on all the insanity of the last two days.

"So you lost it," Marie France says.

"Yes! I lost it. And I feel like maybe I should keep losing it."

Marie France smiles at her. "Good. I think so, too."

"I just . . . I need to know how to get past this grief."

"So you want the secret code."

"Yes, please."

"You don't, Winnie. You don't get past this grief. You rearrange your life around it. There's this Mary Chapin Carpenter song. I don't remember what it's called, but she says she feels 'quietly rearranged.' That's the key here, Winnie. Time doesn't actually heal all wounds."

"Well, that's bleak," Winnie says, staring at the well-traveled checkered floor below her.

"Grief is hard. But here's the thing about time: It doesn't heal, but it allows you to reassemble your life around the wounds."

X

Aaron is back in bed and that's a mixed bag.

He's bone-tired of the bad feelings that have him there. That's for sure. If he never again felt this empty hole in his chest where his heart's supposed to be, it would be very, very nice. And now the new pill. He took the first one an hour ago, and damned if his head doesn't feel a little spinny. Which makes sense because his head has been on a roller coaster these last few days. It would be weird if his head wasn't spinning, maybe.

But it's also safe there. He feels safe. He's in his bed, his dad is back in that chair, and that means he's not on the bridge.

X

He lies there, knowing this will be his home for the foreseeable future, because at least it's safe, and maybe he can't be trusted right now to keep himself protected.

He thinks about what he wants in life. The thing that comes to him isn't an answer he's ever had before.

What Aaron wants more than anything in life is realness. For the thing he feels, the joy, the pain—for it to be as real as the pimple on his chin, to be as true as the fact that he wants to write songs that make the whole world sing, but for now he probably needs to focus on learning how to play actual notes on the piano, not just chords.

That thought makes him wince. Ugh. Wylie and Marissa and all them. He told them he was going to be famous. Ugh. How do you come back from that?

It doesn't matter. It happened. It's over. It wasn't real, and now he wants real.

He's not been a fan of realness before. It feels brand-new. It seems like the kind of thing that could get boring, and that scares him, imagining a staid, unexciting life without too many ups and downs. But lying there, he can imagine, too, a life in which the peaks and valleys of his sine 'graph shrink, and elongate horizontally. That's always scared the shit out of him. The idea that he might not have those peaks that sustain him during the valleys.

But yeah. Lying in bed with a new medicine in his head and his dad sitting there in case he's needed, Aaron gets for once that the x-axis is what's real. Stick close to the x-axis for now. That's what he wants most of all.

"Can I play you a song?" his dad asks.

Aaron, staring up at the ceiling, isn't really sure he feels like listening to music. But he says, "Sure."

His dad fiddles with his phone and soon there's some light percussion and then ambient keyboard, and then a cherubic female voice, the voice of a girl who absolutely, one hundred percent knows there's pain.

He listens, first with his head down on the pillow, looking up, and then he rolls over and looks at his father, watching him.

"When I came home from college, back when I was so down? Nan put this on for me. It wasn't my deal. I mean, grunge rock was just beginning, and liking the über-sentimental pop music of Wilson Phillips wasn't remotely cool. But. It pierced me, you know? I listened to it over and over. *Hold on for one more day.* I'd sit on the window seat in the living room, looking out over the Hudson, while Nan bustled. You know, I don't know if she knew this before she passed, because I'm pretty sure I never told her. But this song . . . saved my life."

His dad's voice is like honey over the chamomile song, which soothes his manic bones, and Aaron knows this. He knows that this is one of those moments he'll remember all his life, and he loves that.

It feels oddly good to be back at school for the talent show, and at the same time, Aaron knows this qualifies as one of those weird and questionable moments, like when someone is too sick for school but not to play baseball, or something like that.

"You sure you want to do this?" Marissa asks.

She and Wylie are sitting on either side of Aaron in the second row, and part of him is totally sure. The other part of him is not sure at all.

"I'm good," he says.

What he is sure about is Wylie and Marissa, who enveloped him in a three-person hug as soon as they saw him outside the auditorium. It was pretty clear that people knew. That people talk, and his behavior had been weird, and then he was gone, and who knew how these things happened? Word had gotten around. He knew it the moment Marissa asked him if he was okay, right after the hug. It was an okay with an unstated *last time you were here, you were decidedly not okay.*

"I'm so embarrassed that you saw me when I . . . wasn't good," he says now.

Marissa squeezes his arm. "Don't be. We kinda got that something was up. It's okay. Like really, really okay. We're just glad you got help."

They don't know about the bridge. Maybe they never will. Who knows? It's all new.

"Why didn't you tell me you thought something was up?" Aaron finds himself asking.

Wylie and Marissa look at each other, and Aaron feels a little like a science experiment, which isn't the greatest feeling ever.

"We weren't sure you should, like, interrupt a manic person," Wylie says.

"Sounds like you're confusing that with 'never wake a sleepwalker,'" Aaron says, and Marissa cracks up and puts her head on his shoulder.

It's odd, having this connection. People who are actual friends, or maybe friend candidates. It's like a language he doesn't know yet, but he likes the idea of it a lot.

And now, the unveiling of something real: "In My Corner." Not the disco dirge version, which Aaron can hardly think about because it's so part of his illness. But, like, the real version, sung slow. He's brought accompaniment, and he already gave the track to the sound girl, and his butterflies have butterflies that have butterflies. It's like the pretty insect version of a Russian doll inside a Russian doll, and on and on and on, living in his chest.

The idea was that a song would be an earnest, emotional way to return to school. He's been home for a week, hibernating and feeling mostly awful with some okay times thrown in. Therapy every day. Dr. Laudner had a lot of questions about whether he ought to return with a song, and Aaron was like, it'll be fine. It'll be good. "In My Corner" is a little depressing, maybe, but that's okay, too, and he's going to be out about his depression. He wants that, because he wants people to know him.

"You sure you're okay?" asks Marissa, when he's been apparently staring off into space for who knows how long.

"Yes, no, maybe."

That's the thing. He has so many more questions than answers, and aside from sitting at home for a couple weeks or months until he's stabilized, it kinda seems like his job is to be okay with the questions, and the unsureness, right now.

"I'm sure the song is really good, Aaron. But you don't, like, have to do this. You can just come back. You can—"

"Let him do it," Wylie says. "I mean, if he wants to?"

There's a question in there, but Aaron has no more answers. Just a lot of fear. In his throat. Down his pipes and into his lungs.

He knows he's afraid he's about to mess up publicly again, adding to whatever legend is forming about Aaron Boroff and his epic weirdness. But there's something even bigger than that rattling around in his brain.

A bigger fear. That he's not going to be able to make it to the next time he is in a good place.

That's a new thought for him. He files it away under things to say to his dad. His dad always knows what to say back. And maybe Dr. Laudner. Yeah, maybe. Maybe he'll start talking more in those sessions.

This makes him feel ever so slightly better.

Then it's his turn, and then he's walking up the stairs, and people are clapping, and then he's standing at a microphone, and it's wrong. Wrong. Wrong.

All wrong.

So when the piano music starts, he takes a deep breath, awkwardly leans into the microphone, and says, "Off. Turn it off, please."

The music goes off. He stands at the microphone, looking out at a sea of expectant faces. Some more friendly than others.

He says, "They say tragedy plus time is comedy. I wonder what mania plus not that much time is?"

A couple laughs. Including, notably, Marissa and Wylie.

Thank god for the Jones-Joneses. He smiles and looks down.

"Maybe mania plus not that much time is singing an okay song at a talent show and hoping people think it's AMAZING." He laughs, a real, half-nervous laugh. More laughter from the audience, and it spurs him on.

"Am I, like, the least likely person to be manic depressive, by the way? I'm the middle-of-the-road kid, except I'm really, really not. That's an awkward place to be. People see me and they're like, 'Aw, he's so nice and quiet' and meanwhile my brain is going . . . AAAAGGGHHHH!"

He pantomimes his brain exploding and people laugh and he laughs, too, because it is, actually, really funny to him. It's a lot of things. It's sad as fuck. But also it's funny, the way he had this mask on all the time.

And his impulse is to go on about all this, because people would laugh, because they'd see the humor, and the best jokes are aimed at oneself, and, man, there's a history of depressive and probably manic comedians, isn't there? All this shoots through his brain in like a nanosecond.

But then his gut steps in.

He doesn't need to do that, actually. To get the laughter. To walk offstage the most popular, the most funny, the most anything.

He smiles, and then he purses his lips.

"So, um. I'm coming back to school Monday. It's gonna be weird, because I guess I'm weird. I don't know. So. I'm kinda scared. But. I'm gonna try it, I guess. Thanks for listening to me. Thanks."

And as he does walk offstage, the craziest thing happens. Raucous applause. Whistles. More than he ever got through singing or performing. He closes his eyes and puts his head down, because a part of him likes it . . . too much, probably. His gut tells him that the best thing for him to do in this situation is keep his head down and hear the applause without soaking it in. To enjoy it without settling in for a huge fantasy of what it all means.

Tillie isn't ready for what happens next.

The boy pulls himself over the railing until he's sitting on the ledge as if he's on a swing set, swaying in the wind, except there's no swing, just a thin piece of metal under him. She's like, *No, wait up. Wait for me.*

But he doesn't wait.

He's gone.

One moment the mysterious boy she'd just walked past was there. The next? Gone.

She squeezes her eyes shut. She cannot watch him fall. When she hears the most distant of clacks, she keeps her eyes locked shut.

What? What just happened? What the—?

She is so, so stupid. She'd walked past the kid, who was about her age, and she thought he was, like, a poet or a painter, looking out at the city, memorizing it for his art. That's seriously the thought she had because she was so fixated on her own crap. *Stupid and selfish*, she thinks. She should have said something and it would have made him not do that. *So, so selfish.*

Also: *Totally not going to jump now. Who jumps off the George Washington Bridge second?*

She slowly walks toward the spot where the boy was, just a minute ago. She feels dizzy, like the time she was mugged when she was eight. An outsize thing has happened and her body doesn't know how to react. It's so weird to her, so random. If she'd come an hour earlier, she'd be dead. Now she isn't, but this stranger is. It's like he saved her life, kind of, because in the echo of that distant clack, she can't really imagine—was she actually going to? Drown in the Hudson? Where it's so cold? Over what? Stupid Molly Tobin and her mean video? Fucking Amir? Was he worth it?

She puts her hand on the dilapidated rail, approximating where the boy's hand was. No spot is particularly warmer than any other. It's like he was a ghost. There are no signs of his existence in the hard-blowing wind. If she leaves and doesn't say anything, no one will ever know. Boy evaporated.

He was looking right at her. Before he jumped. They were staring at each other. She was the last person he saw on this earth. She is so not worthy of that role.

What made him do it? It must have been way worse than what's going on with her.

She walks back toward Manhattan and climbs down the stairs. Totally numb and not knowing what the right thing to do is, she zombie walks to the subway station at 175th Street and Fort Washington Ave.

Once she gets there, the warmth of the station does nothing to stop her chattering teeth.

A boy is dead in the water.

She's pretty sure her teeth will be chattering for a while.

×

Britt is practicing her routine to Cardi B in the living room when Tillie trudges in and drops her backpack on the floor by the coat closet. Her little sister has the moves down, but the feeling is totally wrong, which is a good thing because Britt is ten and Tillie thinks it's super creepy that Mom and Dad think it's okay to let her ten-year-old sister sway her hips so provocatively. That is so clearly part of the reason this world sucks, and here it is, in her living room.

And in such a fucking adorable package. Everyone loves Britt. How could they not? Long blond hair, rail-thin arms and legs, no hips, dimples. Everything Tillie's not, never was, never will be. Watching her little sister shake her tiny butt, she wants to hate her, but she just can't. Instead, she's totally Team Britt. She's the captain. Kind of agrees with her dad, who so clearly feels that the Stanleys should never have adopted a dark, chubby Korean girl because you never know. One day you can't conceive, and the next? Surprise! You can. Oh, joyful day.

"Watch, Tillie!" Britt yells over the music. "I added this new part."

Tillie takes what just happened and scrunches it up into a tiny ball and stores it in her jacket pocket, and she smiles at her little sister, and she watches. Britt bends at the knees and undulates her full body from her knees up to her head. She's all personality, and it jumps off her as she moves, and it looks awesome. Shocker. Who cares if Britt has no fucking clue what she's dancing to and what the moves mean? Who cares if Tillie as a poet does really connect to her art, but since it's not pretty, no one gives a shit?

"So good," Tillie says.

This makes Britt smile. And then, like she has too much love for her tiny body to contain and she has to let it out, she explodes onto Tillie, running over and hugging her big sister tight. It's so weird how all this girl eats is candy, and she's just a rail.

"Now you go," Britt says, pulling at Tillie's arm.

"I go?"

Britt puts her hands on her skinny hips and tilts her head to the side.

"I need backup dancers. Duh."

Tillie laughs, despite herself. Where this girl got her personality, Tillie will never know. Their dad isn't exactly a YouTube celebrity, and she can't even imagine her mom copping an attitude, ever.

"I don't think I'm background dancer material," Tillie says.

"Anyone can!" Britt says. "You just gotta"—and here she undulates her hips in a way that Tillie is pretty sure her hips don't go—"*feel* the beat!" The word *feel* has ten *e*'s, the way Britt says it.

Tillie rolls her eyes, tries to forget about what's there, pulsing in her pocket, that she just witnessed a boy dying, and what kind of person dances after that? After almost—

"Come onnnn," Britt whines, pulling on Tillie's arm.

"Okay. Just once," Tillie says, taking off her coat and putting it on the floor.

"Attagirl," her ten-year-old sister says, and Tillie snorts.

Britt runs over and starts the music again, and as the rap part starts in and Britt starts doing her choreography and Tillie does her best to approximate, she feels dirty, like unclean in the soul. As she unenthusiastically wiggles her midsection, she feels as if she could cry, actually, as if she's left her body and nothing will ever be the same again.

Britt turns and watches, and she shakes her head in frustration.

"No, no, no!" she shouts over the chorus. "Like this!" And she runs over and puts her hand on Tillie's pelvis and on her butt and tries to basically unhinge her older sister's pelvis with an exaggerated, forced undulation. Tillie looks down, momentarily shocked, and Britt looks up, her mouth open and her expression wild, and in a nanosecond Tillie gets that she's being punked, that Britt is freaking hilarious and knows that Tillie is not quite the Twerking Queen, and the sisters make eye contact and everything Tillie's been feeling slips away and the laughter just goes.

Britt collapses on the floor and Tillie gingerly leans down and fake punches her little sister in the shoulder, and Britt grasps her arm like she's been mortally wounded, and, in retaliation, makes the fingers on her left hand into a V and pretends to stab Tillie in the eyes. Tillie falls onto her back, grabbing her face in mock agony, and she hears Britt kneel over her.

"Oh no! And all over a spat between dancers!" Britt wails.

Tillie peeks up at her little sister and her silly, dramatic face is too much and Tillie starts to laugh, for real. Britt drops the act and falls down onto Tillie's ample torso and Tillie wraps her arms around Britt and they laugh until they cry, and Tillie feels the thing in her coat pocket across the room, pulsing. It's her almost death, and she just tries, tries, tries to forget. To pretend it never happened. So she can just laugh with her sister.

Who would have—what? If Tillie had died? She pushes that away, too, and she tries to melt into the moment.

Britt puts her mouth on Tillie's shirt right around the belly button and blows a raspberry.

"You brat," Tillie says.

"You're the brat," Britt says. "I fire you. As a background dancer. Because you're mouthy and you talk back and you don't take direction."

"You diva bitch," says Tillie, mock incredulous.

"That's Miss Diva Bitch to you!" says Britt. She rolls off her sister and they lie on the ground and catch their breath. Tillie glances over at her sister, who is beaming. So happy. And why can't she be? Why can't she just—

"Dinner's ready," her dad yells from the dining room. He sounds like he's already chewing.

Ah, yes. The reason why she can't just.

Tillie sits across from Britt, who sporadically makes funny faces at her. To Tillie's right is her mom, who is a force of nature. Tillie's respirator. Who feels like Tillie's pulse sometimes. And to her left is a huge void, a vacuum. A black hole in her life.

That used to be her father. She remembers the time before Britt, and how her dad played airplane with her. He'd sit down with his legs bent, knees up, and she'd stand on his knees, and he'd grab her small hands in his big ones and lie down, and Tillie would be flying like Superman, arms out in front of her, and they'd lock eyes and laugh, and the roller coaster in her belly would be the thing she'd think about as she squirmed around at night in bed, how her daddy loved her so much. Mom's love was even then like a steady pulse, like a locomotive, and Dad's? Incredible peaks and the valleys of his business travel. It swooned her. She was so much Daddy's little girl back then.

And then Britt, who was unexpected. "A gift from heaven," she heard her grandma Stanley say as she stood there, holding baby Britt. It was the first time she'd seen her grandma since she was a baby. It was like Britt came along and suddenly she had grand-parents. She never understood that.

Dad changed. It was slow and then it was fast. No airplane and split time with her sister, which was fine because she got to watch him make Britt feel so happy, and that made Tillie happy, too. But then her teen years, and Dad went away, almost like. It was subtle at first. He was there but not there. Questions about her day at school at the dinner table, but no roller coaster anymore. That was for Britt only. And sometimes it felt like they were roommates instead of father and daughter, and she'd see him putting Britt to bed and the bottom would drop out and she was all alone in the world, even with her mom the locomotive always there, ever present. And then Amir, and the big fight, and Dad washed his hands of her.

"How's the choreography coming?" her dad asks, not looking up from his corn pudding.

"Good," Britt says, and for a nanosecond Tillie wants to push Britt off the George Washington Bridge. Then she realizes the awfulness of this and she makes that thought disappear.

"Awesome," Dad says, and he digs out a big spoonful of corn pudding and shovels it into his mouth and Tillie watches out of the corner of her eye and she is just out of ideas about how to survive this cold war anymore. This war of no words that plays out, every night, at the dinner table. The war she does not understand even a little. It makes her think of the boy falling, and that just makes it worse, and suddenly she can't breathe. She gasps involuntarily, and thankfully Britt is going on about the dance competition and how she hopes her new choreography will win Spence first place, because no one seems to notice.

But then Tillie's mom gently puts her hand on Tillie's wrist. Tillie wants to pull away because it's like, no, don't. Don't get too attached to this wrist, please. You're already too attached. It might not be here tomorrow. She tenses up slightly and she feels a slight squeeze.

The squeeze means, *I see you're struggling. We'll talk after dinner, okay?*

Her mom. Winnie. The only reason Tillie still is. And even with her mom's love, Tillie almost wasn't. And she's gonna wind up telling her, and that's gonna suck. Tillie always tells her mom everything.

Tillie looks at her dad. She feels sorry for him, in a way. She was plan B, and seven years later plan A happened, and this particular plan B is so not what he would have signed up for. It's a shame that adoption agencies can't say shit like, *Now, just so you know, this cute infant will one day get über dark and do monologues at talent shows about having sex in which she likens herself to a cow, and you'll be super embarrassed in front of the other well-heeled parents. Shall we still proceed?*

She tries to communicate to him through telepathy. To sear into his brain that she's sorry she's so difficult, and she knows she's lost him, and by the way it's not a manageable loss, and she'll change, she'll do anything if he'll love her again. He looks up toward her. Face blank. Eyes boring right through her. Not seeing anything. And her whole body shivers because it puts her right back up on that bridge again.

X

On the Upper East Side, a girl named Molly lazes in her room, thinking about how sucky it is that Spence's zero-tolerance policy on bullying doesn't consider *nuance*.

No doubt it's bad to roast someone for being fat, but that was so not the point. The point is there were three girls there that day. Gretchen's and Isabella's things were way worse, but they didn't get leaked.

Gretchen's sex kitten video totally roasted Tacy Evans, and even though Tacy is a slut and not in the empowering way but in the *you're bringing down the entire gender with your lack of standards* way— she does married men, so come on—it was still way over the line and Molly knew that. It was way worse than what Molly did minutes later. And in between, Isabella's thing on Savanya was way over the line and they didn't even record it, thank God. Molly was embarrassed to be in the room when Isabella was doing it, to be honest.

But then it had been her turn. And yeah, making fun of someone's weight is obviously not cool, but it wasn't meant for public consumption, okay? It was basically a dare. So. Goodbye, Brown. Adios, Michigan. And all over a stupid cow.

×

Up at Montefiore Medical Center in the Bronx, Michael Boroff is finishing up his notes after seeing a girl with severe bulimia when the phone call comes. It's a number he doesn't recognize, and usually that means a telemarketer. For some reason, he answers.

"Is this Michael Boroff?"

He rolls his eyes. What are they selling this time? "Depends who's asking."

"Hello, sir. This is Lieutenant Jonathan Riggs from the Twentieth Precinct. We're at your home and it seems like you're not here. May I ask: Where are you?"

He laughs because his first thought is so . . . not right. Off target. His son, Aaron, shoplifting dirty magazines, which is actually a memory from his own teen years, back when dirty magazines were a thing. Ridiculous idea. Anyway, he's not at all the kind of kid—

"Mr. Boroff?"

"Oh. Right. Um. Can you at least—is my son in trouble? What did he do? He's never done anything—"

"Mr. Boroff. Could you please come home? We can send a car. Would you like that? Would you like us to send a car?"

Michael Boroff loses control of his legs a little. It's so sudden and drastic and unexpected. His head and his body are operating completely on their own. His legs buckle and turn to jelly, and he laughs and then the laugh turns into another sound Michael has never heard from his body before. It's a sound of protest, like he's protesting whatever this is, this unwanted call that has made his legs do one thing, his mouth another, his brain a third.

He says, "What? What's happening?"

"Where are you, Mr. Boroff? We'll come get you and bring you home."

"No. Tell me. You have to. What's going on? Please?"

"Where are you, Mr. Boroff? Please tell us where you are. We're coming your way, okay?"

X

After dinner, Tillie goes to her bedroom, lies on her bed under the sheets, and puts the comforter over her face. In her little cocoon, she tries to imagine where the boy is now. Bottom of the Hudson? Is his soul gone? Is it in outer space? In some kind of heaven place?

It could just as easily be me. It should have been me.

Ten minutes later, she hears the door open and shut softly and hears her mom take her usual seat in the desk chair, rolling it over to the bed. It's gotten so it's embarrassing, how often Winnie has to do this. Tillie is seventeen, and still her mom has to talk her down. Tell her that she is loved, she is appreciated. Why can't it stick?

Tillie pulls the comforter down and stares up at the ceiling. She doesn't say it for maybe a minute. Says nothing, calculates what will happen if she doesn't speak, and what will happen if she does. Finally, she blurts it out:

"I went to the George Washington Bridge after school and thought about jumping."

"Till!" her mom says, and she climbs onto the bed next to her and holds her tight from the side. Tillie can't feel it. Can't feel anything.

It's the right tone, the right movement. The totally wrong feel.

She loves her mom to death and she knows her mom loves her back every bit as much. So why does it feel like she's the girl in the bubble, the girl no one can touch?

What's wrong with her?

"Did you really do that, Till?"

"Yeah," Tillie says, monotone.

Her mother starts crying. Tillie can't.

"I just—I don't know what to do, sweetheart. Has Dr. Brown helped at all?"

Dr. Brown. Tillie thinks it's perfect that her psychologist has the same name as her favorite brand of cream soda. She has been about as effective as soda at helping Tillie deal with, as she says, her *core belief* that she doesn't deserve love.

Tillie shrugs.

"I wonder if we need to put you in someplace. Inpatient, I mean."

This makes Tillie sit up. "No," she says. "*No.*"

The idea of losing her freedom is . . . inconceivable to her. A total deal breaker. Patently unfair. Like it's not enough that she lives her life underwater. She should also, apparently, be told what to eat, when to eat. Who to see, when to sleep. She'd rather die than go inpatient. Martha Sorenson went inpatient for her bulimia. Now Tillie walks in on Martha disgorging the contents of her stomach in the third-floor bathroom twice weekly at a minimum.

"We need to come up with a plan."

Erase what happened with Amir? With the video? Maybe figure out how to get Dad to pretend I'm still alive?

The way her dad has washed his hands of her? Too much. Over lunch, she'd texted her parents about the A-minus she'd gotten on her report on Prohibition. Her mom immediately responded with a "Yay!" No response from Dad. Which in and of itself meant nothing, because of course the cold war, and she wasn't sure if he'd just say a quick good job or ignore it, and sometimes he got busy at work. But then she looked on Facebook, and who do you think was posting pictures of Britt from their weekend outing to Barnegat Lighthouse? Like a half hour after her text? And then a response to a comment about how beautiful Britt was, an hour later, when Tillie checked again after calc class?

Light of my life, he wrote to Uncle Gorman.

Nice, Tillie thought. But no. Not nice. Because sometimes these things made Tillie dark, and sometimes when Tillie got dark, she found herself sitting in the hallway between the senior lounge and the lunchroom, scribbling on a piece of paper because she worried if she stopped, if she lifted the pen a centimeter off the page, she might stand up, walk somewhere, and do something way worse. Because the hollow feeling in her gut actually hurt, like outsize pain, like way worse than it should just because her dad didn't love her as much as he loved his actual, real biological daughter. This sort of thing was the reason weak people hurt themselves. Meanwhile strong people would be in a war and watch their best friends' heads get shot off and be basically fine. She'd read a book about girl soldiers fighting in World War II, and about a million times she thought, *This. This is why I suck. Because these girls kick actual ass, and I would have basically walked into oncoming enemy fire to end it all.*

She hated how weak she was.

"What kind of plan?" Tillie finally asked.

Her mother pressed her hands into the sides of her face, like she was trying to keep her head from exploding.

"Just . . . something that will get you through this hard time," she says. "Maybe have you see a psychiatrist. See about medicine."

Tillie laughs, slightly relieved that at least this plan isn't a freedom-losing one. But still. No. Apparently a therapist like Dr. Brown isn't enough—she's going to need a psychiatrist who can prescribe pills. This was everyone's answer. How many of her friends were on Ritalin or Zoloft or Wellbutrin? *Oh, Mandy has the sadness, give her a pill. Oh, Tonya gets nervous when she has to give an oral report. Shoot her full of diazepam.*

"No," she says.

Her mom says something she rarely says, and she says it in a tone she never uses.

Her mom shouts, "No!"

This gets Tillie's attention.

"No, Tillie," she says. "No to your no. I can't do this anymore. I can't hear, every day, that you're suicidal, and keep allowing you out of my sight. I know how much you're hurting, darling. But do you have any idea how scared I am every day you go off to school, and I have to hope you'll make it back home?"

Tillie throws the blanket over her face. She can't let her mom see the way her face contorts hearing these words. She can't let anyone see. Ever again. She wishes she were under the water in the Hudson. She wishes she were anywhere but here.

Her mother tries to pull the blanket down, but Tillie is too fast. She holds it tight.

"Tillie," her mom pleads.

Nope. She'll hold the blanket over her head until her mother leaves.

No one will ever see her face again.

Dr. Brown's office is down the steps just to the side of the entrance of a fancy prewar building on Park Avenue. The skinny, dark-skinned doorman with an American flag pin on his lapel nods at Tillie. He always nods at her, every time, and she wonders just how much crazy he sees, and how privileged he must think she is, because, well, she's not exactly sure what a session with a Park Avenue shrink costs, but she's pretty sure it's more money than a doorman makes in a day, or maybe even two days. For an hour of whining to a doctor who could not care less.

"I'd like you to ask Dr. Brown if I can join you for the last fifteen minutes," her mom says as she digs through her pocketbook.

Tillie doesn't respond. It feels like she doesn't care, but in a way she does, because she's busy doing math. Dr. Brown plus Winnie equals a brainstorming session about a plan.

"Sweetheart?"

"Fine," Tillie mutters.

"I know this is hard," her mom says, putting a thin, muscular arm that feels a bit too much like a snake right now around her back. "I know. But we need to get you better."

Tillie pulls out her phone and goes to Snapchat, only to realize she had utterly no interest in seeing pictures or communicating with anyone in the entire world. She turns her phone off and glances over at her mother. Winnie's face is like what you might expect of a soldier stationed in Afghanistan. Someone who has been through a long war. Someone who has seen things. Tillie is now at least part of that war. This is an unfortunate result. She looks away. She can't deal with it at all.

Dr. Brown opens the door and peers her vegan face out. "Tillie? Oh, hi, Winnie. How are you?"

Tillie's mother offers as much of a controlled smile as she can in this situation. "I really want to be part of this discussion, if that's okay. We need a plan."

Dr. Brown looks at Tillie. Tillie looks at the floor.

"Let me chat with Tillie for a bit and see where we are," Dr. Brown says in her best Mondo Zen Buddha Bitch voice.

Tillie, head down and without looking back at her mother, whose very presence is sucking the air out of the world, follows Dr. Brown into the danger zone.

"So how are you doing?" Dr. Brown asks as she sits down. As she always asks.

"Pretty good," Tillie answers as *she* sits down. As she always answers.

"Your mother called me and told me what happened, so I don't think you're 'pretty good' at all," Dr. Brown says, as she's never said before.

"Oh."

"What's going on under the hood?" Dr. Brown asks, and Tillie suppresses a grimace. She does not like to be referred to as a car. It makes her feel, for one, fat. She's a human being. She doesn't have a hood.

"I don't know," Tillie says.

Dr. Brown nods and nods. She keeps staring at Tillie in an unnerving manner, and she makes a note in her notebook. Tillie fidgets in the plush red-leather recliner.

"Well, let's start with what you do know."

Tillie takes a deep breath and resists rolling her eyes.

"I went to the bridge. George Washington. I don't know. I wasn't really going to jump, I don't think. It's like. I don't know. Like I'm an artist without a canvas or something."

Tillie's class read *Sula* by Toni Morrison last month, and that was her takeaway: *Like any artist with no art form, she became dangerous*, the line had read, and when Ms. Cruz asked about it in class, Tillie perked up. It had been like reading about herself—and that was before the satire video that forever ended her performance career.

"An artist without a canvas," Dr. Brown repeats, and it sounds totally wrong coming out of her mouth. Tillie just wants to say, *Yes. My canvas was taken away. Now I am dangerous.*

It's so typical that Dr. Brown doesn't elaborate. She almost never does. No advice that would help, even though sometimes Tillie wouldn't mind someone telling her what to do. It's like it's Dr. Brown's only job to get Tillie to say all the really bad things, as if that will make the bad things go away. It won't.

So Dr. Brown doesn't reply, and she writes something else in her book. As much as she sometimes loathes Dr. Brown, Tillie would give, like, a zillion dollars for an hour alone with that book. Maybe *it* has the answers.

Finally, after Tillie digs into her silence, Dr. Brown relents her own silence to say, "So you went to the bridge, but you weren't really going to jump. What were you there for?"

Tillie crosses and uncrosses her legs. She squirms in her seat. This is the part she can't explain.

There was no other option. That's the truth of how it felt. She literally did not know what else to do with the pain so deep down in her throat, the pain that sometimes feels like a string is pulling her shoulders down from the center of her gut. The tension is so taut that she can't even fight against it.

"I thought about it, okay? I thought about it and it wasn't worth it."

"What stopped you?"

Tillie gulps. She doesn't know why but she cannot share about the boy jumping. It feels like that's hers, and hers alone, and also like maybe her not reporting it might be a crime or something. If nothing else, it was a sign that she's too selfish to live.

"I don't know," she says.

Dr. Brown tilts her head sideways, like she's trying to figure Tillie out.

"Well, say one thing about it. One thing you were feeling up there. Or a thought you had."

"That my mom would literally die. That Britt would be sad."

Dr. Brown smiles. "Good. Yes. And what about your father?"

Tillie shrugs and stares at the ceiling. Nope. Ever since the fight with her dad, Dr. Brown is always trying to get Tillie to go there. Reduce that relationship to something understandable, which it most certainly isn't.

"Do you think he would have been sad, had you died by suicide, Tillie?"

Tillie chews her cuticles.

Dr. Brown goes on. "You know what I think? I think he would have been terribly sad."

Tillie's throat tightens. She holds her breath. Nope. And then Dr. Brown does something she almost never does. She shares her opinion.

"I think you tell yourself a story about your father, and that it's terribly difficult for you because some of the story is true. Your father doesn't react to you the way you would like, and I think you feel terribly alone, as if there's a gulf there. And I want you to know I hear that. Your father is not there for you in the way you might like."

Tillie's eyes fill up with water. Nope. She moves her teeth from her cuticle to her finger. She bites down. Ouch.

"Tillie?"

Tillie stares straight ahead.

"I'm concerned you're going to draw blood there. Your pinkie."

Tillie opens her mouth, pulls her finger away, looks at it. No blood. She stares at the clock next to Dr. Brown.

"How much more time do we have today?"

Dr. Brown sighs. "Sometimes it feels like you're not even here. Are you angry? Are you angry at me, for example?"

Tillie feels like laughing. This is a thing adults do. They make it about them. Everything. *It's not about you, Dr. Brown. Go take a long weekend in East Hampton with your perfect family, Dr. Brown. Feast on fava bean chips and water with electrolytes as you motor east on the LIE in your electric car, Dr. Brown. You fuck.*

"Are you angry?" Dr. Brown asks again.

"Nope," Tillie says. "Not angry. Don't worry about it."

Dr. Brown smiles a bit. "But I do worry about it. My gut instinct—and your mother agrees—is that you ought to go somewhere until you feel a bit more stable. Can I bring her in here so we can discuss that?"

Tillie winces. She should never let her guard down. You let your guard down and suddenly you're en route to some horrifying facility in Minnesota. That's a bottom-line no right there. She will jump in front of the first taxi she sees outside if they actually think they're locking her away somewhere. Absolutely one hundred percent fucking not.

"I'm fine," she says, looking directly at Dr. Brown. "I mean, I'm not fine. Obviously. But yesterday I—I guess yesterday was a test and I passed. Or I failed. I mean. Depends which shoulder you're on. Part of me is definitely not fine and definitely wanted things to end yesterday, but the other shoulder? It's a fighter, okay? I'm not going to die. I just want things to be—"

She swallows. The feelings have jumped to her chin and she doesn't want them there. She wants them down. This isn't *get real* time. This is *stay out of institution* time. She swallows, again and again, tasting the salty tears in her throat.

"It's okay," Dr. Brown says. "Let it out, Tillie. Let it out."

No. No. She can't. She won't.

She'll swallow it down again and again and again until the end of time.

"I'm *fine*," she says again, forcing a smile that feels like death to her face.

Dr. Brown writes something down in her book, and Tillie vows to spend the rest of the session elsewhere in her head. A happier place. Because this place?

Nearly unbearable.

"I'm going to bring your mother in now," Dr. Brown says. "We need to put our heads together. I hear what you're saying. You're saying you didn't attempt suicide yesterday, and that you were on the bridge because you're out of ideas. But that's a problem, too. How do we know that you don't wind up there again? This is a hard time for you, Tillie. And as I said, I think we need to protect you right now. Get you on the right track, and I know a place that I'm pretty sure can admit you today. In Vermont. It's private, but I think that's going to be the best choice and I know your parents are on board and no price is too much for your safety. Can I bring her in?"

She hears her father's voice: *Who's gonna pay for your goddamn psych bill?*

Tillie's entire body has gone numb. She pictures herself in a different bed tonight, in Vermont, without her stuff, and she just . . . can't. It's like with a few words, Dr. Brown has torn what's left of Tillie's world down, and her feet and her legs and her arms and her hands buzz and she cannot feel them, and her head is filled with static.

This is it. The big fear. Coming true.

She's all alone in this world.

"Tillie?"

"Let me," Tillie says, barely loud enough to be heard. "I need to tell her something first."

"Okay," Dr. Brown finally says. "Sure. Okay."

Tillie slowly crosses the room. Part of her wishes for a nuclear bomb right now. All of her prays her mom has somehow disappeared, like a black hole swallowed her up in the last fifteen minutes.

She opens the door, steps out into the waiting room.

Somehow, her mom isn't here.

Maybe a black hole?

More likely the bathroom.

Tillie doesn't hesitate. She walks straight out of the office, out onto Park Avenue, out past the skinny doorman with his American flag pin, and south toward who knows where.

Anywhere but here.

✕

Molly is jonesing for her secret love, and her stupid mother just won't leave.

Her mom is lingering over breakfast and Molly is like, *Go! Go to Pilates, please, woman!* She pushes an organic blueberry around her cereal bowl while her mother spoons her morning soft-boiled egg, which sits nested in a pewter egg holder. Molly's thoughts are about interruptions.

People have secrets. A lot of those secrets are about drugs and alcohol and cheating. Molly's secret is . . . not those.

Molly's secret is the wrong thing, on so many levels.

×

Michael Boroff sits and stares at the fishbowl in his son's room.

Britney Spearfish. Tina Tuna. Carpi B.

He stares until his eyes go blurry. He puts his head in his hands and silently weeps.

His ex is coming down from Massachusetts later. He called her. Not a fun conversation. Not the person he wants to see. The other failed parent in this equation.

When his hands are drenched in his own tears, he wills himself to look up, and he takes a deep breath. *Okay. Okay.*

He picks up the little shaker of fish food and sprinkles some flakes into the water.

The least he can do is keep his son's fish alive.

×

Sarah Palmer sobs in the cafeteria. She is surrounded by her friends, and snot is running down her face.

"He was just—why didn't I just say 'you were good'? He was like a wounded puppy, and I just. You know, it's my gut instinct, because, like, I would NOT want to have an elevated sense of who I am, and he seemed to think he and Kelly were like equals and they so weren't, but. Why didn't I just?"

Renee Hampton puts his arm around her. "You didn't know. Nobody knew."

"But maybe we should have known?" Sarah asks.

"Well, who were his friends?"

No one says much. The thing about Aaron was that everybody was okay with him. And nobody was a close friend. He was the kid who was super nice and kinda funny and a bit of a geek and he really, really, really tried on those songs and, like, Sarah's grandmother who was from Dallas would say—bless his heart. You had to kind of love a kid who was that earnest. Who put it out there and seemed totally okay with being, well. Maybe he wasn't. Obviously, he wasn't.

"I just. I will be playing that stupid conversation over and over in my brain forever," Sarah says.

And the response is supportive pats and rubs, because the answer is so obvious.

Yeah, of course you will.

X

The text from Mike comes in during English class.

Lunchtime binge?

Amir Rahimi smiles and shudders. *Binge* refers to bingeing on girls, which means skulking two blocks up Park Avenue and hanging outside Hewitt. While the girls there seem to tolerate the Browning boys, they probably don't know about the points system, about how Mike is at forty-eight, and how Amir has finally gotten away from zero by getting with Tillie, and how not okay he was after, and how a little bit of his soul dies every single time he has to stand there and act interested in whatever every normal boy in the world seems interested in.

Sure, Amir texts back.

There are choices to be made in life. Sacrifices. Being gay is just not—normal. Or even if it is normal, it still isn't—acceptable. At least not to his friends and definitely not to his mom. So that isn't something that's going to happen. Some things are just not possible.

And if wanting to jump out of his skin a little bit every day is the price, so be it. And if hurting Tillie Stanley, whom he truly, really liked, is the price, that is a price he's willing to pay.

Apparently.

X

Tillie scurries down Park Avenue, hardly breathing, her face numb in the chilly morning breeze. She passes joggers in spandex pants, an old lady walking her pug, and two girls wearing long skirts and blazers with a Loyola School insignia on them. She wonders what things would have been like if she'd gone to school there, a school with boys as well as girls. Maybe that would have made the girls in her class nicer.

That thought makes her laugh. Yeah. As if the girls were nicer at coed dances. As if they hadn't made it a fucking death-blow competition to scoop up the cute boys, and hadn't shoved it in Tillie's face that she'd wound up standing on the sidelines with Marcia

Fishbaum and Savanya Booker. As if they hadn't called them the Three Nuns. Fuckers.

She isn't sure where she's going, but one thing is for sure: She is not sticking around to submit to forcible commitment to inpatient or whatever.

Her phone buzzes in her pocket. Twice. Three times. Her whole body shudders. She's upsetting her mom and that's horrible. She knows it. But her hand is being forced. She instinctively grabs for her phone but then stops herself. First she needs to get as far away as she can so they can't find her. Then she can respond.

When she is on a side street several blocks away, under some of New York City's ubiquitous metal scaffolding—do construction projects ever get finished?—Tillie pulls out her phone. There are four texts already.

> Tillie! Sweetheart? Where are you? Please write me back!

> Tillie! I'm SO SCARED right now. You CANNOT do this to me!

> Please? Please?

> Sweetheart!

Tillie's heart twists in her rib cage. She is a terrible, terrible person. But then she remembers, once more, what she's running from. And she knows that on some level, she's right to run.

> I'm sorry mom. I'm not going to hurt myself. I need some time to think. Just a little time, k? I'm not going inpatient. Bottom line. Give me a day to think.

Her mom writes her back immediately: Please tell me where you are. Let me think with you, okay? I want to protect you and I can't if I don't know where you are. Please!

Tillie responds: I need to do this, Mom. I need some time. I'll be okay. I promise.

Her mom doesn't write back right away and Tillie stares at her phone, waiting. Then it comes.

> Dr. Brown and I think you need to be placed in treatment. Today. This isn't negotiable, Till. This is for your safety. Come back and talk to us and we will fill you in on the details. It's going to be good, Till. You need help.

Tillie goes numb again. She doesn't respond, and when she doesn't, her mother writes more.

> Don't do this, Tillie. Don't make me come find you. Don't make me call the police to come pick you up. Do the right thing and come back, OK?

Something about these words makes Tillie study her screen more carefully. That's when she sees the weird icon. Up near the battery icon, next to the one for location. Little black glasses she's never seen before.

Shit.

Her mom must have put some sort of tracking thing on her phone last night after she went to bed. *Just like Winnie*, she thinks. *She never trusts—*

Oh. Well.

She powers the phone off, then realizes that's probably not enough. Shit. She looks left, looks right. She's standing between Park and Lexington on Eighty-Third Street, under scaffolding that looks semipermanent to her well-trained New York City eyes. She spies a divot in the sidewalk, behind a metal scaffolding pole. It goes about four inches below the concrete. She winces, thinking about what lives down there. She looks around her once again, doesn't see anyone watching her. She cringes, unable to imagine life without her phone, but even more unable to picture life in some cold institution, her freedom taken from her. Shit. She leans down and carefully places it in the divot. It barely sticks out. *Bye, phone. I'll miss you. Hope to see you later today, but probably you'll be gone.*

She runs toward Lexington Avenue, her beige skirt blowing in the wind, feeling dangerously, thrillingly free. Her heart is in her mouth and her eyes dart all around her to see if she's been made, as if she's a spy or a covert operative in some movie.

No one will find her. Not today.

X

Once Molly's mom mercifully leaves, Molly quickly grabs her laptop, folds her conscience up into a neat little pile, and watches the most recent video of Jasmine. She skips to minute four, watches twenty awful seconds with bile rising into her esophagus, and pulls out her phone.

She texts Gretchen.

> Oh my god! That eye shadow Jasmine used was SO on point

Gretchen texts right back.

> I know!! Are you dying about Lizzie and Drew breaking up??!?!

Molly swallows down bile.

> Totally dying!! Say hey to Isabella, k?

It's only when she's satisfied that she's done what she needs to do to not be thrown into Spence's scrap heap that she puts her phone away. A smile creeps across her face. An actual smile. Rare since this thing with Tillie.

She pulls the book out from under her mattress.

Molly will finally be doing the thing she loves so much: lying in bed, totally ensconced in the world of Adarlan.

This is the part she loves the most: This is where Celaena Sardothien sort of splits in two, and there's the tough girl, the assassin who kicks ass, and there's the terrifyingly hot girl who the prince is totally into, and you know she's likes him, too, and the tingles she gets reading these pages are not normal, but man. What she wouldn't give to just let her inner Celaena out.

Just once.

She looks up from her book. She puts it down. *No.* She can't. She went through this last year. Last year she started around February, pretty sure she'd finally go, and then, by April, she'd chickened the fuck out. The day of, she walked around furious with herself, that she was at Sephora with Isabella and not at the Marriott Marquis.

Is it possible? Should she check? No. Yes. No.

Ah, fuck it. She picks up her phone and types in the words, and soon she's looking at a date, two weeks from tomorrow, and a list of guests.

And yes, of course, she'll be there.

Sarah J. Maas. At FanCosCon, the biggest, geekiest gathering of fantasy cosplayers in New York.

She imagines Sarah J. Maas herself, seeing Molly in her getup as Celaena and giving her a hug. She imagines the resulting selfie, just the two of them. And yeah, maybe she doesn't have a single person to show it to, not a single friend who wouldn't laugh-in-a-bad-way at it. But she'd have it.

Could she get up the courage to just go alone?

She looks around her room, thinks again about her friends, and her shoulders droop.

Of course not. Get real. Molly Tobin at something called Fan-CosCon? Fat fucking chance.

✕

On the corner of Lexington and Eighty-Third, Tillie sees a red awning for Tal Bagels. A black sign hangs above the door. It reads, APPETIZING. It is unclear to her whether it is a blurb for the bagels or part of the store name. Appetizing Tal Bagels? Normally she'd look on her phone, but. Oh well.

She pops in and orders a sesame bagel with strawberry cream cheese and a large coffee. She sits down in the back and tries to figure out what to do next. What do you do when you have to be off the grid? When you have one day left?

Today she's going to be different, better, more aware, more awake, more—

Her stomach flips. Who is she fooling? When have things ever been different, really?

She laughs when the thought crosses her mind to go to school. She imagines walking into second-period calculus and just sitting down and pretending nothing is wrong. Going through a day like usual, and then going home and when her mom rushes to the door and says, *Sweetheart! I've been so worried*, she could be like, *Why? What's wrong?* And her mom would be like, *This morning? At Dr. Brown's.* And Tillie would be all, *Mom. We didn't go to Dr. Brown's today. I was at school. All day. I have proof.*

She shakes her head and smirks. Nope.

School used to be . . . adequate. Seventh grade was a nightmare, sure. Eighth not much better. But then high school came and Tillie found ninth-grade drama and Ms. Dawson, who *saw* her. She's the only one, really, who ever has.

Ms. Dawson took an interest in her monologues. Tillie performed, and she wrote, and yeah, some of the other girls thought she was weird. Big fucking deal. Ms. Dawson approved. Ms. Dawson applauded. And then Ms. Dawson left, and Tillie was alone again.

Until this year. Eleventh grade. Ms. Cruz in English encouraged her again to write monologues, and for the first time in a while she was seen. Which was good in one way, and bad in another. Because in Tillie's experience, when you're visible, bad things tend to happen.

Molly's video, like a dagger in her heart. Who takes a person's trauma and makes it into a joke? Who does that?

Molly Tobin does that. Former best friend, from like a lifetime ago. And Tillie almost died yesterday, just because—what? Because Samantha Quinn walked by Tillie as she sat alone at lunch and put the back of her hand up against her forehead and said dramatically, "Go, cow"?

It had all started at the talent show two weeks ago. Most of the acts were your basic sexy lip-sync numbers and choreographed dance moves. Kat Lopez did standup that was moderately well received, and a couple of girls sang with piano accompaniment. Tillie's was the only act of its kind.

She had written a monologue that Ms. Cruz had said was "powerful." Tillie had written it in a fit of anger after the Amir debacle. Amir, the fuckhead from Browning. Somehow a teacher's simple compliment led into a decision to perform the piece. And you know what? She performed it damn well. She did it up, and while she was doing it, she could feel the power in her legs, in her arms. She was alive onstage in a way she wasn't anywhere else, and she knew, yeah, that it was dangerous to give girls ammunition. She knew it was vulnerable. But she believed that some things were more important than that. And that if something was good, and real, it deserved to have its moment. She somehow still believed that, against all evidence, people were basically good, and if they saw pain put forth on a stage, they'd see it, and hear it, and honor it for what it was.

So she stood up onstage, in all black, and she belted out the words. She gave them some goddamn life.

> They say, why marry the cow when you can get the
>   milk for free?
> Well, take it from the cow . . .
> That's what he did. He took it.
> My milk.
> My innocence.
> My wonder.
> I will never wonder again, because it's gone.
> GONE.
> He took my udders and squeezed, HARD.
> He took my udders as if they were there for the taking.
> And it's my fault, too, and that's the hard part
>   to deal with.
> That I let him do it.
> No one made me smile at him, approach him and ask if he
>   were
> basic. Which he took as

permission.
After,
I was fucking SAD
because at the moment of truth he closed his eyes
and I knew then that he wasn't with me.
He was with him.
It was all him
and he used me.
My body.

   A substitute for his hand.
   A plaything to be bought and sold
   On the market of love.
Because we're so, so beyond inequality of the sexes.
RIGHT?
So I stand before you
a cow.
Hurting.
And I will not be married anytime soon. Not that I want to
   be. But still.
I will have to think about how sacredly I hold my milk
from this point on.

The moment she finished, she rejoined the room. Almost instantly, she felt it. The awkwardness. Of her life. Seeping into the auditorium. Under the chairs it gathered, in the hearts of the girls and parents watching. She felt it and immediately she wanted to hide, and it took everything she had to walk off the stage slowly, not run, not bolt, to the smattering of uneasy applause.

Her mom, of course, greeted her backstage with an ecstatic hug. Britt, too.

"Sweetheart! Oh my God! That was so, so, so good. So powerful."

Britt draped herself over Tillie's torso like a slinky dress and said, "Moo!" That made Tillie smile despite herself.

Tillie peered around her mom's hovering head. Where was Dad? He'd been there in the audience. Where was he now?

And then, there he was. The three Stanley women exited into the auditorium from backstage and there was her dad, fiddling with his phone.

"Earth to Frank," her mom said, and her dad looked up.

He looked like a stranger. Wearing a polite smile, like the kind you give when you meet the boyfriend of someone you don't really give a shit about at a party, maybe. He gave her this light tap on the shoulder. The kind that says, *Sorry to hear that your great-aunt died, near stranger.*

During the walk home down tree-lined Ninetieth Street, past the Cooper Hewitt Museum, past sandstone brick apartment buildings built for permanence, as if to highlight the collective invincibility of New Yorkers, Britt hung on their dad, pleading that she was too tired to walk and demanding a piggyback ride. Tillie's mom strapped her arm through Tillie's and leaned into her. But all Tillie could think was *What have I done to disappoint him? How can I take it back?*

She felt him pull away then, in the following days. She'd see him in the mornings at the breakfast nook and he'd barely nod, and he'd stare at his phone as if he were the teenager with an attention-span issue and she the parent. Her sudden invisibility had a voice, inside her inner ear, telling her The Truth, which was that she deserved it. She deserved to be cast out. And every time she saw him sitting on the couch with Britt by his side, watching *American Ninja*

Warrior, she felt like pounding her head into the mauve living room wall because of whatever the thing was that made him not love her anymore.

Then one afternoon, last week. Tillie forgot to take the trash out to the compactor. Her dad, who last gave a shit about household chores never, knocked on her door and told her to come out to the living room.

"The trash. Where is it supposed to be?" he asked when she got there. He was hunkered down on the couch, looking tense and also disoriented. She'd never seen him like this before.

"Sorry," she said, lowering her head slightly and lingering in the room. She needed more, had so many questions about what this was, and why. When he'd knocked on her door, she'd gotten this funky feeling in her chest, like something was about to go down. But the trash? Nothing computed.

"Sorry is not good enough. You have to do better, Tillie. You just . . . have to. Do better."

She bit her lip. "Um. Okay. Sorry."

He shook his head. "This is becoming typical. You leave your shit around for other people to deal with. I don't want to have to see . . . I don't want to come home from a long day of work and see all your stuff around. Out of place. In the living room. I'm disappointed in you. I thought you were growing up. I thought you were getting older and more mature, but it seems like everywhere I look, there's your . . . dirty laundry."

Tillie stared just to the right of her dad's face. She felt stunned. What was this? "Sorry," she said for the third time. "But, um. What are you talking about? What dirty laundry? I don't leave—"

"Well . . . actually, you do." His face was red, and he exhaled and balled his left hand into a fist and placed it against his forehead. "You need to stop airing your dirty laundry."

"What?"

"Some things are private, damn it. And you go and spill it at a talent show, in front of all your classmates? It's humiliating, for Christ sake."

Oh. So this was what was up. Tillie stared at her father, suddenly hating him and at the same time totally unable to hate him because he was the person whose love had always meant the most.

"We take care of our own shit. Stuff. And you're not. Instead of dealing with it, you're . . . airing it. No more. I mean it. No more."

She crossed her arms over her chest. "I was performing a piece. It was art. That's what art is. You take from your life. You express it."

"Just stop, Tillie. Stop. It's goddamn humiliating."

"But . . ."

"Who's gonna pay for your goddamn psych bills?" he yelled.

What she heard was a snap, like a bone cracking. A clean break. Numb, she skulked off to her room and gently closed the door and got under the sheets on her bed and held her breath, hoping she could just—cease to be.

It wasn't just what he said; it was what he didn't say, too. Never a moment where he said, as a dad, *I heard what you said up there. You feel like a boy used you. Should we talk about this? Are you okay, Tillie?*

That was the start of the cold war in the Stanley household, and her mom, uncomfortably in the middle, calming everyone down. Tillie was grateful, and also she wanted to smash things.

And then there were the actual voices of her classmates, in

the hallways, mooing. In the cafeteria, saying, "Got milk?"

Did they not get what their words did to her? How they reached inside her chest and tore up her heart?

Damn her stupid need to get onstage. And what for?

But was that worth fucking dying for? How many times had Tillie and her mom gone over this? What is and isn't worthwhile? Sitting in the bagel shop, eating the last bite, Tillie realized she'd kicked to the curb her one ally in the world—two, Britt included—and it was cold outside, and the world didn't know her or care, and she averted her eyes as she felt the tears start to gestate inside them again.

No. No. No.

And worse. Molly. Asshole Molly. Who took the insult and exploded it. Who might as well have said, *Here, Tillie. Why don't you watch this and then maybe kill yourself because you're a waste of space?*

Tillie remembers: last Thursday. The text from Natasha, who wasn't a friend, exactly, but was at least willing to acknowledge Tillie's existence enough to ask for her French homework once in a while.

Did you see it?

See what?

Oh. Um.

See what?

Natasha attached a link and apologized in advance. Tillie's throat constricted. *What now?* she thought. One time this past fall she'd been on Insta and saw a link to an eleventh-grade poll. How her jaw got tight because she just knew, and then she opened it and it was a mixed blessing. Marcia Fishbaum had been voted most likely to die a virgin. Savanya had been voted most likely to die alone surrounded by a hundred cats.

She hadn't been voted anything. And she was relieved, but also kind of pissed, because she had been forgotten again. Tillie liked Rhiannon Kelly's post saying that the poll was mean. Tillie's was one of eleven likes, and that was how she chose to voice her protest, and that was that.

But this time she had been remembered. The video showed Molly in her bedroom. Tillie remembered it from sleepovers back when they were good friends, back in fifth grade. Now the walls were glossy white with polka dots instead of pink. Molly was wearing all black, and had stuffed her midsection with a throw pillow, it looked like. It made her look not just fat, but misshapen. She stood there acting meek, her body curled inward, her face a mask of faux pain—Molly didn't have a fucking clue what pain really was, did she? Tillie's gut twisted, because she knew what was coming, and it felt like insult on top of insult on top of insult, too unfair to be real. There was lots of laughter in the back—was that Isabella? Was that Gretchen? And then came the really horrible part.

Moo.
I'm a cow.
I'm a sad, sad cow.
Who gave her milk
to a boy. The only boy who would take it.
Because I'm gross.
And I'm so, so sad. Look at me! Look at my pain.
Sad cow, I am.
I am a sad cow.

Moo.

Thank you! Thank you!

She bowed, demure, in a way that Tillie read as stereotypically Asian, and Gretchen and Isabella howled in the background, and the video stopped.

As did Tillie's heart for a moment. She gently closed her laptop and got into bed. And when Natasha later wrote a text saying just ??—as if it was up to Tillie to react, as if she owed it to be like, *Yeah, that hurt like fuck.* She put down her phone and decided she wouldn't be going to school for a while.

When she went back on Monday, a lot of people came up to her and were like, *That shit was so not cool.* And then, as if hit by a wave of amnesia, suddenly on Tuesday it was walked back, even though Tillie hadn't said a fucking word about any of it, and the narrative had changed. People were coming up to her and saying shit like, *You know, if you're going to be a performer, you're going to have to toughen up your skin.*

As if she'd said something. Which she hadn't. But the truth didn't matter. Just the story.

And Tillie *still* didn't say anything, because even if it hadn't been her complaining about it, maybe they were right in a larger sense, maybe she was weak and too sensitive, and she should have laughed, but she couldn't, she couldn't quite figure out how to be the girl who laughs along when all the girls laugh at you and call you a freak, and when the mooing started up again on Wednesday— thanks, Samantha, thanks very much—Tillie decided she didn't care anymore. About anything. Because nothing mattered.

"Are you done with that?"

The man who asks wears a red Tal Bagel uniform.

She nods. "Are you hiring?" she asks.

"I don't know. Want me to find out?"

Tillie imagines taking a job at Tal Bagels for the day. Having a place. It's warm here. Safe. If she worked here, she wouldn't wind up on a bridge—which, oddly enough, is kind of where she wants to go. And if she goes, her life might be over, and really she doesn't want it to be over. She just wants it to be different. But Tal Bagel different? She tries to imagine what her mom would say if she came home and said she had a job at a bagel shop. Yep. Institution for sure.

"That's okay. Maybe another time," she says, and the guy walks away. Tillie gets up, reaches into her wallet, and pulls out a hundred. Her allowance for the week.

"Here," she says, tapping the guy on the shoulder.

The guy looks at the money, looks back at Tillie's face.

She averts her eyes. "Bagels. For the people. Take some as a tip, and then maybe give some people their bagels on me, okay? I trust you. Whatever."

"Thanks," he says, confused but not unpleasantly so.

As Tillie walks back out into the cold and replays the moment, she realizes she did it so that if she does actually not make it back home today, if they somehow trace her steps, they'll see this act of kindness and remember that she wasn't all bad.

She stops on Lexington and Eighty-Third and realizes she doesn't know where she's going next.

Until she does. She slowly walks south.

Toward Eightieth and Lexington. She'll never forget where Molly lives. It's the kind of thing you remember: the apartment of a double-crossing former friend.

×

Based on the amount of time it takes for the elderly white doorman with the pale complexion to give Tillie a response when he calls upstairs and says, "I have a Tillie here to see Molly," Tillie's stomach ties in knots.

She knows Molly isn't at school, because she was suspended for a week. That doesn't mean she's definitely at home, but. It probably does.

And this. This was a very bad idea. Who goes over to the apartment of their online bully? Tillie's face purples as she tries to imagine what Molly must be saying on the other end of the intercom, let alone thinking.

She's about to dart back out onto the street when the doorman says, "Eight C," and Tillie, a little stunned at her own ballsiness, lopes toward the elevator.

In the elevator, Tillie feels it, like a knife in her belly. The wrongness of what Molly did. She has no idea what she's going to do when she sees Molly, but one possibility is definitely violent.

The elevator opens; Tillie takes a deep breath and walks out. Molly stands down the hall at her front door, arms across her chest. She is wearing a turquoise tank top, her hair is matted and frizzy, and she doesn't have any makeup on. Tillie hasn't seen Molly without makeup since maybe sixth grade. Possibly fifth. She looks a little like she has the flu minus the red nose.

"What are you doing here?" Molly asks, her voice flat.

The anger freezes in Tillie's stomach and chest. "Hey," she mumbles.

It's as if she's not capable. Not capable of saying the thing she should say, and now, standing here in the middle of the hall-way, she wishes she had thought a little more about this. She's so stupid. She can hear it. See it. Molly, who might as well run eleventh grade at Spence, holding court in the cafeteria, talking about the appearance of that freak at her front door, Tillie, who just stood there while Molly waited for her to say something, like talk, like what human beings do all the time.

"Tillie. What. Are. You. Doing here?"

"I really don't know anymore," she says.

Molly rolls her eyes, goes back inside, and closes the door. Actually closes the door. Tillie just stands there, feeling numb. For a minute, maybe. Feeling like a speck of dirt and totally unable to figure out what she does next, because—shit. Maybe she is a danger to herself? Because here are the feelings again, the creepy, crawly, lower-than-a-dirt-speck feelings. That stomach thing where it feels like she's utterly empty inside and she just wants it all to stop. She needs it to stop.

The door opens again. Molly comes back out and leans against the wall next to the door, crossing her arms.

"You can't just stay here all day, you know? Do I have to call the cops and say you're trespassing? Because I will, you know. You've already ruined my life, okay? Can you, like, please leave me the fuck alone now?"

Tillie makes sure her outside stays very still. Her face tenses. The words are so . . . wrong and unfair and . . . no. No no no. She holds her breath and the hallway goes dizzy.

"Holy Jesus. Why are you so weird? Can you even be normal for three minutes? You came here? Be normal. How were we ever even friends? What do you want? Say words, you freak. Say *something*."

Tillie doesn't know why Molly keeps firing her weapon, or what she even means, and then she's crouching on the floor, and she can't feel her legs, and she needs to be lower, and then she is time, standing still, and the walls go funny and it's madness, madness.

"Shit," Molly says. She disappears and the door swings shut and Tillie's alone in the hallway and her existence goes inside out and sideways and then she's in the sandbox and it's maybe the fours? There were two sandboxes. One for kids who wanted to play rowdy, one for kids who wanted calm. She was in the calm box, but Trevor Rheim wasn't being calm and he kicked sand in Tillie's eyes and Tillie started crying and that's all she remembers, all she—

Tillie is on a rug, lying down on her side, her right arm stretched out above her head. Her shoulder hurts from the position. She has no idea where or why she is. She blinks a few times and her eyes adjust into a room with cream and peach walls, and she turns her head and there, sitting on the floor, leaning up against the cream-colored wall, with her legs splayed out like a rag doll, looking spent, is Molly.

Tillie blinks a few more times and looks into Molly's eyes. She can't read what's in there. Regret? Nothing? It's almost slightly familiar but not quite.

"So are you okay now?" Molly asks, her voice soft in a way that makes Tillie's heart twist because it's like she hasn't experienced this tone from this particular voice since maybe sixth grade.

"Um. I guess."

Neither girl says anything for a while, and slowly Tillie uses her arms to sit herself up. She looks around and she remembers the den from years ago. This same Persian rug, paisley designs in blood red and tan. She runs her fingers across it.

"How did I get here?"

"I dragged you."

"Oh. Um. Thanks."

Molly shrugs. "So why aren't you at school, where I can't be, of course."

Tillie takes a deep breath and decides not to say the thing that would shut Molly up. "I'm just . . . taking time for myself."

"Well. How nice for you."

"Yes. All of this. Extremely very nice," Tillie says, flat.

"You know, you might want to grow a spine," Molly says. "No offense, and I don't want to, like, put you back in whatever that was? But people are going to not like you. Especially if you're . . . Never mind."

"Especially if I'm what?" Tillie feels her heart speed up again and she's so, so tired and on the edge she can't believe it.

"You're different, okay? And yeah, it's good to be different. I'm actually more different than—ugh. Never mind. It's just, if you get up onstage and you bleed your soul out, what do you expect? This is high school. You think people are gonna run to you and be like, *Wow, that was awesome*? No. People are going to use it against you. Welcome to the world, Tillie. This is why I choose not to share every little thing about me to the entire world."

Tillie hangs her head and closes her eyes. What kind of world is this, where people are always looking for ammunition, and is that a world she wishes to be in? But what's the alternative? She doesn't want to die. She just doesn't want to be *here*. And thinking about that totally unfixable contradiction makes her arms go cold, and her head starts to spin, and yeah. She's back in.

"*Tillie*," Molly says. Now her old friend is looming over her, and her face is half-concerned and half-angry. "Are you on drugs?"

"I went to the bridge yesterday," Tillie says, her voice soft, her spirit utterly defeated.

Michael's warrior brothers make a house call.

This is what brothers do, Morris said on the phone earlier, and true to form, every one of them, including Reggie, who is ninety-one and uses a walker, arrives at his front door and makes himself at home, even though none of them but Morris has ever been to the apartment before. All Michael he can do is sit on the couch and stare out at the Hudson River.

Soon they are gathered around him, and Jack is lighting sage and then waving it up and down each man's body as a cleansing ritual, which has always been the part of ManKind Project that means the least to Michael, but he goes along with it because the rest of it has saved his life. And they're going to have to save it again, because he has nothing left.

Instead of a formal meeting, once they've smudged, Morris takes over and asks, "What do you need?"

Michael doesn't answer right away. He can't.

"We're here. We'll just hold space," Morris says. It's something they say, and frankly it's something that, four years ago, before this weekend, Michael would have laughed at. The image of a person holding space. But now he's so glad, because these men, these brothers, are here. Holding his space.

For minutes. Many. He's not sure if it's minutes or hours, and thoughts jump around his addled brain and none of them are worthy of verbalization. Who's coming to the funeral? What's the conversation with the folks at Fieldston going to look like? Will they look at him with so much pity?

Finally, when the thoughts slow to a crawl, he says, "I want to be held."

The men stand, Michael in the middle. And once he is enveloped by them, and their hands are there, strong, on his arms, around his back, he begins to shake. Like a whole-body earthquake. No sound. Just shaking. This horror quakes through him and finally reaches his mouth and he screams, and the sound that comes out of his mouth is not his. It's a raw grief in a tone that seems like it comes from elsewhere. Above or below but not in him. It continues. And the men soak it in, and they hold him tight, and they cry, too, a wailing wall of men, caring for a fallen brother.

X

Molly can't believe what she's just heard. "You what?"

"I went to the bridge. I didn't want to jump but. I also kind of, I don't know. I didn't want to deal with being me anymore. Being me is not a joy."

Molly sits back down against the wall. Her mouth forms an O. And Tillie's glad in a way, that she's finally rendered Molly speechless. And also, in a way, that she knows. So she'll stop saying horrible things.

"Jesus," Molly says.

Tillie nods.

"Did my . . . ?"

Tillie shakes her head. "No. Not really. I mean. Not entirely. My life's shit in lots of ways. It wasn't like, you made a mean video and I jumped off a bridge, okay? You don't have that power over me."

"Okay," Molly says. "God."

The girls sit for a while, breathing like they've just run a marathon. Nothing needs to be said, and everything still needs to be said, and Tillie, for the first time, begins to feel like it's okay to be there, like the weirdness of the situation dissipated the moment she told Molly, and yeah, half of her wants to make sure Molly doesn't tell the whole world, and the other half is like, fuck it. Tell everyone. She doesn't care anymore. She stares at the peach and cream walls, and the rich, dark brown wooden bookshelves built into the far wall. She fixates on this small crack in the concrete on the corner of the white ceiling, inches away from the intersection of the far two corners. She stares, and as she does it's like tunnel vision overtakes her body, and the crack grows, and her head begins to buzz, but not in a bad way. In a way that feels almost serene, almost like she's at home again after a long absence. Which is weird, given she most certainly is not at home.

"Do you ever just stare at a wall and suddenly the size of it gets bigger?" she asks.

Molly laughs a little. "Um. No. Not really."

Tillie laughs, too. "I know. I'm the weirdest person on the planet."

"Not the weirdest. Just. Superlatives. You're superlative girl."

This snaps Tillie out of her odd staring daydream.

"What?"

"You've always been. When we were friends way back when, it was always like, this is the best lipstick ever, or being grounded is the worst thing ever. Superlative girl."

Tillie focuses on her old friend's face. "You know, that's a new one to me. I've never, ever thought of that before."

Molly smiles a little. "Well, you're a bit dramatic. You know that, right?"

"Now that one I've heard."

"Not that it's a terrible thing to be dramatic. I mean, I could be more—never mind."

Tillie doesn't ask what, but a part of her wants—needs—to hear. Needs to go back. To fifth grade, and lying on the rug in Molly's room, talking about random things, like how llamas spit rather than bite when they get angry, or how a narwhal's long unicorn-like horn is actually an enlarged ivory tooth that can weigh more than twenty pounds. And fashion stuff, like trips down to SoHo to buy colorful scarves and even berets for a while, which Tillie could totally get into, and off-the-shoulder tops, which Tillie could not. And the time Molly was mad about being made to clean her room while Tillie was there—they were like sisters back then—and Molly was narrating her cleaning out loud as she did it, angrily, and she took this big stuffed animal bear from her bed and put it on a rocking chair and said, "Bear. Chair." And then they laughed so hard that Molly's anger broke in a millisecond and they both almost had snot running from their noses.

This was before the whole popular-kid dynamic started in sixth grade. When they went to tennis camp and immediately Molly had all these mostly white girls surrounding her, and they were squeaking about makeup and boys, and Tillie felt like she'd arrived on another planet. And Molly made sure Tillie was included that summer, even if she was on the outskirts of cool, the large Asian girl in a sea of mostly white faces. But come sixth grade, it was different, and the sleepovers were different. She felt Molly's urge to be elsewhere as if their friendship were watermelon taffy, its sweet pinkness stretching to the point of almost breaking. And then it did break. Spring of sixth grade. A Friday night in April, the leaves on the ubiquitous London plane trees that line city streets just starting to bloom. The first dance with the Allen-Stevenson boys at the Goddard Gaieties. They arrived together, but then Molly saw Gretchen, and they did this clapping thing Tillie didn't know about, and they laughed and hugged and Molly lifted her right foot back almost coquettishly as they embraced and it was like watching a horror movie, because Gretchen was obviously evil. Tillie backed into the corner and watched, and suddenly there were three girls and three boys dancing in the center of the room to Beyoncé's "XO," and Tillie felt the tears well up, and there was nowhere to run, but there was Molly's mom, chaperoning, so she went to her, because Molly's mom was almost her mom, in a way, with how much time she'd spent at Molly's over the years, and almost immediately she got that it was all wrong. Molly's mom didn't hug her tight, didn't comfort her and tell her it was okay to be excluded, or to be different. She rolled her eyes and said, "Till, get a grip. It's not cute to cry at a dance. Go to the ladies' room and get your act together."

Tillie did go to the restroom, and she stared in the mirror and thought, *This is my life. This is how it's going to be from now on.* And truly that was right. At school on Monday it was different. Molly had new friends and it was understood that Tillie was cut loose. No breakup. Just an understanding.

These memories make Tillie feel like slugging and hugging Molly simultaneously, and she doesn't know what to do with that. So she just says, "What could you be more?"

Molly dramatically sighs. "I don't know," she says, staring at the ceiling, her arms splayed out palms up, exasperated. "Real, maybe? Like I think my rep is probably that I have my shit way together. There are things about me that I don't share, Tillie. Life is like a museum, and you have to curate. And I wish you didn't have to, because sometimes stuff gets lost."

"Yeah?" Tillie asks.

"Yeah. And no offense, because I'm not saying it's your fault, exactly, but the suspension? If you had any idea what Gretchen and

Isabella were doing, moments before I did whatever, and I'm sorry, by the way, that sucked, but theirs were way meaner—not about you, okay—and they're in school right now, and I'm not, and that's on my permanent record, so I can basically say goodbye to Penn, or Brown, even Michigan, probably, because who fat-shames a classmate on video? How the fuck do you explain that one in a letter, and come on. I know we're not, like, friends anymore, but seriously. Does one stupid joke mean I don't deserve to go to a good college? And don't even get me started on Gretchen and Isabella. I just have this sense they've *moved on*, and here I am, and I actually can feel it happening. My popularity, my position, disappearing, over a mistake. So I'm not super rosy, either. Not going to jump off a bridge, but, yeah."

Tillie laughs. It's the only thing she can do. And then the weirdest thing happens. Molly laughs, too.

"Too soon?" Molly asks.

"You think?"

Molly cocks her head in a sympathetic way and says, "Sorry. I don't know why I do that. Or I do, but whatever. I could be nicer, right?"

"I think there may be room for growth in that area," Tillie says, and they both laugh again, and Tillie hopes to god that Molly gets it. That this laugh isn't an *it's all good* laugh. Because it's not all good. There's this fury still in her chest, and if she were an actual visible person, someone might see it. But she is not visible. This is the way you laugh when there's literally nothing else your body can do.

"So why are you here?" Molly asks, crossing her arms in front of her chest. "In my living room? And not in, you know, school? Where I can't be but very much wish I was."

They're still sitting on the living room floor. Tillie hears the edge, and there's a part of her that wants to go off on Molly, but it's like she can't. For whatever reason, she does not have the permission to do that, ever, in her life.

Maybe it's Molly's tone, though, that at least allows Tillie to tell the truth.

"So my mom was like, 'We need to get you help.' Which I get, by the way. I'm depressed. Obvs. But I'm depressed because of things. Yeah, your video wasn't great for me, but it's not just that. It's . . . the guy. From the thing. Amir is his name. I was really into him, and then he was just gone. And what do you do with that? When you finally let a guy get that close to you and you trust him and then it's all gone."

She wipes her eyes, which are totally dry. Molly's looking at the floor in front of Tillie, like there's something there that needs wiping up. There isn't.

"And stuff at home is . . . Never mind. It doesn't matter. It's just hard right now and I got a little whatever. So my mom took me to see a doctor this morning and she's all wanting me to go to some inpatient facility in Vermont. Which I am absolutely not doing. So I bolted. Not, like, I ran while they shouted at me to stay. My mom was in the bathroom I guess when I went out to get her to come in, and I just kept walking. I don't know why. And here I am. So."

Molly's stare continues, but her face gets more and more inscrutable to Tillie. Jaw set, eyes glassy. Is she bored? Alarmed? Annoyed?

When it's clear Tillie is done talking, Molly looks up, not exactly into Tillie's eyes, but at least close. She sits up so that her spine is straight against the wall behind her.

"Okay, then," she says.

"Oh yeah. I have no phone. Because after I left I found out my mom was tracking me, and I just left it on Eighty-Third Street. It lives there now. In this hole in the pavement. That's how serious I am about not going inpatient."

Molly swallows and puts her hand on her throat.

"Okay. So. You have no phone, your mom is looking for you, and she wants to have you committed?"

Committed. The word sounds so wrong to Tillie. She's most definitely not insane. She's sad. *Committed* makes her think of straitjackets and *One Flew Over the Cuckoo's Nest*, which was the main-stage play the spring before Tillie's tenth-grade year. This is different. This is . . . Tillie.

"I'm not crazy," Tillie says, her throat tight.

"Did I say you were?"

"Your tone kind of did."

"God," Molly says. "It's the facts. You're supposed to be in a hospital, but instead you came to my place."

Tillie's insides twist again, and part of her wants to punch Molly in the face, hard. She bites her lip, harder.

"God," Molly repeats, this time muttering it under her breath.

This was a bad idea, Tillie realizes. She doesn't feel better. If anything, she feels worse, because now it's out. That she's hurt. And Molly's right. You put things out there, and people use it as ammunition.

"Come on," Molly says, standing up.

Tillie looks up at her. "Where are we going?"

"My room, okay?"

This is not what Tillie expected Molly to say, but she slowly stands and follows Molly there.

Molly excuses herself for a moment, and Tillie stands there at the door, awkwardly.

Molly's room, unlike Tillie's, is nearly unrecognizable from five years earlier. Whereas Tillie's is still pink—she remembers how much it mattered that she and Molly had matching pink rooms—Molly's pink walls are gone, replaced with glossy white with purple dots that probably were painted by some famous artist, knowing Molly's A-list mom. The wooden floor they used to sit and play jacks on is now concealed with a Persian rug, and turquoise designer sheets cover her unmade bed.

"Wow," Tillie says when Molly returns to the room.

"Wow what?"

"I just haven't been in here in a while."

"Yeah, well," Molly says.

"What's that?" Tillie says, pointing to the book sitting open and facedown on the bed.

"Nothing," Molly says, lunging for the book and putting it behind her back. Tillie almost laughs. "Just . . . mind your own business."

"Okay, then," Tillie says as a twinge of something passes through her chest. Like it's too soon. To be here. As if there's unfinished business. As if a different, better Tillie would—should, maybe—go apeshit on the place, in retaliation for the video that ruined her life.

The girls look at each other and Tillie shrugs and sits in the one chair in the room, a designer wooden desk chair that has seemingly replaced the bear rocking chair. Molly has put the book under her mattress like it's a secret and Tillie is like, *Is it porn or something? How weird.*

"Do you remember Jukebox?" Tillie asks.

Molly laughs despite herself and rolls her eyes. "Oh God. That."

It was maybe fourth grade. They made up a skit for Molly's mom. Molly dressed up all pretty and she was in an old-fashioned bar like they'd seen in this movie and there was this ancient jukebox with all these songs. They used a chair with a blanket over it as the jukebox, adorning it with a piece of paper on which Tillie had written A JUKEBOX.

"What should I play?" Molly said, and then she'd hit a button, say "Boop!" in a high voice like that's what happened when she pressed a button, and then Tillie would start singing a Justin Bieber song, until Molly would "Boop!" again and Tillie would sing a different song.

Tillie could hear Molly's mom cracking up, and it was hard not to laugh herself. They were so funny!

"Or Pony Town," Tillie says. She can't stop remembering.

"Huh?"

"Pony Town?"

Molly shrugs. "Sorry. Must have been someone else."

But it wasn't, and Tillie knows it.

Man. Pony Town. She almost describes it, because she's pretty sure Molly would remember. That lasted until fifth grade for sure. But she knows she can't. That Jukebox or not, Molly is too sophisticated to remember something like that fondly.

These ponies were supposed to be cake decorations, but her mom didn't use them. So Tillie took them into her room, about ten of them, and she made up this world where they were the townspeople and she drew stores and places on loose-leaf paper. The horses all got names, like Jackie and Esmerelda. Some were boys, some were girls. And they'd go to the candy store, or the gym, or the beach. It was kind of based on West Hampton, where they went one summer. And her dad came in that first time, and he loved it, and he made up voices for the different characters, and they just played for the longest time. Tillie wanted that day to never end. And for years later, she'd take out the horses and keep the story going, even when it was probably too young a game for her but she didn't care, and she remembers how she showed Molly, and Molly made it a story about all the girls going for Nathan, this good-looking horse-slash-boy, and Tillie didn't really want it to be about that, but she played along because that's what she did.

Sometimes, Tillie thinks, *I wish the world were more like Pony Town. My version.*

Which was another thing she'd never say to grown-up Molly, whose room she is now feeling super awkward in.

Even then, Tillie realizes, Molly was always the curator of what was cool. Pony Town was not cool, and it was just another place Tillie was an outcast.

The phone from the lobby rings, which means there's a visitor.

It's something about the way Molly glances to the phone and back to Tillie that makes her realize, immediately, who the visitor is.

"You called my mom, didn't you?"

Molly subtly nods and averts her eyes. "I had to, Tillie. I'm sorry. I know you don't want to, but you want to know the truth? I'm worried about you. Okay? The video sucked, but you look like, I don't know. You look so sad. You're, like, making me almost cry, okay? So I texted your mom, because you probably need more help than I can give."

For the first time, Tillie's anger rises into her cheeks and she feels her whole body heat up and her chest get tight.

"You shouldn't have done that," she says.

"Sorry, but . . ."

"Fuck," Tillie says. "I can't."

The phone keeps ringing.

"You can. C'mon. I'm gonna tell the doorman to send your mom up."

"No. Don't. A deal. I get it. I need help. But I also need a day. I needed to make things right with you, and I have to confront Amir, too. Once I do that, if I still need to go, I'll go, okay? But I just need that."

"I don't know."

"I'll make you a deal."

"What kind of deal?"

"How about: If you send my mom away and let me get out of here without her seeing, I promise I'll go to Principal Pembree's office and try to get the thing off your record. Say that we made up, that it was a big misunderstanding."

Tillie feels something leave her body, and she knows it's not good. She also knows she's in a corner, and she's doing the thing she has to do.

"You'd do that?"

"Yes."

Molly takes a deep breath. "I'm gonna regret this."

"You won't."

"I will, but whatever. It's worth a try. One thing, though."

"What?"

"I'm coming with you."

"You're coming with me."

"Yep."

"Why?"

"Because. If I let you go and you jump off the bridge, I'll never forgive myself, okay?"

Tillie nods. This makes some sense to her. The only thing she can't figure out is how they'll be together for even five more minutes without it being so awkward that they'll both pray for a nuclear holocaust.

Molly sighs and pulls out her phone. She hits a button and puts it to her ear.

"Hi, Mrs. Stanley. I'm so sorry. I tried. No . . . She left like five minutes ago and I couldn't stop her . . . Yeah . . . Right, but . . . She was, like, I don't think she's a danger to herself. I think she just needs some time . . . I'm sorry, by the way. I know that's not— Okay, right. I'll let you know if she calls or texts. Yep. Bye."

She hangs up. Molly looks at Tillie and sighs again.

"So where to?"

"Amir goes to Browning, so Browning. It's time. Time to tell him off. Time to fuck that bitch up. With words, I mean. Not violence."

Molly's face goes blank. Tillie translates her expression to mean, *Like you did with me?*

"We'll take the fire stairs. If we can even get out there. Mom stores old Persian rugs there. Blocks the door."

"That's a fire code violation," Tillie says.

Molly laughs. "Yes. That should be your top concern right now. Ugh. Okay. Give me a second. I'm not going out looking like this. I don't want anyone to see me like this."

Tillie stands there, nodding like a marionette and feeling like a speck again. Because it's implicit in what Molly said.

Tillie isn't anyone.

×

If Tillie had made ten guesses about how this day would turn out? If she'd made a hundred? A thousand? None of them would have included walking down Madison Avenue with Molly Tobin, aka the Devil.

Molly walks beside her in her gorgeous pink tweed coat, which makes her look like a million bucks and would make Tillie look like a Pepto-Bismol bottle. Tillie rolls her eyes, thinking about the unfairness of this. *I'm a cow, moo. No. No. Cancel.* This is one of the few things Dr. Brown has taught her. When she has a negative thought, she's supposed to say "cancel" out loud. Because thoughts have power blah blah. Tillie has not been doing this, because if she did, she'd basically walk around saying "cancel, cancel" all day long. She could be a model for people who want to get rid of their cable subscriptions, maybe.

"It's on Sixty-Fourth, right?" Molly asks.

"Sixty-Second."

"Right."

This is the extent of their conversation, and Tillie wants to tear her hair out it's so awkward. If she were fast, she'd sprint away, get away from Molly, void their stupid deal, which she basically made to save her life. But she's not fast, and Molly made it clear: Tillie is not going to be left alone.

As they walk south along cold and windy Madison Avenue, past posh bakeries and posher jewelry shops and French boutiques, Tillie thinks about Amir. His hair impeccably messed with pomade, his slight mouth and nose perfect, his face beautiful despite a smattering of pimples along his chin line. His eyebrows arched in a way that's almost feminine. He'd make a pretty girl, really, which is a weird thing to think about your ex-boyfriend, but it is just so painfully true. He'd been the pretty one in the relationship.

She had no idea what he'd seen in her. Why he'd picked her.

They'd met in front of Spence during lunch hour. It was apparently this Browning thing, which was weird because they had to Uber more than a mile to get to Spence, but they were always there, the omnipresent Browning upperclassmen, out front of the school, almost every lunch period. For a while they'd call out mundane questions to the girls as they left the building, and Tillie found it a little . . . menacing. A little gross. Then they'd do cheesy lines, and that was actually worse, because it was all so staged.

And then, one day, Amir. With his immaculately wild hair and his bright black eyes and that shy smirk of a smile. She saw him, their eyes locked, and she was definitely not grossed out.

He didn't call anything out, and he'd looked away and then quickly back at her, and then away again. A shy boy! Tillie was hooked. So the second time she saw him there, she made the first move. She stood to the side of the doorway, pulled out her phone, and texted no one. She kept glancing up at him, and each time she did so, he'd glance up and then bashfully away, and finally she was like, *This is not 1950*. So she marched up to him, ignored his friends, who seemed to be elbowing him in the ribs and whispering, almost certainly about her since they were finally holding eye contact, and she said the first thing that came to her mind.

"I don't think you're basic. Are you basic?"

Amir was like, "What?"

"Are you basic?"

"Um, no. I'm not . . . basic."

She half smirked and said, "But this. This is über-basic."

That was the first time she heard his melodic laugh. He leaned in close. His breath smelled like pepperoni, in a good way.

"Yes. You're correct. This is very, extremely basic."

"But you're not."

"I'm incontrovertibly not basic."

She flushed a bit. His words told her what she needed to know about him.

So she smiled, crossed her arms in front of her chest, and said, "But if you were. If you were basic, what would you say right now?"

He averted his eyes. God, was he shy! "I'd probably say something cheesy about your smooth skin."

This. This was the best thing he could have said. And it was cheesy, but it was also incredibly sweet, and it was also the first time a guy had ever said anything nice about her . . . Anything. Ever. One of the fabulous perks of an all-girls school. Almost no casual contact with the opposite sex, and, as a result—at least for Tillie—feeling super awkward around boys. She felt herself blushing pink and bit her lip as if she were some coquettish person, which cracked her up a little but she wasn't going to explain to this nameless guy how funny this all was, the idea of her as coquettish, because she was very, um, yeah. Not that. So instead she said, "And if you were to, like, do something basic, what would that be?"

His response sealed it. He started flossing. First slow, and then he picked up his bookbag, put it on, and did it high speed, like Backpack Kid.

All the rest of that day, and the next, she was someone at Spence. Girls were coming up and asking her about that adorable boy who danced the floss for her, and Tillie shrugged a lot, not really knowing how to play it. She was glad when that shit stopped.

Over a series of a few weeks, they started going out. Meals, movies, the park. They went to the Frick, and Amir showed her the textiles exhibit, the beautiful Persian and Indian carpets, which he always went to look at when he was feeling down, and as she took in the lush blues and reds and the intricate floral designs, she felt her guard coming down, and on a walk through Central Park after, she let him see the real her. Which made him the first boy ever to see it.

She told him what it felt like to be adopted, how as a kid it sometimes felt like she had to smile all the time to show she was grateful, even when she felt sad. How embarrassing and lonely it felt when she was in kindergarten and her white mom had the talk with her about racism and the names she was being called. How it was nice and comforting when her parents took her to a meeting of Coalition for Asian American Children and Families downtown one time when she was six, and there were all these people who looked like her, and her mom and dad were the ones who were different, but at the same time she felt like she had to protect them, make them feel comfortable, and she was actually a little relieved when her mom didn't suggest going back the next week. She told him about the time in nursery school when suddenly, out of nowhere, this guy with a guitar showed up and he was Korean, too, and when he sang his folk tunes he stared right at her, smiling, and it was so awkward because she somehow knew, even then, that her mom had gone to the school and asked them to bring in someone who looked like her daughter, and she had made peace with the daily experience of gratitude and isolation, which seemed to lodge in her larynx.

She told him about how it felt when girls who otherwise had never said a word to Tillie suddenly got all chummy and asked about her preparation for the math SAT, even though she was more of a language person. He shared back about what it felt like to hear ISIS jokes and to have Iran confused with every other country in the Middle East, as if they were all interchangeable, as if he and all people of Middle Eastern descent were one, and Tillie felt chagrined because, yeah, those things weren't exactly equal—being singled out as good at math versus being called a terrorist, and then she made a joke to make it clear that she knew that he won, if this were an oppression battle, but he was totally sweet about it.

And then he said, "I get it, though. It's maddening to be seen for one thing when we're all so many things."

Tillie stopped walking. They were on the bridle path near the exit to Eighty-Ninth Street and Fifth Avenue.

"Yes!" she said. "When people see me, I sometimes feel like they are reacting to my looks as if my looks *are* me. Which is so, so weird. I feel as though if I did that to a single person, I would feel horrified for weeks, but people do it thoughtlessly to me all the time."

Amir smiled. "Welcome to my world. Why are people so shitty to each other?"

Tillie said, "I have no idea, but I actually wonder that all the time."

A month later they were in his room, his parents were out, and the physical joined the emotional, because she was already so deep in with him. She felt seen. She felt like he saw her soul, and she saw his, and it was a delicate thing, his soul, and she cradled it in her hands like one of the pony figurines on her shelf.

It was the first time she'd been with a boy, and for her to not feel self-conscious? To not be focused on the size of her butt, or whether her face was pretty enough? Priceless.

Sitting next to him on his bed, his spine so straight she wished she could draw him, she'd leaned over and put her lips near his and looked up at him and said, "Is this okay?" And he nodded almost imperceptibly and suddenly there they were, kissing, this time a little more passionately than the one time at the theater on Eighty-Sixth, which she also started, which didn't feel quite right, which made her wonder if maybe Amir was just a bad kisser. But this time, once they got started, she felt him tuned in, and she felt him open to her, and it was like this electricity connected their chests.

"Where is your brain, Tillie?" Molly asks now.

"What?"

"You're smiling and grimacing and walking down Madison Avenue."

Tillie's gut instinct is to get sarcastic. *I'm thinking about how great it is to spend the day with the person whose video fat-shamed me.* But instead, she decides to just be real for once.

"I was thinking about Amir."

"That's the boy?"

"That's the boy."

Molly nods. "Your first love, huh?"

Tillie nods back.

"And then he ghosted you?"

Another nod.

"Fucking boys. I mean, that does kind of suck."

Tillie thinks, *Thank you for acknowledging that I'm a person.*

"What are you going to say to him?"

Tillie says, "I have no fucking idea."

X

Amir, Mike, and Rich strut up Madison Avenue, commenting on all the girls and women they pass.

Mike says about a waiflike girl with brown hair wearing a gray overcoat, "Doable. Like two a.m. on a Saturday night at JG Melon. With the lights off and she goes home right after."

"For reals," says Rich.

Amir is elsewhere. He has to be. Four months, basically. That's what he has left. Until he goes to college, until he can find new friends who aren't Browning douchebags.

And he knows. Some people have a spine. They don't find

girlfriends and break their hearts or whatever. And he knows: He's not enough to have broken Tillie's heart, exactly. He's not that full of himself. Just did her wrong, really.

Can't think about that. Hurts to.

"We going up to Spence?" Rich asks.

"Too far," says Mike, and he ribs Amir. Because this is bro code. Rich doesn't know about how things ended with Tillie, and he doesn't need to. This is a brother taking care of a brother. And Amir appreciates it.

"Hewitt, then?" asks Rich, and Mike says, "Yup."

×

Molly says, "Maybe you should have a plan? Figure out what you're going to say to him ahead of time? Take today to think, then tomorrow to act? Because I really think what we ought to do is go find your phone, and get it, and get you home."

They stop walking.

"What?" Tillie asks, the blood rushing out of her face.

"T?" Molly asks. Her voice, her tone, has changed. It's gone surprisingly gentle. "Can we pretend for the moment that none of this happened, and make it like we're friends in sixth grade?"

Tillie holds in a gasp. It's such an unexpected thing, to hear Molly Tobin say this, and also it's fucking wrong, because all of it happened, and it's like Molly is saying, *Can we for a moment forget all the mean shit I've done to you, like kicking you out of my life for being nerdy after we were bestest friends, and making fun of you with my friends, and also that heinous video? Can we put that thousand-pound bag of shit aside?* And it's like, no. No, we can't!

But Molly looks surprisingly earnest, and Tillie needs to hear what's next. So she says, "Um. Okay."

Molly runs her hands through her hair, glances each way as if to ensure Gretchen and all them aren't somehow randomly walking down this very street during a school day, and bites her bottom lip.

"I'm worried about you. Like, really worried. The bridge, and. I think you're, like, really depressed."

Tillie stares at the ground, half wishing it would swallow her whole, half wanting this moment not to end.

"And while we're saying things. I'm . . . I know what I did and said wasn't right, and you didn't deserve that and . . ."

Tillie waits for the next words. When they don't come, she glances up into Molly's eyes, and before she just has to look away, she says, "Why did you?"

Molly closes her eyes and shakes her head. "You ever create a drama to keep people away from your drama?"

Tillie tilts her head and thinks about it. No, not really. But she says, "I don't know. Maybe."

"I'm gonna be real with you, okay. But I'm gonna trust that because you're a good person—and you are, Tillie, a really good person, okay—I'm gonna trust that you won't say anything to any-body. And if you do? I guess then I deserve it."

Tillie nods.

Molly rolls her neck and bends it side to side. Then she runs her hands through her hair again.

"I feel like I'm slipping."

"Slipping?"

Molly looks to the sky, her mouth open like a jack-o'-lantern.

"Ugh. You're so not going to get this. Maybe it's just there's nothing to get? I don't know. Let's just drop it, okay?"

Tillie says, "Okay," but she's not sure it is. She doesn't know much of anything right now.

They walk east on Seventy-Fifth, and she sees a bunch of girls swarmed in front of a building. The Hewitt School. A rival girls' school.

And then she sees something that sets her hair on fire. There, standing awkwardly by a nice red car, along with two white guys in blue blazers who are calling out to Hewitt girls, is Amir Rahimi.

Tillie is faster than she realizes, because without thinking, she's left Molly behind and charged over to the car where Amir silently stands. She's so glad he's not talking to a girl right now, because homicide would be an absolute possibility. She grabs him by his red striped tie and pulls him onto the sidewalk. He gasps and grabs his throat. Everyone watches. She doesn't release the pressure. She yanks him against the wall of the building to the left of Hewitt.

"Are you—" Her voice doesn't sound like her. It sounds sharper, heavier. "Are you fucking kidding me?"

Amir mouths words, but no sound comes out. His throat is still constricted. Tillie lets go, hard, and his head bounces against the wall a bit. He cradles it and rubs the spot that made contact.

Everyone is watching. Tillie could not give fewer shits.

"What are you—how could you even DO this to me?"

"Can we—" Amir says.

She yanks his arm and pulls him down the street, hard.

"Do you know what you did to me? Are you aware? Do you know how much you hurt me?"

"I'm sorry. I—"

"No. No. Absolutely not. My turn. You acted like you cared about me. I cared about you, Amir. You were the first boy I ever felt that way about. I'll never get that back. Do you know that? You made me, like, love you, and then you went away. Not a single fucking word. What kind of person does that? What kind?"

All the nerves have gone away. Everything that stopped her from saying to Molly what she needed to say is gone, too, and suddenly Tillie's head is turned and she is screaming in Molly's direction.

"And fuck you, too!" she yells. "No, it's NOT okay! Because of you and because of you"—she looks back at Amir, fury in her eyes—"I almost fucking killed myself yesterday. So no! Not okay! I'm so fucking tired of people shitting on me because they can! It's over. Done!"

The tears start to fall down Amir's face so fast that it unnerves Tillie. She expects him to fight back or run. She does not expect tears.

"You almost killed yourself?"

Tillie's voice goes away again. She nods, holding his eye contact.

"Because of me?"

"Because of you and some other things. Yeah. It was stupid. It's obviously so not worth it. Dying because some boy doesn't like me."

"I do like you," he says quickly.

She laughs, low at first, and then like a cackle.

"I like you, but I'm—"

She stares at him.

He lowers his voice and leans in. "I'm gay and I'm fucking petrified, okay?"

"Oh," she says. "That was not—oh."

As soon as he says it, she gets it, she sees it, she knows it is true, not just something a guy says to cover shitty behavior, though in this case it is, in fact, still highly shitty behavior. And Tillie thinks: *Thank god. Asshole. Poor Amir.* If only there were a word for the combination of relief, fury, and sadness that wells up in her throat.

Amir motions to his friends that he's okay and waves them away, and then he hugs himself into a defensive posture as she stands there, not answering. The power has shifted, and the furious part of her is glad. And the other part can't allow him to go even another second feeling the way he must feel inside.

"Okay, so," she says. She finds herself unable, or maybe just unwilling, to finish the sentence. "I almost killed myself because my gay boyfriend ghosted me. Okay."

"I'm so sorry, T. I wanted to tell you, like a thousand times."

"Why didn't you?"

He looks both ways. "Why don't I tell anybody? As soon as I do, it leads to a path that leads to the inevitability of me not having a family."

"You wouldn't—how do you know? Did your mom say that?"

"I just know, okay?"

Tillie sighs, feeling exhaustion in her shoulders. She looks around. She finds Molly, standing about ten feet away. Too far to hear this conversation, but close enough so Tillie knows she's there.

She waves her hand over at Molly. "And this is Molly. Who I just also yelled at in front of a million people."

Molly tentatively comes over and kind of salutes awkwardly. "Hey."

Tillie turns to Molly, who smiles a bit at her as a sort of apology. "Thank you," Molly says.

It's the last thing Tillie expects to hear.

"Thank me?"

"You at least said it, you know? I deserved it. So, um. Thanks for being real with me."

And the three of them stand, awkwardly, and Tillie looks at both the boy who tormented her and the girl who did so, and she feels angry still, and that anger is useful and useless and also she's hungry. So she says, "And now, maybe you're buying me lunch?"

She's not sure who she's addressing, so it's a relief when they both say, almost in unison, "Yes."

×

When all the men but Morris leave, Michael takes a nap.

"Of course I'm staying," Morris had said. "It's what we do. You don't have to go through this alone." Morris took Michael's phone and said he'd answer calls and texts, and he'll check in with Michael's ex, who is en route by train.

Michael can barely react, and he hopes Morris understands.

Sleep comes fast. So do dreams.

His son is writing a song. The song's lyrics float over his head, and Michael cannot hear what they are. He calls out to his son, to make the lyrics clearer, so he can hear them. He calls out to the world, to lower the volume, so he can hear the song.

Then his son, sitting with his laptop, smiling.

"I wrote something good," he says when his dad walks in. "I wrote something really good."

"Everything you write is good," Michael says.

His son smiles. But the camera goes in, in, in, to his son's bloodstream. Behind the smile. To the inner workings.

He opens his eyes. He sees it now. He sees what he didn't see before, and it's so damn simple. The thing he didn't see. How did he not see it?

The thing is purple and blue and clogs the bloodstream, and it comes with a mournful sound. It's heavy like lead, and it's . . . everywhere.

I let him down, sleeping Michael thinks. *I should have seen. I should have known. I should have done so much better.*

×

Knowing it is potentially her last lunch outside of an institution for a while, and also for once utterly not giving a shit what anyone thinks, Tillie orders a croque-monsieur and a croque-madame at Maison Kayser for lunch. When the two sandwiches arrive, she has them face each other and she says, "Watch this, Amir. Watch how the monsieur does NOT ghost the madame. Even if he likes other monsieurs."

"We all love us some croque," Molly mutters, using the correct French pronunciation—*cruck*—before she takes a nibble of her salade niçoise. Tillie half cracks up. Amir, nursing a gratinée à l'oignon that is still too steamy to eat, does not.

Amir seemed all too happy to skip out on the afternoon. He told his buddies he was going, and Tillie could tell he was scared shitless that they'd heard him. She was pretty sure they hadn't.

"So explain," Tillie says. "Why you can't come out. Why it was worth, you know. Being unimaginably cruel to me."

"I'm guessing I'm going to have to apologize a bunch more times?"

Tillie nods. "Yeah. Like twenty-three. Or a hundred and six. I haven't decided yet."

"But at some point, you'll be able to, like, accept? Because I really am sorry."

"We'll see. Meanwhile, amuse me. Tell me zis story."

The lightness of the bad French accent is bullshit, but something about this whole day has stolen caring or giving a fuck from her entirely. It's also really weird. Her best friend from fifth grade and her ex-boyfriend, who don't know each other, and shouldn't, really. They are so not congruent in her mind.

"My mom," he says.

"Muslim. Religious," Molly says, almost dismissively.

Amir says, "Um. No. Muslim, yes. Not religious. Basically atheist. And just as American as you, so."

Molly shrinks back into herself. "Sorry."

He stares a little longer. "Anyway, Nava, her sister, is lesbian, and my mom basically disowned her. All my childhood I heard about her disgusting sister, my disgusting aunt. I haven't seen her in forever. She lives in DC. My mother as good as told me if I'm gay, better to just not come home and tell her. Better to find a new place to live, and a new family."

The girls listen, intently, and they eat in silence. Tillie is thinking about parents and disappointment, which she could write a book about. But this one. This thing of telling your kid not to come home if he's a certain way? That's a new one to her.

The whole thing makes her feel tired and confused in her bones.

"Sometimes maybe parents say stuff but they don't mean it?" Molly finally says.

Amir shrugs. "Two months till I graduate. Then college. I just need to hold out a little longer, then I don't have to live there, and I don't have to pretend."

"So . . . boyfriends?" Tillie asks. The word is hard to even say. She's not sure how she'll feel when he talks about that side of his life.

He shakes his head, hard. "Oh God no."

"Really? Why not?"

"Are you kidding me? It's what I said. Patience. I'm waiting. Georgetown."

"I want to go there!" Molly says, like it's a reflex, and then, as if something washes over her, she closes her eyes. "Or someplace else, I guess."

"Why does it matter to you so much?" Tillie says, irked, because god forbid Molly should not be the center of attention for two minutes. She wants to know more about this lack-of-boyfriend thing. It makes Amir seem almost noble to her, and knowing that at least he wasn't hiding something like that helps a bit. "Why do you care where you go to school?"

Molly stabs at a piece of lettuce. Forcefully.

"You wouldn't get it," she finally says, not putting the lettuce into her mouth.

"Try us," Amir says, a little anger in his voice, and Tillie is glad he sees it, too.

"Okay, so. No, I'm not jumping off a—sorry, sorry," she says, facing Tillie. "I'm just, I'm aware that you guys are dealing with more, so this all feels a little privileged."

"We're private school kids eating lunch at Maison Kayser. I'm pretty sure we're at a privilege standstill here," Tillie says.

"Ugh," Molly says. "Why am I even—okay. So you know how they always say, 'If I can make it there, I'll make it anywhere'? About New York?"

Tillie and Amir nod.

Molly puts her hand through her blond hair. "Well . . . apparently the converse is true, too, because if you can make it here? Well, he couldn't make it here, either, but the point is, he couldn't make it in Baltimore, either. My uncle Bill. He was an Allen-Stevenson kid. Then Horace Mann. He played football. He was good-looking. Not that I—" She pauses and looks down at her plate.

"You're gorgeous, yes, we know," Tillie says.

Molly rolls her eyes. "So Uncle Bill. He's in Baltimore. He sells Formica countertops. Not well, either. It's so bleak. I'm so, so scared, scared that like him, I'm peaking now, too, because he definitely peaked in high school. And Gretchen and Isabella are absolutely pulling away, okay? Gretchen texts me every day, but it's less and less, and I'm just hanging by a thread. And this suspension thing is not helping, because now forget a good college."

"What do you mean you're hanging by a thread?" Tillie cocks her head. "I mean, really. You're the center of everything."

"Yeah, but I'm actually not."

"Okay . . ."

"They have no idea who I am."

"Who are you?"

"I'm the worst."

"You're the worst?"

"Yes."

"How?"

"I'm a fraud."

"What are you talking about?"

"I'm a geek! Okay? I want to go to things like FanCosCon!" Molly says it so seriously, and so loud, that all three of them look at one another. After a few awkward beats, they each break out laughing.

"What?" asks Tillie.

"It's so much worse than you think," Molly says, masking her face with her hands.

"It really isn't, though, is it?" Tillie says.

"Ugh. It is and it isn't, okay? I'm just . . . I'm supposed to be this one girl, and I'm supposed to, like, care about Jasmine on YouTube and her fucking eyeliner, and I really, truly don't. What I do care about is Sarah J. Maas—her books are everything, and all I want to do is be immersed in that world, and meet Sarah J. Maas, and there are just some things you don't do when you live on Madison Avenue and your mom is my mom, and that is clearly, clearly one of them. So I am kind of hanging by a thread because who I am, like, inside? It's not acceptable. I can't be. So I won't be."

"Oh," Amir says, smirking. "I have no idea what that would be like."

This makes Molly laugh at herself a bit.

Tillie finds herself feeling different than she'd expected as she lunches with the odd combination of Amir and Molly, the two people she most wanted to murder just four hours ago. And she thinks: *How strange. How strange that I might have ended my existence for these two people, and I had no idea, no idea. That they are so not worth that, and that they have their own shit I didn't even know about, and there's something there, a lesson, like.* And she thinks, *Next time I'm there, I need to remember* . . . and then Molly starts talking some more, and she forgets what she was supposed to remember.

She doesn't really hear all that Molly is saying, because she's thinking about belonging. And how, at the moment, she almost feels like she belongs. Almost.

"So?" Molly asks. She is looking at Tillie expectantly.

"Um . . ."

"Quick answer, no hesitation: Are you a danger to yourself?"

"What? No. No. I'm not."

She means it, and the thought makes her smile a bit in realization. Something has changed here. Quickly, something has changed, and it feels like a cloud has lifted. Or two.

"Good," Molly says. "So what's next? Because we're pretty

much in agreement. You deserve a chance. Both of us will talk to your mom. Because I've seen a danger to yourself, Tillie Stanley. And what I see here? What we see? Not that. So if you want, we can, like, go pick up your phone now. Go pick it up and we'll take you home, and we will explain everything, and, I mean, it's not like we can promise that your mom won't send you away, but it's worth a shot, right?"

Tillie looks to Amir, who is smiling shyly at her. To Molly, who's still looking at her expectantly, and with eyes that are nearly kind. Tillie almost says yes. And then she realizes: There's one more cloud. No. Yes. She's doing things today. She's got to continue. She's so close.

"My dad," she says.

"What about your dad?" Molly asks.

"I need to say some things to him. Will you come?"

Molly to Amir. Amir to Molly. Something communicated.

"We're in," Amir says. "Let's go."

✕

Tillie is able to find her dad's office building without too much trouble amid the chaos of businesspeople rushing about on their cell phones at Fifty-First and Third, and a quick elevator trip later, the three teens are in the posh lobby of her dad's hedge fund.

"You say you're his daughter?" the receptionist, a petite white woman with beautiful straight brown hair asks, staring at her perhaps a second too long, and something acrid pours through Tillie's chest. What she wouldn't give to never feel that again.

"Yes," she says.

She calls and then half turns and puts her hand over the

mouth end of the phone. Tillie looks, exasperated, to Amir and Molly. Molly is on her phone, not paying attention, but Amir has seen it.

"That's ridiculous," he says.

"Right?" says Tillie. "There's always an asterisk. I hate it."

The receptionist's nasally voice grabs their attention.

"I'm so sorry," she says. "He's not available."

Tillie looks to Amir and Molly as if they'll have the answer. When she doesn't find it there, she says, "Well, I can wait."

The woman nods almost imperceptibly and picks up the phone again. Tillie crosses her arms and taps her foot, and when the woman does the thing where she half turns again, Tillie looks to the floor.

The woman hangs up the phone. "I'm sorry, but your father is wrapped up today. It's not a good day for this. He says he'll see you at home tonight."

Tillie's throat constricts. Her shoulders sag. "Okay," she says. "I guess we won't wait, then."

She quietly and slowly walks out of the reception area, back toward the elevators, Amir and Molly in tow.

"People get busy," Molly says. "I know you want to talk to him now, but you'll get him later. We'll take you home, okay?"

Tillie says nothing. There's nothing much to say.

And then she thinks about the reality of the situation.

How her mother freaked out when she walked out of the office.

How she dropped her phone, and how her mother must have figured that out.

How her mother must be going crazy, actually, a little crazy, with fear.

How of course her father must know this. They talk all the

time. They're her parents. Of course she's called him. So he knows she's MIA.

And he just said he didn't have time for her.

Something delicate inside her tattered body, a piece she'd always kept safe, even in the moment when she stood there with one leg over the railing, looking at that boy, shatters.

She feels two hands simultaneously reach for her. One lands on her right shoulder blade. The other on her left elbow.

She turns.

She runs. Back toward her father's office.

She's a battering ram. There's nothing that will keep her from where she needs to go now, and she feels dangerously alive and without a net.

She charges past the receptionist, who says, "Hey!" and then, "Excuse me, excuse—"

But Tillie is gone. She finds his nameplate next to a door and pushes.

Her dad's receding blond hair blows a bit as he swivels his chair, and Tillie can tell his feet were, moments ago, up on his desk. He was reclined.

Everything pours into her throat at once, and she drowns in words and feelings.

And what she says, in the smallest voice possible, when their eyes meet, is "Daddy!"

He holds her stare like he's just been caught with another woman. He doesn't say anything. Until he does.

"Hey, Till," he says, his voice casual.

It's all she needs to hear to know that he knows. And that he opted out. Which is all she needs to know about her father.

"How could you?" she says, her voice vulnerable and high, and she wants the other, she wants the one that came out earlier at Amir. But it's gone. The shattering of the thing next to her heart stole her mojo.

"Till," he says.

"Dad."

"What am I supposed to—"

"So you know," Tillie says, and some of that mojo returns because her voice is less eight years old and more seventeen now.

He nods ever so slightly.

"You know that I went to the bridge. That I ran today. I came to you. And you sent me away."

"I don't do well with—" he says. "I'm sorry."

She exhales quickly, almost like a laugh. She stretches out her arms wide, and she doesn't know why. It's as if to say, *This is me! Me! Your Till! Don't you see me?*

But he doesn't, or maybe he can't, because he looks away and very quietly says, again, "Sorry."

She deflates her wide arms. She stands there, feeling inconsequential, feeling like maybe she did when she found out about Santa Claus—she can't really remember. Something has died and nothing's there to replace it, and again the drowning—words, feelings—in her throat. She'd gargle them and spit them out but she's numb there.

She turns and walks out, and it's like she can't see or hear anything.

She's vaguely aware of Amir and Molly, but she walks right by them. She ignores them, not because she wants to, but because she can't not.

And then she's on the street, and she's vaguely aware of them behind her, pulling on her arms, and she's somewhat aware of the altercation, the "Leave me alone!" that someone else must say through her mouth, because she's not there.

And the train is silent but not.

And her beating heart is the only remaining soundtrack to her sad life, and she has to put a stop to that.

×

When Tillie gets off the train at 181st, her hearing is back a little and things feel calmer inside her chest. Every step feels definitive, terminal. She's okay with that.

She cannot bear a single second more of this heart pain. There are no other options but to stop it, once and for all, and she's sorry. Because she knows this will ruin her mom. Ruin her. And Britt, poor Britt! But she tried and she tried and nothing worked.

This. This will work.

So she walks, slowly, head down, back toward the bridge, where she was yesterday, at just about this time, actually.

"So just a question."

The voice jolts her back. The vacuum of sound, the silence, dissipates and suddenly there she is, in the urban scene, cars and horns and all that noise.

She turns around.

The voice belongs to Molly. Amir is with her.

"So just a question," Molly repeats, very calm. "What's the likelihood your dad will ever be who you want him to be?"

A tear falls from Tillie's left eye.

Then another.

More tears. A torrent. And then she's sobbing, louder than

she ever has before, and she's hugging her side like someone's punched her.

It hurts worse than anything she could imagine hurting.

She cries and she cries and she holds herself and she's aware they're with her, standing with her, but they're letting her cry.

"So what's the likelihood?" Molly says again, her voice soft, calm.

When Tillie can finally talk, she says, "He didn't care that I almost tried to kill myself. He *didn't care*. He sent me away."

"What's the likelihood?"

"He had his receptionist send me away on my worst-ever day. He had to know I might do it again, and he sent me away."

"What's the likelihood?"

"Stop asking me that, okay? Nil! Zero! Okay?"

"Okay," Molly says.

"He's a shit dad. I'm not the daughter he wants, I guess, or whatever, and no good person would ever do that to another person, obviously. So he's a shit dad."

"Yeah," says Molly. "My dad, too. Maybe he loves me in his own way. I don't know. He's not there. I don't know. And one day, my therapist asked me that question, and I was like, oh."

"I don't know my dad," Amir says. "I hate not knowing him and I hate that I don't have a dad who loves me. It hurts."

Tillie has tears, still, but the heaving has gone for the moment, and she does a thing that surprises even her. She opens her arms. And these two people, these two people who were almost terminal for her, step in and hold her.

"You have to, like, I don't know. What's something else you could want?" Molly says, her voice like syrup, calming. "Besides that from your dad. Because he can't, obviously."

Nothing has ever made more sense to Tillie than these words, and where no option existed, where the word *terminal* had been posted in her brain, something opens up and options appear, and the word fades.

It hurts. Bad. Unbearably. But she's not so alone with it anymore. So it's no longer terminal.

She turns and she takes a hand in each of hers, and the three walk back toward the subway. She says, "Take me home," and no answer is needed, because that's where they're going.

X

The sun is almost fully set across the Hudson, putting to rest the longest fucking day of his life, when Michael comes back out to the living room to see Morris, seated in the window seat, working away on his laptop.

"Hey," Michael says lamely.

"Hey."

Michael sits down on the couch. Morris walks over and points to the couch across the way. "Here, or where you are?"

"There's fine," Michael says.

They sit in silence for a bit.

"I keep waiting. For him to come home from school. Every time I hear a noise, I think it's him, messing with his keys. The door's about to open."

"Sure, sure," Morris says.

Morris stares intently at Michael. He holds the space.

"The gay thing? I mean, he knew that was totally okay. That I loved him exactly as he is. Exactly."

Morris gets up, goes to the kitchen, and returns with two glasses of water. Michael downs his and starts talking before he's even taken his mouth off the glass.

"I mean. The first thirteen years of his life I was focused elsewhere, and I know that. But I feel like I was making up for it. I feel like I was giving him what he needed, and we checked in every night, and I told him. I told him he could say anything to me. I knew he was a little depressed. So was I as a kid. I was giving him space. I was letting him have space to experience things for himself, and look what I—look what I did."

"You didn't do this," Morris says.

Michael shakes his head, his whole body beginning to shake. "How did I not see this? How stupid—"

"No," Morris says calmly. "No. I'm good to sit with you in sadness. Anger is fine. But I'm not going to cosign this bullshit."

Michael swallows. The anger is right there, lightning fast. Who the fuck says something like that to a man who's lost his kid? Who the fuck does Morris think he is?

"What? Say it," Morris prods.

"Fuck you!"

"Okay."

"Fuck you fuck you fuck you and fuck your touchy-feely fucking shit and fuck fuck fuck FUCK!"

Morris smiles despite himself and then readjusts himself to a more neutral face. "Better?"

Michael exhales and leans back. "A little. Thanks."

"No problem. You'd do the same for me."

╳

Tillie's mother isn't mad. Or if she is, she's decided it's better not to lead with it. Tillie is welcomed with a big hug, and then Amir and Molly get embraced, too.

"You I haven't met, but I've heard about you," Tillie's mom says to Amir, a slight eyebrow raised.

"And you, I haven't seen in years. How are you, sweetheart?" she says to Molly.

"Hi, Mrs. Stanley."

"Thank you so much for returning my lovely daughter to me."

"Oh shit," Tillie says. "My phone. I need to—"

Her mother puts up her hands. "Got it," she says.

"And am I going to get it back?"

"We'll talk."

And then it's the world's most awkward goodbyes, first to the ex-boyfriend who did her wrong but has his own shit to deal with, and then to her best friend from five years ago. And it's unclear where this all will go, these—friendships? Not exactly. They saved her life, so there's that. But *friendship* might not be the word.

"Stay in touch," Molly says, and Tillie nods but she's pretty sure she won't.

Amir doesn't say that, but he does say, "I still owe you like a hundred apologies."

Tillie, in return, says, "Let me know you're okay when you tell your mom. If."

And then she's alone with her mom. Britt is in her room, and Tillie is glad. She doesn't want her sister to know any of this, ever.

"So I went to see Dad," Tillie says.

"You did? He didn't tell me that."

"Mom, will you promise to tell me the truth about something?"

"Of course."

"Did you call Dad after I ran off? Did he know?"

Her mom is still for a moment. Then she slowly nods. "I did."

"I thought so. He sent me away."

Her mother's face registers this with a flinch and a shutting of her eyes.

"I'm so sorry, Till," her mom finally says, and there are tears in her eyes.

She says, "Eh." Which she doesn't mean, but sometimes enough is enough for a day.

They're quiet for a while, and then Tillie says, before she can stop herself, "I saw a boy jump."

"What?"

Tillie takes a deep breath and nods. "Yesterday when I was on the bridge. A boy was there. We looked at each other. And . . ."

"Oh, Till!" her mother says, and she puts her arms around her, and she squeezes, and Tillie isn't sure if it's an admonishment or what until her mother says, "What that must have been like for you, all this time. Holding that in."

Tillie doesn't need to say any more. She's glad she's told. And no, she doesn't know if that information is useful, or if, like, the police should know or something, but one thing she does know is that her mom will take care of it.

And it's decided. Tillie's going to Vermont. No, she has no say in the matter, but yes, something about the day she's just had lets her accept that it's happening, and also that it probably should.

"I'm sorry, by the way."

"Another time," her mom says. "I just . . . You are so loved, Tillie. So loved."

"Okay," she says. "I know, I guess. You are, too, for what it's worth."

"I know," her mom says, a gentle smile across her face. "I do."

Michael's ex, Erica, comes over in the evening, and as they stand in the doorway of Aaron's still-messy room, he watches her take the room in with utterly lost eyes.

He pictures her from back in college, and he thinks, *This isn't what a girl whose son will one day die by suicide looks like.* He's not sure what that looks like, but not the girl with the slightly uneven smile who loved SweeTarts and Smash Mouth. That girl has a different path.

She sits on Aaron's unmade bed. His smelly robe lies on the floor next to it. An empty bowl next to his Xbox controller. Fish food box open and sitting on the radiator.

"You think he's alive if we're still together?" she asks. Her posture is perfect, like it used to be.

Michael breathes in the question. It doesn't matter, really. He's not alive.

"I think he is," she says. "I think this is basically on us. I think—"

"Please," Michael says. "I beg of you. Please."

She nods, absently. And suddenly he has to leave. Like nothing he's ever felt before. He gets it. She needs to process. It just can't be with him. He literally can't.

He stands, a bit unsteady on his feet.

"Stay as long as you want," he says, his voice jittery. "I'm not mad. I just need—" And he walks out.

He gets to his room and collapses on his bed and lets his body shake like he's the victim of a biological attack, like some chemical is sweeping through him and he's powerless. This is just day one, he realizes. There are more, more coming, and sometimes the rain falls and it's good, and it's a Vermont stream, and other times the rain just comes and comes and it seems like it will never, ever end.

That thought petrifies him, like he's skydiving and can't find the cord to his parachute.

X

Tillie knocks on Britt's door.

"Come in," her sister says.

Tillie enters. Britt is lying in her bed playing Candy Crush. Tillie wonders if her mom told her something. She hopes not. Britt shouldn't have to carry that around. That's Tillie's stuff.

"Hey," Tillie says.

"Hey, Tillie Face."

Tillie stares at her sister until her sister looks up. She smiles and puts her phone down. "Did you hear about the guy whose left side was cut off?" Britt asks.

"No."

"He was all right."

Tillie giggles. "You're silly."

"*You're* silly," says Britt, poking her sister.

"So I need to tell you something."

"You're a goblin?"

"What? No, silly."

Britt giggles. "You're a backup dancer in the new Cardi B video?"

"I have to tell you I'm going away for a while. It's all gonna be okay. I just have to go for a bit, okay?"

Britt's eyes search the room. "Do you have to?"

"Yeah."

"I don't want you to."

"I know. Me neither. It won't be long, though. And I'll call you all the time."

Britt nods. "Okay."

Tillie leans down and kisses her sister. "I love you a lot, did you know that?"

"I love you, Tillie Face."

×

Michael awakens to the sound of someone in his room. He turns over, looks up, and sees his ex-wife standing there in a violet night-gown, hugging herself as if she's cold.

"Our son," she says.

He exhales and rubs his eyes. "Yeah."

"It's not supposed to be like this."

"I know."

"Why on earth did he do this?"

"I don't know."

She scratches her chin. He sits up a bit.

"Come here," he says, and there are about a million questions that could be asked, but they don't ask any of them. He doesn't know what it is. He doesn't have to. He just knows that he needs it like oxygen. She gets under the sheets with him in her robe, and he spoons her, putting his arms around her.

"Can we make a deal?" he asks.

She nods and he feels her wipe her right eye.

"I won't blame me if you don't blame you, okay?"

She expels a laugh. Even though she's facing the other way, he catches a whiff of her breath, a bit stale and a bit cinnamon toothpaste. It takes him back.

"Easier said than done."

"Promise?" he says.

She says, softly, "Promise."

Tillie sits in yet another therapist's office. This one is a little different, though. Instead of a view of people's elegant shoes and lower legs tromping down Park Avenue, she is looking at a floor-to-ceiling window view of the Vermont countryside. Pine trees, tall and noble, congregate in a far-off forest, and beyond, a hazy mountain range, gray and blue and eternal. And instead of Dr. Brown and her well-tanned arms, here's a light-skinned Black woman whose eyes immediately pierce into Tillie in an unnerving way. So yeah, a little different, at least on the surface.

She hopes it's different, anyway. But if she were a betting girl? Her money would be on it being exactly the same.

"Tillie," the woman says. "I'm so glad you're here."

Tillie shrugs and rolls her eyes playfully, as if to say, *Not my choice*, and the woman smiles.

"I want you to use this time. I want you to take the time while you're here to breathe."

Tillie holds in a laugh. She's like, *So I went to this place, and I just stopped breathing and I died. In retrospect, going to Vermont was not the best choice for keeping me alive and safe.*

"Also, I want you to know that you're not alone. That's one thing group therapy is going to do for you, and you'll be doing that. It'll help you see that the feelings you have are feelings other people have, too, and that your pain is welcome here. And finally, I want to give you permission to feel whatever the heck it is you feel."

It's all a little New Agey to Tillie, but at the same time, she can see that the woman means what she says, and it's kinda sweet.

"So. Tell me everything."

"Everything?"

"I want to know Tillie Stanley. The things she loves. The things that make her fume. The things that led her to the George Washington Bridge."

"So you know."

"I know the bare details. I want to know more. Will you tell me?"

So Tillie slowly starts talking, realizing that not talking to Dr. Brown didn't do her much good, really. And the thing about Carolyn—she has a first name, this lady—is that she has expressions. Like when Tillie tells the woman about Amir ghosting her, her face falls, and her eyes get red at just the same time Tillie's eyes get moist talking about thinking that she finally wasn't alone, only to find out she was more alone than ever before.

Something about the woman's investment in her story gets Tillie to talk. More than she's talked to Dr. Brown for sure. More than to Molly and Amir for the hour they were at lunch. More than to her mom, even at Tillie's most talkative. She opens up about feeling like a visitor in her own house, and the way her heart felt crushed the moment she walked in on her dad, reclining in his chair at work.

And she cries, which is not a very Tillie thing to do. She lets the tears out and Carolyn's eyes water, too, and they sit across from each other and have a good sob. For Tillie, it feels different inside. Like she's not so afraid that the ache will kill her if she acknowledges that it's there. All her life, it's like she signed some agreement. Don't feel sad. We chose you and gave you a good life. Be happy always.

She says this to Carolyn, and Carolyn's eyes light up.

"Wow," she says. "That has to be almost impossible."

Tillie nods. "Pretty stupid, huh?"

"No! Not stupid at all. I had some of the same messages growing up. Made some of the same agreements. Do you know that I
came here, Tillie? I was a patient here? And then, after it helped me,
I decided I would come back and be a counselor here to help people
like I was helped."

Tillie feels a warmth pass through her midsection. For the very
first time in her life, someone has climbed down into the abyss with
her. Her mom did in her own way, but there was always this feeling
that her mom was going to drown in it, and that wasn't good, either.
With Carolyn, who's been where she is, and her reactive face, Tillie
feels like she has a partner down here, like someone is holding her
hand, and when she mentions the poem she read, Carolyn asks if
she has it memorized, and would she perform it. Tillie says yes, and
the performance is different from the one at the talent show because
she's not saying, *Here, here's my pain, see the pain I'm in*. She's
sharing it, like saying, *Here, experience this*, and Carolyn does, and
when she's done, and when Carolyn applauds after, Tillie gets that
it's not bullshit. This woman really does care.

"So will there ever come a time when I'll be normal?" Tillie
asks.

Carolyn laughs and says, "I sincerely hope not."

×

Michael decides some fresh air might help him. So he wanders to
Central Park and heads south toward the Bethesda Fountain.

Aaron loved it there. The buskers with their music and dancing.
Maybe he imagined himself there. Michael doesn't know. All he
knows is every time they went there, Aaron would have this moment

when his entire chemistry changed. Michael knows that feeling. He gets it at work, when a patient has a breakthrough.

He stands alone, listening to an improvisational musician, a guy with a ponytail who adds recorded loops of various instruments to a drum loop, and then his voice. Standing there, Michael feels the palpable absence like a pain in his rib, like someone has surgically removed part of him, and he holds his breath to stop from screaming out at the agony of the precise, pointless, surgical removal of his son from this universe.

Where he would have so enjoyed being, right at this very moment.

×

"So, Tillie's off at Homestead?"

Winnie nods.

"And where does that leave you?"

And for the first time, Winnie breaks down. She just lets go. She drops her face into her hands and she cries like a baby.

Marie France waits. When Winnie's no longer shaking, she says, "I'm pretty sure my marriage is over."

"Ah," Marie France says.

"He couldn't just . . . comfort her. He knew. He knew what she'd been through and he was physically unable, or mentally, or whatever. And then another business trip. Out of nowhere. Imagine that."

Marie France nods.

"A Fifth Avenue hotel staycation, complete with minibar, it would appear. He lies but he doesn't cover his lies and in some ways that's great and in some ways it's a little insulting. Like I don't matter enough for him to try harder."

"Maybe he's just so sick it doesn't matter," Marie France offers.

Winnie shrugs and wipes her eyes. Marie France doesn't say anything. She just offers Winnie a placid expression.

"Let's just breathe a little. Shall we?"

So the two women sit across from each other and share the air of the room. And Winnie thinks good thoughts. For her daughters. For herself. Because this—this is not going to be easy.

×

Carolyn lets Tillie check her phone one last time before taking it away, giving her five minutes with it. No phones at Homestead.

There's one text.

The text reads: Hey.

The number is a 917 one. She doesn't know who it is, though. Her mom is her only texter, generally.

Tillie texts back: who is this?

Molly

Oh . . . hi

Your mom says you're at a place in Vermont

Yeah

I'm glad. I mean, I'm glad you're getting help

Thanks

Can I tell you something weird?

This is about as surprising a question as Tillie can remember. Molly and weird do not go together too often.

> I know it wasn't a great day by any stretch,
> but I liked hanging out with you.

Tillie has to put the phone down. She wonders: Is her mom paying Molly? Is this another prank? Will this show up on some other video?

But she knows in her heart that it isn't a prank. And oddly enough, the day had been fun, in a way. In a *This is nearly very possibly going to be the last day of your life* sort of way. In an *edge of the universe* sort of way.

She lets the phone sit for a moment.

?? Molly texts.

> Thanks. Is it ok if I just say it might take a while to trust you

Molly texts back three smiley faces.

> Of course. One other thing?

> Ok

> Next year, will you go to a con with me?

Tillie cracks up, and she smiles, and the smile is real.

I would definitely consider that, yes, Tillie texts.

×

"What is it, Amir? What did you want to tell me that was so important that it was worth taking me out of my morning routine? You know I need my morning time. It's important. So what? Tell me. What's going on?"

Amir takes the deepest breath of his life.

Then another one.

"Nothing, Mom. It's nothing."

×

Later, Tillie sits in another room with a similar view but more chairs. The sun is going down, so she watches the peach sunset over the blue-gray mountains, and the room begins to fill. With other teens. With some adults. Some she saw during lunch, when she sat alone at a table in the cafeteria until two older ladies joined her, which was sweet and a little awkward. Some she's never seen before. The facilitator, John, is a tall, lanky white guy with a shaved head who looks like he's maybe a few years out of college.

He goes over the ground rules—one person talking at a time, tell the truth, speak your mind, use "I" statements—and then he asks Tillie to introduce herself.

"I'm Tillie Stanley. I'm seventeen. I'm from New York. I guess . . . that's it?"

He smiles and shakes his head. "That's a start. Who are you, Tillie Stanley?"

A few smartass answers come to her. She thinks about saying she likes taking long walks on the beach and men who aren't afraid to feel. But instead, she thinks of Carolyn and her supportive eyes, and she sees the eyes of these people, all of whom are here for whatever reason, too, like her, and she decides to tell the delicate truth.

"I'm Tillie Stanley. I live in New York City, on the thirty-third floor of a fancy building with a view overlooking Central Park. My parents are white. They adopted me at birth. I've never met my birth parents, but I know my mom is from Korea. I sometimes feel like my family is sorry they adopted me because I have a sister who is ten, and my parents adopted me because they couldn't have kids themselves, so, surprise! My sister is blond and pretty and sweet, and I am none of those things, so.

"I get sad. I think it's in my blood. I'm intense. Anyway, the way I feel things isn't normal, I don't think. And I don't know. I guess the thing about being Asian with white parents is that quite frankly it's exhausting having to be aware, every single minute of my life, of my differences from them."

Tillie stops talking. John says, "Thank you." And he looks around the room and says, "Does anybody here have feedback for Tillie?"

She wasn't expecting this, and her heart flips and she shifts in her seat. She is so not prepared for a critique right now.

And older man with a scruffy beard and a scratchy voice to match says, "I like you right away, Tillie. You're honest and real. I'm intense, too."

"Thank you, Richie," John says. "Anyone else?"

A teenage girl whose skin is gray and who has bandages on both wrists tentatively raises her hand.

"I'm glad—" She stops talking and tucks her chin to her chest.

Tillie leans forward. Like she can sense the girl's pain, and she wants the girl to know it's okay, it's okay. And in that moment, Tillie realizes something. That she's good. She's one of the good ones. She wants good things for people. And that. That feels like something to hold on to, so she files it away.

"—I'm glad you're part of the group," the girl says, a near whisper.

Tillie promises herself to seek the girl out in the cafeteria and sit with her sometime. Maybe tomorrow at breakfast.

"Me too," Tillie says.

Aaron's funeral takes place on Sunday. They do it at Riverside Memorial Chapel, and thank god for Morris, who's done everything. Like Michael would do for him if the situation were reversed, for certain. That and a kidney.

Michael and Erica go together. It's weird and it's not weird for Michael to spend time with his ex. He's looking forward to her going back to the Cape, and he's scared about what being alone will feel like.

Classmates of Aaron's show up. A whole slew of them, most of whom Michael does not recognize because his frame of reference is plays and talent shows. Aaron didn't have friends over much in the last year, and truthfully Michael never thought to push him on that, figured that it was being a junior, and the end of playdates and all that.

But the kids are there, and he sees some of them hugging and some tears, and he is so, so grateful, because it tells him that someone cares, and there's Kelly Jameson, who Michael recognizes as Aaron's girlfriend from the play, and, man, was she good. Aaron was high school good. This girl? She was famous good.

He recognizes Sarah Palmer. She used to come over right around the time Aaron came out, and they'd sit and play music on Spotify and talk and laugh, and Michael liked her.

She is the one who comes over to Michael. "I'm sorry. I'm so, so sorry," she says.

"Thank you, Sarah," Michael says.

"Everyone liked Aaron."

"That's . . . good to know."

Conversation exhausted, she awkwardly bows her head and walks away, and Michael wonders: Did they? Like his son? If so, why was he always so alone?

His warrior brothers are all there. Of course. They stand as one, a posse of men, Michael's protectors, his support. And they sit with him and Erica, and he's glad they're there, so glad, like they're a limb of his body, and when he sees the group of them, in jackets and ties, which is not what he is used to seeing them in, a part of him returns and he can breathe a bit.

The service begins with a playing of "Walking Alone." Aaron's last song. Because that's absolutely what Aaron would have wanted.

> Teardrops fill my sunny Sunday morning
> And emptiness still fills my evenings, too
> One more lonely night awake
> Still in my bed
> While thoughts of you
> Burn through my head
>
> Spending time on my own
> Right now it's all I can do
> Taking walks all alone
> Because I can't be with you

The song hits hard. Michael tries to steady himself but he feels faint. Morris squeezes his shoulder. He thinks, *Who? Who was he singing to? Who couldn't he be with?* It's like a part of his life he'll never be privy to, and he hates hates hates it.

While the rabbi speaks, Michael looks around and tries his best to see the funeral through his son's eyes. Would this have been honoring to him? Would he have been pleased that people showed up and cried? Would he have adored the way they reacted to the song?

Would that have been enough to keep him here? Forever? Or just a little while?

And in that moment, Michael realizes exactly who the song was about, and it cuts him right down the center and he gasps, and he grips his head so it will all stay together.

The one who the song was about, who left him feeling empty? The one he couldn't walk with?

The entire world.

All of it.

It is a terrible ballet.

Like amateur dancers choreographed poorly by an uncaring god, they tilt out toward the blue unknown and lose their balance.

And falling, they—

Time's up for conjecture. Casual musing. Forever.

Wind rushing through hair and popping eardrums and the girl turned upside down and she tries to reach her hand back to grasp but it's far too late for that and her body breaks upon impact.

The boy, inverted to the world, a quick glimpse of New Jersey— what a final vision—the word *fly*, followed by the incomplete concept of—

Michael wishes for wind.

A strong wind that might sweep down First Avenue and prevent him from entering the blue-brick building. One that might pick him up and carry him into yesterday, into before.

He stands under the sign that reads CITY OF NEW YORK, OFFICE OF CHIEF MEDICAL EXAMINER, wanting to disintegrate.

He won't call Morris. There is nothing a person might say that could lessen—no. This pain, devouring him from the inside, is mandatory, unavoidable. How do you breathe when the most crucial part of your life evaporates in an instant?

A blond woman about his age exits the morgue, sobbing. Her whole being convulses. Her wails rise the hairs on the back of his neck.

He wants to help her. That is his instinct. But he can't. He is the same. The very same. The worst is yet to come and he just wishes he were able to run away from this, but he can't.

Michael closes his eyes as the woman passes by.

X

In the moment, Winnie barely registers the frozen man in front of the morgue. Later, after she pieces together that there were two jumpers that day, she will remember his presence and wonder.

Was that the father?

How did their children know each other? Why would they jump together?

But for the moment, all she and Michael share is complete devastation.

Britt loves dances. They're so old school it's not even funny, but the boys from Allen-Stevenson are SO CUTE.

It's her first Goddard Gaieties and she came with Carly and Sadie. She's wearing her favorite Vera Bradley floral-pattern dress with the side windows, and Carly is extra in her white Laura Ashley—so normcore! Sadie is blasting a black bandage dress with a full zipper down the back, very tight and very short. Very 1991.

They dance in a circle, and then some boys start dancing nearby and suddenly they are a group of seven.

First it's a Lizzo jam and they throw their hands in the air and sing along. Then the new Gucci Tran, which isn't Britt's favorite, but the boys go nuts, so it's okay.

Then a familiar sound, something she hasn't heard in a few years.

The bile rises up from her belly into her esophagus so fast that it stuns her. She takes off for the bathroom, arriving at an empty stall seconds before she detonates. The contents of her guts splat into the pristine toilet.

She closes her eyes and tries to breathe. In, out. In, out. Dr. Fitzpatrick has taught her some things. This one works. Sometimes.

The sound of the door swinging open and someone holding it so it doesn't slam shut. Britt senses Carly moments before she feels her hand on her sleeveless shoulder.

"You okay?"

Britt can't speak yet. She nods silently.

"What was it this time?"

Britt takes ten more seconds to catch her breath and to feel the well of sadness bubble into her throat.

"That song," she says. "My sister and I would . . ."

It's all the stuff that was going on three years ago that triggers it. A song or walking past Maison Kayser, one of Tillie's favorites, or a girl doing a monologue onstage or just about any TV show with an older sister. The EMDR has helped some, but clearly not enough.

Carly kisses her on the back and wraps her arms around Britt, who is glad she has a friend who will be with her when she vomits, or shakes uncontrollably, yet again.

She wonders if it will ever, ever go away.

It's the first LGBTQIA+ social of the year at Kenyon, and Hal thinks, *Maybe this time . . .*

The thought makes him roll his eyes.

His love life has not exactly been on fire, his first two years in Ohio.

He came here from Boston because it's a liberal campus with a strong LGBTQIA+ presence and a killer English department. He's going to be a writer. Experimental fiction. And while he's hardly the only quirky gay guy at Kenyon, finding the right match is close to impossible.

Someone who would get his satirical lyrics to pop songs, and the fact that he compiles a weekly Top 10 songs list, and has since he was eight.

Someone who doesn't think it's weird that he has a fishbowl in his dorm room.

Someone whose sense of humor doesn't bore the crap out of him. Someone who says surprising things.

It doesn't seem like a lot to ask for, but it's not here.

He looks around the room as kids start to enter. He likes Darby and her radical feminist poetry a whole lot. He enjoys ogling Dax and his outrageously long legs—who doesn't?—but if he has to listen to one more story about how popular Dax was back in Fayetteville, he might have to slay someone.

No. It's like there's a missing boy. Someone who would truly get him. Someone to be his first. Someone to hold him at night.

Because the holding, or the lack thereof: That's the hard part. Not being held is creating this void, and he's not really sure how much longer he can take it.

"You okay, Hally?" It's Darby, her head newly shaven. She looks awesome, of course.

He forces a smile so she won't know. No one can know how alone he really feels.

"Of course!" he says. "I'm fine."

He keeps looking.

Michael Boroff groans as the alarm goes off in his empty bedroom in Brooklyn, a sense of dread flooding through his veins. It's the tenth anniversary of Aaron's suicide, and he's as prepared for the feelings as he can be, yet his chest still feels heavy and a palpable lack trembles his limbs. Despite all the work he's done and the constant support of his ever-present warrior brothers, he still can't quite believe this is his life. That Aaron is gone.

×

Winnie takes Britt for a Monday-morning breakfast at Cushman's.

It was a popular visiting weekend at UMass Amherst, and Winnie and Frank came separately. Frank left last night. Winnie stayed the extra day.

Unspoken but understood was the fact that today is the tenth anniversary of Tillie.

"I just thought it would be nice to be here," Winnie says, taking a sip of coffee.

Britt instinctively grabs for her phone. She stops herself. Dr. Roberts would be proud. It's taken a while, but she can finally *feel her feelings*, as the great doctor would say.

It sucks.

"Yeah," Britt says, and she twirls her fork around the plate of pancakes.

"Let's each say three things. Three things we are grateful

for. Memories of Tillie, I guess I mean. Okay?"

Britt closes her eyes, and for a moment she hates Tillie. Hates her and the fact that this is never, ever going away. Feelings are shit. And then she realizes, no. She doesn't. She can't hate, ever. That's her Tillie Bear.

When Britt's eyes open, her mother is smiling at her sadly. "I just . . . I want to celebrate her," Winnie says, sighing.

Britt nods. She gets that. She really does. It's just hard to jump to that from what she's really feeling.

She doesn't have the words to express that. She never will.

✕

When the ship docks in Finland, Amir grabs Devon's hand. He can't help it at each new port. It's all so romantic, and he wants to memorialize every feeling.

He can feel Devon smirking next to him. He can hear his voice: "We're going e-biking in Helsinki, not hiking to the top of Mount Everest, sweetheart."

But to Amir, it's freedom from all the chains he once had. He's married! To a guy! His mom even came to the wedding. Now he's on his honeymoon!

He turns and looks at his husband and he is so overcome with love that the straight couple behind him have to clear their throats to remind Amir they're in a moving line.

It's not that he's forgotten Tillie. He's just stopped living there. The first five years were the worst. Feeling responsible. Wishing he could turn back time. And then, over time, less focus there. Still sadness when he thinks of the coolest girl he ever met. And how stupid he was to not just tell her the truth.

X

Molly is in a meeting when her phone buzzes. It's an anniversary reminder. Years ago she set it for 3:30 p.m. instead of all day, and she's never fixed it. So once a year, when she's busy doing something else, she's reminded.

She needs it to be that way.

She excuses herself to go into the bathroom, where she can have a few minutes to think about her once friend. About where Tillie would be today.

Molly runs her hands through her hair as she sits in the stall, thinking the same thought for the millionth time: What if she'd been more true to herself? If she'd just dumped Gretchen and Isabella when she realized they were truly nothing like her. If she'd reached out to Tillie, who was so clearly struggling, instead of being part of the problem. A big part, obviously.

She swallows and blinks a few times. No. She can't. Yes, she could have done something, and no, she didn't. What's done is done. And now she has a meeting to run.

X

The George Washington Bridge shimmers at night, all these years later. So many glimmering stars along its north and south necklaces. We think of its majesty, we marvel at its beauty.

What the throngs of drivers passing from upper Manhattan to Fort Lee, New Jersey, can't see is the despair. They cannot feel it as they drive past the spot where, ten years earlier, two teens threw away their lives.

Ryan's always been a sucker for romance.

Even back in high school, when he was goth. Underneath the black trench coat and the eyeliner beat the true heart of a softie.

Senior year, he had to dress in camouflage in order to go see a revival of *Pretty Woman* at the Rialto. Alone.

And now it's the morning of his wedding—ta-da!—and he's snuck out of bed before dawn to have a little meditation time down by the lake of the Stowe B & B that Askia's family rented out for the occasion.

He sits down in the dewy grass and stares out onto the foggy morning air, watching the slightly shimmering surface of the placid lake.

He's so lucky, he thinks, and a shiver rushes through his body, thinking of the way Askia snores, and her slightly crooked smile, and how she burns turkey bacon every time she cooks it.

And then it's like he sees Her. The other Her. Standing on the water. In a black peacoat with a pink knapsack.

He shakes his head, willing the vision away.

It's his fucking wedding day. He's not going to allow it to—

But oh, those eyes.

Black like perfect marble. Her long hair almost down to her waist. Her fine features, her eyebrows, ever-tilted up at the ends.

He's seen her sporadically, the last decade or so. She always just stands, looking at him with an expression as calm as this placid lake.

×

He's never told anyone. Who would believe him, anyway? An apparition of a girl who shows up five, maybe six times a year, to look at him? It was never that scary to him after the first time. And that first year, back when he was at Brown, once he accepted her as not super creepy, he saw her nearly every day. She was a person in his life, a secret, and the romantic side of him couldn't help but play. This. This was the girl he was to marry. Someday he'd meet her in person, and it would be his little secret, that he'd seen her so often, and she wouldn't even know. Or maybe she would? That idea gave him thrilling tingles up his spine.

"I'm getting married," he says softly to the apparition, his voice cutting into the silent Stowe morning air. When she first appeared, she was just about his age, with a face full of life. Diminutive and beautifully curved. She's aged alongside him. Now she's—stunning. Eyes that command attention, reverence.

She does not speak back. She's an apparition, after all. But perhaps for the first time in their experience together, he swears he sees her lips turn up.

"I waited for you. I looked for you. But this is right. Askia is right."

Her cheeks puff out slightly in an approximation of a smile, and he's transfixed. This is real. It has to be real. And yet it cannot be.

He whispers, "Goodbye."

A tear rolls down her cheek, and she turns and walks across the lake, away from him forever.

Everybody's just . . . wrong for the position.

Wrong aesthetic.

The thing about Hung's first post-college venture is he has such strong opinions on exactly what kind of senior reviewer *Downbeat* needs.

It's snarky at times, yes, but never cynical.

A person who isn't above retro pop but who doesn't live there. Certainly not someone who would put it down, and it seems like every applicant thinks their fucking music's shit doesn't stink.

He dreams of a staff of music experts—perhaps with music backgrounds—but they have to be . . . is the word *real*?

Hung was going to change music journalism forever. Bring the love back without sacrificing a truly critical lens.

Can't anyone write like that anymore?

He goes through the last of the applications. A girl named Tawny who wrote her dissertation at Wesleyan about how Wilson Phillips ruined music forever.

No! They didn't! Can't anyone with a heart apply for this job? Can he get just one unironic-yet-refined piece about how Wilson Phillips SAVED music?

He closes down the file and opens another browser window. He shakes his head. He was so sure he could, but without that missing ingredient, it really feels like he can't.

So he opens up the application for Browning. A part-time music teacher. It's not his dream, but he's gonna have to pay the bills, and his dream of *Downbeat* isn't gonna do that.

Probably ever.

Backstage at her own wedding, the bride sobs.

It's just so hard.

Two fathers. The one she had until everything in her world collapsed, more than fifteen years ago now, who hasn't much been in her life since then, in and out of rehab, mostly out. And the other one. The one who was at her high school and college graduations.

Andy checks all the boxes. Britt can see why her mom chose him. He's such a solid guy. And that's how she feels about him. She solidly likes him. That's all.

And then there's Frank.

She hates him so much.

She loves him so much.

It's confusing. Just like it is with Sean, her future husband. She loves his strength. She hates his strength. She hates his inability to talk. Loves it, too. Lets her off the hook all the time.

And now the feud.

"Sweetheart, it's your day," her mom says. "I didn't think he'd actually show up and demand to walk you down the aisle. You choose. Don't let their drama become your drama, okay?"

Britt smiles. She always smiles. Her mom knows her well enough to know what the smile means in this case: *Too late. It's already my drama.*

If Tillie were here.

Shit. No. She's already done her makeup. No. But if she were. If Tillie were here, she'd run interference. Tell Frank to fuck off. Her sister was so much better at bringing the real than Britt is. She knew that even back then. Even before—no.

Can't.

She clears her throat. She looks at her mom, who looks so old these days. Way older than she really is.

Britt says, "Will you tell Andy? Please?"

She knows her mom so well by now. So she knows that the way she swallows means, *You're putting me in a terrible situation, but I'll do it because it's you.*

And Britt knows that, too. And she knows that Andy, not Frank, deserves to walk her down the aisle today. But just as sure as that is true, the other thing is true, too.

She simply cannot say no to her dad.

The boy in the mirrored fleece wishes someone could see him.

When he passes people, they only see themselves, and that's by design, of course. He picked it out himself on Bork and clicked want. A new look for school that's a little Max, even.

But in practice, as he walks down Seventy-Fourth Street, he realizes that it may not have been the right choice.

When people see you, he thinks as he passes the only original pre-Second-World-War brownstone, the one between the two connected towers, they see themselves. And that's in the best of circumstances. In some ways, he bought the fleece to highlight that, thinking that by drawing attention to it, people might actually realize how little they see of other people. Of him.

When he looks at people, he really sees them. On the inside. He wants so much for someone to see him that way, the way he sees others.

But mostly they just fix their quaffs, check their makeup, smile at their reflections.

He wants one adult to just peer in and say, "Hey there. You okay?"

Because he's not, really. Not too okay.

This street. Seventy-Fourth Street. It's a little different. It's not a major thoroughfare like Seventy-Second or Seventy-Third, which they just revamped and elevated, or Seventy-Fifth or Seventy-Sixth, even, with its multilevels.

It's an old-timey street with concrete sidewalks, and walking down them, he feels it's the most connect-ish place left in the

Mid-UpWest Quadrangle. It's the place where you're most likely to catch someone's eye, which is hard to do with all the holographics on the thoroughfares.

Modern life is lonely, he thinks as he sits on the steps of the one brownstone. It's beige and original-looking, and he thinks of people who might live inside. Maybe it's a gay couple or throuple? Older, with wisdom. Like his dad probably has, he doesn't know. His dad left.

He imagines a guy, maybe his dad's age, coming down the steps. He lives there with his husband. They are both big into running and they read actual books, and they talk to each other. That's not a thing at his house.

He imagines the middle-aged guy stopping, sitting down next to him. Saying something like, "You look like you need to talk to someone. Do you notice that people don't say hi to each other on the street anymore?"

And he'd be, "Yes! Exactly. I long for the old days."

The guy would smirk. "The old days didn't exist," he'd say, or something like that, and it would be the start of a real connection, someone who would see him.

The boy hears a door open and close behind him. His heart catches. Maybe it's . . .

"Nice fleece," says a woman's voice.

She's maybe just out of grad school. She has a mod appearance and her smile is warm. He smiles back.

"Thanks," he says, and she nods and gets on her hover and is gone, just like that, and it's nice and all. But it's not the experience he needed. It's not the guy who would really, truly *see* him, who would understand that need, and understand how damn special this old block is . . .

What Enya Martinez needs, as she walks into the only remaining physical library in New York City, is a book that will tell her what to do.

She presses her fingertips into the sensor and the doors hiss open and she is surrounded by that smell of old books. Part sawdust, part seaweed, part human history. It's her favorite smell and momentarily she feels almost okay inside, like the darkness ebbs in her chest for a nanosecond.

The virtual librarian greets her with a perfunctory "How do you do?" The old-fashioned phrase usually brings her joy and she usually says, "I do quite well, thanks," but this time she just says, "Is there a book for teens about . . ." Then she glances around as if anyone might be listening and might judge her. It's almost entirely empty save for street neighbors, which is not surprising since most normal people with homes just consult the World Wide Bibliotech in the comfort of their own pod. But she doesn't like the WWB nearly as much as she loves this place with its old book smells and memories.

". . . online bullying and skinniness?"

The virtual assistant clears her throat.

"Not precisely," she says. She's one of the nicer virtual assistants; her tone is almost kind. "We have many, many books about online bullying. Would you be interested in online bullying and national origin? Online bullying and gender identity? Online bullying and class? These are the closest matches I can find at this time."

Enya sighs. Most feelings she has full training in. But being singled out for who she is? For not being able to keep meat on her bones? She was born this way. Her parents are both very thin, and she eats and eats and no weight stays. When she told her mother, all she got was a lecture about how in the days of old, she'd have been the one making fun of them for being large, and Enya was like, *What? Why would anyone even do that?*

No. All she wants is a book, maybe in verse, like those old Ellen Hopkins classics, where a person like her writes about how it feels to be singled out for their physical appearance. So she can feel that she's not the only one, because it actually hurts. It hurts a lot and no one seems to understand these feelings at all.

Surely someone, somewhere, has felt this before? Where is the book she needs?

Why hasn't it been written?

Ajax is transfixed by the image.

Their mom left the hologram up on the dining room tablet. It's a young person with Korean features and high cheekbones, and their eyes are deep, soulful. They are wearing retro clothing and something about them looks like they come from a different time.

Sometimes Ajax fantasizes that some other adult is their mother. Not that their mom is the worst, exactly, but they have the feeling sometimes that even if she'd never admit it, if their mother could choose, she'd prefer Ajax to be cis. And that's just not okay.

What would this person be like as a mom? It's a weird thing to think, but that's what Ajax ponders, staring into their eyes.

"Who is this?" Ajax asks when their mother comes through en route to the kitchen.

Their mother stops and purses her lips. "Oh," she says.

"Who, Mom?"

Britt sits down across from Ajax and offers them a patient smile. "That would be your aunt Tillie," she says.

It's a small service, and Mays Jagger is a little irked.

He barely knew the guy. He was a warrior brother, but he was older, and while he'd heard stories from that ancient dude Morris about how powerful a man this Michael Boroff was at one time, it wasn't like he was a friend, exactly. Just a handful of meetings where the guy hadn't said much.

And where was the dude's family? Here he was. Where were they? The guy was alive all these years. But the only people here are a few warrior brothers, most who barely knew him.

Nope. Not a relative in sight.

Mays leans over to Morris, who is sitting three seats away.

"This guy have family?" he asks, barely hiding his annoyance.

Morris's whisper comes with a gust of sour breath. Old people, right? "He really didn't," Morris says, and Mays plugs his nose casually, pretending it's a sniffle.

This ancient-sounding song plays. Like the kind of thing created on an early-twenty-first-century digital. And the singing is like a kid or something.

Mays shifts in his seat. He's not really paying attention.

The song is forgotten the moment it ends.

The boy and the girl straddle the rail one hundred and fifty feet apart on the upper deck of the George Washington Bridge. They stare at each other like they're playing a petrifying game of dare. Minutes go by.

The girl goes through a silent litany of goodbyes, and as she gets to her younger sister, she hears Britt's voice say, "You're silly, Tillie." It startles her, how real the voice sounds in her inner ear.

The boy imagines them both jumping simultaneously, and he imagines a peculiar and spectacularly morbid synchronized swimming routine they'd do in the depths of the Hudson. This strikes him as a particularly stupid final earthly thought.

The boy blinks first. He pulls back from his precarious perch, lifting his skinny leg back over the wall and climbing down. Once he's on firm ground again, he runs his hand through his hair and strides tentatively in her direction, the frantic wind slapping him across the face.

As he approaches, she sits up taller and turns her face away from him, toward the water.

Aaron asks, "Are you okay?"

A puff of air blurts from Tillie's lips before she can swallow it down. It's neither a laugh nor a scoff. More like pent-up incredulity.

"Um," she says, clenching the rail with all her might. Her left hand in front, her right hand behind.

In silence, they listen to the soundtrack of the bridge, the rumbling, perverse, concert-decibel-level row of motors, and tires on asphalt, and wind, and they smell the exhaust, and they see the gray-blue sky, hazy with pain, and they taste motor oil and despair.

She finally twists her face and torso back toward him. "Are *you* okay?"

Now it's his turn to expel a sound he doesn't expect or mean to share. It's a laugh. He looks down at his feet, and laughter escapes his lips like a fart he was trying to hold in, and then she laughs, too, and it's the most inappropriate laughter ever.

She sighs and dismounts, her heart beating too hard and fast for her body.

"So," she manages once she's caught her breath and is standing on solid ground, her eyes glued to the concrete walkway beneath her.

"So," he responds.

They stand there, and she leans momentarily against the fence before recoiling. Without a word, they move to the far side of the pedestrian path, as far from the railing as possible. The bridge shakes beneath their feet.

Neither of them knows what to do now.

"Tillie," she finally says.

He replies, "I'm Aaron, I guess."

Another pause.

Comedy improv comes to Aaron's mind. *Yes, and.* As if they're in a scene, and they both have to commit to everything the other person says by adding, "Yes, and . . ." which is super hard because all he really wants to do is deny reality. It's the hardest scene he's ever played, and the difficulty takes his breath away. Too real for his taste.

Tillie, too, is onstage in her mind. She pictures herself in the spotlight, doing a monologue about this very moment, and she comes up blank for words. Because this moment isn't right. There's not supposed to be an after. You jump and it's over, pain gone, nothing more to say.

"Yes, and," Aaron says, and Tillie is like, *What?* for about half a second. Then, with some dread, she recognizes exactly what he's saying from ninth-grade drama class. She thinks: *I'm maybe one person in a thousand who would understand what you're saying here. Someone else would probably just walk away, and you'd die. That's how lucky you are that I'm here, me.*

"You do improv," she says, monotone.

He shrugs. "Not well, apparently."

"I write and perform monologues. That people make fun of, by the way."

Now there's a look of recognition from Aaron. "Yes, and . . . I would like to see them."

She shakes her head. "No, but . . . you probably wouldn't if you were like any other person in the actual world."

He frowns. "The rules," he says.

She rolls her eyes. "Yes, and . . . whatever. Yes, and . . . I will perform them for you." She is lying. A moment ago she was in, but something about the artifice of this improv thing takes her out. This is her last performance. Once he leaves, she can do what she needs to do.

"I'd like to hear them," he says.

"Yes, and . . . you are not going to jump off this bridge. Because . . ."

Aaron looks up and away and his stomach twinges as he tries to come up with one good reason to stay.

"Donuts," he blurts out.

This is clearly not what the girl was expecting him to say.

"Donuts?" she echoes.

And here's the thing: Usually when he says something weird, it's for effect. To make people laugh. But right now, at this very moment, it's like his mind is pushing something out there, *anything* out there, so the conversation can continue. He wants to keep talking. Which means he doesn't want to jump. *Yes, and . . .*

She doesn't know it yet, but this random conversation about baked goods, by the sheer fact of its continuation, is going to escort them off this bridge.

He repeats it again, with more certainty. "Donuts." And then he explains, "Because we are going to eat three each at the closest donut place."

"Fine. Donuts," she says. "I just need to make a call first. Tell me where. I'll join you."

It's too easy. Aaron feels the void inside the loophole she's creating.

"No," he says.

"No?"

"No," Aaron insists. "We're going together. Now."

Tillie wants to scream at him—*Leave me alone! Can't you see I want to do this alone?* But instead what comes out is "You don't know me. You can't tell me what to do. I am so tired of letting other people dictate my life."

"I'm not dictating anything," the boy responds. "I'm just saying donuts. It's . . . an option."

She shakes her head. Why can't he realize she's out of options?

He goes on. "I think the minute I turn my back, you're jumping. Which makes sense because, if you'd turned your back a minute ago, I'd have jumped. I'd be—"

She swallows. He can't say the word. She doesn't want to hear the word.

But right now, it's the only word. It's behind every single other word.

"Am I wrong?" he asks. "About what you're going to do if I leave?"

She swallows again.

"So donuts," he says.

Tillie tries to find a way to say no to him. She is sure it's there, somewhere inside her. But it's hiding. Of all times for a no to fail.

Options. It's not the donuts that get her. It's the word *options*. She has a choice. Still standing and breathing in the afterburn of her strongest impulses, she asks herself if she really wants to drown in the Hudson. All because of other people's meanness. All because of people who aren't worth it.

"Donuts," she slowly repeats. "And fuck three. Six. This is serious."

He extends his hand and says, "You have yourself a deal."

It's so stupid—the whole world is so stupid—but Tillie shakes his hand. They have themselves a deal. The only terms being: not jumping, and eating donuts.

What a strange fucking deal.

Neither one of them is crying. Neither one of them is laughing. Together, they walk in silence toward Manhattan, the wind beating down on them like a vengeful god who has had enough of their bullshit.

×

The Dunkin' Donuts they go to is a block past Fort Washington Avenue on 181st Street, which is to say nowhere either of them has ever been before. It's hot inside, like the store's been running the heater for decades without stopping, and Aaron takes off his blue down jacket immediately. Tillie puts her peacoat over a chair and goes to the counter, where she orders coffee and six vanilla cream donuts.

"The same, I guess," Aaron says, hoping he has enough allowance left for that. He opens his wallet and spies a five. "Sorry, um, make it four. And a glass of water instead of coffee, please."

Soon they are stuffing their faces with powdered-sugar-coated donuts with a vanilla cream so sweet it hurts their teeth.

"So here we are," Aaron says.

"Yeah," she says, giving away nothing. "We are here."

He studies her without learning a thing. Then he ventures forward with "I'm taking it that we are not going to talk about the bridge?"

"That is correct."

"Instead we will . . ."

"Eat donuts."

It isn't until she's on her third donut and he's on his second that she breaks the uneasy silence that has enveloped their table.

"I just," she says. "I'm not sure what just happened, and I'm thinking that maybe if we just eat donuts for a while, I can go back to my life and try again."

This makes him laugh, and she shoots him a look. He quickly clarifies, "I'm laughing with you, I think. I mean, I'm all about that. Trying again even though I'm pretty sure this is like my hundred-and-thirty-first attempt at starting over."

"Yeah," she says, like she knows. Then she stares out the window like she's waiting for something better to come along.

And that makes him say, "Yeah," too.

"What do you think happens?" she asks, momentarily peering into his eyes.

He swallows. "I think about that all the time. Like, do you just cease to be?"

"God, that would be nice," she says, and something about the way she says it unleashes this thing in her and tears start to well up behind her eyes. She blinks them away.

"I know, right?" he says. "How many times have I wished to stop feeling things?"

"But," she says.

"Yeah. Forever."

"Yeah," she says. "My psychologist says it's a permanent solution to a temporary problem, but so far I haven't really seen as to how this problem"—and with this she points to herself and draws a big circle—"is temporary."

"I figure, like, if you're just gone, then you're just . . . gone," he says.

She snorts. "Deep."

He shrugs and blinks a few times, and she wonders if she's hurt his feelings.

"I mean," she says, "but what if you're not? Like what if your body dies but your soul or whatever stays alive and you just have to live in eternity without a body?"

He takes another bite. "Yeah," he says. "I've thought about that."

"And you still almost?"

He shrugs again. "Well, so did you."

It's surreal to Aaron to be having this conversation. How is he having this conversation? He's used to having it constantly in his head, but he's always supplied all the voices. But now here it is. Out loud. With another person supplying the responses.

It feels more real, like this.

And having it feel so real makes him realize how unreal his life felt.

Before.

That's real, too: The existence of a *before*.

Tillie whisks her chin with the side of her hand, knocking off a puff of powdered sugar. "I'm just really tired," she says.

Aaron surprises her by reaching over and squeezing her arm. It's the most personal thing anyone other than her mom has done with her in eons. Excluding Amir, of course, but he definitely doesn't count anymore.

"I so get that," he says.

She keeps her arm very still, though she wants to move it. She says, "Do you think we'll ever not be tired?"

He puts his forehead down on the table, which is pretty filthy, and he keeps it there for a bit. "God, I hope so," he says to the floor. "Because this is *not* working."

"Yeah," Tillie says. "I feel like I literally cannot take another minute of my life."

Aaron picks his head up from the table. "Ditto."

They sit for a while, chewing and sipping. Tillie wants to ask him why he went with just water, but she figures it's too random a thing to ask. Aaron wants to ask her why she's there, but he's afraid it's too not random a thing to ask.

Finally, Aaron realizes he's going to burst if he keeps silent. So he decides to say things about himself instead of asking things about her. It's safer that way. He says, "Sometimes I feel like my dad is perfect, or at least now he is, post midlife crisis. All day he deals with imperfect, fucked-up kids, and he shouldn't have to come home to that, too."

Tillie laughs and nods. "Right. With me, it's like, when I show how fucked up I am, I just confirm what my mom and dad know. And my mom's way of dealing is to micromanage my existence, and my dad's is to wash his hands of me completely."

"Wow," Aaron says.

Tillie shrugs. "There are kids without clean water. Not just in other countries, but here, in our country. And I'm sad because my dad doesn't love me hard enough. It doesn't really matter."

Aaron chews his cuticle. "Well, it matters a little, because you almost died."

Tillie stares down at the table in front of her. "Ouch."

"Yeah, well. Me too, so."

They both let that sink in for a moment, and the temperature in the room seems to dip some, which is good. Tillie pictures the bridge again, and she's hit with the fact that this attempted intervention isn't working. At some point they'll finish eating donuts, and nothing will have changed.

Aaron chews and ponders the bottom of the Hudson River.

They look up at the same moment and catch each other's eyes, and it's like they both realize in the same moment how unsafe this all is. Two suicidal strangers chewing fried dough in a hot and humid donut shop in the immediate aftermath of a near dual fatality. Aaron remembers one time last summer, being at an amusement park on a roller coaster with some kids from school; the barely interested ride attendant half checked Aaron's safety bar, and Aaron kind of knew it wasn't tight enough, and for half a moment he thought, *Don't say anything. It'll be quick and easy.* But then he called out and the guy came back and tightened it, glowering as if Aaron was annoying for asking for the thing he needed to stay alive.

Tillie sees the pain in Aaron's face, and she experiences a comparable feeling of hopelessness wafting through her chest.

"Jesus," she says.

"Jesus," echoes Aaron.

"Every instinct I have is broken. Nothing is even close to acceptable." A tear wants to escape from her left eye and she tenses to stop it. It works, and her face stays dry. "Fuck. I am so done with me."

The door swings open. A lost-looking girl maybe a couple years older than them in a tattered brown down jacket skulks up to the counter.

They can't hear what she says to the man there, but they sure can hear his response. "You go," he demands. "*Out.*"

"Please?" she says.

"You people never buy. Always take take take. Out, you."

"You people? How am I *people*? I'm a person. I've never done this before in my life."

"Out!" he yells.

She turns and skulks out of the store, her head down. The door slams behind her.

Tillie looks at Aaron. Aaron looks at Tillie. It's Tillie who stands first, steps up to the counter, and pulls out her wallet. "One coffee, please," she says.

Aaron follows and takes out his wallet. There's just the change from before, but it's enough. "And one donut, please. Cinnamon?"

He says it like a question. With him, it's always a question. But this question has an answer. A slight nod from Tillie, and suddenly they are both thinking the same stupid, infuriating thought.

Yes . . . and.

They step outside onto noisy, bustling 181st. The girl is standing to the side of the shop's entrance, toward the street corner. Her head is down, her hands are on her hips.

"Excuse me," Tillie says to the girl.

The girl doesn't move. Tillie taps her, and she jumps away defensively.

"What the fuck?" the girl asks.

Tillie hands her the coffee. "Here."

The girl doesn't take it at first. She eyes Tillie, and then Aaron, a bit suspiciously.

"You put any sugar in that? I don't eat that shit."

"No," Tillie says.

Aaron gently extends his bag to her. "Donut?"

She shakes her head. "Are you kidding me with this? You trying to kill a person?"

"Oh," says Aaron. "Okay. Sorry."

The girl shakes her head like she's disappointed with them. "Gotta stay away from that shit. That shit'll kill you."

She nods at them and walks up Fort Washington Avenue, and Tillie and Aaron are left on the street, not sure what's next.

They stand there for a moment, watching the girl walk north, and then, when she's out of view, they turn and start walking south. Neither knows where they're going.

Aaron is thinking that he'd really like to be home, sitting on his radiator, listening to his music, watching his fish swim around their aquarium. And yet there's a part of him that knows he can't do that. Because a couple hours ago, he chose to go up to the bridge, and nothing has changed since then, really. Which means that he's not safe being alone. And also he's not sure exactly when his dad will be home, but the thought of talking to Dad right now fills him with dread because he'll have to act like everything is fine, and everything isn't fine. He feels it inside him, like an actual physical presence.

Tillie is thinking that it's not enough. Donuts and coffee with someone random isn't enough. She half hopes he'll say, *Well, it was nice meeting you, I guess I'll see ya around*, so that she can go back to the bridge and finish what she started. And she's half petrified that he'll say that and she'll have to figure out how to not follow through. The pull is so, so strong, but there's this fierce, small part of her that doesn't want to die. Who knows she just . . . can't. Die. It would kill Britt.

They walk aimlessly down Fort Washington, retracing their steps from the bridge. As they traverse the underpass of the George Washington Bridge's bus station, a sense of utter doom closes in on Aaron. This. This is it. He tried, he failed. Time to exit mundi. He stops walking.

"So," he says.

Tillie looks at the ground and puts her hands in her coat pockets. "So."

"I guess . . ."

Tillie swallows. She's not sure what he guesses, but she knows it's the end. Of what, she isn't sure. Their acquaintance? The world? Are they both going to the bridge? Together? Will they take turns, go one at a time? Cold, cold water. She shivers. She's not at all ready for an ending.

They are interrupted.

"Have you heard the good news?" an older white woman with too-bright orangey lipstick asks them. She has a red-and-brown knit cap pulled down so low that she almost doesn't have eyes. She smells of too much perfume.

Tillie and Aaron look at each other and they break out laughing.

The woman flinches, a tentative smile disappearing from her face.

Aaron steps forward and stretches his arms down, hands open, as if he wants to catch something the woman is about to throw at him that will change his life.

"Tell me!" he says. "Please. I need some fucking good news."

The woman smiles politely. "Okay, now," she says, retreating. "No need to—"

"No, seriously," Aaron says. "This isn't a day for just good news. It has to be incredible. And yes, I mean fucking incredible, don't pardon my language. So lay it on me, lovely woman of good news. Tell me. Please."

The woman walks away, shaking her head.

Tillie looks at Aaron like he's a stranger. "Where did that come from?"

"I don't know. It just felt right in the moment. I really did want the good news, by the way. I wanted it to be all Jesus-y good news, and then I wanted to tell her I am an unrepentant gay boy and see her head explode."

Tillie laughs. "Okay," she says. "I get that."

"Feel like walking?" Aaron asks. "I suddenly feel like walking all the way downtown. Or downer-town. Where do you live?"

They start walking. "Upper East Side," Tillie says.

"I'm Upper West. Praise the fucking lord."

"You're a little weird, aren't you?"

"I'm a lot weird," Aaron says.

"Good. I'm weird, too."

"Amen to that. Let's be two weird people walking down through Washington Heights, speaking only of light things. I have no more heavy in me."

"Deal."

As they walk, Tillie thinks about how arbitrary life is. Not just with Aaron, but how she has no idea why she wound up on the Upper East Side of Manhattan in her life, like a sort of lottery winning that's a bit like the lottery in Shirley Jackson's short story, where the winner is stoned to death. Because surely she is lucky, and surely she has been stoned, emotionally, for so long now, and this neighborhood, these quiet, tree-lined streets, might well be more like where she belongs, but in reality she doesn't know where she belongs because she doesn't know where she's from. She knows she was born in Gyeongsangnam-do Province, but she doesn't know what that means, really, in terms of who her birth parents were, why they gave her up, any of that. And living a life where you don't know your starting point is just . . . Sometimes she just feels utterly without a base.

Aaron thinks about music. About how it would feel to perform at a talent show and NOT leave the stage and feel like maybe the people saying he did good are lying, maybe they're all laughing at him, and yet. The compulsion. He can't not. It's in his DNA, almost. This need to say certain things, do certain things. He hates it sometimes, and other times he loves it very, very much. It keeps him alive.

Fort Washington curves onto Broadway at 159th, and finally things look, if not specifically familiar, at least more like what Aaron thinks of as New York City. The green scaffolding, the discount shoe stores and bodegas with oranges and mangoes and tomatoes in cartons out front. Aaron asks Tillie about her favorite band, and Tillie says she likes everything, and Aaron says, "Oh." Tillie asks Aaron one thing he's looking forward to, and that one takes a while to answer.

"Hugging my dad, I guess," he says.

This hits Tillie so hard that she actually cannot speak. She walks and lets the cold evening wind keep her eyes bone-dry.

As they pass the entrance to Columbia University on 116th Street, Aaron says, "What's your favorite bacteria?" and Tillie, more because of the pent-up tension in her throat and less because this amuses her, cackles. Aaron smiles, grateful. Making people laugh. It's up there with masturbation, Froot Loops, and having people like his songs.

"I like good bacteria," she says.

"Ah, yes. But more specifically. What kind?"

"Um, the kind that come from probiotic yogurt?"

"Mmm, yes," he says. "Deliciously good bacteria."

By the time they're south of Ninety-Sixth Street, the streetlights are on. By the time they hit Seventy-Ninth Street, their feet are tired, and Tillie is extremely aware that this walk has probably saved her life, because she's now too exhausted to jump off a bridge.

Aaron, too. He's aware that all he wants to do now is sleep.

They stand, not looking at each other, in a quiet sort of comfort.

"So are you gonna be . . . ?" Aaron asks.

"I think so," Tillie says.

"Me too," Aaron says.

It's not like they've just got the magic cure for suicidal thoughts, and they both know that. But at least they're still here.

"So maybe we should text in the morning?" Aaron asks.

Tillie takes his phone and plugs in her number. "Yeah," she says.

"Thanks for, um . . ."

"Yeah," Tillie repeats.

They aren't looking at each other.

The *saving my life* is understood.

Aaron wakes up, and here's his old best-worst friend again, the empty bone crush. He knows he's supposed to get out of this bed and keep on doing what he's been doing, as if nothing's wrong. But he doesn't want to move, at all. There are thousands of decisions to make in a given day, and he feels as if he can't make a single one of them.

His dad's typical knock-pause-knock-knock-pause-knock-knock-knock rhythm takes Aaron out of his half slumber.

"How's Aaron?" Dad asks from behind the door.

Aaron can't do this one more time. *How does anyone do anything?* he wonders. But he knows he can't ask his dad, because that conversation would be unbearable. So instead he groans dramatically, because it's part of the routine.

"Aaron is vaguely okay," Aaron mutters. "Come in."

His dad opens the door, looking ready to take on the universe. He's wearing a beige polo shirt that is slightly too short for his growing paunch. It's all so sad, the human body. Someday Aaron's gonna look like that, and that's if things go well.

Aaron yawns and stretches. "You are aware, of course, that you have a head start? That by waking up earlier than me, you have time to get your brain and mouth working together, right? Because I have not had that luxury."

His dad scratches his head in a mocking way. "Well, gee. I wonder how you could get a better head start so you could match wits with your father?"

Aaron smirks. "I wish I could figure out where I get my sarcasm."

His dad bows, which is a total Aaron move.

Then he raises his eyebrows and asks, "Is there a withhold going on here, Aaron?"

Aaron laughs. He's a really good actor, and nonchalant, irreverent Aaron is one of his best characters.

It always throws his dad offtrack.

X

Tillie wakes up and looks around her very pink room and thinks about how it's way more pink than she wants it to be.

Sometimes Tillie is two different people. There's the real Tillie, the one in her brain, the one whose voice she hears. That Tillie's room should definitely be black. And there's the person who is, aside from when she's performing, always trying to be what everyone else wants her to be. Looking at her pink room, which has been mostly unchanged since prepuberty, she realizes this lack of update is how she tries to keep her exterior looking a certain way, in case her dad wants to come in some night and just hang out and talk like they used to do.

As she showers, as the water pelts her back, she thinks about how the times she gets really hurt are the times she lets her guard down. Like with Amir. Like how he let her in, lured her into dropping her guard. He danced the floss for her day they met. When a guy is willing to do that, it's like, yeah, Tillie's gonna open right up, too, and she did. She let him see the real her, the pink and the black, and she told him about what it feels like to be adopted, which is not something she shares. And he said, "I get it. It's maddening sometimes to be seen for one thing and yet to really be so many things."

YES. *That*, Tillie thinks, rinsing the soap off her legs. When people see her, she sometimes feels like they are reacting to her looks as if her looks ARE her. Which is so, so wrong. She'd never do that to someone, but people do it to her all the time like it's no big deal.

As she puts on her acne medication, she looks in the mirror.

I'm Tillie Stanley. Today's going to be different. I'm going to not worry if someone decides to confuse me with my labels. I'm going to let the whole thing with the video wash over me like it never happened. And I'm not going to think about my dad, because it's not worth it.

She stares at her reflection in the mirror, and she smiles ruefully.

Yeah, right.

×

Aaron sits next to Topher Flaherty on the subway. Topher goes on and on about some group called Rage, the Flower and a rave that was, apparently, lit, and as Aaron half listens, he is trying to remember whether Topher was on the email list he'd sent out two nights ago with "Walking Alone." Topher is kind of an on-the-bubble friend. They know a lot of the same people but have never hung out outside of school. Probably he wasn't on the list. Aaron doesn't want to have to wonder if Topher hated his song. It's not a very Rage, the Flower song. Probably. He has no idea.

He could ask, but no. He's learned his lesson. Asking too many questions on the subway yesterday got him up on a bridge. The hollowness in his gut is still there today, but it's a different shape. Because yesterday, walking not alone, helped. He felt just the slightest bit connected to something, and now instead of being able to park a motorcycle in his gut, maybe a small tricycle would fit better.

He thinks of Tillie. He hopes she feels the same slight improvement that he's feeling, that her yurt of emptiness has been reduced to a single-person tent, perhaps, and that weird analogy makes him laugh.

"What, dude?" Topher asks.

"It wouldn't translate," Aaron says.

"You okay?"

Aaron says yeah. "Just thinking of something."

"Cool," Topher says, because he doesn't care. No one really cares.

Sarah, who sat down next to him when she got on at Eighty-Sixth, asks him about Spanish homework, which he has not done.

"No hice nada," he says.

"And how, exactly, does that help me?" she asks.

"In no way that I can explain at this juncture."

"Maybe Ms. Higuera won't check?"

"Maybe. As long as she's wearing something floral, I'm cool with it."

Sarah laughs. "I'm guessing yes."

"Oh good," says Aaron. "I may fail out of school, but at least I'll get to see another lovely floral pattern on Ms. Higuera."

X

Walking to homeroom, he quickly scans for an *Avenue Q* cast list. Nothing yet. There is, however, a sign-up sheet for the talent show two weeks from Saturday. He grunts. These people can't even be bothered to listen to one song—

He stops himself. *That doesn't mean they didn't like it. It means they didn't hear it.*

He stares at the Sharpie hanging from a string off the bottom of the sign-up sheet, and he has this delicious fantasy about singing "Walking Alone" in front of the whole school, and the applause, applause, and how, after, kids will congratulate him and see him in a different light. And Evan Hanson. He'll come up after everyone else is gone, and he'll have a special gift for Aaron, who is such a talented singer-songwriter and deserving of extremely special gifts.

Aaron smiles dopily and adds his name to the bottom of the list.

×

Winnie pops a couple slices of twelve-grain bread in the toaster and goes looking for the Fage yogurt. She doesn't say good morning. She doesn't say anything. A pit forms in Tillie's stomach. It always does when they fight. It's like a part of her, a part she needs in order to breathe, is gone, and at the same time, she was the one who sent it away.

It happened when she got home last night.

"Where have you been?" her mom asked. She was sitting on the couch in the living room, and Tillie could see the anger and fear in her creased forehead.

"Out," Tillie said, and she knew it wasn't the right answer. She knew she needed to have a story, and not be evasive, because evasive never works with her mom.

"Tillie. It's eight fifteen. Where have you been?"

Tillie glances around, hoping against hope that her dad is concerned, too. He is nowhere to be found. Probably in his fucking man cave.

"I . . . took a walk, okay?"

"You took a *four-hour* walk."

"I had some thinking to do."

"Till. Are you okay? I'm worried about you."

The truth was caught in her throat. It was the kind of thing she'd normally tell her mom, who knows she's struggling, who knows about Amir, mostly, and knows about the video, and knows some streamlined version of what happened with her and Dad. But something warned her: *danger.* This was the kind of story that would make her mom take over, and she just couldn't right now.

So Tillie said, "Mind your business."

The moment it was out of her mouth, she knew she'd fucked up. She felt like covering her mouth with her hands. Instead, she stayed very still.

"Did you just—?"

"Mom. Please. I'm fine, okay. I'm sorry. I just need some space, okay?"

In response, her mom had stormed out of the living room, and apparently it's no better this morning.

There have been times Tillie's walked over and hugged her mom after a squabble, even though she was feeling not so huggy. But she can't take her mom along on this one.

Britt skips into the kitchen, sneaks up on the back of Tillie's chair, and gives the chair and its occupant a big squeeze. Her arms barely reach Tillie's biceps.

Britt yells, "Tandoori chicken at lunch today! And I'm gonna try the mulligatawny this time."

Tillie suppresses a smile. "Cool," she says.

"Cool," repeats Britt, who then goes and hugs Winnie, and for

Tillie, it's like they've hugged by perky conduit, and that feels a slight bit better.

×

Creative writing turns into a shit show for Aaron. It starts out nice enough, with Ms. Hooper complimenting him on "Walking Alone," to which Aaron replies that he knows it's pretty bad, which the Google-to-Aaron dictionary translates as *Please say more nice things!* But then, because it's his day, he winds up reading this story he has on his computer because he hasn't written anything new. It doesn't go well. And Aaron is like, *I should have just jumped yesterday. I'm a bad person and don't deserve to be alive.*

At lunch he sits alone, his rib crush pushing out on him, feeling like it could explode his whole midsection. Then Kwan comes to sit with him, and short of running out of school and never coming back, he realizes he's stuck in a situation his body and brain can't really deal with today.

Ratiya and Ebony and Josh join them, and he winds up saying sorry about sixty-seven times, and when they leave the table, he thinks it is possible that he's never felt less worthy as a person ever, in his entire life.

×

It's hard for Aaron to pay attention in physics, and the difference between centripetal and centrifugal goes right through him, and he realizes that despite his adventure yesterday, he's not significantly different, or better. Things don't improve. They never do, and he's trying to listen to Dr. Sengupta as he prattles on and on about how centrifugal force results from inertia and how centripetal is a *true* force, whatever that means. And he thinks about how his life is actually inertia, like it's his natural state, his true force, and it will always be, and that's hard for him to take, actually, this idea that nothing moves, nothing changes, and it never, ever will, and a chill forms in his gut and freezes him solid into his chair.

When the bell rings, the funniest thing happens.

He doesn't move. He can't.

Aaron stares at a crack in the upper-left quadrant of the whiteboard, one that almost reaches the top-left corner but not quite, and Aaron tries to move it with his mind so that it's not so imperfect and random.

"Aaron?" Dr. Sengupta says from the front of the classroom. It might be empty, it might be emptying. Aaron doesn't know. He can't move his head.

Hmm, he thinks. *This is new. This is interesting.* It's petrifying because he literally cannot move and if he had feelings left he would feel so very deeply scared.

"Aaron?" Dr. Sengupta repeats, and it's as if Aaron is watching a movie about a boy whose life is falling away. What the soundtrack is saying is that this is that pivotal point in the story, the point after which the die is cast and there's no going back. This shakes whatever part of him is still sentient, and it snaps him to attention.

"Yes," he says.

"Are you okay, Aaron?"

"Fine," he says. "Yes. I'm fine."

He gets up and walks toward math class thinking, *Well, this isn't great.* This thing where he couldn't actually move. Was he just being dramatic? Could he have moved if he'd really tried? In the end he was able to, but it felt like it took everything he had. He remembers how he stared at the wall the night before he went to the bridge, like something had taken over his body—was this the same thing? This is the kind of thing he's supposed to share with his father, who is just the kind of father with whom one could share such a thing. But he's an idiot loser and that's not going to happen.

Before he walks into his Spanish class, he texts Tillie.

> You ever have a thing where you stop being able to move?

The response comes fast.

> Um. No. You ok?

> You tell me. Because I basically stopped being able to move.

> What are you talking about?

> Never mind

> No. Seriously. What are you talking about?

> I was in physics and when class was dismissed I was basically . . .

> I just sat there. Couldn't move.

> Jesus. You think you're depressed?

> I don't know. I just think I'm fucked up and sad.

> Yeah that's called depressed. Wanna meet?

> Like leave school? You would do that for me?

> And leave the place where everyone hates me? Yeah

> Donut place?

Lol absolutely not. A place where we are not near a bridge.

So the lowest point in the city

Lol you are really weird

Thanks. That's what I needed to hear right now.

I mean that in a good way. Ok. What's the lowest point in the city?

Aaron is numb, but not too numb for research. So he looks it up.

The Atlantic Ocean. Wherever the ocean meets land.

So the beach?

I guess.

Meet at Coney Island?

Now? Are we really leaving school to go to Coney Island?

Do you have a better idea?

He doesn't.

×

Aaron meets Tillie outside Nathan's Famous on Surf Avenue. He feels like a pain in the ass as he waves tentatively, and she meekly waves back, looking like someone on the worst blind date ever.

"I'm sensing a pattern?" he says lamely, pointing at the sign.

"What pattern?"

"Fatty foods?"

She fixes him with that blank, unreadable look. She says, "Ha."

The cold response weakens the layer that's currently swaddling the bone-crush-best-worst-friend thing in his gut. Aaron stares at his feet and makes up a story.

She must be thinking: How long till I can drop this idiot? I have no patience for this weird guy. I only came here because he's so pathetic and he's gonna kill himself and I can't have that on my conscience. And can you believe he actually made me travel an hour just because of some stupid joke about the lowest point in New York City? Get me the fuck out of here. This guy is so not worth my time.

X

Tillie's throat feels so tight, like if she opens her mouth, she might scream. Somewhere along the way on the Q train, Tillie pictured Amir, and he got stuck in her head. Even though Aaron told her he's gay and Amir is . . . Amir, she cannot understand what in the world made her open up even a little yesterday. Last time she did this, it didn't go well, and when Aaron makes some infuriating comment about fatty foods that hits way too close to her inner cow, she's out.

But then she remembers yesterday. The way they seemed to understand each other without judgment. Her heart tenderizes just a smidge.

She rolls her eyes and leads him into Nathan's as she says, "Yes . . ."

He breaks into a relieved smile and says, ". . . and."

They get to the counter and examine their options. Aaron looks disappointed when the order arrives.

"So these are actually just hot dogs," he says once they settle in.

Tillie looks at their hot dogs and wonders what else they'd be. "Um. What?" she asks.

"Nathan's Famous hot dogs. They make them sound like they're special, but I'm pretty sure they're just intestines like any other hot dog."

"So, *moving on*."

He laughs. "I'm just saying. I hate things like that. That seem special but aren't."

They eat in silence for a while, and then she says, "Like people."

"Like people?"

"People who seem special, but they aren't."

"Yes," he says, not at all sure what she means but sure it means something.

"Yes."

After lunch, they walk the boardwalk in silence. Aaron wants to ask why she came. Would he have done this for her?

He'd like to think he would have, but it's hard to say, really. A girl he just met yesterday writes him while he's in Spanish class and says, *Hey, I need you. Meet me in Brooklyn?* Hard to say what he does. And yet he gets it. The inscrutable bond of the bridge. Makes you do screwy things.

"So remember yesterday, when we said maybe let's not talk about it?" Aaron says.

"Yeah?"

"Let's maybe instead . . . talk about things? Because I meant it earlier. I couldn't move. In physics class. There was this part of me that was looking down at myself and I feel like if I didn't move the moment I did, I would have been paralyzed. Which is pretty much freaking me out. And the truth is . . ."

He stops walking. She stops, too.

He drops his head and starts weeping. Full-on weeping.

Tillie feels stuck, watching him cry. She hates this about herself. This obvious contradiction, that she's a feminist and so completely against the idea that men have to be strong at all costs but in reality she doesn't want to see a boy or man cry unless a piano just fell on him. But she can feel the pain in his face.

It's just them. On the boardwalk. Other people who may or may not be walking by cease to exist. Aaron weeps. Tillie watches. And finally she just says "Shit" under her breath, and reaches out, grabs his arm, and pulls him to a nearby bench, one that faces the surf and the empty beach, empty except the gulls haplessly seeking hot dog buns and spilled liquid from the abandoned soda cans on the sand.

They sit and he weeps in near silence, and she sits there and looks out at the ocean, wondering about the connection between this water, the Atlantic, and that water, the Hudson, where she almost landed yesterday. The thought shivers her.

"Sorry," Aaron says. He dries his eyes, looks out at the water. "I'm at land's end."

"Yep. We are."

"So, um, if you want to go. If you just—don't want to be here. With a loser idiot who cries to strangers, who is so pathetic—"

"Oh my god. Stop," she says. "You're not. Or if you are, so am I. I want to be here, okay?"

"Sorry," he says again, and she sighs, and he laughs.

"You *are* sorry."

He laughs some more, and the laugh turns into a convulsion, which turns into more tears.

"Yes!" he finally says. "I'm deeply, deeply sorry. My whole life. I'm the problem here."

A woman in a sanitation outfit leans down to scoop some of the hot dog bun detritus into her black garbage bag. A couple gulls flap their wings powerlessly.

"The gull lobby is not going to be pleased with these sanitation people stealing their food," Aaron says.

"The gull lobby?"

"You know. Big Bird."

Tillie smiles. Even depressed, this is a silly boy. She thinks of Britt. Who is also silly. But unlike Aaron, Britt has never felt the need to apologize for her existence. And while Tillie loves that little sister of hers, at a moment like this, watching a boy who can't stop saying sorry, and being a person whose apology is unspoken but nevertheless eternally internalized, she is also really, profoundly jealous of her self-assurance.

Aaron takes a breath and explains his existence to the ocean:

"Sometimes I honestly can't even explain what it is. It's just this thing. This feeling in the pit of my stomach. It's disappointment with myself. That I'm not better. That I'm not someone people like more, or someone who's more talented, or better loved, or worthy of the attention I seem to need just to survive. To be more like my fish, but the human version."

"More like human fish?"

He rubs his forehead. "I love my fish. I have a sixty-gallon tank and—currently—seven goldfish. There's Britney Spearfish, Tina Tuna—"

"Oh my god," she says, and she rolls her eyes, and her face heats up a bit.

He cracks a smile. "You're going to leave now, aren't you?"

She stands up like she's about to walk away, then sits down again.

"So anyway . . . they just—swim around all the time. You know when you look at something and you know there's no sadness there? That's my fish. There's a nobility to being a fish, I think."

"Fish nobility."

"They aren't swimming around in a circle thinking, *Oh, kill me. This is so boring.* Which is exactly what I'd be thinking. That's the connection, I think."

She crosses her legs and leans back on the bench. "You know what? I actually really get that."

"You do?"

"I do."

"Ugh," he says. "It's hard because the problem is me. Obviously."

Tillie scratches her forehead in a way she hopes translates as *Yes, I, too, am the problem* without her having to say it.

Aaron goes on. "I have no real problems. My dad has enough money to survive, even after quitting his bank job and becoming a social worker during his midlife crisis. I have a scholarship to Fieldston. I don't get bullied, and, I don't know. It's like I know I should be happy, but nothing gets through."

She does something that surprises her then. She touches his knee lightly with her fingertips. Then she removes her hands and averts her eyes, embarrassed. She shouldn't have touched him. She hates when people touch her without her permission. But yeah. It just sort of felt like it was a moment that she needed to make contact a little.

"What about the gay thing?" she asks.

"Huh? What about it?"

"Is that a problem in your life? I mean, is it an issue?"

He shrugs. "Maybe for other people. I mean, at Fieldston it's pretty much a nonissue. The guys who would disagree with it or whatever? I don't like them, either. They leave me alone because they know if they didn't, they'd get in trouble. So I feel safe. At home, I have my dad, who is the gayest straight guy I've ever met. He goes and sits with other men and they work on themselves, I guess, and it makes him—well, it's made him better, to be honest."

"I should get my dad to do that," Tillie says ruefully.

Aaron hears it and knows intrinsically that there's a story there. He looks her in the eye, and she looks away.

Instead of trying to fill the silence, Aaron waits.

Eventually, Tillie asks, "So . . . what are we gonna do?"

Aaron hears the *we*. He likes it. It's been a long time, or maybe since never, that another person other than his dad has referred to him as part of a *we*. He looks up at the sky. "I have no idea."

"What have you been doing? Because whatever that is, it isn't working. Maybe do the opposite?"

"Solid advice." Aaron rubs his eyes.

"I'm super good at fixing other people—just not so good at fixing myself."

"Yeah. I'm kinda like that, too."

Tillie crosses her legs. "So—and I say this because I know it's a super-healthy idea, and most psychologists would suggest it—how about I fix you, and you fix me?"

"Ha. Totally. We'll fix each other. That's not codependent *at all*."

He expects her to laugh along, or say something equally sarcastic. But instead she looks him right in the eye and says, "So, you know you're depressed, right?"

He turns to stare out at the ocean. The blue-green rising and falling, the mist kicking off the waves. It's so beautiful, and it's like he can't access the beauty. He can't feel it, internalize it. It's part of a scene and he's not in it. And something about that makes him not do what he would normally do, which is to explain the intricate difference between depression and his thing. Because he's different. He's not a statistic or a case. He's Aaron, and no textbook can quite explain Aaron's thing, and definitely not in one word.

Instead of saying that, he sighs and says, "I don't know. Maybe. Sorry."

Tillie slumps back on the bench. "So what's the opposite of what you've been doing?"

"I don't know. I go to school, I go home. I write songs and no one listens to them. I lie to my dad. Well, more like, I don't tell him what's up."

"So the opposite for you would be to not go to school, not go home, not write songs, or maybe have people listen to your songs. And telling your dad what's up."

"Yeah, well, the last isn't gonna happen. So maybe not going to school? Instead I—"

"*We,*" she interrupts. "Have adventures. Go explore life. Starting tomorrow. How do you feel out here?"

He thinks about it, staring at the sky. "Not terrible, I guess. I don't feel like I'm about to be paralyzed in one position, so that's something. I mean, it's kind of cool talking like this. I never, ever, ever talk like this with anyone."

"Sometimes I do with my mom, but I feel like—maybe I should grow the fuck up and talk like this with a friend and not my mom?"

"So. Talk. What about you? Are you depressed?"

Tillie bites her lip and chews on it a bit. "Well, yeah. I mean, non-depressed people don't almost jump off bridges, do they? But it's like, there are reasons. I feel like shit because—never mind."

"What?" he says.

"You don't need this, on top of all that." She motions circularly at his body.

"I kinda do, actually. I'd love a vacation from my own shit right about now."

She looks out at the ocean and thinks: *Am I doing this?*

And then she realizes: *No. Not yet.* She smiles, looks down, and shakes her head.

"It's funny," she says. "In art I can say things. But in life? I tend to keep my room pretty pink."

"I am guessing that means something to you. Maybe you could let me in on it?"

She kicks the ground and says, "Next time, definitely."

On Friday morning, Tillie finds herself thinking that compromise is a dangerous, ill-advised concept. She thinks this as she climbs a steep, narrow, circular staircase, eyes averted as much as possible from the random elderly butt right in front of her face, tugging her tuba case behind her.

On the train home last night, she and Aaron came up with a plan of how to do the opposite of what they've been doing with their lives. The specifics were hammered out via text around midnight.

> So remind me again, Tillie, how being suspended from school two months before the end of 11th grade is a good idea?

> Fine. Go to school. That seemed to work out really well for you yesterday

> I'm scared, okay? This is not what I do

> Which is why we have to do it. Sometimes you just have to say what the fuck

> Isn't that from a bad 90s movie?

> Maybe. Doesn't make it wrong. I honestly don't think I can take another day at Spence. I almost don't care at this point. If I don't move on to senior year. Don't care even a little.

> So what are we doing instead?

The answer is compromise, in a way. Or perhaps it's just proof of their insanity, because the specifics that came up when they decided to simultaneously have Aaron text the activity, and Tillie text the place they'd do it, don't make a ton of sense.

Which is why she's lugging her tuba to the top of the upper tower at Belvedere Castle in the middle of Central Park on a Friday morning. When she emerges into the open air of the observation deck, there's Aaron, who is cradling his laptop like it's a football.

"Hey," he says, smiling brightly.

She scowls at his brightness. He didn't just haul a cumbersome tuba case up a steep, narrow, winding staircase. She lays the instrument at her feet and wipes sweat off her forehead. "Let's just do this," she says.

He raises an eyebrow. "That's not—no. The whole purpose of this is to be happy."

She wants to kick him. Or something. This is what guys do. They fundamentally misread her moods and say exactly the wrong thing. Of course girls are terrible, too. Why is everyone terrible?

This last thought makes her crack a smile.

"What?" Aaron says, smiling back.

"Hard to explain," she says. "I'm busy having thoughts that ignore my own innate awfulness."

Aaron shrugs, unsure what to do with that comment. While she opens her massive case and takes out her tuba, he opens his laptop and perches it on the edge of the northern deck, overlooking the empty softball fields of the Great Lawn. He tinkers with windows until he finds Guitar Pro, where "The Palm of Your Beautiful Hand" is waiting.

No way is he going to do "Walking Alone" again. Too soon.

"Palm" is a safe bet. He performed that at the talent show last year, and some kids he didn't even know came up and said they really liked it, that it had this cool retro vibe.

Aaron watches as Tillie puts the mouthpiece in the receiver. "So I don't exactly know how to do a duet with a tuba," he says, "but seeing as you can actually play your instrument—"

"I'm really not good," she says.

"Seeing as you couldn't be less proficient at the tuba than I am at the—whatever—I'm thinking I should probably just play you this song I wrote and maybe you can figure out how to harmonize?"

She uses her throat to blow a whisper breath and hits a placid, funereal F as a response.

He laughs.

"What?" she asks.

He shakes his head. There's something hilarious about the noise that just came out of that instrument, which is nearly as big as Tillie, but he's pretty sure nothing good can come from saying that. "No," he tells her. "It's good."

She cocks her head to the side. "Yeah, sure."

"So can I play you the song?" he asks, a little too willingly.

She nods, her face blank. He pauses for a second, looking at her as if trying to figure out if it's safe. Then he presses play. He closes his eyes in concentration, his head down.

Tillie listens carefully to the intro. What she hears is a guy who plays chords on the keyboard as opposed to notes, and she's not sure if he does that because he wants to or because it's the limit of his ability. Her gut instinct is the latter. It sounds as if he's doing what he can, and when the drumbeat comes in, she is relieved.

Then he raises his head and sings, and it surprises her that he's singing, live.

We sit across from each other and stare
And look right through each other
We're searching for something far too deep
The price of which is much too steep

The lyrics are kind of cerebral. His voice is: It's hard to explain. It's not pleasant or unpleasant. What she hears is someone who can carry a tune, but what his voice doesn't have is inflection. It's like the lyrics and the singing of them don't connect. Instead of feeling the song, what she senses is that he really, really wants people to like it. Or him. Or both. And recognizing that makes her like him more, because she knows that feeling, that wish to be seen and loved, and she gets in a nanosecond that he probably hasn't gotten that sort of response much, because, let's face it, it's not a great song, not by any means. It's . . . okay. Its heart is on its sleeve, which is lovely, but the words are not inspired and in general there's an old-school feel to it. He sings a verse where he actually says something about having "the butterflies" and it reminds her of bad theater. Its sincerity also makes her kind of love Aaron.

Can I fake you out
With a fake moral stand?
Or do you know me
Like the palm of your beautiful hand?

That's the chorus, she guesses, and he stops singing and he looks at the ground as if he's having a moment, but the thing is, he isn't. It's an approximation of a moment. It's like he wants her to think he means it, but she doesn't believe he's ever had such a moment with a guy. She's sure of it, actually. It's not a real moment at all, and she wants to reach out and tell him it's okay.

×

When the music fades, she claps enthusiastically. An elderly couple, the only other people on the deck, clap as well. She goes to him and for the first time she hugs him. She feels his body melt a little into hers.

"Oh my god," she says. "That was so . . . real."

"Real," he repeats into her shoulder.

"Well, yeah. Like real to life. Relatable."

"It needs work," he says.

"No. I mean, I don't know. You can work on anything and make it better. But . . . thanks, Aaron. Thanks for sharing that with me. I—loved it."

And she's not lying, exactly. She loved something. If not the song, what she loved was him putting himself out there. This is a boy who has no defenses, and yeah, the last boy who took his defenses down messed her up, but this is a different boy, and there's something about that that makes her glad she's standing on the top of Belvedere Castle on a Friday morning with him.

×

While Tillie hugs Aaron after he sings his song, he goes over every single moment of the performance. Did he go flat when he sang the *You watch as I write* line? Sometimes he does that. Did the feeling come through in the refrain? He's not thinking about a specific person when he sings it. More a general idea of a potential connection.

That moment when you hope someone gets you, hope someone hears your song and sees inside your soul, but they might only have an idea of you, and it might not even be correct. Kind of like this moment right now.

Does Tillie really get it? The hug feels like she does. The word *real* that she used to describe it, too. But she didn't say anything about his voice. Did she like it? Does he have what it takes to be a singer, professionally?

He needs to have it. Because without it, he has nothing.

×

It turns out the tuba is superfluous to the visit to Central Park, as Aaron's and Tillie's musical skills are not a match. Aaron shows himself to have just enough ability on Guitar Pro to be dangerous, just well versed enough to create songs using keyboard, drums, and vocals. Tillie has a loose sense of harmony, but she tends to find the harmonies moments or two after the notes have come and gone.

So they walk to Tillie's place and leave her tuba in the lobby— she's supposed to be at school, so a drop-off is all she can get away with—and then they head south on Lexington Avenue, unsure of what is next but knowing they have to keep going with whatever it is they're doing. A new way of living, kind of.

As they walk, Aaron talks about his dreams of being a musician.

"I think the vibe is kind of Ed Sheeran meets Julien Baker?"

"Yeah?"

"Or like Rufus Wainwright, if you've heard of him? Like it's all about the lyrics and the feelings, and I'm not going to, I don't know. Dumb it down."

"Sure," she says.

"Maybe in college I'll study composition? Or at least singing. I took some singing lessons but that was a couple years ago. I think I kind of figured out singing on my own. I know I'm not like Sam Smith or something. But people like Bob Dylan, too."

"Right."

"I think what people really want is what you said about real, anyway."

Tillie doesn't say anything now, though she has two things that she really feels like she ought to say. One is that real is good, and she tries to deliver the real, too. But the thing about real is that people are cruel. And when you're really real, and people critique that real, it cuts too deep. The other is that real is best when combined with craft, and what would be really good is if he put in the time to get more than just "dangerous on Guitar Pro." Because what she loved about the song wasn't the craft but the vulnerability, but she's special, she's different, she gets it. The world will eat Aaron alive. But she can't say that, because who says to a boy they met on a bridge, a boy who almost jumped two days earlier, "I need to be honest. That song is sweet but needs work." No.

They subway down to Grand Central on the 6 line. It's mid-morning and the train is half-full, and when it stops at Fifty-First Street, the door opens and there, standing like a passenger reading a newspaper and waiting for the express, is not a person but a rat.

"Do you ever just want to get out of New York?" Aaron asks once the doors close without the rat boarding. "Like run off to somewhere warm and pretty and clean and never look back?"

"Not really," Tillie says.

The train squeaks as it goes around a bend, like it needs some oil and hasn't been tended to in a century. Aaron grabs the bar that a million other people have probably touched—in the last week. "Yeah, me neither," he says.

They take the 7 train west and wind up on the High Line—Aaron's idea—sitting and doing nothing, which is Tillie's, because she's tired and it's already been a lot.

✕

They enter on Thirty-Third and wander south along the narrow paths of the former elevated rail line that is now a gorgeous public park, a narrow greenway with paths featuring pristine gardens and eclectic artwork.

Aaron is about to ask where they ought to sit when a balding guy with a big gut wearing an Empire State Building T-shirt says, "Would you mind?" He sticks out his phone. Aaron takes it and happily obliges by taking a few snaps with the Hudson River as the backdrop.

They wander past an enclosed amphitheater of gray wooden steps and seats and a small enclosed garden of purple flowers that remind Tillie of little lavender Christmas trees. Aaron spots a bench facing the water and as he turns to ask Tillie if that would work, he nearly runs into two women trying to maneuver a selfie stick.

"Most sorry," one of them says. She has an accent, maybe Russian.

Tillie motions awkwardly in a way that she hopes indicates that she'd be willing to divest them of their gadget and take a picture for them, and they look confused until she pulls out her phone and pantomimes taking a photo. This brings smiles and nods, and soon Tillie is snapping shots of them from various angles.

"Does anyone from New York actually come here?" Aaron asks,

just as a middle-aged Chinese woman taps Tillie on the shoulder, smiles, and hands her a camera.

"Unclear," Tillie says before obliging the woman.

Once they've fulfilled their duties as emissaries for their city, Tillie lies fully down on the closest bench and stares up at the blue sky. Aaron lies down the other direction, with the top of his head inches from hers. The two of them fill one bench just about perfectly.

"You know, I actually don't feel that depressed right now," Aaron says.

"Me neither."

"So maybe there's a lesson there?"

"Sure," Tillie says. "Next time I'm about to jump off a bridge, I'll make sure to take a photo of a tourist."

"Yes, that's exactly what I meant," Aaron says.

They catch their breath and study the sky for a few minutes.

"So," Aaron says. "It's another time."

"Huh?"

"You said yesterday you'd tell me what's up with you another time."

"Ugh. I'd rather not."

"Really?"

Tillie thinks about this for a bit. She scratches her scalp, the backs of her fingers grazing Aaron's forearm along the way. She thinks: *No. Not really. I kind of do want to talk about it.* And she feels still short of breath but now also jittery in her throat. *This is a dangerous place to be. If he leaves, if he ends up ghosting me, I might not be able to take it.*

She sits up, and so does he. She tentatively starts to tell him about Amir, and as she does, she feels his energy to her right, and occasionally she glances over and she watches him take it in, and she watches his face change, his expression. He gets it, he totally gets it. And watching him understand what it's like to be that open and have a boy just disappear on you emboldens her, and she starts telling him more details, which is very not her. Like how alone in this world she feels, and how Amir seemed to get that and it gave her just a tiny bit of hope, and then it was pulled away. Suddenly she's sharing her innermost secrets and feelings with this still near stranger, and she feels the tears there, on the insides of her eyelids, but she won't let them fall, no, she won't, and she tenses her chin and talks about the video, and what it feels like to have a skinny girl put a pillow under her shirt to imitate you and call you a cow, and have other girls laughing in the video, and then all the online comments about how hysterical it is, and watching him get it makes her relive it a little, and damn it, the first tear breaks out, from the outside of her right eye, and she wants to push it back in but she can't, and once the first one is out, others come, and she realizes where all that moisture came from inside him yesterday, because she's crying more tears than she knew she had. He reaches out to touch her shoulder, and she flinches away. He puts his arm back, away from her, and she tells him more about Amir, about Molly. Not her dad, though. It's like when she gets close to there, she's just so exhausted that she can't.

Aaron finds himself crying because she's crying, and he wonders if this is the first time strangers have ever cried together on this particular bench along the High Line. Probably not. It just intrinsically feels like the place this happens sometimes.

When she's done telling him all that she's going to tell him, they sit in silence for a while, which feels right. Tillie then turns and looks into Aaron's eyes and says something that surprises him. And her, a little, too.

"So not to be too whatever, but if you ghost me after this, I will either come and kill you, or I will kill myself and haunt your dreams forever. No joke. Do you get that?"

He's like, *Whoa*. And also like, *Yep. Got it.* He nods.

"Just saying," she says.

"Just hearing" is his response.

×

Tillie angles for a lunch of savory crepes at La Bergamote on Ninth Avenue and Twenty-First Street. Aaron doesn't want her pity and is about to make up an excuse involving an aversion to French foods when Tillie saves him.

"It's on me," she says.

The feeling is relief and shame, balled into one. Aaron hates being a charity case in general, but the way Tillie is so breezy about things with money puts him at ease.

"Thanks," he says, deciding later he'll take her for hot dogs at Papaya King, which is more his speed and budget.

After, Tillie and Aaron wander down Ninth Avenue, with its odd combination of old tenements and posh eateries, and then Hudson Street, where the efficient grid of Manhattan breaks down into the chaos of Greenwich Village and its cobblestoned, catawampus lanes barely wide enough for one-way car traffic. Sometimes Aaron takes the subway down to the Village and aimlessly wanders these small, tree-lined backstreets and alleys, imagining himself as a famous singer living in one of those multimillion-dollar brownstones. This time, he's thinking about Tillie's story, and how, when she told him what was up in her life, he felt his heart break a bit. He gets that he doesn't really know how it would be to feel so alone in your own house. To fall for a guy and then have him ghost you when you're at your most open and vulnerable. If somebody at school made a video lampooning him and everyone watched it— okay, that humiliation *is* something he gets completely.

×

When the school day is over, they descend into the subway station at West Fourth, where the plan is for Tillie to take the E to the Upper East Side, while Aaron will take the C up to Central Park West. As it gets closer to the time to say goodbye, Tillie feels this twinge of sorrow enter her chest. As they stand on the platform, they hear a thunderous cacophony down the track, a booming, reverberating melody that sounds like it's coming from a grand piano. Which it cannot be, Tillie realizes, as it would be nearly impossible to get a grand piano down into the subway.

But lo and behold, that's exactly what it is. They approach and see a young Black guy playing what sounds like a Bach concerto, and the melody hits her in the heart, and she looks over and sees that Aaron, too, seems moved by the odd juxtaposition of classical music and subway station, and they are not alone. A crowd of disparate New Yorkers has gathered to watch and listen, and Aaron and Tillie look at each other and smile. Aaron loops his arm through Tillie's and they lock elbows, and in that moment their friendship is solidified. They both know, Tillie can tell that this is a story they will share forever, and that forever might actually last more than a couple more days. Somehow their connection has lengthened forever for both of them.

The crowd bursts into applause as the pianist finishes the concerto, and trains come and go, and somehow Aaron and Tillie don't board any uptown trains. They are content to hear more music. And then Tillie watches Aaron fiddle around in his pocket, and she's glad because he's going to give the guy a tip, which he deserves, not only for the playing but for the effort of bringing an actual grand piano into the subway station.

Aaron approaches and kneels down to murmur something to the pianist, who is preparing to start his next song. The guy says something back, raising an eyebrow, and a conversation ensues, and Tillie gets this uncomfortable feeling in her gut, and her instinct is to go and pull her new friend back.

The guy stands up, and Aaron sits down, and Tillie thinks, *Don't do this.*

Aaron shouts to those watching that he'd like to play a song he wrote. He says that he's been sad, but that he's not sad today, and he points to Tillie, who tentatively waves. He says that it was meeting her that helped make him un-sad. A few people clap at this, but there's a runaway-train feeling in Tillie's chest and she just wants to grab him out of there, protect him, but she cannot move.

He starts to play his un-nuanced, clunky chords, which, coming after the gorgeous concerto, sounds particularly underwhelming. Then he adds his scratchy young Bob Dylan voice, and the lyrics warble and wiggle and fall essentially flat in the cavernous subway station.

> *I called you yesterday*
> *And let the phone ring*
> *Though I knew*
> *You couldn't answer*
>
> *I must remind myself*
> *Constantly*

I have to make do
With a memory of you

The crowd starts to disperse. Some people walk away. Not scoffing, exactly. More like they have places to go, and this is not worthy of their time in the same way the concerto was. And Tillie's heart breaks for Aaron, and she can see that he's aware of the people moving away, and that he soldiers on anyway, raising his voice as if maybe they can't hear him, which is so brave. She tries to send that message to him telepathically, that he's damn courageous.

When he's done, there's a smattering of polite applause that is drowned out by an arriving uptown E train. No way is Tillie getting on that train. She shouts and whistles and woos for her friend, doing everything she can to sound like many, many people, and it feels absurd but she'll do it again and she'll do it longer if it means Aaron won't be sad.

But he will be, she realizes. This seems like just the kind of thing that would make him really, really sad.

He skulks over, his head bent down, his posture defeated.

As much as she doesn't love hugging, she wraps her arms around his midsection and squeezes.

She feels his body disengaging.

"I just . . ." he says.

"You were great," she says as the piano music starts thundering up again.

He sits down in the center of the chaotic platform and puts his head in his hands, and despite the people rushing this way and that, she has no choice but to sit down on the filthy subway floor, too, though really she wants to pull his arm and take him somewhere—anywhere—else. To Belvedere Castle. To the High Line. Someplace with air and relative quiet. She feels his deflation and the extent of the feeling surprises her. It's heavy and it's a lot.

He sits in the same spot, unmoving, his head not down, just staring at what would be the train tracks, but she's pretty sure he isn't seeing anything. She wants to shake him, take him out of whatever this is. But she also somehow knows that won't work.

She gently puts her hand on his back but yells the words over the cacophony of piano and subway sounds. "Is this like what happened in physics?"

He ever so slightly nods.

"Can you move?"

He doesn't move.

She inhales deeply. "So what do we do?"

He takes so long to answer that when he does, what he says is drowned out by an express train coming into the station. So she asks again, and she hears him say, monotone, "Take me home, please."

Which she does. She helps him stand, she takes his bag, and she holds his hand. They grab the next C train, and they hold on to a pole and jostle and jangle into strangers, and she watches his increasingly vacant eyes and knows: He's not here. Aaron is missing. It scares the shit out of her.

X

She's able to get him home with a minimum of words. He hands her the key and he lets her lead him into his bedroom, where he numbly gets into bed without taking off his clothes or his shoes. He lies flat on his back, staring at the ceiling. She pulls over his desk chair and sits with him in silence.

She texts her mom:

> I'll explain later. I love you. I'm helping a friend who isn't okay. I am okay but I wasn't okay a couple days ago and I don't want to talk about it but I will when I'm ready. Okay? Home later. Need to stay with him until his dad gets home. He's not okay at all.

Her mom texts back immediately.

> Do you need me to come? Oh Till. I know you're struggling and I want to make everything better and I can't and that makes me feel powerless.

> I know. Love you. More later.

> Love you so much. Call if you need backup.

×

They sit in silence from 7:00 to 8:00 to 8:29, when she hears the door opening. She yells, "Mr.—Aaron's dad?"

Footsteps quicken to a run.

"What's—what's happening?"

"I'm Tillie. I'm Aaron's friend. He's not okay."

"Okay, okay. Thank you. Hi. Aar—Aar—?"

Aaron doesn't stir.

"Aaron," his dad says, his voice calmer than her mother's would be. "Talk to me, kiddo. I'm here. I'll help you however is possible. Please just say something, kiddo."

Aaron mumbles something. Neither Tillie nor his dad hears it. They both move closer.

"I don't deserve to live," Aaron says, and his dad reaches down and envelops his son, who doesn't move, and Tillie stands and gives them room.

She gives them so much room that she can't hear the rest of the conversation, but she knows enough so that when there's a pause, she says, "So. Do you need me? I can stay—" She tells his dad a little bit more about what happened, how Aaron froze on the platform. She doesn't mention the bridge, and doesn't mention cutting school—those are Aaron's things to tell. But she has to help with what's going on right now. She tells Aaron's dad she thinks this happened to Aaron in class yesterday, too, that this isn't the first time.

"Thank you so much," his father says, offering her a sympathetic smile. "You have no idea how grateful I am to you. I can take it from here."

She says, "Bye, Aaron. I love you, okay?" There's no answer, and she walks out of the room and the apartment, thinking, *I don't know but I think I may have just saved a life.* Which should feel great. But all it really feels is exhausting.

X

Tillie's mom is waiting by the door when Tillie gets home. She wraps Tillie in a breath-stealing hug, takes her hand, and leads her to the couch.

Britt is sleeping over at a friend's house. Dad is who knows where. In his office, hiding? Asleep? What would it be like to have a dad who cared? Who came out at a time like this and soothed her?

But he doesn't, so when Tillie's mom asks her what happened, Tillie just tells her. Everything. Even the bridge.

Tillie's mom is a cryer, and the story makes her sob.

"Till!" she says. "What am I going to do with you?"

Tillie doesn't have an answer to that.

"Do we need to put you somewhere?"

"No," Tillie says, too fast. "I mean, I should probably see Dr. Brown, like, pronto."

"I'll see if I can get you in tomorrow. Whatever it takes."

Tillie rubs her tired eyes. "I know you won't get this, but hanging out with Aaron the last couple days has actually really helped. I know I probably won't see him for a bit, but I needed a friend, Mom."

"I get that. Sweetheart? Can I ask you one thing?"

"Sure, Mom."

"Will you promise me you'll tell me if things get that bad again? Can I have your word? I simply would not be able to live with myself if you . . . I can't even say it."

Tillie is so glad her mom says this. A few days ago it might have bugged her. But something about her reawakening with Aaron makes it the perfect thing to say.

"I promise," she says.

By the time Aaron wakes up on Saturday morning, his dad has already organized everything. There's an appointment with a shrink named Dr. Laudner. There's a plan in place to get Aaron on meds for depression. And Aaron has no idea how this happened, but there's a summit with Tillie Stanley and her mother set for Aaron's living room at four p.m.

"Is this like the G-Four?" Aaron asks, playing a role, really, because he just doesn't have a lot of humor in him this morning. "Are we going to discuss nuclear disarmament with the Russians, Chinese, and Germans?"

Aaron's father turns the blue rocking chair in which he's sitting to face Aaron's bed. It squeaks against the floor angrily, like it needs an oil change.

"Well, if keeping you and your friend safe is nuclear disarmament, then yes," Aaron's dad says. "Not sure the Germans will be there, however. How's your head?"

"Medium rare," Aaron says, and his father has no follow-up questions.

✕

Tillie and her mother curl up on the couch on Saturday morning and watch some terrible old movie on TCM about a cop guarding a gangster on a train ride. Tillie's mother's face is more lined than usual, and mostly Tillie wishes she could just say, *You're released, you're free*, and let her mom go and be a happy person without the burden of the disaster that is her older daughter. And she knows that if she said that, her mom would tell her to stop it, and that she's loved so much, and there are lots of things Tillie can take right now, but with her dad still not around and her sister sleeping over at Carly's like a regular kid, hearing that she is so loved and so normal is not one of them.

"They don't make movies like this anymore," Tillie's mom says.

"All white and all male?"

Her mom laughs. "They still make plenty of those."

"I wish I could make a movie." Tillie puts her head in her mother's lap.

Tillie's mom strokes her shoulder. "What would it be?"

"It would be about the awfulness of people."

"Sounds like a real summer blockbuster."

Tillie goes on. "Aaron is, like . . . You know when someone's heart is so tender that they probably can't live? It was like that. He sang in the subway, Mom. It was, like, he just put his pure heart out there and he so wanted everyone to, like, love him. And they didn't, because people are the worst. It broke my heart."

Her mother bends down and kisses her ear. "I certainly don't know any teens with that sort of tender-heart problem," she says.

X

Dr. Laudner's office is on West End Avenue and Ninety-First. He's a blond, bearded guy with kind eyes and thinning hair, and he sits in a room filled with too many plants, like maybe his doctorate is in horticulture or something.

The doctor asks Aaron all sorts of questions and Aaron gives minimal answers, not wanting to piss the doctor off but also not really feeling up to a lot of conversation.

"So on a scale of one to ten, Aaron, with ten meaning as happy as ever and one being as despondent as ever, where are you today?"

Aaron looks out the second-story window. The newly green leaves of flowing trees blow tranquilly in the early spring wind. "Is negative six an option?"

"Oh dear," Dr. Laudner says, making Aaron wonder if he's gay. He hopes so. If he had a sex drive, Laudner would definitely be fantasy material. Aaron really doesn't, though. Not at the moment, thank you very much. It would just be nice to talk to an adult gay male once in a while, maybe.

Aaron is given a test to take with multiple choice answers, about just how depressed he really is. He takes it as honestly as possible.

"Seventy-six," the doctor says.

"Is that good?"

The doctor smiles sympathetically.

"Anything above fifty-four is severely depressed."

Aaron closes his eyes. "A fine time to start getting C-pluses," he says, and this makes the doctor laugh a bit, at least.

X

Tillie's appointment with Dr. Brown is at one. Tillie considered asking her mother if she could see someone else, someone not so . . . stick-in-ass. Dr. Brown is the kind of skinny blond lady who probably sends her kids to Spence. Whose kids probably are still laughing about Molly's cow video. But in the end, she decided not to make a big deal about it. She's high maintenance enough, after all.

"So what's going on under the hood?" the doctor asks.

Tillie wants to dramatically study her own shell and report on her lack of a hood. But she knows any such action will not help her right now.

"I'm fine, basically."

"Your mom told me about the bridge."

"It was stupid."

"Stupid? How do you mean?"

"I don't know."

"Well, if you did know."

This is Tillie's least favorite of Dr. Brown's greatest hits. It's like a cute way of saying, *Bullshit.*

Tillie shrugs and starts pulling at a strand of brown fabric sticking out from the couch upon which she reclines. She imagines unraveling the couch while sitting on it, so that at the end she's sitting in a pile of unwound brown fabric and cream-colored cushion.

"Please don't do that," Dr. Brown says, pointing.

"Sorry," says Tillie.

X

Aaron fires off a quick text to Tillie an hour before the upcoming tête-à-tête.

> Ugh. Sorry about this. I think I got us in trouble. Really sorry.

It's fine. How are you?

> Just took my first Petralor (antidepressant). I'm cured. The world is a beautiful place. Yay.

Is there a sarcasm emoji?

> I will make it my life's work to create one.
> Guessing my music career is over, so

Stop.

> Sorry. See you in a bit when we get whatever horrible punishment
> two sad kids get after emergency therapy appointments

You heard about mine

> Just that you had it. You get on meds too

Nah we'll see.

> It's fun. Like amusement park fun.

Sarcasm emoji

> Major sarcasm emoji

X

At the door to Aaron's apartment, Aaron and Tillie give each other a sort of awkward side embrace that makes them both want to die a bit. Aaron shakes Tillie's mom's hand. Tillie says hey to Aaron's dad as if they've known each other for more than two awkward minutes last night.

The two families sit opposite each other on two peach couches in the living room. Tillie sees the view of New Jersey and the Hudson from the twelfth floor and can't help but wonder how many times Aaron has stared out at it, maybe from the window seats right against the huge picture windows, wondering whether life is worth living. She also can't help but imagine the coldness of the water that, just three days ago, she almost jumped into.

"So this is maybe a little strange, but I set this meeting up as a chance to discuss what's been going on this last week," Aaron's dad says. "I don't mean to speak for Mrs. Stanley, but I know I'm really concerned and thought the best thing we could do is put everything out on the table."

Aaron tenses. He looks at Tillie, who looks back at him. She looks tense, too, around the jaw.

Aaron's dad continues. "I first want to say how glad I am—"

He swallows, and he averts his eyes, and then he wipes them, though they are dry. But not for long. The wetness comes, and then the redness, and Aaron wants to die, because he's made his father cry, and his father is the kind of dad who would cry in front of others, and yeah, he would, too, and that should be something to be proud of, but at the moment he just wants to disappear.

"Tillie. I am so sorry you were there, because it must mean you're really struggling. But I am so forever grateful, too, because you—saved my boy's life."

At this point, Aaron's dad begins to bawl, and Aaron steals a glance at Mrs. Stanley, and she, too, is crying, and Aaron imagines taking Tillie by the hand and running down all twelve flights and out into the street and into the world and never looking back because this is too real, too awful, and it's his fault, totally his fault, or half his fault, anyway, and he could just disappear forever.

Tillie, too, ducks her head, as if by staring at her lap and blinking several times, she might magically extricate herself.

Tillie's mom dries her eyes, blows into a Kleenex she's pulled from her purse, and takes over.

"So the big thing here is that we need to have a plan. And it's not clear you're both in the same place, but you're both battling right now. So. Can we ask a few questions?"

Both kids nod. The parents look at each other. They share a subliminal nod, too.

Tillie's mom continues. "So the only rule here is this: You have to be totally honest with us. You're not in trouble. The opposite. This is about helping you however we can, okay?"

Aaron and Tillie nod again.

Tillie's mom turns to Aaron. "Aaron, are you right now a danger to yourself?"

He thinks about it. "Um. Not at this moment, no. It's better when I'm not alone, I guess. I'm scared of the next time I go back to being alone."

Aaron's dad says, "Okay. Thank you for your honesty. Tillie?"

"Uh. No."

The four of them sit in silence for a while.

Finally, Mrs. Stanley speaks. "Aaron, what would you do if you were together and Tillie suddenly was in danger?"

"I'd . . . um. Do anything. I wouldn't let her—"

"Could you be one hundred percent trusted to call me? Even if Tillie said 'don't'?"

Aaron looks at Tillie and he realizes that yes, he'd absolutely do that, no question. "Yes," he tells her mom.

"Same question, Tillie," Aaron's dad says.

Tillie doesn't hesitate. "I'd do what I did yesterday."

"Okay. Good."

Tillie's mother says, "I think for right now, obviously you two need us to be close and available, and you need each other. I think we're both afraid." She points to Aaron's dad when she says that. "But less afraid when we're with you or when you're together. So this is all to say that we're around and we're here for you, anytime. You're our priority. And also, if you need a break from us, you have each other."

Tillie and Aaron share an openmouthed look. Like, *what?*

Tillie's mom keeps going. "But we need to know everything. Where you are when you're not with us. Where you're going. If you need us. If school isn't safe, you tell us and we'll take care of it, but no secrets, got it? We will release you both into each other's care, but we will be aware of your whereabouts at every moment. How does that sound?"

Tillie feels as if she's been sent to the principal's office and praised instead of disciplined, which has never happened but if it did, it would surely feel like this. Something about her mother accepting that she's not fully okay without trying to fix it all sets Tillie free.

For Aaron's part, it's as if their parents have spent time lamenting behind their backs that their kids are such lost causes that they've decided to pair them up, see what happens, and hope for the best. But at the same time, it's also really, really good.

"Sounds okay," Aaron says.

"Yeah," Tillie says, and they both crack up at the same moment, because something about this is so awkward and funny and neither can describe what it is, or why.

Released into each other's custody, on Sunday Aaron and Tillie meet at the Seventy-Ninth Street bus station on Broadway and wander aimlessly downtown, walking the whole way despite Tillie's not-so-subtle hints that Ubers are fun and educational and might be a good idea.

"You know what would be so cool? If there was some sort of car you could take, and it would, like, pick you up and drop you off at the movie, or wherever you're going. They should invent that," she says as they pass Lincoln Center.

"What's the rush?" Aaron says. "The movie doesn't start for another hour."

"I'm just saying. Could be fun. On an unrelated topic, my feet are ever so slightly tired."

He stops short. "Oh. Okay. Is it bad? We can. Sorry."

She thinks about this for a bit. "Nah. I'm just being whiny."

He laughs and starts walking again. "That's sort of my thing," he says. "Don't be co-opting my things."

"I will try not to," she says.

The silence is awkward as they walk through the fashion district and then Chelsea, and Aaron wonders if it's possible that they've permanently misplaced their conversational groove.

Tillie is thinking that it's weird that they chose a dark, artsy movie, because for all of her weirdness and darkness, she tends to fall asleep at artsy movies. But when Aaron asked what she liked to do, she felt like her options were to say the truth—*I have no idea, because I hate most people and I'm going to be a female hermit and I have exorbitantly limited social experience*—or make up some shit. She chose the latter.

The movie is Chinese with English subtitles, and the somber mood and monochromatic colors of the desolate Manchurian landscape deepen the rut both of them feel after their awkward walk. Then, about an hour into the endless film, there's a huge-ass elephant, filling up the screen. The camera stays on it for a painfully long time.

Aaron cracks up, and Tillie is momentarily annoyed by the outburst, but then she cracks up, too, because here they are, two depressed kids, watching a motionless Manchurian elephant.

They eye each other and Tillie motions with her hand that they need to be serious. Aaron sucks in his cheeks and nods.

And the elephant. Just sits there. Not moving. For an eternity.

This time it's Tillie snorting, and it's like when you're at a funeral, and you know laughing is the last thing you should do, but simply having that thought makes the laughter creep into your throat and suddenly you cannot breathe, you cannot move, because if you do, you're going to cackle, and you can't just cackle, except that's exactly what you do and then your family hates you for the rest of eternity. And Aaron snorts, and Tillie snorts again, and then they are both bent over in hysterics, and every "Shh!" that comes their way makes it worse and finally Tillie is the one who just bellows out a laugh, and it's like everything held in for the past however long just shoots out her mouth, and Aaron, too, lets go, and it's not that long before the usher, who is their age and a total hipster who looks like every other hipster ever, escorts them out, and they laugh and laugh and laugh until they run out of gas in front of the Quad Cinema.

"Woo," says Tillie. "Whose fucking shitty idea was that, to go see a sad foreign film when we're both, like, at death's door?"

"Yours," Aaron says, and they laugh some more, and finally Aaron adds, "Pact: nothing but fun stuff the rest of the day?"

"Pact," Tillie says.

Tillie buys them each a Lucky Charms cookie and a glass of milk at Chip NYC. Aaron's eyes get wide when he sees that this behemoth, muffin-size cookie is covered in vanilla glaze and Lucky Charms marshmallows. Before they dig in, he excuses himself to the restroom.

Once inside and seated, he takes out his phone and texts his dad.

> I've gone out with my sweater. At Chip NYC. Two cookies and milk have been ordered. I am now in the bathroom clearing the way for said cookies.

Sigh. Why does it not surprise me that you are taking this checking in thing to the extreme?

> One sec.

> Pooping . . .

> Right . . .

> Now

Double sigh. Love you kid.

> Roger that.

Back at the table, Tillie has not waited. Aaron's first clue is the white gunk all around her lips.

"Um," he says. "Don't mind me."

"You can't put Lucky Charms cookies at a table with me and go off and expect me not to eat. That's a form of torture. Can you believe there's marshmallow fluff inside?"

He bites into it and his mouth is assaulted by the commingling textures. His eyes go wide, and he chews in disbelief.

"Oh my god. We are moving here. I will spend the rest of my days subsisting on cookies and I will be happy forevermore. Happy and fat."

Tillie's expression changes, and Aaron, oblivious, talks over it. "I will write songs about cookies, I will blog about cookies, maybe even write a play about them. And then, when I've decided I've had enough, I will drown in a bathtub of marshmallow fluff. Which has always been my life goal."

Tillie doesn't respond for a while, and Aaron stares at her, expecting her to say something. "What? What did I say?"

"You're skinny, Aaron."

"Duh," he says.

"So. I'm not. Skinny. And it kind of pisses me off that you, like, talk about becoming fat like it's this—I don't know. I just."

"Oh god," he says. "I'm sorry. I don't know if you know this, but I used to be called Pretzel Stick Man. People have been making fun of me for my weight all my life."

She shakes her head. "It's not the same."

"It isn't?"

"Skinny is good. Fat is bad. That's just how it is."

"For girls, maybe."

"What?"

"Well. Boys are supposed to be, I don't know. Muscular. Not waiflike."

Tillie thinks about this for a bit. "So you'd rather be fat than skinny?"

Aaron shrugs. "Fat is substantial. Like you have a right to exist."

Tillie chugs her milk. "Wow. That's different."

"That's me," Aaron says. "By the way, you're totally beautiful."

Tillie rolls her eyes. "Yeah, right."

"Just the truth. If I were straight? I'd absolutely want to go out with you. You're beautiful and smart and funny and magnetic."

Running her hands through her hair and shrinking into herself, Tillie giggles, and then she hates so much that she's just giggled because a boy complimented her. Aaron sees it and laughs. She catches his eye and laughs, too.

"We're ridiculous, aren't we?" she asks.

"We really are."

X

After gorging on too many muffin-size cookies, they wander over to the Museum of Sex on Fifth Avenue, where they find a huge breast to jump in. Only a few people are allowed in at a time, as it should be, anytime you find yourself bouncing around a bunch of breasts.

"Try the areola," Tillie yells as she bounces against a pink protuberance in the center of one of the seven or eight boobs inside the bounce house, which is also shaped like a breast.

"This is probably the only time I will," says Aaron, who does a mosh pit bounce, arms wide open, into the areola, which springs him backward.

The weird truth for Aaron, the one he feels in his body as he jumps up and down, up and down, is that the fun, free feeling of jumping is pressing against the rib crush that is, to him, depression, and it feels weird to be momentarily happy, even very happy, and also the thing that almost killed him is still there.

None of which are useful thoughts as he jumps inside a mammary gland, so he puts them away.

×

They follow up their bosom adventure with hot chocolate at Max Brenner near Union Square, and then they wander south as the sun goes down.

"I feel sort of out of time," Aaron says as they walk along Spring Street in SoHo, amid fashionable people he will never be like. "Time is suspended, life is suspended. It's a Sunday afternoon and school is tomorrow or maybe not, and I don't know. All of a sudden, this window's opened up and you've appeared and I keep wondering— where I'd be if you'd . . . Never mind."

"I get it," Tillie says. "I thought about that last night. What could have happened on the bridge."

"Yeah."

"That is, like, the scariest thought I've ever had."

As they walk, Aaron leans his head against Tillie's shoulder. They walk that way for a bit, connected head to shoulder, like their lives depend on it.

"So I think I'm faking," Aaron tells Dr. Laudner when he's in his office the next morning. He and Tillie convinced their parents that therapy, not school, was the best way to spend a Monday.

Dr. Laudner cocks his head to the left. "You do?"

"I think it's like when I was in third grade and I decided to fake being sick so I didn't have to go to school. I put the thermometer against the radiator and it didn't register, then I put it under hot water and it didn't because I guess it was the kind you run across your forehead. So I got the idea to put a hot, wet towel on my forehead and then do it, and suddenly I had a temperature of one-oh-eight."

Dr. Laudner laughs.

"My dad told me he'd pick out a grave site for me, because clearly I was near death or maybe already dead, which at the moment seemed mean but now that I think about it it's pretty funny. And I wound up going to school."

"And this is what you think is happening now?"

"Well, I don't know what else it could be, because yesterday I hung out all day with Tillie and it was maybe the best day of my life. We had so much fun, and depressed people don't do that, so what the fuck is going on?"

"I think what's going on is that you had a good day. And that's great. And also just two days ago you had trouble getting out of bed. You can have happiness within depression. Both can be true simultaneously."

Aaron rolls his eyes into the back of his head. "I just want to have the good stuff. Can I just have every day be like yesterday?"

"So let me ask you: What was different yesterday?"

Aaron tells him a little about Tillie, and the connection they have. And also how he was glad to have alone time this morning, because being with a friend was a lot.

Dr. Laudner nods. "Sure. So maybe the key is getting more connected but still sometimes having time for yourself?"

Aaron hates how easy Dr. Laudner makes that sound.

X

Tillie spends her morning with her mother, who's found a psychiatrist for her to talk to. Even though that could mean medicine, Tillie agrees to make an appointment because at least it isn't Dr. Brown.

Tillie knows she can't stay away from school forever. Her mom is humoring her, but that will only last so long. Also, she knows she can't hide from life. She has to deal with it. She wants to go and tell Amir what he can do with his—whatever. And Molly, too. Just screw them. She doesn't care what they think anymore.

Once school is out and she knows Amir will be home, she texts Aaron and asks him to ride shotgun on her first attempt at tying up loose ends. They meet outside Tillie's building. Aaron is wearing a jacket that might be worn by a lesbian clown, a multicolored flannel extravaganza that Tillie is certain no gay boy has ever worn before, or hopefully will ever again.

"You sure you want to do this?" he asks.

She looks down the street longingly in a way that makes Aaron wonder if she'll ever be really happy. "I'm pretty sure," she says.

As they walk in silence to Amir's place, Tillie runs through all the possibilities of things he'll say, and what she should say in each case; the feeling of despair is so palpable that Aaron feels it and puts his arm around her.

When they get there, Tillie stops and takes a deep breath.

"Am I really doing this?" she asks.

"Seems like it," Aaron observes.

"I need to do it alone. Can you stand back a bit?"

He starts to back up. "Should we have a safe word? Some sort of code in case you need me to charge in and save you?"

She rolls her eyes. "Yeah, I think we're good."

"Good luck," he says. "I'm here if you need me. And maybe the code could be 'Hey, Aaron' or something."

"Sure. That sounds like a foolproof plan."

Aaron backs off about twenty-five feet. He stands next to a parked Volvo, feeling conspicuous and awkward.

Amir's apartment building has always seemed to have a personality to Tillie. It's tall, beige, and judgmental, like a nineteenth-century politician. It doesn't approve of people like her. When she stands in front of the buzzer and gets ready to buzz 5A, she can't help but think that the building is on Amir's side, that it thinks she's a pathetic freak, too. She feels the overwhelming urge to run, and yet she persists. She stands and catches her breath, and she presses the button.

"Hello?"

"Hey. Amir? It's Tillie."

Silence on the other end. For quite a while. Her chest begins to curl in as a minute goes by, and then a minute and a half, and she is experiencing the trauma all over again, of being made invisible, of being told that she's inconsequential, and fuck your feelings, all the things that make up the world she lives in, a world where she really doesn't belong. She wants to call "Hey, Aaron" and have him come and hold her, and—

"Coming down," Amir says. Tillie snaps back to reality and says "thanks" so softly she can barely hear her own word.

She looks back at Aaron, who gives her a meek thumbs-up. It makes her grin a bit despite the situation, seeing him in his flannel monstrosity, standing there so gawkily, on her side.

Two minutes later, Amir appears, his hair impeccably Dippity-Do'd, his slight mouth and nose perfect, his face beautiful despite a smattering of pimples along his chin line. He looks smaller than she remembers, like he's shrunk at least three inches. His shoulders are drooped and he looks shy, which he normally isn't, and sensitive, which he normally is, which is why the whole thing is so—fucked up. Being ghosted by someone sensitive? A zillion times worse than being ghosted by someone who's obviously an asshole.

"Hey," he says. His voice is light, like he's embarrassed, and sorry, and the part of Tillie that she hates jumps sides immediately and forgets why she's there, and how she's felt, and what this all did to her. Without Amir ghosting her, she would have never written the poem, would have never performed it, would have never had to see Molly Tobin put a pillow under her shirt and mock her and her words, would have never had to experience an entire school laughing at her naked pain.

"Hey," she says, staring at his chest. He's wearing a blue Brooks Brothers shirt and jeans and loafers, even though he was at home minding his own business. She's the one who actively chose to do this, to come confront Amir, and she's wearing black sweatpants and a gray hoodie, her hair pulled into a not-so-neat ponytail.

This. This is why she's not fit to live. She is so much less presentable than every other person on earth. It would have taken her hours to be the equivalent of what he probably just threw on, and that sucks.

"I've been meaning to text you," he says.

The only response she can have to this is to laugh.

"No, I really have. I'm sorry, Tillie."

"You're sorry," she repeats.

He nods, averts his eyes, and then looks back at her.

"There's a weird guy standing there, pretending not to be watching us."

"Is there?"

"Yeah. Should we walk? I don't mean to be phobic of homeless people, but—"

"He's not homeless. He's my friend Aaron." Tillie turns and waves, and Aaron gives a tentative wave back, like he's unsure if it's okay that he's been made.

"You brought a friend?"

"Well, I had to. Ever since I nearly jumped off a bridge, I'm not allowed to be alone. He's my chaperone, sort of."

Amir stands there, looking like he's been punched in the face. He seems to have no words. He becomes a frozen statue of Amir, shocked.

"Can we . . . take a walk?" he finally says. "I need to tell you something. Explain. But not here. I can't."

"Why not?"

"My mom."

Tillie can't quite figure out how that sentence could possibly be finished to make sense. *My mom . . . doesn't want me to apologize to you?*

They walk in silence toward the park, Aaron trailing a half block behind.

They enter the park at Eighty-Ninth Street and take a left on the bridle path, where they'd been a few times before. Once they're on the dirt path, he stops walking.

"I'm so sorry," he says.

"For what, exactly?"

He crosses his arms over his chest and then uncrosses them. "If you're serious about nearly jumping off a bridge . . . I'm sorry for being a part of that. Because I must have been."

She looks to the sky. "Um. Kind of. It's complicated. But yeah. I thought you loved me. I thought I loved you. You made me take my guard down and then you ghosted me."

Now it's Amir who looks like he might want to jump off a bridge. "Oh my god," he says, almost to himself. "I am the worst person."

She stares at him.

He glances around to make sure they are basically alone—which they aren't, because Aaron is about twenty feet away, leaning against a fence post. Amir starts talking anyway, in a soft, controlled, fearful voice. She can hear the quavering and it makes her hate him.

"I've had a bunch of things on my mind and I knew at some point I'd have to, you know, talk to you about them."

Her imaginary alter ego, the one who reacts to things from the heart, smashes him over the head with a green metal trash receptacle, the closest heavy object she can find.

Her actual self, though, nods and says, "Okay."

"So first off, I'm so sorry. About everything. About how I acted. I am so deeply, deeply sorry and I might never forgive myself, actually. This is my fault. And this next thing? I don't know how you'll react. Or even if you will. You might just walk off and never talk to me again, and I wouldn't blame you because I probably would do the same if I were in your shoes. And you might just tell everyone and ruin my life. Which would suck, but I'm gonna take the chance anyway. So. Here goes: I'm gay, Tillie. Not like, I kissed you and that led me to realize—nothing like that. More like, I'm a gay person, I always was a gay person, and I've been totally, utterly unable to talk about it because I'm pretty sure it's not gonna be okay. At school or at home. My mom has basically said if I'm gay I'd better find another place to live." He wrings his hands, fixes his shirt, glances around to see if anyone else has heard him say what he's said.

Tillie stares. She bites her lip. She feels so many things all at once. *What? Fuck! Huh? Oh! Um, what?*

Amir hugs himself into a defensive posture as she stands there, not answering. The power has shifted, and the furious part of her is glad. And the other part can't allow him to go even another second feeling the way he must feel inside.

"Okay, so," she says. She finds herself unable, or maybe just unwilling, to finish the sentence. The two of them stand there like dunces on the bridle path near the Eighty-Ninth Street entrance to Central Park, watching the caravan of cute children with their parents and joggers and bikers and horses while they remain motionless.

Finally Tillie laughs. Which catches Amir off guard, and she watches his body react, put up its barriers.

"So there's a story my dad once told me. You know, back when he used to—tell me things," she says. "It was from when he was in high school. In English class, they read the Bible and talked about parables, and they were given an assignment to write a parable. So my dad went home and wrote this story about a man and his wife, and how they had a bad marriage, so to fix the marriage they decided to have a child, which they did. And they had this son, and he was a challenging kid who was always getting into trouble. He'd slash the tires on their car and have parties when they went out of town. The father finally was pushed too far one day, when the son emptied their bank account. So the father took his son to the edge of town and pushed him off a cliff, and he died. The end. My dad hands it in and then when the teacher returns the parables, he gives my dad the paper with a confused look on his face. The teacher says to him, 'Well, I can't say I understand how this is a parable. What's the lesson?' And my dad says, 'Never have children.'"

"Um," Amir says. "So the moral of this story is?" He looks utterly confused.

"I don't know. You have an issue. Don't be an asshole about it? Don't, like, use a person to try and solve it, and then, like, push them off a cliff?"

Amir looks at Tillie. Then he cracks up. Which is fine with her, actually, because she's so damn tired of anger. And she's about to laugh, too, as his little laugh becomes a big one, and his shoulders start to convulse, and then of course the damn tears—so many people in her life crying these days, herself included—and she weighs the options of putting her hand on him somewhere as comfort, and not doing so, and she decides to not do it. But she does say something.

"First off, that's crazy. Your mom saying that. That's so wrong. And. I'm sorry that's hard for you."

He nods and murmurs, "Thanks."

"Second: Get your shit together, Amir. Everyone's gay. It's a million percent fine with me. The ghosting thing was less fine. Like gloriously, incredibly not fine."

Amir hugs her tight. She is not really ready for the hug, nor is she ready to not be hugged. So she kinda hugs him back while all sorts of things churn inside her.

"I'm so, so, so sorry," he says.

"It's fine," she says. "I mean, by that I mean not completely fine."

"I get it," he says. "I owe you a lot."

"Damn right you do," she says. "Come with me."

She walks over to Aaron, who is standing there with his hands in his jacket pockets. She shakes her head.

"Do you think it's too cold to be without a jacket?"

Aaron shrugs. "Not really. I'm pretty warm, actually."

"Good," she says, and she pulls it off him, left side first, then right. Then she finds a nearby trash bin and throws it in there.

"Hey," he says.

"Bozo the feminist needed her jacket back."

"I liked that jacket."

"Face it. I'm doing you a favor," Tillie says. "And no way am I introducing you to another gay boy while you wear that monstrosity."

"Hey!" says Amir. "That's not—"

And Aaron says, "Oh."

"Yeah. Gay," Tillie deadpans. "All the good ones are gay, as my mother says."

"Wait. I'm a good one?" Aaron asks.

She ignores him. "Aaron, Amir. Amir, Aaron. You have boys in common, apparently. If I sound angry and bitter, it's because I am."

She walks toward the reservoir, leaving them alone together.

"Hi, I guess?" says Amir.

"Um, hi," Aaron replies. Then he looks over his shoulder. "I think I have to go follow her."

"Yeah. Please tell her I'm sorry again, and that I'm willing to talk and to apologize many more times. Also tell her to please, please not say anything about this to anyone, okay? I'm not ready."

Aaron says, "Sure." Then he walks over to Tillie, who is crying on a bench facing the reservoir. Joggers zip by, oblivious to the drama that is Tillie's life; she wants to be that oblivious to it as well.

"So," Aaron says. "That happened."

"Jesus," Tillie says.

"Sorry. You okay?"

"Does this look like I'm okay?"

"Sorry."

"I'm not mad at you. I'm just. How do you ghost someone you care about? Even when you have a secret?"

"He told me to tell you he's sorry and that he'll apologize a million more times if you want him to."

"Whatever. Can we not talk about him? I think I need to forget. Like get drunk or something."

Aaron laughs. "That sounds like a brilliant idea. Everyone says that depressed people should add alcohol."

She smiles despite herself. "Shut up."

He bends down and kisses her shoulder. "So I'm a good one, eh?"

"If you ever mention that again, no, you're not."

"Point taken," says Aaron.

Tillie stares out at the reservoir and thinks about the power of water. How it is life and death at once. We subsist on it and would die without the drinking water in front of us, and yet an overabundance of it, like the rushing Hudson River less than a week ago, can kill a person.

People are like that, too. And love. Life-saving and life-taking, and it's almost too much to navigate, that there's this thing out there we need so much, that also hurts and destroys as it does.

She wants Aaron to ask her what she's thinking about. And also she's so glad he doesn't, because she might scream.

And if there's a single person in the world who would get that, he's sitting right next to her.

How are you, T?

Been better, A.

Can I ask a weird question?

Almost exclusively

Ha. Did him being gay make it worse or better?

I don't know. Probably better, but it pissed me off. That a person could act like that for such a stupid reason. He could have just told me

Yeah, why didn't he?

His mom is really homophobic I guess

Oh

So now part of me wants to text him and talk again, and part of me feels like I'm going through the whole thing again.

You need me to come over?

Nah. Thanks though. How are you?

Fucking weird. Like half okay and then half not

Can you feel the medicine?

There are moments it feels like I can hear my head

What?!?

It's like I can feel the neurotransmitters changing. On an unrelated note I should probably not research drugs I'm taking on the internet

I totally get that

Yeah, it was like one minute I'm taking Petralor and I'm fine, the next minute I'm reading about it and I'm like, yeah, my mouth IS dry

I kinda love you

You seem to have a type

😩 😩 😩

Too soon?

Ya

Later:

So why do you think adults become therapists?

I don't know, Aaron. Why do adults become therapists?

I think they're sadists. Like they've waited all their lives to be like, how can I get this kid to say the one thing that's gonna make him so sad he'll want to die?

Oh wow. Mine just did that too

Really

Oh yeah. It was awful.

I feel like if I finally just said whatever they wanted, some alarms would go off and maybe balloons would fall from the ceiling and they'd be like "congratulations Aaron, you've just said the magic word! You win!" And then I'd go cut myself or whatever

You are so weird

Quod erat demonstratum

Mine wants me to say the one thing and I'm just like, stop. No. I don't trust you. I don't want to talk about that.

Do you think we should do it here?

What

Like just to spite them? We both just type the thing they want us to say that we're never going to say and then never talk about it again

hmm.

hmm?

hmm meaning that's not the worst idea ever. But if I do that and you don't I will never speak to you again and will come and cut your body into pieces

do you think maybe you ought to spend some time in therapy talking about your violent tendencies?

Ignoring . . . so are we doing this?

yes

Ready?

as i'll ever be

1 . . . 2 . . . 3 . . .

My dad hates me

Not at all special

So we're just gonna let that lie, right?

those were the rules

K. I love you.

Love you too

I'm going back to school tomorrow

I think I'm ready

That's great. I'm just afraid that means by the transitive property I'm going to be going back tomorrow, too.

How do you feel?

It's weird. I find myself laughing at shows on TV and I think maybe I'm totally okay. Other times I feel like I wanna curl up in a ball. My therapist says you can be happy and depressed at the same time. I don't know.

Amir keeps texting me

!!! What did you do? Did you text back??

I texted back something really passive aggressive

What?

"I am in receipt of your text, so you won't go crazy wondering why I haven't texted you. Please give me two to three business days to respond. Sincerely, Tillie"

HAHAHAHA You are literally the best person

☺

Except when you threw out my jacket. That was mean

I honestly feel like we need to get you Queer Eyed.
Like get some gay dude to take you shopping

Can it be Amir? He's kinda cute

What did we say about too soon, Aaron Boroff?

Sorry couldn't resist

Later:

So here's the thing . . . what do I do about Molly?

The girl who did the video?

Ya

What is there to do?

I'll see her at school tomorrow. I'm pretty sure her
suspension is over

What do you think you'll do?

Part of me wants closure. Like to just put it out there
that I'm over it and over her and make her know she
has no power over me anymore

That's great. Does she?

No. Yes. I don't know. I mean, I get that she's the
problem. She's like that Brandi Carlile song. The
joke's on her, not me

I love that song

I've been listening to it all day

brb . . .

Okay. Now it's on in the background in your honor

Thank you. So if the joke's on her, why does it hurt me?

That's like the trillion dollar question. Solve that and nerds everywhere will buy you a lifetime supply of Max Brenner hot chocolate for you and a friend

I'd rather have cookies

Oh yes. Damn you Tillie Stanley. Now I want cookies.

You gonna go back to school?

Not tomorrow, but probably soon. Feeling good today tbh

☺

☺ Good luck tomorrow. Text me every five minutes

K

Tillie's first day back at school is anticlimactic, to say the least.

Savanya gives her a hug and asks where she's been, but otherwise, it's like nothing has happened. Which is good—no one trolls you for perceived weaknesses they don't know about—and not so good—if a Tillie falls in the forest and no one hears, did Tillie exist in the first place?

She wonders what would have happened had she jumped. Had she died. Would anyone have cared?

None of these thoughts are helpful to Tillie in homeroom, so she tries to put them out of her mind. Under her desk, she texts her lifeline.

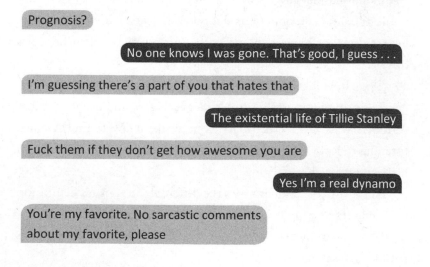

It's been five minutes

Prognosis?

No one knows I was gone. That's good, I guess . . .

I'm guessing there's a part of you that hates that

The existential life of Tillie Stanley

Fuck them if they don't get how awesome you are

Yes I'm a real dynamo

You're my favorite. No sarcastic comments about my favorite, please

Tillie smiles despite herself. Being someone's favorite counts for something, she guesses.

The bell rings, and she heads off to class.

"Moo-ve," Samantha Quinn says as Tillie attempts to maneuver the crowded hallway.

Tillie's palm hits Samantha in the forehead in a way that shocks everyone who sees it. Tillie looks down at her hand, which is in a claw position, the palm red from contact, like it belongs to someone else. Samantha looks like Tillie hitting her in the face with her palm was the last thing she'd expected, which it surely was. The girls who witness the assault share looks with one another that vary from appalled to impressed, and when Ms. Steinke grabs Tillie's hand and brings her to the principal's office, Tillie wonders if this will be the shortest return to school in human history.

X

The clouds have begun to lift. Aaron tells his dad he's okay to walk to his appointment alone. His dad, who has taken a week off from his residency to hang at home with Aaron, smiles when he hears this.

"I see it, you know."

The grin that crosses Aaron's face feels true and deeply good to Aaron, and he just about floats as he walks up West End Avenue, listening to Robyn, who he hasn't listened to in a while. He needs a little up-tempo this morning.

At the office, Laudner notes the difference in Aaron's demeanor, too, and says he wonders if the meds have already begun to kick in.

"You mean there's more?" Aaron asks, and then he pumps his fist like he's saying, *Score!*

Laudner laughs and hands over the test Aaron does every day. Little bubbles to fill in. Anything above fifty-four is severely depressed. Today he scores a thirty-one.

"Mild to moderate depression," the doctor says. "That's a big difference in a short time. Five days. Congratulations!"

And yeah, it's a weird thing to celebrate being moderately depressed. But Aaron feels the difference in his brain. He actually feels it. So it's a little hard for him to not break into another smile.

×

"I honestly didn't mean to," Tillie tells Principal Pembree. "Seriously. It was like my hand acted without my consent."

The principal tilts her head and scratches her chin. "Was this about the video?"

Tillie nods.

"What did Samantha say to you?"

"She said, 'Moo-ve.'"

The principal frowns. "Yeah, that's not okay with me."

Tillie stays still.

"Comments like that are not acceptable. Neither is punching, but frankly, I get it even though I don't endorse the action. Are you okay, Tillie?"

A week ago, Tillie would have nodded, said little, and been relieved when she was excused to go back to class. But now she says, "No. Not really. I mean, I'm getting better and I'm not a danger to myself, but no, this hasn't been okay at all. Basically everyone seems to think I got Molly suspended, and everyone seems to hate me for it, and last week was probably the worst of my life."

Principal Pembree nods. "I heard you'd needed some mental health days. Do you need some more?"

Tillie struggles not to raise her voice.

"What I need is to know the school has my back."

"We do!"

Tillie's face feels hot. "I appreciate that, but. You suspended Molly for a few days. Why didn't we talk about it as a community?"

"Okay. Thank you, Tillie. You're always so quiet. This is the most I've ever heard you say."

"Well, no more. I'm done not speaking up, because it almost . . ."

The principal's face changes, like the unspoken words have gotten through anyway.

"Are you feeling brave?" Pembree asks.

"What? Why?"

"Just an idea I want to float. Feel free to say no . . ."

×

Aaron finds himself singing as he walks home. He twirls once, too. He feels like he's just gotten out of jail. Like this new thing is happening and it feels like the sun has just come out after a long and endless winter. He sings "Can't Forget Your Smile" aloud, not caring in the least if people hear him. He's finally free! Or getting free. From the hell of depression.

His dad is out doing errands when Aaron gets home from therapy, and he breaks out the notebook his dad gave him. He writes his name on the front in big letters and then entitles the notebook *Thoughts from Up High, Never to Fall*. He stares at the words and smiles.

He does, actually, feel good. Surprisingly good. Stupid *not good enough* thing aside—and he's put it aside because what good does it do to focus on it all day? The clouds overhead have parted and the sky is shining bright blue, and he feels himself lighter in the shoulders than he has in a long while. They said it would take weeks for the medicine to work, but here he is, five days in, and he's just about cured.

He should write a song! Yes. He's written plenty of songs when he's been sad. What if he writes a happy song? The idea makes him smile. Yes. A happy song.

He closes his eyes and thinks. What is happy? What does he like to do?

He likes walking. He likes being in communion with nature, or, well, whatever New York City is. Nature adjacent. Central Park? Nah. What's his favorite place to walk?

He thinks of the block between Amsterdam and Columbus on Seventy-Fourth. The gray brownstones, all in a row, the curved windows, the quiet. He imagines people smiling, walking down the street, as if this street were the antidote, the antidote to all the things wrong with this hell of a civilization we've created.

He writes.

On Seventy-Fourth Street
they all held hand
there's a twinkle
And no shit mean
or at all unclear
On Seventy-Fourth, Seventy-Fourth Street

He reads what he's written. Interesting. People don't really express happiness openly these days. Everything is so jaded. This sort of song expresses happiness and hope. That's new. It's what the world needs more of.

He lies back on his bed, shuts his eyes, and thinks to himself: *Maybe I'll be the one. The person who brings kindness back. Happiness.*

Yeah. Maybe that'll be me.

×

Tillie is buzzing as she walks the hallway en route to chemistry from the principal's office. Funny how things work. She was summoned there for punching Samantha Quinn, and left with the possibility of running an assembly on online bullying. And she isn't sure how that will go over, if she chooses to do it. She doesn't have the best track record when it comes to being open and vulnerable at school, and surely some of the girls will double down on their cruelty. It's what happens when you're real.

A thought stops her in her tracks.

I'd rather be real and made fun of than fake and safe.

The biggest smile she can remember having at school crosses her face, and she is glad that classes are going on at the moment so she's alone, although when she thinks about it for a second she finds herself wishing that everyone *could* see it, because this is her, this is Tillie Stanley, and she almost didn't make it, but she did, and now she knows. She knows! The joke isn't on her. It's on them.

She feels her eyes welling up, and even though no one is in the hallway, she steals into the quiet restroom almost no one uses because it's tucked in the science wing, along a less-used hallway.

She opens the door and standing there, staring in the mirror, is Molly Tobin.

Tillie stops in her tracks, like she's hiking and she's just come across a bear.

Molly turns toward her. Her eyes are rimmed red, and she frowns, exasperated.

"What? Jesus. What the hell do you want?"

Tillie is stunned into silence. So she stands there, voiceless.

Molly huffs. "Oh, you probably love this."

And there's a part of Tillie that does. But she pushes that part down, because there's a crying girl standing in front of her, in the rarely used bathroom along the science corridor.

"You okay?" Tillie finds herself asking.

"Peachy. I'm *perfect*. I'm *wonderful*. Can you just go, please? You've already ruined my life."

But Tillie doesn't go. "Nope," she says.

"You won't go?"

"Nope. Not going."

"So you're just going to gloat? Fine. Terrific."

"Molly," Tillie says, "shut up. Stop talking."

Molly's expression is maybe even more shocked than Samantha's was.

Tillie goes on. "So what's wrong?"

Molly runs her fingers through her hair and looks away. "Why would you even care, anyway?"

Tillie leans against a sink. "Because you're a person?"

"A person who made a video about you."

"Yeah, about that. What the fuck. Why would you—"

Molly puts her hands over her eyes. "I don't know. I really, really don't. Could you just go, please? I'm really not in a place—"

"I was suicidal, Molly."

"Because of—"

"Not really. I mean. Not entirely. My life's been shitty in lots of ways. It wasn't like, you made a mean video and I decided to jump off a bridge, okay? You don't have that power over me. But yeah. That wasn't fun. How would you feel if someone made a video like that about you?"

Molly slinks down the wall until she's sitting on the floor. "Jesus."

"I can't actually imagine why a person would do that, but you did it. So . . ."

"I'm sorry," Molly whispers.

Hearing these two words just about takes Tillie's breath away. It's like she'd imagined confronting Molly a zillion times, and none of the times did Molly simply say she was sorry.

"Thank you."

"Sure. I suck. That's basically the consensus right now."

"What happened?"

"It's over," Molly says.

"What's over?"

Molly snorts. "The reign of Molly Tobin. Over. It's like I left for a week, and I came back and it's all gone."

Tillie comes and leans against the closest sink to Molly. "Is that really so bad?"

Molly screws her face up, and it's like Tillie can see the split. Between the Molly she used to know and the new one.

Molly stares at nothing. Like several inches to the side of Tillie. "I don't know."

"I'm sorry. That must suck, I guess."

"Why are you being so nice?" Molly pulls her knees up and rests her chin on them.

Tillie says, "This is what nice people do when they see some-one struggling. They don't, like, tease them."

"I guess I deserve that."

"Yeah. You do."

Molly wipes her eyes. "Sorry. Really."

"Thanks. I'm better now. I mean, not a hundred percent better, but I've figured some shit out. I'm done being quiet about all that shit. I punched Samantha Quinn about twenty minutes ago."

Molly flinches. "You did?"

Tillie nods.

"Wow," Molly says. "What happened? You used to be happy."

Tillie flashes on sixth grade, and Saturday mornings with Molly. She remembers Dylan's Candy Bar and candy binges. Something about narwhals and llamas. Lots of laughter. It feels like another lifetime, actually. "Was I? I don't remember."

"You were happier. I mean, somewhere around ninth grade you got kinda . . . severe. Fashion-wise for sure, but also your expres-sion. The way you glowered at people. I was like—*I used to know that girl.*"

"Well, you changed, too."

Molly chuckles under her breath. "Maybe not quite as much as I should have."

"What?"

"Nothing. It's hard, okay? Try being Molly Tobin and liking . . ."

"Liking what?"

Molly sits up again. "Okay. So I know it won't equalize anything. But what if I tell you a secret? And you know what? If you want to, like, tell everyone? I don't fucking care. It's not like Gretchen and Isabella have the time of day for me anymore."

"Molly, if you're about to tell me you're a lesbian, you'll be the second person in two days to come out to me as an excuse for being a jerk."

This makes Molly smile in a way that Tillie remembers from all those years ago, this sweet, sunny smile with the dimples spreading wide.

"You ever hear of Throne of Glass?"

Tillie shakes her head.

"So I'm kind of obsessed."

"Really?"

"Yeah. Celaena Sardothien is everything. I've read the entire series like twelve times. I cyberstalk Sarah J. Maas's Instagram, hoping against hope that one day she'll answer. My absolutely biggest dream is to go to a con dressed like Celaena and meet Ms. Maas."

Tillie breaks out laughing. Molly stares at her for a moment, and then she realizes it's okay and laughs, too.

"I guess it's kinda stupid," she says.

"No, not at all. This would be, like, my favorite thing about you, probably, at this point."

"Are you into fantasy?"

"Not particularly. But I like that you are. That you're not some Spence robot. No offense."

"Some offense. But yeah. I get it. So are we good?"

Tillie snorts. "Yeah, Molly. We're great. All's totally forgiven. No, we're not good."

Molly offers Tillie a sad smile. "But are we better?"

Tillie can't remember the last time she had this. Power. Of any sort.

"We'll see," she says.

Good morning, sweet cheeks!

Um . . . what, Aaron?

Can I call you that?

You definitely cannot. Who is this and what have you done to my friend Aaron?

I'm happy today! I know it's weird but it's like the birds are singing and the frogs are chirping and the cows are bleating and all that

Okay . . . so this is you chipper then

Yes! Do you like it? Do you like it?

Um. Sure?

Yay! I think the world should be filled with happy people. Like we should start a movement on the streets where we say hello to people and if they don't say hi back we shame them but they will because people intrinsically like to be happy.

Okay . . .

This is the start of something BIG!

Yay, big things

Aaron sits with Sarah Palmer on the subway, she of the ungenerous view of Aaron's performance in *Rent* the day he almost died. But this time, they don't talk about acting. Aaron has other things on his mind.

"I wrote this song yesterday," he tells her. "It's called 'Seventy-Fourth Street' and I don't know if it's good but anyway it got me thinking. Do you think we could start a movement? Like of people saying hi to each other on the street?"

"Um. Why would we do that?"

"To be nice to each other! That's maybe the takeaway out of all of this. I guess I was depressed or whatever—"

Sarah puts her sneakers up against the bottom of the pole people hold on to when it's crowded. "Yeah, I heard about that. How are you? A lot of us have been really worried."

Aaron almost stops to ask how she knows, how people know, but it's so beside the point right now he skips right over it.

"I'm fine and that's what I'm saying. I was depressed and then my eyes opened and I realized that a lot of depression is closed-off-ness. Like I was closed off to niceness because I was . . . I don't know, but now I just feel like we should all be nicer to each other, you know?"

"Well, yeah."

"But could you just imagine? What if we all wore name tags and people called you by your name?"

"Like at school?"

"No! Like on Seventy-Fourth Street. Which was the vision I had. Of this one street where everyone was nice. Like people on the street decided to do it as an experiment."

Sarah gives Aaron side eye. "Wait, what?"

"Maybe it would be a city ordinance or a proclamation . . ."

"Are you okay? You're actually scaring me a little." She picks up her book bag and hugs it to her chest.

Aaron cackles. "I'm scaring you? Is talking about being nice actually scary now?"

She opens her bag. "I'm gonna . . . I think I'm gonna study for my Spanish test."

"Sarah, come on. I'm just. I'm kind of joking, okay?"

Sarah glances sideways at Aaron but won't look him in the eye. "Okay. But yeah. Gonna study."

"Suit yourself."

×

Tillie approaches the principal's office feeling totally conflicted. Everything is new, and everything is tentative. Which makes her wonder. No major decisions—that was her mom's advice this morning. She's changing in a big way, and her life is new and different and tentative. Maybe she should pass on the assembly and just focus on being the Tillie who's not willing to take anybody's shit anymore. Maybe she should focus on how weird it was that Molly passed her in the hallway this morning and said, "Hey."

That was as surprising as anything.

She sits and waits for Pembree to be free, and she goes through all the pros and cons.

Pros: She'd be expressing herself. She'd be real.

Cons: Real hasn't always gone over well at school, and does she really owe these people anything?

Yeah, no. This isn't her job. Surely they could find an expert to come in and talk about online bullying, and everyone can ignore it like every other time some outside speaker has come in to talk about the issue of the day. And everything will remain the same, forever.

"Tillie! So does this mean you've thought about what I talked to you about yesterday?" the principal asks.

Tillie swallows hard. "Yes," she says. "Sign me up. Let's do this thing."

The principal smiles, and damned if Tillie doesn't feel this new sensation of pride ride up her spine.

×

At lunch, Aaron heads to his usual table companions, mostly band geeks and theater people. Wylie and Marissa Jones, who are boyfriend and girlfriend and NOT brother and sister, wave him over.

"Aaron!" Marissa says. "I'm so glad you're back!"

"Yeah," Aaron says. "I'm back, baby."

Marissa screws up her face at him like, *What?* And then she awkwardly laughs.

"So how are you doing?" Wylie asks.

"I'm actually really good. I think the time off cleared my mind a lot, and they put me on these pills? And they say they take months to work sometimes, but mine worked really, really, really fast, because this is day six, and I feel really clear, like essentially clear, like to my essence, clear. Which makes me wonder if I wasn't really depressed in the first place? That it's just in the head? Ha-ha, in the head. But you know what I mean, right? Like I made it up. I was being dramatic about my feelings, maybe, because honestly, I can't even remember what took me up there. Oh! The bridge! I don't even know if people know about that. Did you know? A week ago

Wednesday. Yeah. I went to the GWB. But honestly I don't think I was really going to jump because . . . ta-da! Here I am, a week later, and I'm fine, I'm totally fine."

Marissa, who has rarely heard Aaron say more than a simple sentence outside of a play or musical, says, "Oh my god, Aaron. Wow. Okay."

Wylie says, as calmly as possible, "We're glad you're back."

"Me too. Me too!"

✕

Tillie has been ignoring Amir's texts, but on Friday afternoon, she decides to respond. Amir's written, Can I please buy you coffee after school? Just to apologize. Promise.

She replies, Fine. Midnight Express Diner, half hour. And I get food if I want.

✕

Amir is waiting at a booth when she arrives, and it bugs the shit out of her but she gets this little flutter when she sees him.

Conversation is scarce, and Tillie is relieved when the waiter finally arrives. Amir orders the Cubano chicken panini and Tillie gets her favorite, the French fry burger, because who wouldn't want a burger topped with French fries?

"So what's been going on in your life?" Amir asks.

Tillie swallows and grabs her burger to bide time. She chews methodically and, once she can, she says, "Not much. Gonna do an assembly on online bullying."

"Oh," he says. "Cool. Were you online bullied?"

It takes just about everything for Tillie not to smack him, but then she realizes of course he has no idea. So she is merciful and says, "Yep."

Amir pushes his sandwich around his plate. "I'm really sorry. And the funny thing is, there were lots of times I really wanted to write you just because you're Tillie and I like you. I didn't know how to deal with the thing, though."

Tillie cringes. Is going out with her now better known as "the thing"? "Yeah," she says. "That all kinda sucks."

"But you get it, right? That it wasn't about you? That you're great? Because, um . . ." Amir looks around and lowers his voice. "If I were even bi? I would so be your boyfriend. And I'm not just saying that like some jackass dude. I'm saying it because it's incontrovertibly true."

"Oh, gee, thanks," Tillie says, flat. But in reality, part of her feels lighter for him saying it so clearly. "It's good to know that my gay ex-boyfriend thinks I'm a righteous babe."

He looks around like he's afraid someone heard. "Yeah, can you maybe not say that so loud?"

"Jeez. Your mom has spies everywhere?"

"That's my assumption."

"Well, that sucks."

"Yeah."

Tillie mashes down her bun on the once-crispy, now-soggy French fries. She says, "So assuming I ever forgive you, are we, like, friends again, in your twisted mind?"

Amir gives her a funny look. "I would like to be, yeah."

Tillie swigs her Coke. "Well, we'll see. A few more meals on you, for starters . . ."

He smirks. Her phone goes off.

Tillie mutters, "Shit." Is he suicidal again? He went back to school today. Was it a really bad day?

"What's up?" Amir asks.

"It's a long story. A friend in need."

Where are you?

I'm coming your way. Couldn't sit back at home and just let this happen. Tell you when I get there. Where am I going?

She gives him the address and he shoots her a thumbs-up sign.

When she looks up at Amir to explain, a weird wave of something like jealousy runs through her midsection. No. She is not ready for Amir and Aaron to see each other again. She isn't ready to share Aaron. Or Amir.

"So maybe we should call it a day?" she asks.

Amir laughs and raises an eyebrow. "Would it be okay if I finish my panini first, or are half-eaten meals part of this extensive apology tour?"

"Just . . . finish, okay?"

He takes a comically slow bite, and she groans.

"It feels like there's something you're not telling me," he says while chewing.

"No. Yes. Kind of. It's complicated. Aaron and me. We're complicated."

"Oh! Wait. He's gay, too, right?"

"Yes, asshole. Not everything complicated is about dating."

"You've changed a little," he observes. "You kind of say everything that's on your mind now."

She matches his eye. "When I didn't, I wound up on a bridge, so."

347

"Right," he says, and they go back to eating.

About five minutes later, there's a flash of motion and the energy in the restaurant shifts. It's just a door opening, and the door has opened numerous times since they've been sitting in the booth across the way. But something about this particular entrance sucks the energy away from the booth. Both Amir and Tillie look its way.

"Hi, hi, hi," Aaron says, bursting in and sitting right next to Tillie. Then he kisses her forehead with such abruptness that it makes Tillie cringe and wipe her brow with the back of her hand.

"Ugh," she says.

Aaron laughs. "Sorry. Out of breath and need water. Ran like a million miles to get here fast. Actually outran the bus, thank you very much, all the way from Seventy-Ninth. Water, please!"

He yells that part to no one in particular, and Tillie's eyes get big.

"Um, hi," she says slowly.

"Oh my God. I didn't realize HE would be here. Did he apologize like a zillion times? Did you punch him like you did that girl?"

"Aaron!" Tillie says, shocked.

Aaron turns to Amir. "And I didn't say this before, but, wow. You're stunning."

Amir ducks his head, and Tillie says, "Um."

Aaron giggles. "I mean, look at me. I actually can't take my eyes off of you. For realsies. No joke. Yes homo."

"Aaron!" Tillie says, slapping his shoulder. "Stop. Really."

"Just . . . wow." Finally he does what he has to in order to look away from Amir, and he says, "It's been a day. I don't even know where to start."

"Just start. Are you okay? You seem . . . something."

"I feel reborn!" he just about shouts. "The meds are working this magic and I feel better than I ever have in my life!"

"That's great!" Tillie says, lowering her voice in the hopes that Aaron will take the hint.

He does not. Aaron turns to Amir and says, loudly enough so that the closest tables can't help but hear, "So I went on antidepressants like six days ago. They say they take a few months but BAM! Not so much. I feel so alive and that's why I'm here. To tell you about the idea!"

"You said it was an *emergency*," Tillie points out.

"Well, it is! I don't know how to get started, and I did some research and you can actually trademark an idea, but I don't know what to call it, so I thought maybe just copyright the song, or call the organization 'Seventy-Fourth Street,' because that's the name of the song, though really it's just one verse so far. I—"

For a moment, Tillie considers grabbing both his shoulders and getting him to look her in the eye so she can see if he's high or something. Instead, she puts up both hands. "Aaron. Slow down. What are you talking about?"

"The idea! One street. There's one street, and we get them to institute a law or a rule or something where everyone has to wear name tags and greet each other by name, and also the law is everyone is kind to each other. This is the thing. This is what will put me on the map!"

He looks at Tillie, then Amir. Then back to Tillie.

"Do you get it? This will change the world!"

"Seriously?" she says. "What are you even talking about, Aaron?"

"Don't tell me you don't see it. We were just talking the other day about doing the opposite of everything because obviously with the bridge—"

"Okay," Tillie says, pushing Aaron to stand up, which he does. Even though Amir knows about the bridge, Tillie feels he doesn't need to hear this. "Can we talk, just us, for a second?"

"Sure!" Aaron says.

"Give us a second, please," Tillie says to Amir, and she pushes Aaron across the restaurant and outside in about two seconds.

Out on the sidewalk, Aaron says, "He's gorgeous! I am utterly in love."

"Don't. Even. Think. About. It," Tillie says. "Seriously. I'm not that over him, and you're my—"

"What?" he says, his eyes wide open.

"Friend. So don't even think about hitting on my ex. I'm going to pretend I didn't see that before, got it?"

"Got it," he says. "But cheekbones. Oh my god. What's Amir's last name?"

She punches him lightly in the shoulder. "Stop."

"What is it?"

"Rahimi. Now just stop. You're freaking me out."

Aaron composes himself and says, "All right. Fine. I'm just so excited." He starts jumping up and down.

Tillie presses down on his shoulders until he stops. "What's wrong with you? Are you high? You're being all kinds of weird."

Aaron smirks and his face animates; his eyes jump left and right. "I'm just happy, you know? Relieved. I never thought I'd feel this way again and—"

He stops talking and rubs his eyes.

"Please don't cry on Eighty-Ninth Street," Tillie says, but Aaron is crying.

"I feel new! I am just so goddamn happy and, yeah, I'm doing this thing. I don't know how to do it, but someone climbed Mount Everest, right? Lots of people."

"Some people get hypothermia and die trying."

"Well, that's the spirit!"

They talk some more, and by the time Tillie hugs Aaron good-bye, his tears are dried, his smile is wide, and she feels a little more okay with the fact that Aaron is just on some kind of after-depression trip that she doesn't understand.

"What the hell was that?" Amir asks when Tillie returns to the table.

"I have no fucking idea," she says.

✕

In bed that night, Aaron stares at the wall, transfixed. But unlike a week ago when he couldn't stop staring at the wall, this time, it's a happy stare, a juicy, excited, life-has-an-actual-taste-and-it's-brilliant-like-the-best-ribeye-ever stare.

He's thinking about Amir's eyes. So deeply black, like onyx, almost. In those eyes he saw glorious sunshine and his future, like it all played out in those two beautiful orbs, nestled above those sculpted cheekbones.

This is his forever guy. He's been waiting. He's been patient—well, who is he kidding? There haven't been a lot of applicants as yet—but still he's held out and now he can see his life's horizon and he can't believe it's so good, and so perfect, and he could writhe out of his skin right now, and he twists from side to side and does just about everything he can not to scream out in joy.

His dad knocks on his door. Knock-pause-knock-knock-pause-knock-knock-knock. Aaron jumps up from the bed, sashays across the room, and opens the door with a flourish.

"Hola!"

His dad smirks and raises his eyebrows. "Well, isn't someone chipper for ten p.m.? Sorry I'm working so late these days."

"It's fine," Aaron says. "In fact, it's good. I got a lot going on. Gives me time to live this new way."

"Oh," his dad says. "What new way?"

I'm in love! he wants to shout, but he also doesn't want to jinx it. Not yet. Once it's solidified, then yeah, for sure. From various Manhattan rooftops at midnight.

He puts his palms wide on both sides of his face and he says, "I'm not depressed anymore, Dad! It's amazing. This thing? The way I feel? Is this, like, how people who are normal feel?"

His dad laughs. "You're plenty normal. And yes. Happiness is a normal emotion, and frankly I should have seen that. I saw it but I didn't. Your depression. I'm sorry, kiddo. So deeply sorry."

"Water under the bridge," Aaron says, and his dad seems affected by the word, and Aaron laughs a bit. "Sorry. Word choice. So I need to tell you about Project Seventy-Fourth Street at some point, and there's this other thing I can't tell you yet but hopefully soon and it's gonna be different. From now on I'm gonna be way different."

"Whoa," his dad says. "Who is this energetic person, and what have you done to my son?"

Aaron laughs. "This is it. The new me! Multitasking and changing the world because the world definitely needs changing, and I'm pretty sure I was born to do this. Born for this."

His dad studies him. It takes a little bit, but a smile blooms on his face. "Well, this is quite a change," he says.

"More to come!" Aaron says. "More to come!"

X

When his dad goes off to bed, Aaron goes back to writhing between the sheets and finding all the various ways to say that name. A-MEER Ra-HE-ME. Am-ur RA-he-ME. Such a melodic name. Someday Aaron will write a song about him.

All his life, Aaron's wanted—needed, actually—a boyfriend. Someone who really knows him and likes him anyway, and more than that, someone like a kindred spirit, who shares this need, this yearning. His dad gave him the talk and he knows—it's natural, blah blah—but how do you find that person? Negotiate such a thing? Because all his life, or all since he was fourteen, has been yearning, yearning, needing, and that seems like a hard thing to communicate, and a hard thing to ask for. What if they say no? What if they say yes? He's not been sure which is scarier.

But this. This will change all that. Amir. This is the first time in his life—his whole life!—that he can even imagine broaching that topic with another boy. Telling him whatever. That he likes him. That he wants to be with him.

You can't choose who you love. And Tillie won't get that at first, but over time? She'll get it. He's gay, not straight. What, should she wait for him to fall for someone they don't even know? That's a waste of a perfect guy.

Aaron wakes up at 5:26 a.m. on Saturday with a passion for life and the song "History Has Its Eyes on You" blaring in his brain.

Some people are meant for special things. How did he not know? That he's special? That his ideas would change the world?

And Amir! Yes, there was definitely a vibe. Forget boyfriend. This was lover material. Husband. Those eyes, those cheekbones.

What to do at 5:28 a.m.? What can be accomplished on his life's new mission, on his need to tell Amir he's the one in a special, special way? Oh! Breakfast in bed! His dad!

He jumps out of bed thinking, man, if this is what being un-depressed is like, why didn't he do this years ago? Jesus, he would have been the happiest person alive, because he feels like he could jump out of his skin, it all feels so electric.

He has a lyric in his head. What about rap? He likes rap. Could he write a rap?

I am who I am and that's important, very

What you think of me is secondary

And he means it. He is done living his life the way others would have him live it. He's spent enough of his days in some kind of mental prison and now his brain is out and his body, too, and—*Do we have a bike? In the basement?* He used to have a bike locked up down there.

So he gets dressed—tight pink T-shirt because he can, and he looks in the mirror and sees his skinny frame and thinks: *Am I a twink? Am I kind of hot?* He giggles at the thought. All his life he's thought he was ugly. All his life has been without that special someone, but not anymore. That crap is over, over!

He takes the elevator downstairs, and no bike is familiar and he laughs because he should have asked his dad but his dad is asleep and—he scans the other bikes and, wait, is that one—when he gets closer he can see the actual lock is open so he snakes the coiled lock off the bike, hoists it up over the stall where it's been resting, and wheels it out of the basement.

He's borrowing a bike. It happens to be a really nice one *but let's face it, I have expensive taste.*

Out on the early-morning streets, the sky is still mostly dark and Seventy-Eighth Street is quiet and he wonders if he's all alone out here. Why doesn't he always wake up this early and enjoy this perfect time of the day? The streets are devoid of moving cars, his heart is light and his skin is reborn, and he thinks: *Zabar's! Yes!* Imagine his dad's face when he comes home with bagels and lox and fresh-squeezed orange juice from Zabar's, and that's expensive but he should be able to—*Where is that tray? The one Magda used to use when she ate on her bed in the back room?* No idea. He'll have to search when he gets home with the loot.

Zabar's is closed, though. The sign says they open at eight, and his watch says 5:41. He laughs, loud. Then louder. It's really funny, if he thinks about it. Here he is, on a bike that technically isn't his, and, oh yeah, he should have borrowed a helmet, too, but he forgot, and it's two and a half hours before the store opens. That's nearly a full sleep cycle. A decrepit-looking man in tattered jeans and a stocking cap that's too small for his head walks by and says, "The heck is wrong with you?" and Aaron's heart soars as he thinks about Seventy-Fourth Street and he yells back, "Good morning!" And then the guy stops like Aaron has just challenged him, and Aaron says, "No, no. I only have good thoughts in my head for you," and he pulls out his wallet and he hands the guy his only twenty, and the guy just looks down at the money in his hand, and then he closes his fist, crinkling the cash, and he walks off, shaking his head, and Aaron thinks, *This is how you change the world.*

And he could change the world, definitely. The depression has lifted—by a lot—and if he is going to feel like this all the time, he could create a new way of being in the world. He'll talk to strangers and give people anything he has because, face it, Dad has money, he's not going to miss it, and Dad will be so proud because he's a giver, too, and he wants good things for the world, too, and now they can do it together, and for the moment maybe a turn around the loop in Central Park? Yes. A lap around the park on this beautiful bike, in this splendid morning air, while he figures out this brand-new plan for fixing the world, one communication at a time.

Climbing the incline from 110th southbound on the west side as he's finishing up his first lap, he hears his breathing, glances down at his pale, skinny arms and the pink shirt and thinks—*I should work out. I should get strong.* Inside match outside. He shouts "Yeah!" to the world around him. The few bikers ahead glance backward, a little fear in their eyes.

A middle-aged lady in a yellow helmet, biking fast forward while looking back at him, yells, "Nice shirt!"

"Thanks!" he yells back, and he starts pedaling as fast as he can to catch up to her. She's faster, though, and he finds himself laughing about the fact that he can't catch a middle-aged lady in a yellow helmet, and still all is good in the world. Great, really.

He finds himself in front of Amir's apartment building. Sometimes life is surprising, because this isn't planned, but that makes it more romantic, more of a gesture, which Amir will surely appreciate.

He's not sure which apartment to buzz. He should have paid closer attention when Tillie did it. Momentarily he thinks: buzz them all. That cracks him up, the idea of all these people buzzing down like, "What? What do you want, strange person?" Then he thinks, text Tillie! But no, she's not so okay with this—*yet*, she will be, but not yet—so no.

So he stands out front, stares up the building—maybe twelve floors, maybe eight—and thinking of *A Streetcar Named Desire* and "STELLA!" he widens his arms and yells, "AMIR!"

It feels so good to say the name. Names that start with a vowel are—oh! His! Ha!

"AMIR! AMIR! AMIR!"

A window opens on the third floor. A head pops out. A lady with a pasty face and raccoon eyes. "Shut the hell up, idiot!" she yells.

"Sorry! Good day to you!"

She gives him the finger, which hits him a little in the heart. Not so nice. Is he a little—no. This is a romantic gesture. People lose sleep for less important things.

"AMIR! BE MINE!"

Another window, on the fifth floor, and this head is most definitely Amir's. Aaron's too far away to see his expression, but he *can* see Amir raise a non-middle finger that Aaron takes to mean, "I'll be right down," and Aaron's heart pounds because he's put it out there, and this? This is progress. This is a boy who is realizing his dreams, who is becoming his best self, who is slaying demons left and right, and the world would be proud of him if it knew, and maybe it does know? It kind of feels like—fuck that. It absolutely feels like the world knows. Aaron is done with kind of. He's done with sorry. He's done with so many things. More lyrics come to him.

So you don't like what you see
Well, blow me
I don't give a shit
I don't need you, homie
You don't own me
I don't care about you, care about me only
Lonely? No more
Only? Folklore
Postwar
Hold more
Gettin' in ground floor
This thing is about to explode
Like source code

His heart is racing. Has there been an out gay white rapper?
He's never rapped but this thing that's happening, it's in his socks,
it's in his thighs, it's in his groin, it's real.

Aaron leans his bike against a parked car and paces, his
thoughts beautifully racing—*Seventy-Fourth Street, Amir, Amir,*
rapper, Amir. He paces back and forth in front of the building's
lobby for several minutes, beginning to worry, beginning to think
maybe he needs to call up again, but then Amir, in a pair of sweats
and a stained yellow T-shirt he must have slept in, his hair pointy in
spots, darts out into the street, grabs Aaron by the shoulder, and
pulls him down the street.

As he is pulled in almost a run, Aaron is thinking *meet-cute.* He
is thinking of the perfect thing to say that will solidify—the thing
they'll tell their kids about this moment.

He's about to go with *Fancy meeting you here* when Amir turns
to him, his face tight, his forehead creased, panic in his eyes.

"What are you doing? What the hell is this?"

"I love you! There, I said it. I actually love you. I couldn't wait to tell you."

"What? What the—Aaron, right?"

Aaron laughs. Amir doesn't know his name? What the—Aaron nods, a lump growing in his throat, his mouth drying to desert level in a heartbeat.

Amir goes on. "I don't know you, but what you are doing is inappropriate, you hear me? My mother doesn't even know I'm"—he looks down the street. They are alone—"gay, okay? You almost just outed me. You almost just ruined my life, you idiot."

Aaron feels his body do something he's never felt before. Power off. Curl into itself.

He turns and runs down the street. He speeds as fast as he's ever run. He doesn't stop at Fifth Avenue, and luckily only one car is coming and he pauses so he's not hit, and he runs into the park at Seventy-Ninth Street and collapses under a tree.

X

Tillie wakes up feeling ready to take on the world, too.

This is the day. The day she's ready to do it. Confront her dad. At her next therapy session, she'll talk about it. She can do this. She can confront her last, biggest, saddest demon. Tell her dad—more like ask him. *Why don't you love me anymore? What did I do to make you drop me so completely?*

Her heart lurches and she closes her eyes. Damn. All the stuff about Molly and Amir hurt her a lot, but nothing compares to this one.

How's she going to—

A text interrupts her. It's from Amir.

> Your friend Aaron was just here, yelling outside my window. What the fuck is wrong with him?

> What are you talking about? Is this a joke

> No joke.

> ??? I'm lost. Are you kidding???

There's no response.

Her body feels shaken. Like attacked. All the good feeling about being ready to deal with her dad? It's all gone. She doesn't know what to do. Except—

Her fingers could nearly break her phone she texts Aaron so hard.

> What the fuck did you do? Call me right now

There's no response. She groans. What's happening, how did this happen, and what the hell can she do about it? She flops down on her bed and covers her body and face with a comforter.

Her mom knocks on the door. "You okay?"

"Fine," she says. How do you even explain something you don't understand? At all?

She walks into the kitchen to get a soda, because a root beer might help her think, might help her put this all together. Amir being pissed. Aaron being weird and doing—what? Why would he—

Her dad walks into the kitchen in his blue sleeping shorts and an old gray T-shirt.

She pauses in front of the refrigerator, takes a breath, and turns toward him. Suddenly her midsection is swimming in too much stuff, and she feels almost dizzy. Wrong time. But also right, because— it's here. It's happening.

He opens a cabinet, takes out a protein bar, and stands there, at the counter, looking down at it, totally ignoring her existence.

It's so personal; it's such an affront to her being. And she is so done with the silence. She won't hit. She won't yell. But she will end whatever this is. Right now.

"Okay, so," she says softly.

He doesn't look up.

"Dad."

He slowly turns his head toward her. "Hey," he says, as if nothing's wrong, nothing's been wrong. As if they have been talking all this time.

"So can we just . . . talk? About whatever this is? I hate this," she says.

He tears open his protein bar and takes a big bite. "Sure," he says, as if he's all innocent, as if the thing he said never happened. As if he hasn't been ignoring her.

He tentatively sits down on a wooden stool at the kitchen table. She sits down at the other end, her heart pounding.

"Why are you ignoring me?" she asks.

"I'm not," he says.

"Dad."

"Not talking is not the same as—"

"Dad. What is this? Seriously. You haven't said a word to me since that fight."

He scratches his ear. "What, exactly, is it you'd have me say?"

She feels like screaming at him, but she knows it won't help. She just has to bridge this weird gap that's formed between them. There used to be none. She has to just connect again. So she summons all the strength she can, and she says the delicate truth.

"I feel like you don't love me anymore. Like you did, and then you just sort of . . . I got to be too much for you or something, and it's like I'm not even your daughter anymore. You have Britt and she's easy, and I'm super hard to deal with, and it's not worth it or whatever."

He doesn't move a millimeter. Tears start to form in the corners of her eyes, and unlike usual, she doesn't even try to mask it. Because this is true. It's real, it's true, and he needs to know it.

"I love you so much, Daddy. I'm your girl, and I know I'm getting older but I still need you and that you don't seem to want me around anymore . . . hurts my heart. So I'm sorry I'm so hard. But please, Daddy. Talk to me again."

She places her head in her hands and sobs. It all rushes out of her, and it feels terrible and also wonderful, because finally, finally she's said it to him, and he knows. And he doesn't move, he doesn't come to her but also he doesn't leave. He gives her space. Which is nice.

She manages to look up at him and wipe her eyes. He's looking at her with some sort of feeling she's never seen—regret?—in his eyes. She wants to go hug him.

"Tillie," he says. "I'm . . ."

"Just say it, Daddy. Please."

"I'm not good with emotion. I'm not good with weakness. And I don't get why you . . . have this need to put your weakness out there."

It's like a knife going through her stomach. The word. *Weakness*. He thinks she's weak. He thinks she's frail. And she's all out there, in the open, and he's just sitting there, like a man who can't do anything.

She hugs her arms around her chest, and she thinks, *Oh my god. How did I not know this before?*

Her dad is unfixable. He is deficient in a peculiar way, and it's never going to change. He's the problem, not her, and it's always going to feel like she's lacking something essential, because she is.

She is lacking a father who can be there for her in any real way.

She stands up, at once trembling and totally clear, and she heads back to her bedroom, sodaless. He watches her as she leaves the kitchen like he's watching a goddamn movie, and she just wishes he could say something to make it better, but of course he can't, and she wishes she could fix him, but of course she can't.

She pauses at the kitchen door and glances back. The expression she makes at him is like a wince. She hopes it communicates everything to him. The understanding. The gulf between them.

The wreckage.

X

Aaron makes two realizations while his brain spins as he lies facedown under a tree.

One is that he forgot the bike. Fuck.

Two is that it's all a lie.

Shit. He doesn't want to deal with—Amir had it right; he's such an idiot. What's wrong with him? What's happening? His body feels zapped of energy, like he can't move.

His phone buzzes in his pocket. He can't even. He's done talking. Possibly forever. This level of embarrassment—what if people find out? Seventy-Fourth Street—what a joke. He's such a fool. Worse, really. Something that doesn't deserve to exist.

He almost ruined Amir's life. With his stupid idea. What was he thinking?

His phone buzzes again. He reaches down into his pocket.

It's Tillie.

> What the fuck did you do? Call me right now

Shit. Shit shit shit.

Aaron starts to cry. He wants his mother. He's not sure why. And maybe not his mother. Just *a* mother. Someone to wipe the slate clean and make it all better. Someone who will hug and hold him and not judge him.

His hand shakes as he replies.

> Sorry

> Sorry? What did you do? What the fuck???

> Sorry

> Did you really go over there? That's exactly what I told you not to do.

Aaron dies a little inside. He feels parts of his body numbing, maybe permanently.

> You can't be more angry at me than I am. I honestly don't know what happened there

> Actually I can be. And just so you know I just figured out my dad can't love me in any meaningful way. So that happened.

> I'm so sorry. Take care of yourself, Tillie. You have value. I have none. I'm worthless.

> Join the fucking club. I'm done. Just done

Aaron turns off his phone and puts it away, perhaps for the last time.

✕

Tillie's instinct is to walk out the door, unsure if she'll ever come back. Her body feels like it could combust. She is so fucking done with people.

She walks to the door and stops.

Because she promised. And yeah. She's feeling suddenly pretty . . . something. Unsafe.

So she sighs deeply, turns around, and knocks on her mom's door.

"Are you okay, sweetheart?"

Tillie bursts into tears. "No. Very not okay."

✕

Talking to her mom helps some. Not enough to feel okay, but enough to climb down from the figurative ledge, which is definitely where she was. She tells her about Aaron doing the one thing she asked him not to do. And about what her dad said about weakness, and they have a good cry together.

"You're the opposite of weak," her mom says.

"Yeah, sure."

"No, you are. You're very brave. You don't know that yet, but you are."

Tillie leans her head against her mom and says, "Thanks."

"You promise me you're okay? That you're not going to hurt yourself?"

"Not promising I won't hurt someone else."

"Well, that's not ideal, either. I have to say I'm shocked that Aaron would do that. That doesn't sound like him at all. Should we call his dad?"

"I don't care what you do about Aaron, to be honest. I'm done with him. I'll never trust him again."

Her mom hugs her tight. They're sitting on the daybed in the corner of her parents' bedroom. "I know this hurts, but forever is a long, long time."

"And Dad? That's basically over. I'm not his daughter anymore. I can't be."

Her mother sighs and strokes her hair. "Your father is very limited, I'm afraid. And that he's hurting you? That isn't okay with me. I don't know how to fix it, but it's not okay. And just so you know? Right now? If you made me choose? I choose you. No question."

Tillie hugs her mom tighter than she has in a long time. "Thanks, Mom."

It takes a lot to convince her mom that she's okay to go take a walk. But the truth is she is. She just needs to clear her head, do some thinking.

And when she walks down Fifth Avenue along the park, she does feel a little better. Angry still, for sure. Sad, too. But at least her mom knows, and that changes things, in a way.

She's thinking about Aaron as she passes Eighty-Sixth Street, her chin jittering with fury. It was like he'd stopped being himself. Suddenly his texts were bonkers, and he was so inappropriate at the diner, and—

Oh.

She stops walking. In the middle of the street, she slams on the brakes. How did it not occur to her? Even when she was telling her mom what Aaron did with Amir, it didn't cross her mind.

Something is really not right with Aaron. She looks at his last text: Take care of yourself, Tillie.

She tries texting him again.

No response.

She calls.

Straight to voice mail.

She calls for an Uber. Not sure he's there, but it's worth a try.

✕

Under the tree, Aaron comes to the understanding.

He's been wrong. Utterly, truly wrong. Something's come over him, and he's humiliated, and part of him feels like game over. But a bigger part knows. It's okay. He can go to his dad, who is at home. Who will love him through anything, even this. And yeah, it's probably the medicine, and no, it's probably not normal, like, not-depressed normal—did he see how the Jones-Joneses reacted at lunch yesterday? How did he not notice? And then with Amir, and the bike, and Tillie.

Poor Tillie. Who said she was done in her text before he turned off his phone.

He sits up suddenly.

Done. He'd taken it to mean about their friendship, and he'd gone into pity mode. But the thing with her dad, and the thing with Amir, and the thing with him . . .

Oh shit.

He has no money. He gave his last twenty to some homeless guy in front of Zabar's. But there's no time. Sometimes you have to just act, even if it isn't right. And that means jumping the turnstile if he has to, because he's not a hundred percent sure, but he's close.

He knows where Tillie is.

×

The bridge is just as terrible as it was ten days ago. Tillie rushes up the stairs, ignoring how winded it makes her. As she ascends, she feels the ghosts of all the jumpers howling inside her skull, and she wishes she were lightning fast, and she's ready to rush to him, hopeful she isn't too late. It's like she knows. She feels his presence there, somehow.

But he's not there.

She rushes anyway, needing to feel the railing the whole way, hoping against hope it'll all be cold to the touch so she won't have to think about the unthinkable.

She was angry, yes, but how could she have been so oblivious? How could she not have known that something wasn't right with him?

Please. Don't let me be too late.

×

"Tillie!"

Tillie turns quickly. Aaron is behind her, running toward her, frantic.

"Don't! Please! Don't!"

She turns and runs toward him. "I'm so sorry! So sorry, Aaron!"

They run into each other's arms, and they embrace, and they let the tears fly.

"God. Please. Don't," Aaron says.

Tillie pulls back. "Wait. *You. You* don't."

"Wait, what?"

"I came here to make sure you didn't . . ."

Aaron's eyes light up. "Me too."

×

They sit on the concrete of the walkway, legs splayed out, backs safely against the barrier, looking at the metal railing in front of them and beyond that, the infinite blue of the sky and the mass of skyscrapers that is New York City.

They hold hands, tightly, like letting go would be fatal.

They don't talk for quite a while.

Aaron is thinking about imperfection, and all the things he seemingly doesn't know about himself, and that he's lived his life to this point like he knows everything. How depression snuck up on him, and then this other thing, this whatever, that raised him up so high he became a different person. And how do you trust your brain when it's so empty of knowledge, so unaware of what's real? And will that ever go away, or will life always be like this?

And will it always be so precarious? So scary, so *it could all go away tomorrow*? Because that's what the bridge symbolizes to him. The sense of impermanence. Because it could have all ended here. It could have.

But all that is real in the moment, it seems, is the brown-and-black-speckled concrete beneath them with little chunks of gray and white stone that shine intermittently as the sun breaks through the clouds, and the slightly chilly air that sweeps through his hair, and the frantic sound and harsh smell of vehicles speeding between

New York and New Jersey, and his friend, still grasping his hand so tightly. She is real. And she is safe. And he is so grateful for that. And so willing to do whatever he has to do to make it right after almost screwing everything up. If she'll let him.

Tillie is pondering weakness as the bridge rumbles and vibrates through her body. That word, and how her father used it, but her mother said brave. Is she weak or brave? What would other people in her life say?

And who the hell cares? What would she say?

She just sped up the stairs of the George Washington Bridge to make sure a friend she was mad at didn't jump. Is that weak?

She stares at the rusted metal that was nearly the last thing she touched in this world just over a week ago, and she thinks about how she didn't jump, and that's brave. To stay when things are so shitty-feeling is brave.

That makes her smile. Because it's probably the first time in her life she's ever felt courageous.

"This is gonna suck," Aaron finally says, staring at a rust spot on the railing.

Tillie doesn't even need to ask what he means. "Yeah. Some of it. And some of it will be good."

"The medication thing, for me, is gonna suck. And coming back from all the people who saw me like that. You, for example. I'm so sorry, Tillie. I would never, ever do that."

"You did, though. But yeah. I know. You weren't in your right head."

He leans his head against her shoulder and nuzzles up against her.

"Are you now?" she asks.

"Kinda sorta. It's like I woke out of it. But I have just about no confidence that I can trust my judgment, like maybe ever again. Do you know I stole a bike today?"

She turns her body a bit toward him and his head slips off her shoulders. He straightens up. The bridge shakes beneath and around them.

"I did not know that."

"In the moment, neither did I."

"Wow."

"Yeah, wow. You gonna be okay? With your dad?"

"Nah," she says. "I think that's probably never, ever gonna be okay."

He doesn't need to answer. "So we just . . . keep going?"

"I guess. What's the alternative?"

And they look out at the sky and know that the alternative is so precariously close that it can't even be spoken.

It's a different test entirely that Dr. Laudner hands Aaron the next morning.

Still the same options for answers: *Quite a Lot, Not at All*, etc. But this time the questions make Aaron feel like someone's been listening to his thoughts.

Did he have special plans for the world?

Had his mind never been sharper?

So he aces it, basically, and he knows, while acing it, that this is not the greatest news.

Dr. Laudner scores it, writes a note on top, and doesn't even give Aaron the score. It's that bad.

"So it would appear the Petralor kicked you up into a manic episode. That can happen," the doctor says.

Aaron stares at him. Wouldn't that have been good to communicate prior to it actually happening?

"We'll put you on something that is more appropriate for bipolar disorder."

"So is this, like, something I have now? Like I caught a virus and it's forever?"

Dr. Laudner shakes his head. "What's not clear to me is whether this is a one-shot thing, or if this is a pattern in your life. We can talk about that and eventually we'll figure it out."

Aaron stares out the window. *Bipolar.* The word had never had any real meaning to him. Suddenly it does.

"So we don't know whether this is a thing that could happen to me at any time?"

"One of the most important questions is, has it been happening without you or anyone around you noticing?"

Aaron scans his life for times he felt energized like he did yesterday and the day before. He comes up blank.

"I really don't think so."

"Then it's probably just a one-off, and probably tied to the medication. But we'll keep an eye on it and keep talking about it, okay? Sometimes people are less aware of their lives than they'd think."

The truth of this hits Aaron hard, and he clams up. He doesn't really want to discuss anything at the moment. He wants his bed. He wants to be able to erase the past forty-eight hours.

"How will I know?" Aaron finally asks.

"Know what?"

"If my happiness is real?" His voice is soft, tentative.

"My guess is you'll just know."

Aaron isn't sure what to do with that. How can he trust himself ever again?

×

After a lot of back and forth, Amir agrees to meet with Tillie. This time it's Tillie who feels awkward and apologetic.

They meet in Central Park, not too far from the spot where, unbeknownst to them, Aaron collapsed yesterday. They sit on a park bench, with room for a very large person to sit in between them.

"So I'm sorry," Tillie says.

"There's a lot of that with us."

"I'm not sorry because I did anything wrong," she says. "Because I actually didn't. I told him hands off with you, because that would be weird. He did it all himself. I'm sorry it happened, and that's all."

Amir stretches his arms up. "Well, I guess that does take you off the hook. Sorry I jumped to conclusions."

"Ugh. So much sorry," Tillie says, and Amir nods.

"So is he getting help? 'Cause he really needs help. Did you know he was fucking crazy or was this new to you, too?"

Tillie frowns and looks into Amir's eyes. "Maybe stop with the 'crazy' stuff."

"Okay. Sorry. Whatever he is. Manic?"

"I guess. I didn't know about that manic thing. I don't think he did, either. A medicine kicked him up."

"Ah. Well, that's a lot to deal with."

Tillie laughs. "That's been the theme of the past few weeks."

"Can you and I maybe do a thing where we say a blanket apology? Because there's been a lot of sorry in our conversations."

Tillie says, "I don't think the sorrys will change anything. I think what's going to happen is we'll learn to trust each other again. Or not."

"But you're willing to try?"

She gives him a half smile. "I think I am."

X

Aaron is writing in his journal when his dad knocks on the door around lunchtime.

"How are you holding up?" his dad asks.

Aaron sighs. "Been better." It's been an hour since he took his first new pill. He was aware he wouldn't feel anything right away, but there was a bit of a sadness along with the relief. Relief that this would help his brain stop tripping over itself and stop the wave after wave of thoughts and excitement. Sadness because . . . excitement. He'd miss this, in a way. Even now, even digging out of a deep crater of his own making, one he hates, he knows. He'll miss the way his brain was firing on all cylinders.

"What'cha doing there?"

"The journal you gave me. I called it 'Thoughts from Up High, Never to Fall.' Irony alert."

His dad sits in the blue rocking chair and pushes until he's steadily swaying back and forth. "No one could have guessed—"

"But could we have, maybe?" Aaron says. "I've been thinking all morning about this. Is my songwriting kind of—embarrassing?"

His dad stops the chair with his toes. "Are you kidding me? I love your songs!"

"Yeah, but."

"No buts. Your songs are terrific. It's amazing how you figured out how to put music to them without any lessons. I'm always telling my MKP buddies—"

"Yeah, but that's the thing. I've never had lessons, and I'm always thinking about how I'm gonna be all famous."

His dad starts to slowly rock again. "Ah. Okay. That's a little different."

"So is that manic?"

"Why do you want to be famous?"

"Just so that people . . . I don't know. Know me. Hear me. Love me. Respect me."

"So getting famous is how you'll become loved and respected?

I can think of maybe hundreds of former child actors and singers who would tell you that doesn't work so well."

Aaron laughs. "Is it weird that I never thought of it that way? I just feel like, I need to be like a shooting star. Like I need my wins to be big just to . . ."

"Just to what?"

Aaron puts his hands over his face and pushes his hair back. "I don't know. I don't want to talk about it. Ugh."

"That's fine," his dad says.

But Aaron does know. The words he didn't say. *Just to be enough.*

It's been quite a twenty-four-hour period, and it's like his brain has run a marathon and is in need of a massive amount of electrolytes or something. He's embarrassed. Majorly so. What he did with Amir seemed so normal at the time, like he didn't give it a second thought, and the bicycle, which he hasn't even told his dad about, because, man. He can't even deal with that. Hopefully there's no camera downstairs, or in the lobby. Of course there is. Shit.

"So I may have stolen a bike from the basement."

"Oh," his dad says, stopping his rocking again.

"It's like it didn't occur to me in the moment that it was even weird to do. I was so—*driven. So gotta go do this thing.*"

"What was that thing, by the way? You were trying to explain it to me and I didn't get it."

Aaron sighs again and covers himself with the blanket. "It doesn't matter. It wasn't real. And that's what sucks. It wasn't real. None of it. And I did some of it at school, which is humiliating."

His dad comes and sits next to him.

"You know what? The old me would have told you it wasn't. But you're right. That's pretty humiliating."

Aaron laughs ruefully. "Thanks, Dad."

"No, I just mean maybe it'll be better to meet you in the real world rather than try to make it all better for you. You were manic. You probably acted in some ways that people noted. It's embarrassing, yes. But you can come back from it. People embarrass themselves all the time. Then they go back in and deal with it. They apologize to people if they wronged them."

Aaron snuggles in. His dad continues.

"I know you don't always want to talk to me, because I'm your dad, and it's a crime or whatever to actually talk real to your dad. But I see you, Aaron. And you have nothing to be embarrassed about with me, okay? I am nothing but proud of you, ever. I have nothing but love and admiration for you. You always have that, always. Hear me?"

Aaron feels the words and their warmth pass through his entire body and park themselves in his chest. He closes his eyes and accepts them.

"I hear you," he says.

✕

The text comes in from an unknown number. It just says: Hey

Tillie texts back: Who is this?

Molly

Oh. hi

I just thought you'd appreciate knowing that I've been outed

What

I decided to go to a con. My mom walked in on me

Tillie stifles a laugh. This seems pretty much like a first-world problem.

Oh no

Oh yes. She screamed.

Ok so that made me laugh. Sorry?

Why do you think I'm telling you? It's funny.
I mean, come on

So she screamed?

she was so disappointed

poor molly

no shit. She was even sadder when she found
out i was going to a con as Celaena Sardothien.

Uh oh. what did she think you were doing

Being a hooker

This makes Tillie cackle.

this whole story leaves me . . . speechless.
I'm not sure what to do with this?

maybe come over later and commiserate? Also I can tell you
about the con, because I'm totally going. Alone, by the way

Tillie has not been this surprised by anything in a long time.
And it's been a rather surprising few weeks.

gotta see my depressed friend, but maybe after

sure. I'm up late

I'll bring fiddle faddle

yes!

×

Aaron's not used to company on Sunday nights. He also not used to greeting company of any sort in pajamas. But with Tillie, and with how he's feeling, he indeed does answer the door in his pajamas.

Scooby-Doo pajamas.

"You are not serious," she says.

"What was your first clue?"

She laughs. "I kind of like them. They're very . . . you."

"And what does 'very me' mean? Please edify me."

"Very *I stay home a lot but also I'm adorable and if people only knew how great I was, I wouldn't be home as much.* Kind of like me, plus the adorable."

Aaron blushes. "First of all, that's the nicest thing anyone has ever, ever said about me. Secondly, you are totes adorbs. Did I say that right?"

"I don't think you saying those words will ever sound quite right."

"Could you pull it off?"

"Definitely not."

They go into his bedroom and Aaron allows Tillie to feed Carpi B and Britney Spearfish, and then he puts on his dad's playlist, the one with the Wilson Phillips song.

"This is my new favorite song," he says.

"Ironically?"

He shakes his head. "My dad played it for me this afternoon, after we had this talk about being real with each other. And it really hit me, the way a song can do, you know? It feels like my life, or at least one possibility of what my life could be. So no. Totally unironically."

Tillie listens to it. Aaron isn't sure if she gets it, but when it's over, she says, "I love it, too. It's sweet."

"It's Seventy-Fourth Street sweet," he says.

"I don't know what that means. Wanna explain?"

Aaron runs his hands through his hair. "Maybe another time. Maybe never. I'm so embarrassed about that. About everything. Really. I'm—"

"No. We're not doing sorry. I get it, Aaron. You weren't fully there. Apology not needed, okay?"

"Thanks. Want a whiskey or something to wash down your sorrow?"

She raises one eyebrow.

"It's what I call LaCroix seltzer. Makes me feel less ridiculous about being a sixteen-year-old boy drinking seltzer in his room."

She laughs. "Yes, please."

While Aaron is out getting two cans of seltzer, Aaron's dad sticks his head in the room.

"Thanks for everything," he says. "What you did yesterday, when you went up to the bridge? That was heroic, okay? You've earned your place on my indebted-forever list."

Tillie blushes. "He did it for me, too."

"No. Thank you. Thank you a lot," Aaron's dad says, and he gives her a thumbs-up and walks away.

"Your dad is awesome," Tillie says when Aaron comes back and hands her a peach can of seltzer. It says PAMPLEMOUSSE on it, which she knows means *grapefruit* in French.

Aaron swigs his coconut LaCroix. "He is kinda okay, isn't he?"

"I'm jealous."

"I wish I could make your thing better. Your thing with your dad. He sounds sucky."

"He really is. Do you know he just sat there? I, like, sobbed, and you know what he said?"

"What?"

"Nothing. Not a word."

"Wow."

"Yeah."

"So what are you gonna do about it? You did amazing with the girl and with the guy who shall not be named. What about your dad?"

Tillie pinches the flesh of her right oblique between her left thumb and forefinger. "I don't think there's anything to be done. That's just who he is. I could disown him, I guess. Or I could—I don't know. Ugh. I'm so tired of having to do everything, you know? I just want it to be wireless."

"Wireless?"

"Yeah. Like here's how things work. You plug it in, the battery charges, and then your phone can run the app. And you need the app to run. The app may save your life, or make your day okay. But it doesn't just happen, you know. I have to plug it in. I plug it in, and then things happen."

The weirdest thing occurs then. She starts to feel tears rolling down her cheeks and she just lets them. She had no idea. That she felt so strongly. About wires.

"I just want things to happen without me, you know?"

"Wow," Aaron says.

"Especially with my dad, you know? He should know. He should be different but he just isn't. And that's . . . sad, I guess."

"It is."

Tillie wipes her eyes. "I just think it's his move."

"How's that working so far?"

"How's what working?"

"Waiting for your dad to do something you want him to do?"

Tillie bites her lip, hard.

"I hate you, you know."

"I hate you, too."

"How can you be so smart about my shit, and so dumb about your own shit?"

Aaron rolls backward on his spine like some sort of yoga thing, then rolls up into a seated position. "It's a gift," he says.

X

Her parents and Britt are asleep, so Tillie is extra quiet when she gets home after hanging out first with Aaron, then with Molly.

It's new, this thing of her being out late at night. Being with multiple friends. She can't even count the number of nights she spent alone at home, and in just a couple weeks, everything's changed.

She smiles. She thinks of Aaron, who is a real, true friend already. She thinks of Molly. They laughed a lot tonight. It was a little surreal. Amir, with whom she has major baggage, but also? They're gonna be okay. She's gonna be okay. And just thinking that makes her feel proud of herself. She's brave. Very.

She takes chocolate hearts out of a plastic bag. She hopes her dad focuses on the message rather than the chocolate itself, because this is a CVS special, and she's pretty sure they're leftovers from Valentine's Day, which was more than two months ago.

Tillie grabs a Post-it and a pen, and she writes, in her fanciest cursive:

She thinks about his silence earlier. And how wrong that was. And also, how that's not her. She won't be good at this and it's gonna hurt, if he's going to continue to act this way. And that's how you get hurt. Opening your heart allows you to get hurt. But it's also who she is.

So she places the chocolate hearts wrapped in red tinfoil in the shape of a big heart. Underneath, she signs her name.

As she turns off the lights and gets into bed, she prays that her dad will see the message and understand where it comes from. She prays he still has enough feeling in his closed heart to take that in.

The only way his dad would allow Aaron to go to the talent show is if either he went or Tillie went. Or both. Aaron decided on Tillie.

It's weird being on the Fieldston campus for the first time in more than a week and it's not even a school day. He feels like one of those jock kids who has a football game on Saturday and plays in it despite having too much of a cold to hit classes on Friday.

"This is posh," Tillie says as they get out of the Uber and walk up the driveway toward the main building.

"Is it? More posh than Spence? Really?"

"Well . . . it's more outdoorsy. More suburban, I guess. I'm kinda jealous. Must be nice to sit out on the picnic tables and eat lunch. Can you do that?"

"Sure, if you want to watch Archie and Veronica swap spit while you eat gluten-free pizza," he says, and Tillie smirks as they head on to the theater.

Aaron's still scheduled to sing, but, yeah. No. At one moment in the Uber, he had this thought: *What if I just decide to sing at the last moment?* He knows Tillie thinks it's a bad idea, but what if this one time—

No. That time is over for him now. Not singing, necessarily. He may sing again at some point. What's over is the fantasy world of him becoming a star. He's just not star material. It hurts to think about, but all Aaron's ever gonna be, musically or otherwise, is Aaron.

Tillie says that's not such a bad thing.

So Aaron goes up to Sasha Turner, who holds the clipboard with all the acts, and he says, "Hey, Sasha."

Her eyes light up. "Oh my gosh, Aaron! I wasn't sure if you were going to—"

"I'm not," he says. "I'm not ready. It's like I've grown up, in a way, this whole experience—"

"Okay," she says, cutting him off. "Sorry. Swamped."

He nods and walks away, and as he does so, he grins a bit.

Yes, he's still a little Aaron-ish, he guesses. And maybe that's not such a terrible thing.

"So are you ready for this awful show?" he asks, and Tillie nods.

"You know, a talent show was where I did my thing about Amir."

"Well, now that I've seen him—"

"Nope. Stop."

He grins to tell her he's kidding. Which he really is. He gets it now. Amir is off-limits and always will be.

"So how's Daddy?" Aaron asks as they sit in their seats, exaggerating the length of the *A* sound in between the *D*'s.

"He's fine. It's all just . . . fine."

Tillie still doesn't really want to talk much about that. On Monday morning, she woke up and her dad was in the kitchen getting coffee, and she peeked her head in and he noticed and turned. He smiled at her.

"You're a really special person, Tillie," he said.

Her shoulders lifted. She put her head down and adjusted her mouth so that the smile wasn't too eager.

"Sometimes a person—me in this case—is an asshole. I don't know why I am. And then there are people like you. You shouldn't have to do that."

He went back to making his coffee and she stood there, unsure what to say, not wanting to upset this delicate balance that had suddenly been struck.

But then he grabbed his coffee and smiled at her as he brushed by her, reaching back one hand to tickle the small of her back, which is an old thing he used to do.

That was it. No further conversation. Not that day, not the next, not since.

She wasn't sure if the cold war was over, if this was just . . . business as usual between her and her dad.

And somehow, it actually did bother her less now. The simple words he said to her had done something, at least.

"What's it like to be back?" Tillie asks Aaron instead.

Aaron smiles gently, knowing he's hit a spot Tillie can't talk about yet.

"Fucking weird," he says. "In fact, you wanna . . ."

He stands and walks toward the exit. The show's about to start, and Tillie doesn't understand, but she follows him, in case he's not okay, in case it was, as she thought, too soon to come back. Too loaded because of the talent show and him not singing.

Outside, he runs to a picnic table. She chases him, a little worried. He lies down on the table and pats the space next to him.

"Okay," she says, and she climbs up and puts her head next to his, her body in the opposite direction, so that their heads are touching.

"I've always wanted to do this," he says.

"Flame out and get depressed and miss school and come back for a talent show and not sing in it?"

He blows a raspberry. "I've always wanted to lie like this, on this table, and look up at the underside of this tree, with a friend.

But I've never really had a friend I would trust enough to ask, who wouldn't blow me off or reject me."

"Aw," she says quietly, her body heating up from the compliment.

"And here you go and besmirch me, just when I'm being emotional, and nice, and it's just too much . . ."

He makes sure his tone shows her that he knows he's doing that thing, where he acts all emotional. It's because of all they've been through. She knows it. She does it, too, sometimes. Melodrama is easier than constant real emotion.

×

Tillie stares up at the tree and thinks of branches. The interconnectedness of them all, and the base, the tree, as their source. How one decision, one branch, may seem disconnected from the others but they're all banded together. And one seemingly simple decision leads to another, and on, and how glad she is that she didn't jump that day. If she'd jumped, she'd never have had . . . this. An odd moment of serenity under a tree that she'll probably always remember. And Aaron. And everything. She'd never have learned that she's stronger than she thought.

"I've decided to paint my room," Tillie says.

"Yeah? What color?"

"I dunno yet. It's pink, and that's over."

"You want help?"

"Sure," she says, and they enjoy the night air, the faint sounds of talent show wafting in the breeze. "This is kinda fun."

"Yup."

She asks, "Do you like it?"

He takes the question to mean more than it means, because that's what Aaron does, often. He thinks: *Do I like what's just happened, these last few weeks? All the shit I've gone through—we have*—he corrects himself. *No, of course not.* He's still not quite right in the head. But he's better. Better than he was, that's for sure. And he has Tillie. And she has him, and she's definitely better. And that's big.

He turns his head to the side and kisses, and even though the kiss lands above her head, he knows she feels it. "I like it a whole great deal," he says.

AUTHOR'S NOTE AND RESOURCES

While on tour a few years ago, I got reprimanded. It was one of the first times I had spoken about suicide publicly, and despite the fact that the organization knew I was there representing The Trevor Project, I got called into an office by the person in charge of the youth group after my talk.

She told me it was deeply irresponsible of me to talk about suicide to young LGBTQIA+ people. That I may have done significant damage by doing so.

I was taken aback. In the end, we agreed to disagree, and we parted on less-than-pleasant terms. As I drove away, I wondered: Had I, in fact, done something irresponsible? Might I have, unknowingly, contributed to a teenager's downward spiral by discussing my own battle with severe depression, my suicide attempt at twenty-seven, and my gratitude that I got a second chance at life?

In the end, I'll say two things: One, I am not a trained counselor and I don't have all the answers, so anything is possible; I could be wrong. That said, to my innermost self I believe that person was wrong. I know she had the young people of that organization's best interests at heart, but I think she was incorrect about the impact of a person talking about depression and suicide to teens.

My strong belief is that talking about suicide does not, in general, lead young people to kill themselves. In fact, we need to talk MORE about suicide, to demystify it. We need to discuss the feelings of despair and depression, as well as the entirety of suicide, including the impacts. Including the alternatives. The discussion needs to be a complete one. In talking about suicide, we must be careful not to glamorize it. Not to create fantasies or magical thinking about suicide as some sort of answer to anyone's struggles.

This book is my attempt at a complete discussion of suicide. To show, as objectively as possible in a fictional environment, all the possibilities for two young people who are struggling with suicidal ideation. What might happen if they jump, and what might happen if they don't. The potential impacts on people we know as well as on people we don't know. I know when I was at my lowest, I believed that if I were to not be alive anymore, no one would care.

That's the thing about depression: It makes our brains lie to us. I believed that it wouldn't matter if I were here or not, and I don't imagine anyone could have convinced me otherwise. Looking back now, I realize with a sense of wonder that the world would be different if I had not lived past twenty-seven. For one thing, this book in your hands would not be here.

This is known as the butterfly effect, and it's rather hard, in a moment of severe depression, to think about the impacts of your absence, and how they might compound over time. At twenty-seven, I could not have understood what it would have meant for me to die by suicide.

For those of you who struggle with depression, sadness, feelings of deep despair: You are not alone. You are never alone. There are no new feelings in the world. If you are feeling it, someone else has felt it before, and somebody else is probably feeling it right now.

If you are feeling depressed and hopeless, I beg of you: Talk about it! DO NOT keep it to yourself. Depression loves to linger in the dark and silent, and it is most dangerous there. Find a person who feels safe to talk to, at home or at school. A parent, a teacher, a counselor, a friend. If no such person exists, know that resources exist. I am including some of them below.

If a friend or loved one tells you that they're depressed, listen to them. It can be easy to pass off depression as a phase, or something to "get over." For someone with chemical depression, this is not how it works. Professional help is often needed. I've sat with teens from across the country, and the stories I've heard have chilled me. One young person told their father they were struggling. He responded, "You have nothing to be depressed about."

This is a fundamental misunderstanding about how depression works. It can be about something, but also it can be about nothing. For some, it's a disability at the neurotransmitter level, and being told to not feel the way we feel is a very hopeless feeling indeed. Or worse than that. Denial of depression often leads to untreated depression, which can be deadly.

Last but most crucially: You matter. You really, really matter. We want you here. The world wants you here, even when it feels like the opposite is true. It took me so many years to understand that I matter, and I'm extremely grateful that I stayed around long enough to learn that lesson.

RESOURCES:

If you or a loved one is experiencing suicidal thoughts, it is crucial that you get help immediately. There are many helplines you can call, and there may be one in your area that you can find online. Nationally in the United States, you can call 1-800-SUICIDE or 1-800-273-TALK. Either will put you in contact with a trained volunteer who will understand what you're going through, will listen to you, and will offer resources about how to get help. These are available twenty-four hours a day, seven days a week. If you prefer to communicate via chat, you can go to imalive.org and chat with a trained volunteer at any time. In Canada you can call 1-833-456-4566, text 45645, or go to crisisservicescanada.ca. You can also call the Association québécoise de prévention du suicide at 1-866-277-3553 or Kids Help Phone at 1-800-668-6868 or kidshelpphone.ca.

LGBTQIA+ youth are particularly prone to suicidal ideation. According to a 2016 study by the Centers for Disease Control and Prevention, LGB youth are almost five times as likely to have attempted suicide compared to heterosexual youth. The statistics are even more devastating for transgender youth. According to a 2015 study by the National Center for

Transgender Equality, 40 percent of transgender adults have attempted suicide, and 92 percent of those questioned reported a suicide attempt before the age of 25. If you identify as LGBTQIA+ and are under 25, check out thetrevorproject.org. The organization offers a national hotline at 1-866-488-7386, and also offers options at its website for instant messaging (TrevorChat), over text messaging (TrevorText), and a social networking site for LGBTQIA+ under the age of 25 (TrevorSpace). If you're concerned about an LGBTQIA+ friend, check out The Trevor Project's resource page for tips on helping a friend who is struggling:

thetrevorproject.org/resources/preventing-suicide/

A quick note on the importance of allies to LGBTQIA+ youth: According to a 2019 study by The Trevor Project, LGBTQIA+ youth with at least one accepting adult in their lives were 40 percent less likely to report a suicide attempt in the previous year. For resources on how to be an ally to LGBTQIA+ youth, check out:

engage.youth.gov/resources/being-ally-lgbt-people

ACKNOWLEDGMENTS

Writing this book was an overwhelming process, and as I sit here, trying to figure out whom to thank, it feels similarly daunting. It took more than two years to write this, and during that time countless people helped me.

First, I feel the need to thank the people who were there for me when I almost didn't make it. I will start there. Thanks to Rhonda Ross, Brigit Beyea, Sonia Pinto-Torres, Adam Strassburg, Joanna Gajewski, Telisa Fowlkes, Josh Singer, Alain Silverio, Ratiya Ruangsuwana, Jebeze Alexander, Vagnes De La Rosa, Terry Mullane, Justin Blake, Peter Flamm, Samera Nasereddin, Eliza Mason, and the rest of my incredible support system back when I was a teenager. Without you, I'm not here anymore. That's just a fact.

Thanks to my chosen family in the present. You know who you are, and I would feel terrible if I left out any names. Special thanks to Lisa McMann, who is always there for me. I love you.

To my family: Chuck Cahoy, my person. I don't how I got so lucky in life to find you. To quote a Patti LaBelle song, "I've been looking around and you were here all the time." To my mother, Shelley Doctors; my father, Bob Konigsberg; my stepmother, Roz Konigsberg; my sister, Pam Yoss; and my brother, Dan Konigsberg: I love you all very much.

To Nick Thomas, who was with me through the first and second drafts, and who championed this novel. Your brilliant footprint is all over this book. You are part of it and always will be. Thank you.

To David Levithan, who took on the gargantuan task of editing this monster: I will be forever grateful to you for your keen eye and brilliance.

Linda Epstein, my agent, friend, and biggest fan: Thank you for your love and support.

Thanks to Annika Browne and Kate Moehler for talking to me about mental health issues, including mania and hypomania. Thanks to Miguel Guillon for housing me in Washington Heights when I was doing my research. Big thanks to Lisa Athan and Scotty Fried for talking to me about grief from a counseling perspective. Thanks to Laila Fowlkes, Helen Pinto-Scherstuhl, Bree Irvin, and Rosalyn Collings Eves for giving me the inside scoop on fifth-grade girls. Officer Trever Sweeney was helpful in understanding how police handle notifying families in the case of a suicide. Imi Jackson gave me insight into the world of Throne of Glass and Sarah J. Maas fans.

Huge assist to my first-draft readers, who had to wade through quite a lot of mess to see the beginnings of a story: Pamela Kirkland, Cindy Minnich, Travis Reyes, Alice Hayes, Jaymie Theissen, Francine Rockney, Brigid Kemmerer, Chris Unger, Dave Hughes, Julie Stokes, and Wendy Poteet.

And last but never, ever least: my Scholastic family. I don't know where I am without your huge assistance, but it's certainly not doing the thing I love so much.

ABOUT THE AUTHOR

Bill Konigsberg is the author of six novels, including the Stonewall Book Award– and PEN Center USA Literary Award–winning *The Porcupine of Truth* and the Sid Fleischman Award for Humor–winning *Openly Straight*. In 2018, the National Council of Teachers of English's Assembly on Literature for Adolescents (ALAN) established the Bill Konigsberg Award for Acts and Activism for Equity and Inclusion through Young Adult Literature. Bill loves all Labradoodles, including his best friends Mabel and Buford, and many people, including his husband, Chuck. They live in Phoenix.